Along the Perimeter

Book One of the
Amboy Series

Steven Healt

This is a work of fiction. All of the characters, organizations, and events portrayed in this novel are either products of the author's imagination or are used fictitiously. Any resemblance to actual persons, living or dead, is coincidental.

Maps by Steven Healt

Illustration © Tom Edwards
TomEdwardDesign.com

For Jess with love

Contents

Maps.. v,vi

Silhouettes... 1

The Capital City 15

Amber Waves..34

The Diplomat...45

Companions 60

The Scientist..73

A Job...90

An Old Friend..99

The Beginnings of a Web....................................... 113

Contact... 124

Into the Haze 139

Information 147

Something Lost, Something Gained 162

Port Amboy.. 172

Memories of an Old World 190

The Council.. 208

Homecoming.. 220

Smoke Rising.. 235

To East Edge 247

Another Thread to Pluck 257

Patterns in the Web... 271

Gathering in the Night 281

The Streets of East Edge.. 291

A Kind of Diplomacy.. 302

Among the Crowd.. 314

Setting Sun... 324

A Meeting..…..335

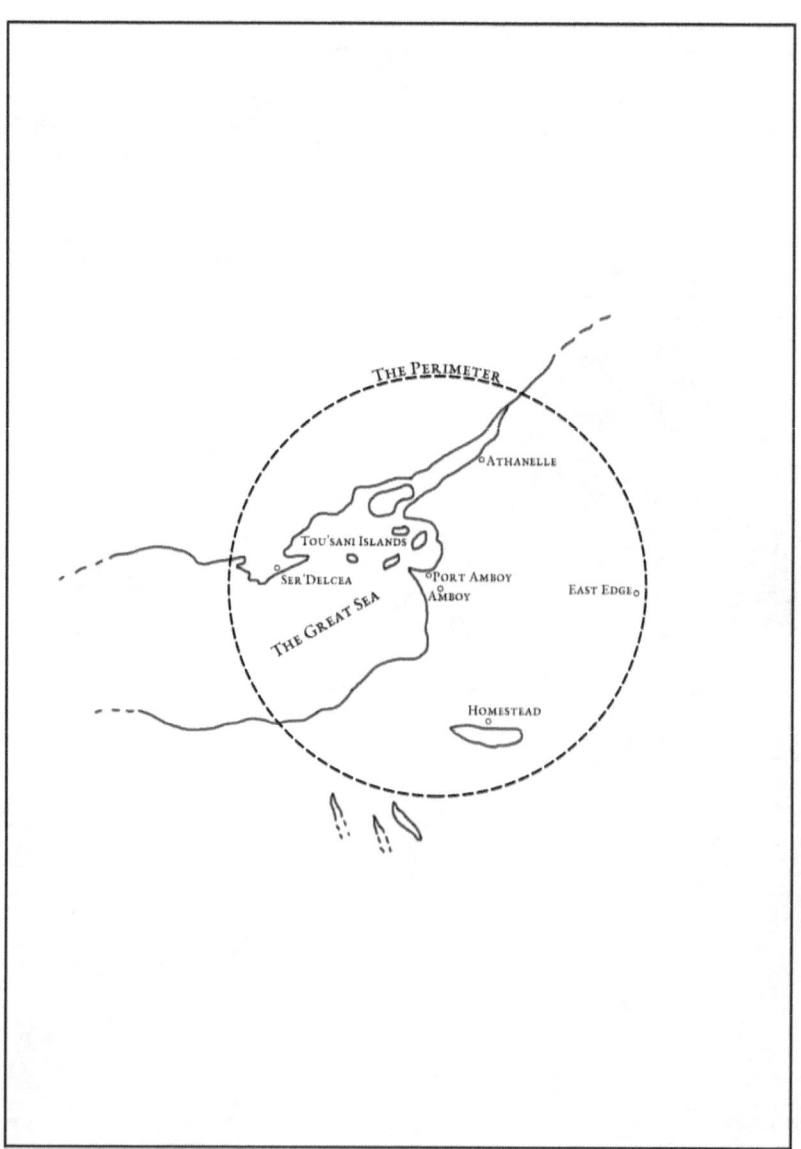

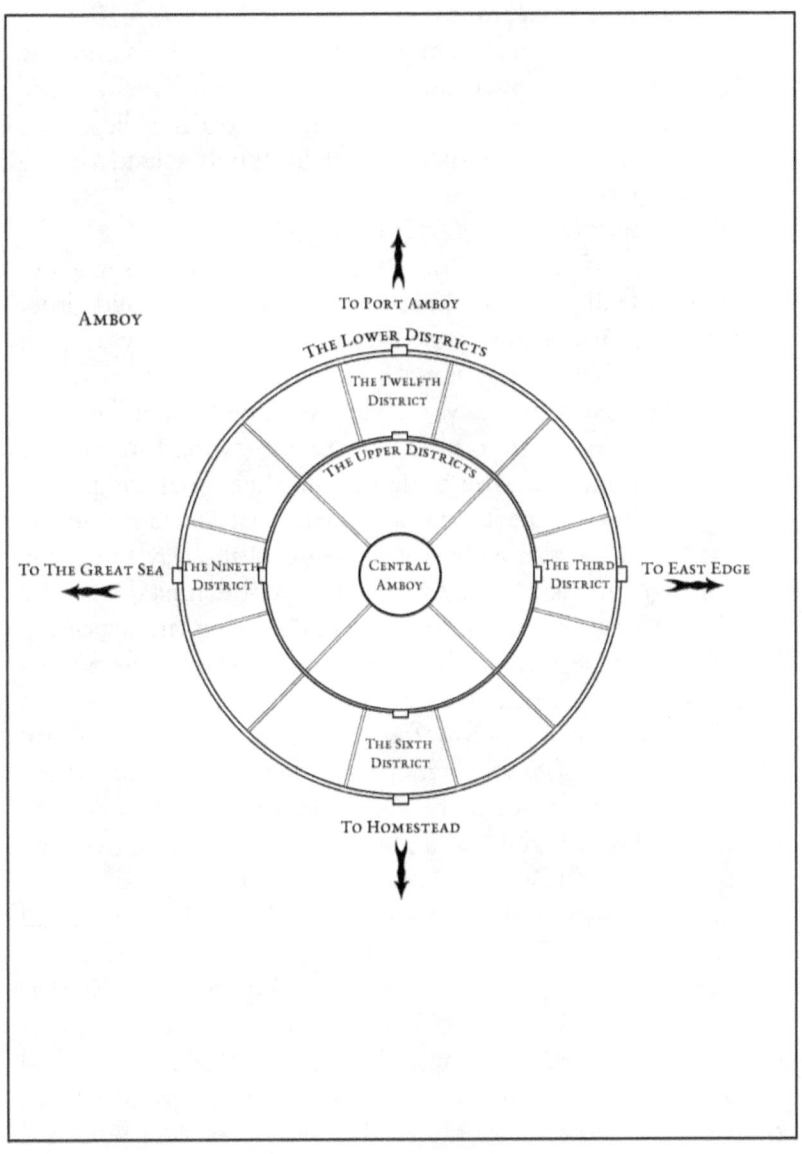

AMBOY

TO PORT AMBOY

TO THE GREAT SEA

TO EAST EDGE

TO HOMESTEAD

THE LOWER DISTRICTS

THE UPPER DISTRICTS

THE TWELFTH DISTRICT

THE NINETH DISTRICT

CENTRAL AMBOY

THE THIRD DISTRICT

THE SIXTH DISTRICT

Silhouettes

The sun had begun to dip below the horizon as Ben lay in the field on his family's farm. With today's end, the harvest was over, and he felt he could finally relax.

Ben and his younger brothers would often lie in the tall grass of the rolling fields on their family's land during their midday breaks.

This was different, Ben was alone now.

His two younger brothers were inside with his mother and father. Had they been here with him the two would either be wrestling in the grass or running about hollering at each other. How they had so much energy left after working all day on their farm was beyond him. In their absence he was able to listen to the sound of the breeze blowing through the tall grass around him, the birds singing their final songs, and enjoy the glow of the Perimeter Shield that stretched across the sky. He always thought it was beautiful the way the pastel blue and green wisps of the protective bubble mixed with the purples and reds of the sky at sunset. The transparency of the Shield also made it possible to see what it was protecting its inhabitants from: The Haze.

The thick murky yellow fog rose higher than the silo on their farm. *Several times higher,* Ben thought as he turned his head to the east toward the direction of the farm. At this hour, the Haze looked like a black shadow looming over the small town. When Ben was younger, he and his friends would sneak out at night and test their bravery by seeing who could get closest to the Perimeter. At the time it seemed like they were in arm's length of passing through the protective barrier.

Thinking back, Ben guessed they hadn't been nearly as close as they had imagined. It seemed that if they had stretched out their hands, they would have passed right through into the danger on the other side. The older boys had said they had gone beyond it before, but even as a child Ben

1

knew they were lying. They would always say anything they thought would impress the others. In truth, anything that passed through would no doubt meet a slow and painful death, or so he had been told.

Travelers who passed through always mentioned how exciting it must be to live so close to the Perimeter. The truth of it was that not much ever happened in his village. Their test of courage had been the only excitement he had experienced growing up.

Ben stood up and brushed some dried grass off of his pant legs. Of course, now at the age of eighteen it would be reckless to do such a thing. Not that it was necessarily prohibited to go out near the Perimeter. It was just considered very foolish. If his parents had ever found out he had gone out there, he would be doing every chore imaginable for the rest of his life. Even still he found himself thinking about visiting their old proving grounds once more, and he began walking toward town.

The sun had completely passed the horizon. The cool air was welcome after a day working in the sun. With the exception of some noise from the Shepherd's Crook, the town was settling in for the night. He entered the light pouring out from the tavern windows; he could see a handful of familiar faces at the bar. The first floor of the Shepherd's Crook was a large room with several tables, and a massive stone hearth on one wall that always had a fire blazing during the colder seasons. Colder weather was still weeks off, so there would be no fire tonight. Every now and then a village meeting would be held in the tavern. The second floor had a few modest rooms for the rare traveler. Ben didn't care much for listening to the arguments between the old men and women about the happenings and plans for the village.

He thought about walking in to join them for a drink. Mistress Olm's apple cobbler was Ben's favorite. Sometimes, Ben and his family would walk into the village together to share a cobbler. As tempting as it was to stop in for a moment, Ben kept walking past the door and down the road. Tomorrow the town would throw a celebration for the end of harvest season. There would be plenty of time for cobbler and ale then. Although, it seemed some were getting a head start. Ben chuckled to himself as he walked by and continued through town.

Farr Plain was sufficient for the needs of those that lived in it. There were those who lived beyond the small village that benefited from it as well. Once a week Ben would take the trip north with his mother or father to East Edge to pick up any supplies they needed and to get news from Amboy, the capital city. The town of East Edge seemed too large to Ben. Rows of streets all crossing this way and that. Stores, all selling something different, and some that sold the same thing as another just a few streets over. It even had *two* inns! That considered, he struggled to imagine the size of the capital. Ben was content to never experience the madness he could only imagine in Amboy. He enjoyed his trips to East Edge, and that was enough for him.

It was only another short walk from Farr Plain to where the Perimeter Shield met the ground. Ben enjoyed living in the rolling fields of the New Ring. Even though they were so close to the Perimeter, he always felt safe behind the protection of the dome. Ben approached the glowing wall and stopped about twenty feet from it. Even though he was much older now, he still felt a mixture of fear and excitement. The wall in front of him looked like the surface of a pond on a calm day. The Haze was like sediment that had been kicked up from below and was now swirling in the water. A breeze came from behind him and passed through the wall as if it wasn't there and churned the murky cloud. Ben took a few steps forward and picked up a small stone and threw it toward the wall. Unlike a pond, there were no ripples. The stone sailed right through and disappeared into the darkness.

After he tossed a few more stones, Ben had had his fill of excitement. Maybe there were still some of those familiar faces at the tavern, and maybe they would be drunk enough to be easily convinced to buy him a drink. Ben was pulled from his thoughts of the tavern when he heard a soft thump behind him.

He turned to see a small stone lying in the grass only a few feet away from where he had stood. His eyes traveled up from the stone to the soft glow of the Perimeter. In the darkness of the Haze, he could see three silhouettes. Ben's heart pounded so hard it felt like it was making his entire body move back and forth. The figures in the Haze moved closer to him. As they breached through the surface of the Perimeter Ben could see them much better. Ben dropped to the ground and tried to lie as flat as possible and remain still.

"No need to hide boy. We already saw you," a muffled voice called out.

Ben felt chills throughout his entire body but didn't dare respond or move. The strangers were still moving closer to him. They spoke to each other, but Ben couldn't hear well enough to understand what was being said. The footsteps drew closer. A light flashed from above and covered him.

"C'mon boy."

Ben looked up with an outstretched hand to block the blinding light. Before his eyes could adjust, the light was shut off and he was being pulled to his feet.

"You live in that small farming town nearby?" A new voice this time, still muffled though. In the darkness Ben could see that the three were wearing masks that covered their entire faces. Tubes connected from a mouthpiece to tanks on their hips. They were wearing bulky brown and gray suits and large packs on their backs. He hadn't seen anything like it before.

"He's gotta be. There's no way he would have come from further away," one of them said while removing their mask and revealing their face. He pulled a tight-fitting hood off his head. "Can you take us there?" The man was about the same age as his father, the lines in his face proved enough. Unlike

4

his father, this man had long brown hair that was tied back in a bun, a short beard, and dark-brown eyes. Now that his mask was off his voice was no longer muffled, and Ben noticed it was slightly hoarse.

The two others removed their masks and hoods. Another man, and a woman.

"It's nice to breathe fresh air again," the second man said after taking a deep breath and exhaling. He was younger than the first, with darker skin and short dark hair. This man's voice was also slightly rough, Ben noticed. He flashed a smile when he saw him looking in his direction.

The stories Ben was told as a child described the people who lived in the Haze as monsters. These three had no boils on their skin, or other disfigurements. Without their odd suits they would look like any other person in Farr Plain. Ben couldn't imagine a person with a smile like that ever harming anyone.

"Who are you?" Ben finally managed to say. He heard Mistress Olm's voice in his head, *they will come out of that Haze over there and snatch you up! Take you in there, and you will never see your family again!*

"What's your name?" the woman said as she walked up to him. She was slightly shorter than Ben. Her long dark hair was woven into a braid that fell out of her hood when she had removed it. As she got closer her bright-blue eyes pierced through him. Her pale skin seemed to glow in the dim light of the Perimeter.

"Uh, Ben. Ben Meadows," he replied, still surprised at his ability to speak given the circumstances.

"I'm Annika. Look, Ben, you're from the farming town nearby. We know you're close to the end of the harvest. You're going to take us to one of the storage houses. We'll take what we need and leave." The woman spoke calmly and didn't break eye contact with Ben the entire time she spoke.

"I don't think—" Ben began.

The short-haired man moved closer to Ben and put his

5

hand on the black handle of a small blade on his waist. "We don't want to have to hurt you or anyone else. We just need supplies for our people." Maybe that smile hadn't been as kind as Ben had thought.

"Take it easy, Jonas," the other man said.

"We don't have time for this." Jonas turned away from Ben and toward the other man. "We need to get back to the Outpost before dawn, and this kid can help us get in and out faster." The two men stared at each other for a moment, unblinking.

"Ben, can you just help out a couple of travelers in need?" the first man said looking away from Jonas.

Ben clenched his fist and mustered all the courage he had. "I can't."

The man looked down at his feet and sighed. He stepped toward Ben, put a hand on his shoulder. "I'll be honest with you Ben. We've got a lot of hungry people; we need those supplies, or our friends and family are going to die." Ben tried to keep his gaze with the man. Fear made it torturous.

"Our harvest feeds our town as well as others in the area. We have hungry people too." It was almost as if the words were coming out of Ben's mouth before he could think.

Jonas shoved the other man to the side. The man stumbled but found his footing. Immediately after the man was out of the way Jonas grabbed Ben by his shoulders and lifted him into the air. Ben felt his shoulders creak under the pressure. Jonas was inches from his face. "We tried being nice to you. Now here's what's going to happen—"

"*Jonas! Enough!*" the other man hissed. Jonas set Ben down with a sigh. "Ben. The storehouse. Now."

Ben rubbed his shoulders. The ache was pulsing through his upper torso. He gave a nod and turned toward the village.

The town was completely silent now as the four moved between buildings. If Ben was lucky, there were a few stragglers left in the tavern and they could help. *What could drunken farmers do against three people who lived beyond the Perimeter?*

Ben stopped at the edge of an alleyway that opened onto the main street he had been walking along only moments ago. During that walk it seemed so peaceful. Now the silence and darkness loomed over him.

"We have to cut across the street and then we can continue west toward the storehouse on my family's land." He winced after he spoke. Why did he tell them it was his family's farm? *What a fool.* He had been a fool to walk out to the Perimeter and was even more of a fool now.

"Okay, kid. How much further is that?" the man whispered as he moved next to Ben. Annika and Jonas were crouched behind them. He hoped none of them had noticed he had said it was his family's farm.

"Not much. If we move quickly, we could be there in a few minutes." Ben looked down both ends of the street and saw no one. Maybe if he brought them along the backside of the tavern he could get someone's attention. He wanted to wait a bit longer before moving out into the street just in case someone might come by. A hand shoved him from behind.

They ran across the street and into the small space between the buildings on the other side. The buildings beyond the main road were mostly houses. Their dark windows only filled him with more dread. If he yelled, he might be able to wake someone, and they might be able to help him. How many would it take? How many might get hurt?

Ben pushed the thought down and turned left along the backside of the building that shared a wall with the Shepherd's Crook. "This way," Ben whispered over his shoulder.

As they approached the tavern Ben could see some light coming from the back door that led to the kitchen. Two figures stepped out. Ben had felt relieved at the sight of the two men stepping out of the Shepherd's Crook, but it disappeared when he felt a hand pull him backward.

"Hold up. There's people up there." The still-unnamed man pulled Ben backward between himself and Annika.

If Ben yelled someone would definitely hear him. These three said they didn't want to hurt anyone. It was Jonas that worried Ben. The other man seemed to be in charge, but would he stop Jonas from hurting anyone else if it came to it? There wouldn't be another chance. Ben pushed himself away from the three and sprinted toward the two figures in the alley.

"H—" Ben tried to yell but was knocked down and his mouth covered. He tried to roll to get free, but the stabbing pain in his shoulders was too much under the weight of the person on top of him.

"Why?" Annika whispered through clenched teeth, still holding a hand over his mouth.

"Hello? Who's there?" a voice said as they walked over. Ben tried to yell. He wasn't sure if his muffled shouting would even be heard.

"*Shut up.*" Annika put a knife to Ben's face, and he fell silent. She pulled the knife away, but only slightly.

"Hey, what are you—"

Ben heard the man began to speak. Then saw him fall to the ground next to him; he immediately recognized Doc Tymbers. He was one of the town elders and ran the clinic in town. Jonas was on top of him; the black-handled blade had slashed Doc Tymbers' throat open. Ben was face to face with him as he choked on his own blood. He was locked on the old man's eyes until the gurgling sound ceased. There was a difference in the lifeless gaze. Blood pooled toward him. Again, he tried to squirm away from it, but Annika still held him down. He craned his neck as Jonas ran after the other man. There was a yelp. Then nothing.

Annika got off Ben and pulled him up. "You just got those two killed." The knife was no longer in her hands, but Ben didn't think that she would hesitate to pull it out again if she felt she needed to.

The last shred of hope Ben had for rescue was lost when he saw Jonas step into the light. "You said this place we're going to is on your family's farm, right?" Jonas walked toward Ben, his face and clothes covered in blood. "Don't make us kill them too."

Ben felt hollow as he led the intruders through the rest of the town and into the field outside the farm. Crouching, they moved through the tall grass in single file. Annika had kept her hands on his back since he had tried to run. She wasn't going to let him get too far from her.

He had seen animals slaughtered for the farm, but this was the first time he had ever seen someone murdered. Thoughts of someone being around to help Ben now were replaced with the hope that his family was still asleep inside the house.

He kept them as far from the house as possible, before bringing them to the large storage building in the back. He moved along the side of the store house, keeping his eyes on the dark windows of his home. The group rounded the corner and moved toward the main door. Ben grabbed the handle and opened the door enough for the three to get inside. He waited for the three to enter, but Annika grabbed him and pulled him in with her.

Ben was about to flip a switch on the wall when Jonas grabbed his hand. "Don't want to wake up the family." Jonas reached for his shoulder where a small light was mounted and turned it on. Annika and the other man did the same.

"Alright, Ben, let's move," the man said.

In the main room of the storage building a long table ran down the middle. Harvested crops were brought in and cleaned here. Clean crops were then sorted and packed away in crates along the walls of the room. Hoses for washing the produce hung down from the ceiling. Not all had been put away properly and lengths of hose were draped over the table. Even now Ben still found himself annoyed that someone hadn't cleaned up after themselves. In the back of the building were dozens of crates that were prepared for nearby towns and villages

"I won't let you take from those crates there. Other towns rely on these shipments." Ben waited for a response; the man nodded. Jonas and Annika looked at the crates and then each other without saying anything.

Ben walked toward a stairway on the left side of the room that led down to a basement. "Down here is where we store some of the food for our town. You can take from that." He walked down the stairs, using the light from his captors behind him to guide the way.

The storage cellar seemed especially dark and cold tonight. Even the air felt heavy. Jonas and Annika pushed past Ben and began looking through the rows of crates. After they searched through a few, the two took off their packs and began filling them. Occasionally, Jonas would pause to smell something he pulled out or hold it to his light to get a better look. Annika seemed to be focused on filling her pack. She grabbed handfuls of potatoes, carrots and other vegetables and stuffed them into the pack at her feet, in such a hurry most of the handfuls were falling to the floor.

The man walked over to a crate, pulled the lid off, and sighed. "Apples." He turned toward Ben. "I haven't even seen an apple since I was younger than you." He took one out of the crate and bit into it. It was difficult to tell in the dim light, but the man's eyes seemed to be glistening with tears.

"Dimitri, there's more than enough food here for the Outpost! If we take some back with us, we can convince the others to come and help us bring even more back."

"I see that, Jonas." Dimitri's response seemed cold in comparison to Jonas' excitement. He closed the lid of the crate of apples and sighed.

10

The scale of what was happening had finally hit Ben. After the three of them left, they would return with others. Thoughts of invaders pouring out of the Haze and into his small town overcame him. Images of the people he cared for being murdered. Buildings burned as they overtook the town. Doc Tymbers' lifeless eyes flashed in his mind. Blood spilled from his neck and bubbled from his mouth. The fear in his eyes.

Jonas and Dimitri walked toward the other crates and looked through each as they talked amongst themselves. Ben moved slowly to the stairs, keeping his eyes on the two of them. Then he realized he could only see two lights in the dark. He strained as he looked around the room for Annika. Could she have gotten by him and gone back upstairs without him noticing? He leaned over the handrail and looked up the stairs. The door was still open. He could barely see into the space up at the top. Had she been near the door, he would be able to see some of the light cast from her shoulder mount. He made his way up the stairs.

He looked out into the room and couldn't see much in the darkness. The lack of light might mean she wasn't up here either. He slid out of the doorway and moved toward the back of the room to the crates that had been prepared for the other towns and villages. A quick glance was all that was needed to tell they had been undisturbed. Ben's shadow cast across the boxes in front of him as a light shone behind him.

"Trying to sneak off?" Dimitri stalked from the stairway.

"I just wanted to make sure no one was stealing from the shipments."

The light obscured Dimitri's face. Frustration filled his voice. He took a step closer. "We aren't bad people. We're only trying to help our own."

Ben took a step back and bumped against the crates; something tumbled onto the floor around his feet. He took a step to his left and tried to put more space between himself and Dimitri. "What about the people in this town? If you

11

come back with others and continue to steal, what about the people in the towns we help supply?" Ben moved along the table in the center of the room.

"Then maybe we can work out a deal?" The light wobbled as Dimitri shrugged. Calm had replaced frustration. "We'll come back every now and then, and you'll sneak us in. We'll take what we need and leave. Like I said before *no one has to get hurt.*"

The air in the room solidified as the two passed around each other. Ben's legs felt like logs. He felt a sting in his palms and unclenched his fists. They shook when he relaxed them.

"Someone would notice a light shipment or things missing from storage downstairs. How would that get explained?" Ben walked backward away from Dimitri. He reached out to put his hand on the table for balance and it fell onto one of the hoses that had been left out. Before he even realized what he was doing he lunged at Dimitri with a length of hose in his hand. Dimitri must have been as surprised as Ben was. He let out a yelp and stumbled backward as he was knocked over. Ben put both his knees on Dimitri's arms and wrapped the hose around his neck and pulled hard. He had wrestled with his brothers and friends, but he had never fought with the intention to hurt someone before. He could no longer feel the pain in his shoulders from earlier.

Dimitri's eyes widened. He gasped for air. Ben could feel hands pulling at his legs and the man's knees hitting him in the back. In one motion Dimitri's legs wrapped around Ben's shoulders and he felt himself being rocked backward. Dimitri was now on top of him in a tangled mess of hose line and limbs. The hose was still tight around his neck, but he was now punching Ben in the chest and face in a wild attempt to break free. Ben could feel his grip loosening on the hose. He let go and repositioned his hands on the nozzle and twisted. A blast of water shot out and hit Dimitri in the eyes causing him to grab at his face and fall to the side. Ben took this

12

opportunity to get back on top and wrapped the hose around his neck once more. As he pulled on the hose, he felt a sharp pain in his left side and arms grabbing him.

"Dimitri!" Jonas shouted as Ben was thrown to the side. When Ben hit the ground the pain in his side felt immeasurable. He looked down and saw the dark wooden handle of Jonas' blade sticking out of him. His breathing felt labored. He coughed up a small amount of blood.

"We need to leave." Annika helped Jonas get Dimitri untangled and off the ground. Dimitri waved the two others off as he stood up.

"Not before I kill this—" Jonas turned toward Ben, but Dimitri put a hand on his shoulder.

"You may have already." Dimitri's voice sounded even more hoarse now, and even in the darkness Ben could see red marks around his neck. "He was only trying to take care of the people he feels responsible for." Dimitri coughed and gasped for air. "His motivations are exactly the same as ours. Let's go." Dimitri took his pack from Jonas and the three of them moved toward the door on the opposite side of the room that they had entered through.

Ben waited as long as he could after he heard the three leave and the door close. He rolled to his right side and began crawling toward the door. He had to keep his left arm at his side to avoid moving the still-embedded knife around in the wound. At least it would stop some of the bleeding. Most of his movement was done with his right arm and leg. He used his left leg as little as possible as he shuffled along the floor of the processing room.

It felt as if he were drowning.

After what seemed like an eternity, he finally reached the door. Ben rolled onto his back and wormed his way up, so he was sitting with his back against the door. He pushed against it and used his legs to force himself up. The room began to sway. His head felt as though it weighed twice as much.

After turning the handle on the door, he nearly fell out

13

into the yard between the storage house and his home. Even though he was on the brink of passing out he couldn't help but laugh that he must have looked like a drunk returning home from a night at the tavern. If only he had actually been able to make it to the tavern.

The ground swayed again. It took all of his remaining energy to keep his head up and his eyes open. His feet were barely leaving the ground as he shuffled toward the back porch.

Then he fell.

He didn't feel the pain in his side anymore and he assumed that probably wasn't good. A blanketing calm came over him.

He rolled onto his back and looked up at the sky. There wasn't a cloud in the sky tonight and he could see thousands of stars. Wisps of blues and greens danced along the surface of the veil of the protective shield.

This was different, Ben was alone now.

He felt tears rolling down the sides of his face and into the folds of his ears.

He could hear the breeze through the grass.

He could feel his eyes closing.

CHAPTER ONE

The Capital City

Cordelia wasn't familiar with this tavern, the Stone Hearth, but it wasn't much different from any other inn or tavern in the Lower Districts. From where she was seated, she could see the entire room and everyone who came and went. The front door, the only entrance for customers and any natural light, was located in the middle of the longer section of the L-shaped room. Wooden booths lined the wall, and stools sat along the bar that followed the shape of the room. The kitchen was located in a separate room behind the bar. She had walked the exterior before entering. The door in the back alley must have led to the kitchen. She could always make an exit out the back if it came to it.

The same song had been selected on the music box for the fourth time now. There was a cheer from two drunk men at the bar. Cordelia preferred a real performer to the small waxy disks that played inside the box. The four other patrons spread out along the bar didn't seem to care, or if they did, she couldn't see from where she was sitting in the opposite corner of the room. The only other person seated was another woman a few booths away. Her head was in her arms on the table, empty bottles surrounded her.

The door to the kitchen swung open and a very large man swayed into the main bar area. What was left of the brown hair on the top of his head was matted down from the heat of the kitchen. The shirt beneath his gray apron was yellowed from sweat. He grabbed a bottle from behind the bar and two small glasses. He smiled as he walked over to the booth that she was seated in. "Glad you could make it, Haze Walker." The man grunted as he squeezed himself into the booth. One of the patrons turned their head at the man's greeting. The woman picked her head up, apparently not passed out, and looked at Cordelia with her mouth agape.

She didn't say anything. The man smelled of smoke, body odor, and cooked meats.

"Right to business then," he said while pouring brown liquid from the bottle into the two glasses. "I like that."

"My contact said you need someone to scavenge the Haze for you," she said as the man pushed one of the small glasses across the table toward her. "What is it that you're looking for?"

"This place may not look like it, but I have important regulars come through once a week. I'm talkin' *Upper District* types. You understand?" The man pointed one finger to the sky while the others gripped the glass in his hand. "I overheard them talking last time they were here. Found out they like antiques from way back. If you can bring me something to impress them with, it would improve my status with them." The man brought the drink to his lips and poured the contents down his throat.

"I've come across a lot out there. I'm going to need some specifics." Cordelia pulled out her data pad and opened up the note file she had made for the job. "Are you looking for tech to refurbish, or just any Old World object?"

The man folded his arms across his chest. "Yeah, I'm looking for something that I can display behind the bar.

Something that'll catch their eye."

"I can do that," Cordelia said as she typed on her data pad. She looked up. "Anything else?"

"That'll be it," the man grunted as he got up. "If I understand, it's thirty credits up front and the rest can be negotiated depending on the quality of the haul?" He adjusted his apron as he spoke.

"Correct." She put away her data pad and shifted toward the end of the booth.

"I can start the thirty-credit transfer now." The man pulled his own data pad from the back of his waistband and tapped the almost-transparent screen with one large thumb. He spoke without looking away from the screen, "You can have what's left of that bottle there, on the house." He tucked the data pad back behind himself.

"Thank you." She grabbed her pack that was on the ground next to the booth and swung it over her shoulder, putting her arms through the straps. "You'll get notified prior to my return. Then we can meet up and make the swap." She shrugged her pack on her shoulders to adjust it to a more comfortable position.

"Sounds good to me." The man smiled and turned away. "Stay safe out there," he said before disappearing into the kitchen as the door swung closed.

Cordelia eyed the drink on the table. She picked it up and brought it to her nose and sniffed. Some kind of grain alcohol. She put the glass to her lips and gulped the drink down in one motion. She grimaced. This was a lot stronger than she was used to. She slid the small bottle into a side pouch on her bag and walked toward the bar.

"Tell the cook I said thanks," she said as she placed the empty glass on the bar top and nodded to the bartender.

One of the men at the bar turned to her. "Did I hear right? You're a Haze Walker?" The man reeked of alcohol. She took a step back to escape the stench that emanated from his body.

"I am."

"Now *that* is an interesting profession. I bet you have all kinds of crazy stories," the man said as he leaned on the bar. "Maybe you could share them with me some time over a drink." He moved a hand toward her. She took a step back and kicked the stool out from under him. He tried to move his outstretched hand toward the bar top, but inebriation slowed down his reaction and his head hit the bar with a loud crack. He fell to the floor writhing in pain as he held the side of his head.

The other man who was with him stood up and pulled a knife from his belt. "I bet the Knights would pay a fair price for some information on you." He wasn't as intoxicated as his friend. She reached into her sleeve and readied a blade.

"That'll be enough!" Cordelia recognized the cook's voice. She didn't take her eyes off the man in front of her. "How about you pick your friend up off the ground and get out of here before I have to call the City Guard. And you, Haze Walker, I'd like you to leave before you hurt more of my customers. I don't want to regret doing business with you." The cook was out of sight before she turned to look at him. He must have been talking through the window that connected the back of the bar to the kitchen.

Cordelia took out her data pad and held it above a scanner at the bar. There was a quick beep and a text box appeared on the screen. She entered the number two and accepted the transaction. "Sorry about that," she said to the bartender. He shrugged and continued cleaning glasses behind the bar. The drunk man let out a groan as he was picked up from the floor.

The brightness of the afternoon welcomed her as she exited the bar and walked down the crowded side street of the Third District. Vendors shouted from their stalls that lined the street as they tried to get the attention of passersby. The heat from the midday sun seemed to double within the crowd. She pushed her way through the small gaps she found

18

between people. At the first opportunity she ducked into a side street. Not many people used the side streets. These streets were mostly used by the waste carts that moved from building to building picking up what was left out for collection. Thankfully, the Lower Districts had a sewer system that ran throughout the districts, so there was no human waste to be collected. Cordelia would have preferred wading through the crowded streets if that were the case.

She knew District Three well enough to find her way to one of the Exterior Gates. From here her best options to get out into the New Ring were the North or East Gate. She could picture the layout of the district in her head and settled on the East Gate. She turned left down another branching side street. Footsteps behind her made her reach into her sleeves once more, but she relaxed when she heard a familiar voice.

"Cordelia? How'd the meet up go?" Howlen Norre was a plump man just past his middle years. His horseshoe of brown hair and his always-pink cheeks reminded Cordelia of a baker or a cook. The least likely man to be a contact for someone who regularly goes out into the Haze. He huffed as he caught up. She slowed her pace to match his.

"Ran into some trouble with some drunks at the bar," she said. Howlen raised an eyebrow. "Nothing to worry about. Just another scavenge job. Oh." Cordelia pulled the bottle of dark alcohol out of the side pouch on her bag. "A gift from the cook."

"Well!" Howlen took the cork from the mouth of the bottle and tipped it back. He let out a hiss, "*Shield protect me.*" The man wheezed and cleared his throat. "Thank you." He chuckled.

"Gladly." Cordelia looked around them. There was no sign of anyone else within earshot. "I'm going to resupply at a friend's place out in the New Ring before I go out." Howlen nodded. He never asked question about the specifics of how she got out into the Haze, or who her friend was out on the

Perimeter. "District Three seems more crowded than usual today. It's like Market District out there."

"One of the Diplomatic Councilors is giving a speech today in the Sixth District. Gotta try to keep the people happy."

Out of the corner of her eye she saw him shake his head. Relations between the Upper and Lower Districts had always been tense. Things had gotten worse as of late. More and more settlers in the New Ring were coming to the capital. The idea of living out in the openness of the New Ring was appealing, but the excitement of living out there seemed to mask the danger for some. Life wasn't always better on the other side of the wall. That counted both ways.

"Good to know. They'll be increasing security between the districts. I need to get out before that." Cordelia picked up her pace. Without a word Howlen turned down a separate street.

The City Guard always seemed to randomly select who to harass when leaving or entering the capital. Getting back in was certainly more challenging. She could return through any of the gates along the massive Exterior Wall. Any choice would be risky depending on what she was bringing in with her. If the guards caught her with something from the Haze, it would be obvious she went out. That would raise some flags. She would probably end up in a cell and questioned.

She had been taken inside one of the checkpoints years ago for questioning. She made the mistake of coming through with some of her Haze gear. At the time she was scolding herself for being so forgetful, but in hindsight it gave her a chance to get an idea of the layout of the guard post. She eventually got away by playing naive and saying she bought it off a trader in the New Ring. They confiscated her gear, but she hadn't been detained any longer than the questioning took. Some were not so lucky.

The capital did have a place for those who broke the laws set in place by the Council. Most of what Cordelia had heard

20

about the dungeons were rumor. The walls of the city weren't actually solid, but a catacomb of cells. There actually was no dungeon at all, instead the Council forced lawbreakers out into the Haze. There was a secret underground city beneath the capital where all the outcasts were forced to live. Cells within the Exterior Wall seemed to be the most realistic. She wasn't interested in finding out for herself.

There was always the option to wait for a chance to sneak in amongst the crowds who seek refuge in the city. Smugglers were always bringing people in and out of Amboy. She had only considered it once when Howlen had brought a big job to her. The risk of getting caught outweighed the payout of any job.

Cordelia exited a side street and entered back into the mass of people. She made her way through the crowd on one of the main streets of the Third District toward the East Gate. Wagon drivers shouted from atop their seats at people who walked by. Some didn't even bother to shout and just plowed through the crowd. There was always a sense of urgency in the Industrial District. Raw materials from the New Ring were constantly coming in to be processed. There were several large factories within the district as well as smaller shops that focused on specialized jobs. The filtering systems on the factories removed a majority of the pollution, but even on cooler days the air was hot, and the smell of the factories weighed heavy on the area.

She approached the security checkpoint along with a small number of others who were on their way out to the New Ring. The colossal stone wall towered over everyone. Being this close, Cordelia had to crane her neck to see the top. Two turrets extended out from the wall roughly twelve feet above the checkpoint, one on each side. There would be two guards stationed in each. There were even more in the rooms inside the wall. She counted six guards around the tunnel. Two were stood facing into the district and the other four were searching a merchant's carts. There would be a few more in an observation room off to the side of the tunnel that led through to the East Gate. The merchants being searched would likely take the attention off her, making it easy to walk right through without any questioning.

"Please sir, this is unnecessary. I pass through here twice a week. I know you've seen me before," the merchant pleaded to an Amboian guard.

The Amboian grabbed the merchant and pushed him against his cart. "I do not care if you pass through these gates every day. We will search these carts. We will search them as many times as we deem necessary." The guard towered over the man. Cordelia had seen plenty of angered guards while living in the city. She pictured the Amboian's blue skin becoming flushed with anger behind his silver helmet.

The merchant turned to a Human guard. "Can you do something to help me here?" Humans had only been allowed to join the City Guard recently. It was uncommon to see a Human posted at one of the Exterior Gates. The Amboian still held the merchant against his cart. He turned to the Human guardsman and grunted.

The man cleared his throat before he spoke, "We check every cart that is flagged to be searched. You would do well to stand by while the search is underway. If nothing is out of place you can go about your business." The Amboian let go of the merchant, who stepped beside his cart and removed the large canvas that was covering it. She glanced over as she passed. The cart was packed with lumber and several canvas sacks. Construction supplies, she guessed.

Cordelia continued through the tunnel toward the gate. A string of dim lights ran along the top of the high vaulted ceiling. The air was much cooler within the tan-gray stone walls. She thought of the rumored holding cells and shuddered. She wanted to quicken her pace but held back. That may look suspicious to the guards. As she neared the end, the wicket door within the massive East Gate opened. Light filled the dim tunnel. She squinted as she continued to the opening. An arm holding a spear shot out from the other side of the door and a massive Amboian Guard stepped out in front of her. The sunlight made it difficult to make out his features. Not that she would be able to see his face behind that silvery helmet.

"What's your business outside the city?" the Amboian snapped.

"Visiting a friend in East Edge," she replied. She focused on the vast green fields in front of her.

"Travel safe." The guard moved back to his position against the gateway.

The Sun Road was the fastest way to travel to East Edge. It was mostly flat aside from some rolling hills. Without any trouble she would be able to make it there in a few days. She checked the pocket on her jacket for her coin pouch. There was a muffled jingle of the few coins she kept. Within the walls of the city credits were the common currency. The further one traveled from the city the worse the transfer speed became for any sort of data, whether it was a simple message or a transfer of credits. Along the Perimeter a message sent between two people standing shoulder to shoulder could take days to receive. She had heard that there were emergency channels that could be hacked into to improve communication speed, but the risk didn't seem worth it.

Her fair skin never did well in the heat, and she often contemplated cutting her long, curly auburn hair short. She would likely regret cutting it once she had, so she tied it up for now. Cordelia pulled out a pair of tinted glasses from inside her jacket and wrapped a loose scarf around her head to protect her from the intensity of the sun. She tightened the shoulder straps of her pack and began her journey to East Edge.

From where he stood on top of the Exterior Wall of the

capital city of Amboy, Carter Gerro could see for miles out into the New Ring; the rolling plains of tall grass dotted with farm houses, the hard-packed dirt roads that led into the dark, green forests. Beyond the horizon was the Perimeter, and then The Haze. The Perimeter dome was barely noticeable against the bright blue sky as Carter looked around him. The only visible representation of the protective barrier were the tiny glints of sunlight reflecting off the floating Shield Generators as they hovered in the sky. It was a hot day and being stationed on top of the stone wall didn't help. The occasional breeze was the only small retreat Carter would have. He had hardly spent time outside the walls that surrounded Amboy. He never saw reason to. Everything he needed was within the capital.

Behind him was the city itself, more specifically the Third District. The circular city of Amboy was sectioned into twelve radial districts on the outermost ring. These were known as the Lower Districts. Further inward toward the center of the city were the four Upper Districts. Carter didn't know much of them. Then there was Central Amboy. In his twenty-five years of living in the city, all he had learned about Central Amboy was that it was where the Council lived and performed their governmental duties.

Although the wall Carter was currently stationed on was three hundred feet tall and fifty feet thick, it was nothing compared to the separation between the Lower and Upper Districts. About a mile and a half away from where Carter was currently standing was another wall, much taller than the exterior wall, and as far as he could guess probably thicker too. The only time he came close to those gates was when he was lost as a kid. He had tried to ask a guard for help, but they hardly acknowledged him. So, he waited. He was afraid but didn't cry. Eventually his older brother who he had been walking the streets with found him and took him home. When they had gotten home neither he nor his brother had mentioned anything about Carter getting lost. His father worked long days at one of the smaller processing factories, and his mother worked longer days at a clinic in the Seventh District, known to most as the Holy District.

Carter was part of the first group of Humans to join the City Guard. Prior to their inclusion it was composed of Amboians led by the Knights of Amboy. The first time he had seen a Knight was during his time in training. Even after having been a member of the City Guard for years, he still found the presence of the Knights intimidating. Even a *regular* Amboy guardsman was intimidating, but there was something exceptional about the Knights.

A loud train whistle snapped Carter back to attention. Shipping trains brought supplies and workers to and from Amboy, throughout the New Ring, and to the Perimeter where new settlements were being built. The New Ring consisted mostly of farms and small towns, but that didn't mean that it was free of threats. Carter had to be on the lookout for anything. He looked down along the wall to see two large metal doors open. A hole in the ground appeared as the gray-blue metal train cars came from below. A circular track ran beneath the Exterior Wall with junctions at various points that allowed the train to travel on the above ground tracks throughout the New Ring. A group of City Guards kept people back, as they attempted to force their way into the now-open doors. The large walls must have seemed more protective than the openness and uncertainty of the New Ring. Those that didn't make it into the city in a proper way always tried to sneak in. Many found success, which only added to the overpopulation in the districts.

Carter was glad to be stationed atop the wall. His safety was never entirely ensured while he was posted at one of the archways between districts. Especially the Eighth District. He never felt safe anywhere near District Eight. It was referred to among those in the Lower Districts as the Forgotten District. There were many rumors, some believed were a hard truth, that the wealthier Upper Districts used their power to control the Lower Districts while the Council was distracted with other matters. Carter didn't mind dealing with the random drunk, or thief. It was the more organized groups that worried him.

"Guardsman!"

Carter snapped to attention. An Amboian was approaching. The Human guards were few enough that they all knew each other by name.

"Sir." If Carter were able to appear more at attention he would have.

The Amboian was at least seven feet tall, about average as far as Carter had known. From the corner of his eye, he could already tell this wasn't a normal City Guard. Carter turned and held a fist to his chest. A Knight might return an Amboian guardsman's salute, but this Knight didn't return Carter's.

The crest of the Amboian Council was on his chest plate. Two circles, one smaller inside the other. Sets of lines sectioned the circles, making them look like the Upper and Lower districts. Sunlight bounced off the Knight's silver armor. The Knight's helmet had a rounded Y-shape visor on the front that was tinted black. It faded and became clear. Behind the now see-through visor, Carter could see his blue skin, dark piercing eyes, and thin lips. "Diplomatic Councilor Gaelcean will be touring Districts Four, Five, and Six today. We are increasing security down in the lower levels. You are to report to the security post between Five and Six."

Far enough away from Eight at least. "Yes sir. Right away." Carter pressed a closed fist to his chest again.

Getting used to being around the Knights and Amboian guards had taken time. He had focused on the similarities between their species and Humans, but in doing so it was easy to notice the differences. Their appearance was Human enough, if you ignored their blue skin, or purple as it had been in some cases. Where a Human's nose stuck out from their face, an Amboians was a slight mound with a slit on

26

either side. Their ears were flat against the sides of their heads. Their sold black eyes still unsettled him, and likely would for some time. He was never quite sure of exactly where they were looking.

The Amboian Knight passed Carter along the wall. Carter walked in the opposite direction to one of the turrets that contained a speed lift that would bring him down to the city streets. The checkpoint between the Fifth and Sixth District wasn't far off. The cool air within the stone walls was welcoming after being out in the sun. He hit the lift button and waited. After a moment, the doors opened, and he stepped inside and pressed the button for the guard post below.

The lift doors opened, and Carter stepped into the foyer of a small barracks that was located at the post between Districts Three and Four. The square room was about twenty feet across and had several rooms on each side. Some were used for interrogations; others were designated areas where guards were allowed their break. During his own break Carter would find a cot to rest for a moment or play a game of Twelve with the other Human guards. He had taken breaks with Amboian guards when they worked the same shifts, but they never occupied the same rooms if they could avoid it.

Once a group of Amboians entered a room where he and others had been. They sat as far as possible from Carter and the others, and in silence. There were plenty of open cots and none of them took the opportunity to lie down. Others had said they had experienced the same. Rumors started that their species didn't need to sleep and that they had no native language. Which was absurd, everything must rest at some point. He opened a door to one of the restrooms in the foyer and locked it behind him. Once inside he took his helmet off and set it on a small wooden table next to the wash basin and looked at himself in the mirror. His brown skin was glistening from the sweat that still covered it.

He looked tired. *Everything must rest.* His hazel eyes were slightly bloodshot from the long hours of work.

Carter unfastened the armor covering his chest and set it on the floor beside him. The matte-gray chest piece was made in the Upper Districts for the City Guards. His consisted of two shoulder straps that connected the front and back plate. Sets of clasps on each side locked the two plates together. The armor was incredibly light, surprisingly durable. It fit his body perfectly. When he passed the training, they had scanned his entire body and made a full suit for him. While on guard duty, the minimum requirement was the chest and helmet, and he appreciated that. His helmet wasn't as involved as the Knights, but it served its purpose. The same matte-gray color as his chest piece. It was made to match the shape of the human head. There was a T-shaped opening in the front that made room for the wearer's face so they could see and be heard without issue. During combat a visor slid down from inside the brow of the helmet to protect the eyes. Much like the visor, two pieces of metal met in the middle, perpendicular to the visor, to protect the face. If he was to be deployed to combat, he had a full suit that protected his body made from the same lightweight metal.

Carter rolled up the sleeves of his shirt, turned on the faucet and splashed some water on his face. He pulled up his shirt to wipe his face only taking a second to admire himself in the mirror. He didn't consider himself vain; he was proud of how well he took care of himself. He picked up his chest piece and put it back on. He grabbed his helmet off the wooden table and walked back out into the foyer.

Carter turned left to the secure door that led outside. He pulled out his data pad and held it up to a scanning device next to the door. A light flashed blue and there was a loud metal clunk from inside the door as the lock mechanism released. Carter put the data pad back into the pouch on his waist belt and grabbed a metal cylinder from a loop on the same belt. The small metal cylinder fit in his hand perfectly. He pushed a button near his middle finger and the cylinder expanded into a long shaft only slightly taller than him. Once completely extended the top end formed to a point. Much like how his armor was made to fit only his body, his weapons would only activate in his hands. He pushed the large metal door open and stepped out into the archway that connected the Third and Fourth Districts.

The two guards standing on duty turned and looked in his direction as he stepped out. Carter recognized them immediately. "Myra. Ronald," he greeted them as the door shut behind him. The metal clunk sounded again announcing the engaged lock. He walked forward so they stood shoulder to shoulder facing the opposite side of the arch that separated the districts. The amount of people that passed through would have been surprising any other day. It seemed the Lower Districts had been informed much earlier than he about the Diplomatic Councilor's speeches. Carter scanned the mass of bodies moving along in front of them.

"Done with your shift up top already, Carter?" Ronald asked in his usual sarcastic tone.

"Apparently. A Diplomatic Councilor is giving a speech today and the Knights are increasing security in some areas."

"I heard word this morning on a patrol. A Knight must have asked you to assist with the event today." Myra elbowed Carter. "They must really like you."

"Even if they did, how could you even tell? The only time I've seen a Knight show emotion is when he's trying to intimidate someone," Carter said half-jokingly.

"When was the last time you went more than a day without being assigned to the Wall?" Carter couldn't tell if Myra was annoyed or continuing the jest. Most likely both.

"I guess you're right." He was stationed up there regularly. He hadn't been on foot patrol in well over a week.

"See. You spend so much time up there, you forget what a privilege it is." Ronald shook his head. "The last time I was posted up there had to have been before Harvest season began in the New Ring." He let out a laugh.

29

"I think I recall hearing that you fell asleep during your shift," Myra said. Ronald's laugh was cut short. If he didn't have to keep a watch on the crowd, Carter would have guessed Ronald was staring daggers. Myra continued, "You're making us look bad. They're going to regret allowing Humans to become guards in the first place."

Ronald scoffed, "That wasn't me. How many times have I told you?"

"Alright." Carter stepped forward. "I'm off to the Fifth and Sixth. I'll see you around." Carter brought a fist to his chest.

"Be safe, Carter," Ronald said as he mirrored the salute. Myra did the same.

Most of the people in District Four were heading in the direction of District Six. Carter moved through the crowd with ease. Being a member of the City Guard didn't hurt either, people usually got out of his way.

"Carter! Carter!" a voice behind him called out. He turned to see where the shout was coming from. A boy ran and weaved between the stalls and vendors along the side of the crowd. Carter recognized Waleed when the boy's head popped up above the others. He was a baker's apprentice in the Fourth District if Carter remembered correctly.

"Hey, Waleed!" Carter kept moving with the crowd but kept the boy in sight.

Waleed stopped at a stall and climbed up some crates as the vendor shouted at him. "Can you stop by the shop sometime soon? We were robbed last week and no one's doin' anything about it!"

"I'll see what I can do about that, Waleed," Carter shouted as he walked past. "Get back to your shop before you cause trouble for that man." Carter heard a thank you but couldn't see Waleed as he continued through the crowd.

The crowd shuffled through the street. Occasionally, Carter would raise his voice to get people to move out of the way. Never threatening, just to allow him to keep his pace.

30

He didn't want to give the Knights reason to regret asking for his assistance. Knights were stationed at the archway between the Fourth and Fifth Districts. There wasn't a regular Amboian guard at the post that Carter could see. He approached the nearest Knight and saluted. "Sir. Carter Gerro."

The Amboian Knight turned to him as his visor became clear. This Knight had the same dark piercing eyes as any. His skin was a deep blue and his face seemed harder than the stone that made the walls of the city. "Yes. Gerro." The Knight looked away and his visor went black again. "Councilor Gaelcean will begin his speech once all City Guards are in place and proper protocols have been completed. Get to your post."

"Understood, sir." Carter moved back into the crowd and passed through the archway and into the Fifth District.

The Fifth was similar to most of other Lower Districts. A wide main street ran the length of it, with shops and stalls lining both sides. Residences stacked on top usually three or four high. Parallel to the main street there were smaller streets that followed the curvature of the district with more of the same. Halfway, the main street was intersected by a similarly sized street. On one end was the gate between the district and the New Ring, and on the other end the gate between the Lower and the Upper Districts.

The only Lower District that strayed from the layout of the others was the Eighth. Carter didn't have to try hard to remember his first patrol through the Forgotten District. Every street seemed to be closing in on him. The widest he walked on wouldn't have fit more than ten guards shoulder to shoulder. There was at one time an order to its chaos, but once the city started to become overpopulated residences could no longer be built upward and had to spread out into the streets. The first obvious choice was the broad main streets that intersected the district, much like the intersection Carter was approaching now. In the Eighth, a row of

31

residences were built to divide the two main streets into separate smaller streets. That was the last major planning done by the Council.

This was long before Carter's time, so he had no firsthand understanding of why this was. There were stories of trouble with some of the towns and villages that lived outside of the city walls and that took priority over planning. Back then the New Ring must have only consisted of a fraction of what it was now. Nothing like the vast space it was today. Maybe the rushed inclusion of those outside the wall caused the haphazard settlement that existed in Eight now.

Carter's thoughts of city planning faded from his mind as he walked up to the archway that divided Five and Six. Again, only Amboian Knights were present. No Amboian City Guards. Were there no other regular Amboian Guardsmen available for the position? Nervousness crept into Carter's mind. He struggled to keep his composure.

"Guardsman!"

"Reporting, sir."

"You are wanted inside the barracks." The Knight's visor remained black. He didn't even look in Carter's direction.

"Yes, sir." Carter moved into the archway and walked toward the security door. He retracted his spear and returned it to his belt. When he reached for his data pad he found himself fumbling with it. He paused for a moment to steady his hands. No other regular guards were present. What was this all about? He managed to hold the data pad up to the scanner long enough for the light to flash blue. The lock disengaged. The familiar sound brought some comfort.

"Breathe." He hadn't meant to say it out loud. He pushed the metal door and stepped inside the barracks.

It was almost exactly the same as the one he had just left, a square foyer, with rooms along the sides, a speed lift in the back. Knights were moving about the space with intent. He was so caught up in the commotion he hadn't even noticed the unarmored Knight looking at him.

"Sir. Carter Gerro." He had brought his fist to his chest a little too fast and could feel a sting in his hand. His mouth was dry, and he struggled to work up some moisture. The Knight seemed shorter than the others moving about the room. Maybe it was the armor that made them seem so large. No, this Amboian was shorter. Carter's nerves were getting to him, the Amboian looked like he was actually smiling at him.

"Hello, Carter Gerro. I am Diplomatic Councilor Gaelcean."

Sweat beaded on his brow. He wished he was standing atop the wall in the hot sun.

CHAPTER TWO

Amber Waves

Caleb Fields stood under the only pine tree that stuck out from the forest behind him, the shade of the tall tree was a welcome respite from the blazing sun above. Caleb looked out across the expansive grassy plain toward the walled city. In his forty-five years he had been inside the walls many times but was always impressed when he looked upon the structure. It truly was massive. He hadn't grown up inside the city, but rather in the town of Homestead to the southeast of the capital. Compared to the other towns in the New Ring, Homestead was a monolith. He enjoyed the bustling streets and the beauty of Farmer's Lake that spanned the length of the town.

"You're thinking about Homestead, aren't you?" Lucas said as he walked up to Caleb's side.

"I am." Caleb laughed. He looked at his old friend. The grays in Lucas' dirty blond hair seemed more noticeable now, as well as the creases at the corners of his eyes. His olive skin was beginning to sag, but he knew his childhood friend was underneath all his signs of age. He couldn't judge Lucas too much anyway; deep valleys had formed on his own face years ago and underneath his hood he was as smooth as a newborn. He raked a hand through his thick black beard. At least he still had that.

"You always have that look on your face when you're thinking about home." Lucas' hand clasped Caleb on the shoulder.

"As if you don't as well." Caleb shook his shoulder and stepped away laughing.

"I hated that place, you know that. Couldn't wait to leave." Lucas looked toward the city and sighed. Caleb and Lucas had joined the Homestead Town Watch and patrolled the streets together. Caleb had found a sense of pride in protecting the people of his town. "We still planning on heading in tomorrow?"

"It's midday now." Caleb looked up to the sky through the branches of the pine. "Less than a half day's travel to the city. We'll stay here and camp another night." Caleb turned and walked in the direction Lucas had come from. "The next job can wait."

The corruption from the capital had spread throughout the New Ring, and placed roots in Homestead. Caleb tried to fight it, but when half the Town Watch was being paid to look the other way, it made his job difficult. Eventually he left, just like Lucas had years before him. That was a long time ago now though and thinking about that would only ruin such a beautiful day. He searched the New Ring to find Lucas. When he did, he convinced Lucas to join him in rooting out that corruption. That was when the two of them founded the Amber Waves Company. They settled on a name that would remind them of Homestead.

Caleb continued walking with Lucas at his side down into the depression that hid their camp. Three tan canvas tents were pitched in a circle around a small cook fire. Their friend and companion, Omar Cross, was seated at the fire. Caleb would often tell Omar he was built like the strongest oak in the forest, and he truly meant it. Omar was a tall, solid man.

35

He had a clean-shaven face and head, and the day's light seemed to bounce off his dark skin.

"How's it coming, Omar?" Caleb asked. Omar was once a member of the Church of Amboy. They were hired to protect him and the other members of the Church while they walked the city streets doing charity work.

"Not sure we have enough seasoning for these," Omar said as he gestured to several rabbits that had been cleaned and skewered on sticks. "We'll have to see about picking up some more. If we're lucky we'll catch a merchant coming back from the city along the Spice Road, maybe we can get a deal."

"We'll keep that in mind." Lucas sat down in front of his tent. "Any word from Ana and Levi?"

"Neither of them have contacted me. They know to meet here though," Caleb said as he sat down across from Lucas and reached back to grab his long sword. He pulled a whetstone from his pack. He poured a bit of water on the stone and began running it along the length of the blade.

"What's the name of our contact in the city again?" Omar removed the skewered rabbits from the flame to get a better look at his work.

"There wasn't one. Just a meeting location in the Ninth District." Lucas was also looking toward the rabbits.

"Few more minutes." Omar chuckled when he saw Lucas' gaze. He looked at Caleb. "Cold drop then?"

"I don't think so. Normally I'd be hesitant to take a job with such little info, but they paid fifty credits up front." The repetitive motion of sharpening his blade had his focus. The information for the job came out of him almost reflexively. Every detail about the job was cemented in his mind. Caleb's companions were like family to him. He felt responsible for each of them, even Lucas.

"Good enough for me." Omar wiped the sweat off his brow with his forearm.

"Probably just another gang looking for us to take out

another gang's leader, then they'll take the credit. Probably keeping their name out of the contact information to avoid anyone fishing for hits," Lucas said as he lay back and covered his eyes with one arm. They had only taken those sorts of jobs when times became tough. Caleb justified it in his mind by focusing on the removal of one gang, and not the bolstering of another.

"I haven't known any gangs to pay credits up front, let alone fifty." Omar wiped his forearm on his pant leg.

"Agreed. I say three of us go to the meet up, while the other two stay back and keep an eye out." Caleb moved back from the fire. Even though it was only a small cooking fire, the midday heat was enough for him. He made room to sit beneath the shade of his tent by rolling his bedding toward the back and set his unstrung bow to the side. The tent had trapped some of the heat from the sun, but the shade was nice.

"I'm done sitting in this heat as well. Let's call it." Omar pulled the rabbits from the fire. He turned back and pulled a knife from the side of his pack. They passed rabbits around as each took a piece for themselves.

"Not bad for having little seasoning left," Lucas said. The words barely made it past the food in his mouth. Omar nodded in appreciation and agreement. Seasoned or not, Caleb had been looking forward to the meal.

"Looks like we're just in time!" a voice called from over the hill opposite the one Caleb had been standing on before.

"Not much left now," Omar yelled without looking behind him and smiled toward Lucas and Caleb. Ana Brooks walked down the hill toward the small camp. Ana was of average height for a woman her age with light-brown skin that reminded Caleb of the flowing fields of wheat that surrounded his hometown. Her eyes were as deep blue as the sea they sailed across when she left Ser'Delcea to join the Amber Waves. Walking next to her was the most recent addition, Levi. His long brown hair was usually neatly parted

37

down the middle and tucked behind his ears on either side. The two were the youngest of the group.

"There's plenty to go around." Caleb cut off a piece for himself and held out what was left.

"Thanks!" Ana laughed as she lunged forward to beat Levi to the rabbit.

"Here's some for you, Levi." Omar handed what was left of his to Levi.

"Thanks, Omar," Levi said. As he chewed on the meat, he unstrung his longbow. Long was an understatement. The bow was taller than Levi, almost taller than Caleb himself. He had once seen Levi hit a badger from across a field, much like the one they were camped in now.

"Only three rabbits, huh?" Ana smiled as she slid her arms out of her pack one at a time and sat down. "If I were here probably could have gotten at least two more." She looked across the fire pit toward Omar and smiled before taking a bite out of the rabbit. She wiped her mouth on a gray sleeve of her undershirt.

Even though she had left Ser'Delcea all those years ago she still only wore clothes in the fashion of her home. She had cut the sleeves of her light wool jacket turning it into a vest that flared at the waist, and the legs of her tan pants were tucked into her tall boots. Caleb and Lucas and Omar had met Ana when they sailed across the Great Sea to Ser'Delcea after receiving a job from her father who owned a shipping company in the port of Ser'Delcea.

"You've been walking through the New Ring all day, and yet you show up empty handed? Couldn't catch anything on the way here?" Omar returned sarcastically without looking up from fire as he smothered it.

"Well, you see..." Ana trailed off and then laughed to herself.

"Ah, yes." Omar looked up and smiled.

"How was the travel this morning?" Caleb interjected.

"Not bad. Not many people on the southern roads today.

At first, we stuck to the less traveled roads, but then decided we would make better time on Farmer's Road." Levi said and then picked a piece of meat from his teeth with his fingers. Levi quickly wiped his hand on the leg of his pants and gave a wry smile.

Caleb shook his head and smiled as well. "End of Harvest. Everyone is probably taking a break from their travels. I know Homestead and other towns have celebrations at the end of this season." Fewer people on the roads could be useful to make good time. It could also bring trouble if someone tried to take advantage of the lack of eyes on them. More than once Caleb had been set upon by someone trying to take some coin from him while traveling. Thankfully, he didn't keep much coin on him when traveling in the New Ring. Most of his wealth was stored in his account he could access with his data pad.

Caleb found himself thinking back to the Harvest's End celebration in Homestead. Days of drinking and feasting. Celebration throughout the town. When he was younger, he was most fond of finding a pretty girl who would dance with him. If there was one thing he knew for certain, it was that a girl from Homestead always liked a boy who knew how to dance well.

"Fewer crowds moving toward the city might make it hard to get in," Omar thought aloud, "Not that we have anything to worry about. Right?"

"True. Fewer people coming and going, might make the guards a bit relaxed though," Lucas replied.

"Have you ever known an Amboian guard to be relaxed?" Ana threw a small bone into the fire pit. "I haven't."

"Have they put Human guards on duty outside the gates yet?" Levi asked.

"Not that I've seen," Omar said, "but even if they did, there would most likely be an Amboian with them. The only time I've seen all Human guards is at the archways between Districts."

39

"We've been able to sneak in before. Why not go in tonight instead of tomorrow?" Ana suggested.

"I'm not sure that we'll need to sneak in. We're not bringing anything in with us. If the Guards decide to check us, they won't find anything unusual." Caleb stroked his thick black beard. "Besides, I don't remember the last time all five of us needed to sneak into the city."

There was a silence as they all thought. In the distance a bird called out and shortly after there was a response.

Lucas snapped his fingers and pointed toward Caleb, "Two winters ago. Remember that bad storm?"

"Right." Even in this heat Caleb felt a chill. "We got caught traveling from Homestead and the snows piled up against the outer wall blocking the gates on the western and northern sides. Everyone was trying to force their way into the gates that hadn't been blocked. I still can't believe they were keeping people out during that."

"At least it was warmer in the crowd." Omar gathered the emptied skewers and tossed them into the blackened fire pit.

"We got lucky taking turns sneaking by the guards while they dealt with the others trying to get in." Levi took his pack off and began rummaging through it.

"It wasn't the first time one or all of us has had luck on our side," Caleb said as he leaned back into the shade of his tent.

"*Chance,*" Omar said smiling. He was referencing the Salvation of Humanity. The Salvation was the scripture that members of the Church of Amboy learned from and preached to others. It wasn't much for Caleb, but he understood what others could see in it and how it helped them.

Caleb saw Ana roll her eyes. "I've only just finished eating, Omar. Can we hold off on the sermon?" Omar had only smiled in response.

Levi pulled a small hammer out of his pack and dropped it on the ground beside him. He undid the straps that held his canvas roll to the top of his pack. "I'll get my tent in order and then gather some more wood for the fire," Levi said, and he unrolled the canvas.

"Sounds like a good idea," Lucas said, "I'll go with you when you're ready."

"I think I'll sleep under the stars tonight." Ana stretched her arms up above her head and lay back onto the grass and let out a long sigh.

"It'll be a good night for it, I bet." Omar looked toward the sky, "Hardly any clouds today, could say the same for tonight."

"If only one of us had been trained as a Sky Watcher," Ana said with her eyes closed.

"I'm not trained, but I think Omar has it right." Levi tossed his tent stakes next to his canvas on the ground and picked up his hammer.

"The Sky Watcher in Homestead was wrong half the time anyway," Lucas said. He wasn't wrong. The old, withered man Caleb remembered would spread the word that the worst rainstorm they had ever seen was on the way. The entire town had to board up the windows and call for more thatch for the houses that needed it. The next week would turn out to have clear skies, but no one would remove their window boards out of fear that the storm would come.

"We should all make sure to get a good night's rest," Lucas said, changing the subject. "We'll enter through the Southern Gate at sun up and head to the Ninth District. We should get to the meeting location ahead of our contact so we can get a feel for things."

The fifty credits they had received upfront was appreciated and it would likely mean the person they were meeting was serious about the job they had in store. *Serious payout for a serious job.* It excited him, but the uncertainty of everything created worry in his thoughts. He couldn't tell which out-weighed the other.

It was beginning to get dark when Lucas and Levi had returned. Caleb got up from his seat near his tent and ran toward Lucas, who was carrying Levi over his shoulders. Caleb had reached them in an instant and help Lucas carry Levi.

"What happened?" Caleb asked. Levi's fair skin seemed much paler, and his hair was matted with sweat. Leaves and small twigs stuck out here and there.

Lucas looked at Caleb. "Found him sitting at the base of a tree. Just rocking back and forth, mumbling to himself." Just like how they had found him those few years ago. He was frail and as thin as a sapling then. Levi was much healthier now, but it pained Caleb to see him like this.

"Is he okay?" Omar asked. He was standing at the edge of the ring of tents as they approached, his iron-capped staff in his hands. Ana was standing beside him with a concerned look on her face.

"He'll be alright. Just needs some rest is all," Caleb said as they carried him to his tent.

"I shouldn't have left him," Lucas mumbled as they covered Levi with his brown travel-worn cloak.

"You couldn't have known this would happen, Lucas."

"He was my responsibility."

"We're both responsible for all of them." Caleb put a hand on Lucas' shoulder.

"How long before he'll speak again this time, you think?" Ana was crouched behind Caleb and Levi.

"Ana—" Caleb began.

"I only mean that I'm worried about him." she sighed.

"We just need to let him rest," Caleb said as he stepped out of the opening of Levi's tent. Lucas undid the ties and closed the flaps of the tent.

The four of them sat around the fire. Levi's whimpers and mumbling could be faintly heard over the crackling and popping of the fire.

42

"Levi has been with us for so long now," Lucas began. "I just wasn't thinking."

"It's fine, Lucas." Caleb continued to reassure his friend.

"I'm just as surprised as you are," Ana said as she poked a stick in the fire. "When was the last time this has even happened."

"I'm not sure. Long enough for me to have difficulty remembering, I guess," Caleb replied.

"It's just like you said, Caleb." Omar was the one doing the consoling now. "He just needs some rest. He has experienced a trauma we know nothing about."

Levi had been covered in cuts and bruises when they found him. They asked him to explain who he was or where he was from, but he wouldn't speak. The four of them took him in and fed him. Days later, he finally spoke. He had told them he would stay with them to repay the debt he owed. At the time he could barely swing a sword or ride a horse. While they were in the Market District during a trip into the city, Levi had purchased his long bow. Caleb had suggested against it, but Levi insisted. He never explained how easily he took to using the bow, and Caleb never asked. When the day came that Levi wanted to talk about his past, Caleb would be there to listen.

"Should we cancel tomorrow's meeting?" Ana asked.

"No." Lucas shook his head. "I'll stay here with Levi if he needs to rest more. You all go on without us, and we'll meet back here."

"We can all stay here together." Omar nodded to himself.

"Lucas is right. We'll go on while he stays here with Levi." Caleb hated to admit it, and it may make him seem cold, but they needed the credits from this job.

"Are we sure—" Omar's sentence was cut short by a rustling sound coming from Levi's tent.

"I'm fine," Levi said as he looked out at them. "I'll rest up tonight, and tomorrow we'll head into the city like we planned." He let the canvas fall back into place.

"I'm going to turn in as well," Lucas said as he stood up.

"We all should get some rest." Caleb rolled to the side and crouch walked into his tent. They would all need their rest for tomorrow's job.

CHAPTER THREE

The Diplomat

The Amboian crossed the room. Even though he was slightly shorter than the three Knights that were accompanying him, he stood a foot taller than Carter. His blue high-necked coat was a much darker shade than his light-blue skin. The coat had flat shoulders with silver trim. Silver buttons ran down the front, and all were buttoned. On his left breast was a pin of the Amboian crest. The crest was present on armor of the Knights of Amboy. It was a simplified version of a top-down view of the city. On his right breast was another pin. A bird of some kind. Carter had seen plenty of birds while he was stationed atop the Exterior Wall but was never any good at identifying them. The coat ended at mid-thigh, and his pants were pressed with one crease that ran down the sides. He wore black flats that seemed a bit out of place with the rest of his attire.

"I am glad that you are able to be a part of my security for this event." Gaelcean held out an open hand toward Carter.

"Of course, sir. I am honored." Carter reached out and shook his hand. It was the first time he hadn't felt an air of intimidation when speaking with an Amboian. There was even a sense of kindness in Gaelcean's pitch-black eyes.

"Under different circumstances I would have enjoyed getting to know you a bit more. I am embarrassed to admit, my only knowledge of you is from what the Knights have told me." Gaelcean released Carter's hand and moved toward the foyer. "Let us go over the plan for today's events." Carter walked side by side with Gaelcean into the foyer with the three Knights towering over them. They entered a room that was normally a mess hall. Three tables were in the center of the room and there was a map on each. Carter immediately recognized the curved sections of Districts Four, Five and Six on each map. There was a Knight at each table standing at attention as Gaelcean and Carter approached.

Behind the table were Amboians talking amongst each other. In his twenty-six years of living within the city walls, he had never heard the Amboian language. Some said they didn't have a native language, others said they spoke telepathically, and Carter had also heard they never spoke their language in public out of secrecy. The Amboian language sounded complex, yet strangely slurred. The Amboians noticed Carter was looking at them and stopped talking.

"I imagine you will be among a very small group of Humans who have heard the Amboian language and continued living." Gaelcean walked up to the edge of the table that was the leftmost of the three. "The more information that one has, the more power they have. Our species agreed to only speak our language behind the safety of closed doors. All of the Knights and City Guards understand your position here today. Do not fear for your life." Gaelcean looked over the map of the Fourth District as he spoke.

"I understand, sir." Carter hadn't felt threatened. Was it Gaelcean's manner of speaking, or was it his own focus?

Gaelcean walked to the map on the opposite end of the tables. "I will be giving my speech here in District Six, at the

District Center. A stage has been set up at the main road crossing. I want you to be on the stage with me along with my personal guard," Gaelcean said while looking over the map.

"You want me on stage with your personal guard, sir?" Carter felt a lump forming in his throat, like a small pebble he had accidentally swallowed somehow.

"Correct. The other Knights here will be positioned around the stage." Gaelcean traced a line around one side of the stage, across the front, and around the opposite side. Carter could feel his heart pounding against his ribcage. He was trying to do everything he could to appear calm. "The Knights have spoken highly of you, Carter Gerro. Although this is our first meeting, I trust you. I trust you because I trust the Knights' assessment of your abilities."

"What's the plan?" If he had something to focus on, he could avoid collapsing under the sudden pressure. He was sure his jaw had almost dropped when Gaelcean told him he would be on the stage with his personal guard. What would the crowd think? No. He had to focus.

"We will move from our location here and walk down the main street toward the stage." Gaelcean traced the map as he spoke. "Once at the stage I will position myself behind the podium, and you will stand to my right. My personal guard is there now to ensure everything is going to plan upon our arrival." Nothing existed outside of the words Carter was hearing, and the path that Gaelcean traced on the map.

"I will give a short speech about Humanity and Amboian co-existence and our future together. Then we will proceed off the stage and begin walking back through District Six, through Five, and Four. Once at the main street intersection in District Four, we will turn toward the Upper District gates and proceed toward them." Gaelcean continued to trace the maps and walk to the other maps on the tables as he spoke.

A short speech. Walk through the districts. Proceed to the Upper District gate.

"Once at the gate you will be dismissed. As a reward for your service today, you will receive the rest of the day off. Your duties will continue tomorrow as normal." Gaelcean folded his arms behind his back and smiled at Carter.

"Thank you, sir." A day off? Carter couldn't remember the last time he had a day off. He once had fallen ill and still made it to his post on time. He was sure he must have passed out during his shift, he hardly remembered it. In hindsight, probably not the safest of choices. Had he fallen off the wall there would be nothing recognizable of him left.

"If you have no questions, we will begin."

"What other security measures have been put into place other than guards stationed around the stage, and those at checkpoints in the districts?"

"There are guards stationed along the route. As we speak a twenty-foot-wide walking perimeter has been secured. If anyone were to try and make an attempt on my life, they would have to make it through the guards along the sides of the path, through the Knights who will be walking with us, and through you." Gaelcean smiled again. "I would be truly impressed with the individuals who would try such a foolish thing." All the Amboians Carter had known seemed to be cut from the same hard stone that made the Exterior Walls. Gaelcean seemed far from that.

Carter had had one more question, but he was unsure about asking it. Gaelcean must have seen his hesitancy. "What else, Carter Gerro?"

He tried to clear the pebble from his throat. "Why me, sir? Why not Mayor Sindaine?" Terrim Sindaine had been the representative for the Sixth District for several years. Since before Carter had joined the City Guard. The people in the Sixth District seemed to like the man. They would prefer a familiar face to Carter.

Gaelcean thought for a moment. "Terrim Sindaine. Yes. A fine man." The Amboian paused again. "However, I believe he is not the *right* man. I believe you are, Carter

48

Gerro."

Carter didn't understand. He would rather not continue to question a Diplomatic Councilor on the matters of politics. Certainly not strengthening relations between two species. "No further questions, sir." Carter looked over the maps. Focusing on the details would be the only thing tethering him to reality.

Another group of Knights entered the room. Gaelcean spoke to them in their native tongue. The Knights seemed uneasy for a moment, and a few of them eyed Carter. Gaelcean spoke again and one of the Knights responded.

"Excellent. We will begin immediately." Gaelcean replied.

With twelve Knights on each side and Gaelcean in front of him, the procession made its way toward the security door. He would have to use the gaps in the Knights formation to see anything once they began walking the Lower Districts.

Each Knight had a two-handed longsword on their backs, and a shortsword at their waist. The dark-gray blades of the long swords were longer than Carter's arm from shoulder to fingertips. Two fullers running down the flat of the blade both met a ridge that continued to the tip. The cross-guards were almost as long as the grip, which had room to accommodate both hands of the Knights.

Carter removed a metal cylinder from a loop on his belt. The dark gray cylinder felt right in his hand. He pressed with his middle finger twice and a short sword began forming in his hand. A polished silver blade extended out from a dark-gray guard. It wasn't as impressive as the Knights massive two-handed swords. It would be perfect for him, though. He slid the blade back into the belt at his waist.

The first Knight on the left flank opened the security door and the right flank walked through the door single file followed by Gaelcean, Carter and the Knights that made up the left flank. Once outside they assumed the same formation and began walking through the Sixth District toward the District Center. Twelve Knights on either side with Carter behind Gaelcean in the center.

Carter kept his head forward and scanned in front of him as they walked. Occasionally Gaelcean would turn from one side of the street to the other and wave to the crowds on both sides. The shouts and cheers from the crowd were deafening. Over the din Carter heard, 'Amboy be praised!' and 'May the Shield protect us!' He had also heard 'Haze the Council!'

Many of the people who lived in the Lower Districts blamed the Council for their current state of living. Several faces in the crowd were dirty. Many wore clothes that had seen years of use and had been mended repeatedly.

The procession continued through the street. Without slowing his pace or lowering his waving hand, Gaelcean turned his head to the side. The crowds continued shouting a mixture of praise and disapproval. Still, none of them dare pass through the Amboians that lined the street. However angry some of the crowd were, their fear of the Knights and City Guard outweighed it.

"How are you feeling, Carter Gerro?" Gaelcean said over his shoulder.

"Fine, sir." Although this was far from his usual patrols through the city, he found that he *was* actually doing fine. He was sure he had heard someone shout a curse at him. Something about an Amboian pet. Earlier in the day he was daydreaming atop the Exterior Wall and now he was guarding one of the most important people in the capital, and he was fine. The shouts continued.

"The Sixth District supports the Council! You saved Humanity!"

"The Council is corrupt!"

"May the Shield protect us all!" It seemed there were members of the Church of Amboy in the crowd. Everyone would be out today.

As the procession approached the District Center, Carter

50

could see a large stage was set up facing out into the space where the two wide main streets crossed. The walls of the Upper Districts were a distant backdrop. The stage was supported by a black metal frame that lifted it several feet off the ground. In the front center of the stage was a large white cylindrical podium with steps that led the speaker to the top. A woman in a tan cloak stood on the podium's left. Two large blue banners hung on each side toward the back of the stage. The Amboian crest in gold glinted as the sunlight hit it. Two concentric circles, one larger than the other. Lines crossed over the larger of the two circles dividing it into twelve equal pieces: The Lower Districts. The smaller was divided into four to represent the Upper Districts. A golden dot at the center of it all represented Amboy Central.

The left flank continued walking down in front of the stage while six of the Knights from the right flank crossed the stage and marched down the steps on the opposite side, positioning themselves along the right side of the stage. As Carter followed Gaelcean up the stairs the six remaining Knights from the right flank stopped and took their posts along the left side of the stage.

Now that Carter was also on the stage, he could see the woman much better. She had pale, almost gray, skin, and bright yellow-orange eyes. Her skin was smooth, and her hair was completely clean shaven. She was slightly shorter than Carter and had exceptionally defined facial features, as if a master artist had sculpted her from clay. Her large tan cloak draped over her shoulders and extended down past her knees and covered her arms. Her chest plate was visible and seemed to be made from the same material as the Knights and similar to Carter's. Her armor extended upward forming a protective collar around her neck. She also had full plate covering her legs and feet.

"Carter Gerro, this is my personal guard, Weleya." Carter held out his hand to greet Weleya. As she revealed her own from underneath her cloak Carter could see she had the same full plates covering her entire arms; the only skin showing was on her hands. Her skin was surprisingly cold against his.

"A pleasure to meet you, Carter." Weleya's voice had a distinct sound to it that Carter had never heard in another's.

"The pacing of today's events keeps us on a tight schedule. Perhaps another day we will all have time to enjoy each other's company, but the people are waiting." Gaelcean stepped toward the podium. Carter took his place on the stage to Gaelcean's right and looked out across the sea of people that had gathered for the speech. There must have been tens of thousands packed into the street. It was almost incomprehensible. If something were to happen, how would the Knights, Carter, and Weleya protect Gaelcean? Among the mass of faces looking up at the stage, few seemed happy or content.

"People of Amboy City!" Gaelcean's voice filled the District Square. "The Harvest season has ended in the New Ring, and we begin preparing for the Winter season ahead…"

Carter's attention was split between listening to the speech and watching the crowd. And Weleya. There was something about her.

"For over two hundred years Amboians and Humans have lived and worked together to survive! We work together to ensure our survival!" Gaelcean continued.

"May the Shield protect us!" a voice shouted. Carter's eyes scanned the crowd.

"There are some in this city who would seek to drive a spike between our species…"

Carter knew every Human that was on the city guard, and yet he had never met her, and she was Gaelcean's personal bodyguard. *Were there Human guards in the Upper District?* Carter was among the first Humans allowed to join the City Guard; he would have known if anyone had been stationed in the Upper Districts. Then again, those that lived in the Lower Districts knew so little about what went on in the Upper Districts, himself included. Her armor was similar to his own, made from the same material that the Knights' armor had been made from.

"That is why it is important that we put an end to those that would choose to divide us. We must work together to pursue peace." A cheer rose from the crowd.

"What about the attacks on the Perimeter? What about those that live in the Haze?" Carter looked toward the direction of the shouting. There were too many faces to tell who exactly where it had come from.

"Indeed." Gaelcean looked in the direction of the shout. "There are those who live in the harsh conditions of the Haze. As the Perimeter expands, we will welcome them into our society. As we always have. The safety of those who live in our city, and the New Ring will always be of the highest priority." More shouting erupted from the audience. This time though it sounded cheerful.

Weleya's armor was form fitting like his own. Possibly even more so. It was almost as if the metal had replaced the skin on her body. Carter had seen people in the Lower Districts with mechanical limb replacements. Some had even been able to afford enhancements for cosmetic purposes. It wasn't uncommon to lose an arm or a hand working in the Industrial District; those prosthetics were built with function in mind, never appearance. If Weleya had limb replacements, they were far more advanced than anything Carter had seen.

Gaelcean had finished speaking and there was another cheer from the crowd. "Thank you, all!" Gaelcean waved both his hands and stepped back from the podium.

The Knights resumed their positions on either side of Gaelcean and Carter. Weleya walked in front of Gaelcean. They proceeded through Districts Six and Five, stopping occasionally so Gaelcean could wave to the crowds and repeat parts of his speech to the crowds along the way who weren't able to fit into the District Center. Again, there was a mixture of shouts from the crowds.

"We would be lost without your guidance!"

"To the Haze with your kind!"

An Amboian City Guard pushed into the crowd and grabbed a man. The man pushed back against the Amboians in wasted effort. Several of the other guards pushed toward the crowd making space around the two.

"Guardsman." Gaelcean had barely raised his voice. The Amboian let go of the man's arm. Carter could see a dark-purple bruise where the guard had grabbed the man. It was likely broken by the way the man was holding himself. Gaelcean motioned for the Knights around them to move aside and Gaelcean stepped out of the procession toward the edge of the street where the man was standing, surrounded by the City Guard who had been lining the street. Weleya was already steps ahead of Gaelcean. Had she known he would move toward the man? Carter followed Gaelcean through the space made by the Knights.

The man lifted himself up higher as they approached. Gaelcean waited until he was inches away before he spoke. "What is your name?"

"Bovram." The man held his head high. "Bovram Norellin." Bovram's once fine red jacket was tattered now. The sleeves torn off just past his shoulders. There had once been four buttons down the center; only the second from the top remained now. His brown pants were made of rough wool and could use a wash. It was possible Bovram himself hadn't been cleaned in sometime as well.

"Bovram Norellin." Gaelcean regarded the man standing in front of him as if he were speaking to an equal. "How is it that you make your living?"

"How do I make my living?" The man laughed. A hoarse cackle. "Is the Council so blind?"

"Perhaps we have been."

Bovram's eyes widened. He cleared his throat before he spoke, "I was a spice trader. Successful one, at that." Bovram's chest puffed out. Even in his tattered clothing Carter could see by the way the man held himself there was

54

truth to his claim. "Bad winter, a terribly bad one. I never recovered." The man sighed and seemed to sink into himself.

"Yes. Times have been difficult." Gaelcean addressed the crowd around them now. "It is during challenging times like these that we find our true limits." He looked back to Bovram. "It is how we address those challenges that define us. I am sure someone who once found success may find it again." Gaelcean held out a hand and Bovram shook it. Gaelcean looked to the crowd once more. "I will bring a proposition to the Council Hall. I will see that the proper resources are brought to the Lower Districts for those who are in need. The Lower Districts are the foundation of the capital. Without the Lower Districts, our capital would soon fall." Gaelcean turned away and walked back into the procession. Weleya was scanning the mass of people around them. He realized he had been paying attention to the conversation the entire time. She nodded to him and followed Gaelcean. The Knights and guards had been around too, at least. He felt a sinking feeling in his stomach as he took his place back in the group behind Gaelcean.

When the procession arrived at the District Four crossing, they turned toward the Upper Gates. The Knights parted the crowd that was lined up across the intersection. Once the path was clear Weleya, Gaelcean and Carter passed through. The street leading toward the gate was completely empty as they walked toward the Upper District gates. The Knights had remained back with other City Guards to contain the crowd from following them and begin moving everyone along.

"I want to thank you again for standing on that stage with me today." Gaelcean looked forward toward the end of the long empty street that stretch in front of them.

"It was an honor, sir." It truly was. Nothing would compare to today. Nothing. He had seen the Amboians in a completely different light now. Gaelcean had shown him that.

"I am going to be entirely candid with you, Carter Gerro." Gaelcean's tone changed slightly and even though there were no others around he spoke softly. The classic Amboian stone appearance overcame Gaelcean. "It is obvious that being in a position of power comes with a certain amount of risk."

"Of course, sir." The number of City Guards that lined the streets, and Knights made that obvious alone.

"Lately I feel that amount of risk has increased and will continue to increase. It is because of this that I would like to extend to you an offer to join my personal security detail." Gaelcean stopped walking and turned toward Carter. This was the second time today he was met with an impossibly unexpected proposal. The lump in his throat returned. "I truly meant what I said before. Amboians and Humans must work together to maintain peace. I will do what I believe is necessary to maintain that peace." Gaelcean looked directly at Carter with his hands held behind his back. "What do you say Carter Gerro?"

"Again, sir, I would be honored." Carter finally found the words.

"I am glad to hear that." A smile returned to Gaelcean's face and the stone exterior had broken down. "As we agreed, you will have the rest of the day off. Tomorrow afternoon you will meet with Weleya here at this gate. She will take you through the rest of the process, and I will see you after." Carter looked toward Weleya, but her attention was on the empty street ahead, and the alleys they passed as they walked.

"Thank you, sir." Carter said.

"You may call me Gaelcean, if you like."

"Thank you, Gaelcean. You can just call me Carter."

"It is good to have met you, Carter. I look forward to the days to come."

The three had reached the gate that led to the Upper

District. It was here where they would go their separate ways until tomorrow. Gaelcean and Weleya bid Carter farewell and passed through the wicket gate into the large tunnel between the districts. Tomorrow, Carter would be passing through the same gate for the first time in his life.

He turned from the gate and walked back down the street. A few people that began trickling back into the area. He continued walking and reached the intersection of the two main streets and found his way into the crowd and walked back toward District Three.

"Back already?" Ronald's eyebrows climbed his face. Then one of them arched. "Did they not need you?"

Ronald and Myra hadn't moved from their post at the Third District archway. The crowd passing through had thinned and was dense with usual traffic. Carter fell in between them as before. "Councilor Gaelcean asked me to stand on the stage with him as he gave his speech."

Ronald's eyebrows shot back up.

"What?" Myra turned away from the crowd to look at Carter, then quickly snapped back to attention. "Can you tell us anything?"

"I got to the District Six barracks, they had turned it into a sort of base of operations for the speech, and Gaelcean was there." Carter felt dizzy for a moment as he recalled what had happened. "He shook my hand and we spoke." He told his fellow Guardsmen all that had happened. The only part he left out was hearing the Amboians speak. He intended to remain among the Humans to hear the language and live.

"Personal guard?" Ronald was no longer paying attention to the passersby and Myra reflexively turned to look at Carter during his retelling.

"I know." Carter shook his head. "I'm struggling to comprehend everything."

"Carter Gerro." Myra laughed. "Personal guard to Diplomatic Councilor Gaelcean." Now she was shaking her head. "The Amboians *are* playing favorites with you." Was Myra angry? She was difficult to read sometimes.

"Gaelcean said he didn't know much about you, right?" Ronald had remembered to return his attention to the crowd. "The Knights put in a good word for you? That doesn't make sense to me."

"Probably because they never have anything good to say about you." Myra chuckled to herself.

Ronald continued on as if he hadn't heard. "And what about the other personal guard, Weleya?"

"I've been running it all over in my head. We would have heard if a Human guard had been promoted. And even still, we all know each other. I have never seen her before."

"You said she had *orange* eyes?" The realization brought concern into Myra's voice. "Okay. I don't want to sound like a drunk spinning tales at a tavern." She paused and sighed. "A few days ago, one of the other guards told me this woman with orange eyes was asking questions in the Forgotten District. Said she was looking for some preacher, but not one with the Church." Carter stared intently as he listened to Myra's story. "He said there was something odd about her, other than the eyes of course." Myra noticed his stare. "I don't know. It's just hearsay."

"I heard the same." Ronald almost whispered. "I was approached by some men and women while I was on patrol in the Ninth District the other night. She had been causing trouble in a few of the taverns and inns. Apparently, she bloodied some people pretty badly. I don't remember anything about a preacher though."

"I wonder if Gaelcean knows his personal guard is letting off steam in the Lower Districts." Myra had regained her composure.

"More questions. I need to gather my things. I can't imagine I'll be staying in any of the Lower Districts barracks anymore."

Ronald and Myra put a fist to the chest in salute.

"Maybe you can put in a good word for us, Carter." The smile on Myra's face was warm. Ronald's eyes seemed to be shimmering. The salute had taken Carter off guard. He quickly returned a salute to his fellow City Guards. Well, he wasn't a City Guard any longer. Did he outrank them now? Hopefully, their friendship would remain the same. Would he even see them again?

"Stay safe, and away from the Forgotten District." Carter gave them a nod and turned to the security door.

There wasn't much to pack up in the barracks. Guards were moved from post to post so frequently it was best to live light. In the chest at the foot of the cot he had been using since being stationed at the Third District barracks he had two black long-sleeve shirts and two gray. He had three pairs of pants similar to the ones he wore now. And the remainder of his armor, of course. An extra pair of boots were tucked under the cot. After arranging everything in his pack he laced the boots together and tied them to the pack. The empty cot and chest would likely be taken up by his replacement tomorrow. Maybe Myra would get his shift on the Exterior Wall. If he could, he would refer her to a better post. Maybe even Ronald. Carter laughed to himself and turned away from the empty cot. He had the rest of the day off and was unsure of what to do with his time. A shower would be nice and maybe he would find himself out in the grassy fields beyond the wall. *Everything must rest.*

CHAPTER FOUR

Companions

The sky behind Cordelia had transitioned to deep purples and reds as she traveled the Sun Road. The dirt path she walked on had been compacted from years of use. She hadn't seen many others traveling the road since the sun began to set; there had even been fewer than normal while the sun had been out. Cordelia's only companions now were the cool breeze that blew past occasionally and the birds singing in the trees around her. Towering, skinny trunks of needle-bearing trees, some had called them seamstress trees, because of the long, pointed needles. There were also the stout, maple trees. Their long branches covered in numerous leaves the size of Cordelia's hand. There were others as well, needle bearing and leaf, but Cordelia had never been good at remembering the names of plants and trees.

Her feet were beginning to get sore and the straps from her pack were digging into her shoulders. And while she was at it, her lower back hurt too. Based on her rough estimations she had traveled twenty miles and was about to come upon a small roadhouse called the Woodsman's Axe.

Cordelia had stopped at the Woodsman's Axe a few times as she traveled to and from the city, and the edge of the New Ring. Tonight was cool, but Cordelia doubted they would have a fire blazing in the large stone hearth. Last time she had stopped to rest they served a delicious meat and vegetable stew with fresh baked bread. A low grumble came from Cordelia's stomach. She had packed some traveling rations—nuts, berries, and dried meat—but the thought of a warm meal and fresh bread made her pick up her pace. There was also mulled wine and ale, which would be appreciated after a long day of traveling.

The shadowy shape of the structure appeared as Cordelia topped one of the shallow hills along the road. The modest wood and stone building served its purpose. Light was pouring out of the windows and the front door. A rough-looking stable had been constructed along the side of the building and a stable hand was tending to one of the horses. She counted three horses total and as well as two carts. That didn't mean there weren't others who had traveled by foot like her. As she got closer, raucous laughter and hollering could be heard from inside. Exhaustion was beginning to settle in, but she had to keep her wits about her.

The stable hand didn't seem to notice her approach. If he was as inattentive as he seemed, she might be able to sneak into the hayloft and sleep up there. The night was fine enough for making camp though, and the innkeepers might not appreciate someone taking advantage of them if they found her. Cordelia crept up to a window to get a look inside.

The spacious first floor had long tables in the center that ran the length of the room and some smaller tables were placed here and there. A set of stairs led up to a balcony that wrapped around the room. The rooms were reasonably priced, if they hadn't changed since Cordelia had last stopped in. The room she had had was small, but it suited her. The bed was just large enough for her to lie comfortably and there was an old wooden cabinet for her to put her things in. The woman who had shown her to her room had even offered to run a bath for her in the house attached to the inn where the owners lived. Cordelia had been tempted to accept the offer, but respectfully declined. The bed was enough for her. *A nice drink and a comfortable bed.*

Three men and two women were sitting at a table. They were the source of the cheering and laughter. One of the men was much larger than the others. His short dark hair was close cut to his head. He had a round, clean-shaven face that his smile stretched across as he laughed. Another man had long black hair that was parted in the middle and flowed down the sides of this head. The third man was much older than the rest. His long brown beard disappeared beneath the edge of the table. One of the women had her back to Cordelia. She could only see her short blond hair and the back of her leather armor. The brown leather was marked and scuffed. A single left shoulder guard was connected to the torso. The other woman had long brown hair that was woven back into a single braid; she had deep green eyes and freckles across her cheeks and nose.

Beyond the five seated at the table, a woman and a young boy sat sharing a bowl of something between the two of them. A door on the left side of the room opened and a woman carrying five large mugs in her hands appeared. She had a familiar face. The innkeeper's wife? There were two wooden mugs in each of her hands and the fifth was stacked on top. Even with this encumbrance the woman seemed to glide across the room. She wasn't even halfway to the table when more cheering erupted from the party of five. Mostly from the larger man, as he got up to help her. Once the drinks were set on the table, he placed a silver coin in the woman's hand. She smiled and laughed along with them before returning to the door from where she had entered.

Satisfied with her short reconnaissance, Cordelia moved away from the window and rounded the corner. A massive axe carved from dark wood was stuck into the side of the building above the door. In the low light coming from inside Cordelia could see 'The Woodsman's Axe' painted on the long handle.

"Ah, the evening brings yet another traveler to our midst! Have a drink and join us. We're trading stories." The larger man was smiling with eyes half open. His head was shifting back and forth ever so slightly. Cordelia wondered if the man's cheeks were always so rosy. He held up his beer in one hand. The other was beckoning her over.

"I could certainly use a drink." None of the five seemed threatening. If they were as drunk as this man, she could easily handle the situation if something were to happen.

"Another drink!" the round-faced man shouted as he stood up and grabbed a chair from another table.

"Thank you," Cordelia said as she took the chair. She removed the scarf that covered her head and let down her hair.

"What a lovely red!" the brown-haired woman said. "I hear, in the Upper District, they change the color of their hair as often as the weather changes. Cordelia smiled and nodded.

The innkeeper's wife appeared again from the door and placed a mug in front of Cordelia. The white foam at the mouth of the wooden mug was a welcome sight. Her exhaustion had begun to fade with the first sip.

"My name is Victor Aymin." The large man slapped an open hand to his chest as he spoke.

"Cordelia," she replied, wiping foam from her upper lip with the back of her hand.

"*Cordelia.* What a name that is!" Victor laughed. He extended a wobbly arm and pointed around the table as he listed off the other's names. "Elina, Conroy, Sean, and Tallie. We are companions for the evening!"

The group lifted up their mugs and Cordelia raised hers along with them. The cheer went silent as the table drank.

"What brings you to the Woodsman's Axe, Cordelia?" Conroy, the man with long dark hair, asked after putting his mug back on the table.

"Traveling to East Edge," she replied. Cordelia took another drink from her mug. The cold beverage was an oasis. She wondered if the beer was actually any good, or if it was a day on the roads that made it so good. Either way she enjoyed it.

"I am from East Edge!" Victor shouted all too loud for how close the group had been sitting. "I made a good profit in the Market District this week. It is always nice to bring an empty cart back home." Victor smiled. Then, in a lower voice, low for Victor it seemed, he said, "An empty cart, means a full coin purse." Victor threw his head back as he laughed.

Conroy nodded curtly toward Victor. "A lovely town, no doubt. I would be nervous living so close to the Perimeter." He looked over his mug as he drank as if to gauge the table's reactions.

"It can be equally, if not, more dangerous in the city," Elina, the woman in the leather armor, replied almost immediately. Her voice was slightly deep for a woman and her short blond hair framed her face.

"But what of the attacks from the Haze?" Conroy raised his eyebrows as he took another drink.

"He's not wrong. The reports have grown lately." The older man named Sean stroked his beard, gazing toward the center of the table. He spoke slowly. Age was present in his voice.

Conroy looked about the table expectantly.

"It's all I heard about during my deliveries to towns in the northern and eastern parts of the New Ring," Tallie said as she set her mug down. The hollow sound it made as it hit the table brought a smile to Victor's face. "It's all anyone is really talking about out here." Tallie pulled her braid in front of her and began idly fumbling with it.

"How many attacks have there been?" Cordelia set her mug down and was surprised when she heard the same hollow sound.

"I would say, three or four in the past few days," Sean said, still stroking his beard.

"The reports say they're small raiding parties, maybe four to six people. They come in, steal supplies, and leave. A village south of East Edge reported at least three deaths." Conroy leaned into the table as he spoke. The man enjoyed the gossip.

Victor threw his arms up in frustration. "We were having such fun. Why do we need to talk about these terrible things?"

"Have the raiding parties left any messages or made demands?" Cordelia was asking Conroy directly now.

"Not that I've heard. Seems like they just need supplies."

"Any indication of if they're working together? Maybe it was coordinated?"

"Coordinated?" Tallie laughed. "I would be impressed if *those* people were anything more than the wild pack they seem to be."

"I had planned on walking the rest of the way to East Edge." Cordelia turned to Victor whose eyes were beginning to close. "Victor, would it be too much to ask for a ride to East Edge. You mentioned you were from there, correct?"

Victor's eyes shot open. "Gladly! I love to travel with others." As soon as he was done speaking his eyes began to close again.

"Thank you, Victor."

"Got family out that way?" Elina asked Cordelia. The mug in front of the woman had hardly been touched.

"A friend. He lives just north of East Edge." Cordelia looked into her empty mug.

"I wouldn't worry, Cordelia. Worry doesn't do much good for anyone." Sean smiled as he tried to comfort her. she smiled back at the old man, but she found it difficult. It made no sense to her. Raiding parties weren't uncommon, especially near the end of the Harvest.

65

It was the killing that concerned her. Cordelia had never known them to kill. What had changed?

"A song!" Victor shouted as he reanimated. "I shall sing you all a song." There was another cheer from the table. "Cordelia. What song would you like to hear?" It was as if the man hadn't just been on the verge of passing out.

"Oh, I'm not sure." She knew most of the well-known songs, and she did prefer performers over music boxes. Taverns and inns in the Lower Districts all seemed to have music boxes that played those grainy recordings.

"I know several! Songs about battle. Songs about travel. Songs about *love*." Victor made different poses as he made his list. He was now seated on the edge of his chair with cupped hands brought to the side of his smiling face.

"I don't think I have a preference really. I'm sure anything will be good."

Victor sat for a moment with his hand on his chin. Then he began pounding the table with his hands in an upbeat rhythm. "Well, the road is long, an' the sun is high. The trees in the wood reach toward the sky." Victor's voice was as warm as his personality. "Many miles lie ahead, oh aye. On the long road before us. An' the rains come down, an' the winds do blow. But soon I return home, I know. Many miles lie ahead, oh oh. On the long road before us." Cordelia and the rest of the table began pounding along to Victor's rhythm as he sang. As if on cue, the innkeeper's wife came out once again, this time with six drinks in hand. As she floated over to the table Victor stood up and continued singing. "In the tavern hall the drink is good. The best around, it's understood." He danced around the woman as he sang. Even while holding the drinks the woman managed to match his movements. She set them down and let Victor spin her around as he sang. "Return to the road, I know I should. There's a long road before us!" Laughing, the woman returned to the kitchen. Tallie stood up to dance with Victor. "Well, the journey's done, an' I've had my fun. Soon away,

66

another one." Victor looked toward everyone and conducted the group before they all sang in chorus. "There's a long road before us!"

The group erupted in laughter and cheering. The others in the room cheered as Victor and Tallie returned to the table. They all held up their mugs and drank.

Victor had his head tilted upward as he drank. Most spilled down the sides of his face. He slammed the mug down as he finished. "That," he gasped, "is one of my favorite songs!"

Sean stood up from his seat and gave a slight bow to the table. "It is getting a bit late for me. I do have a long road before me."

"Sean, my friend." Victor's words were almost completely slurred together now. "It was a pleasure."

As the evening went on more travelers had come into the tavern, and several drinks had come to the table. She was beginning to feel their effects. She would have to stop soon to keep her wits about her. That, and a sickness tomorrow would make for a rough day of traveling.

"I think he's had his fill," Cordelia said. She laughed as she nodded toward Victor, who sat arms folded snoring in his chair. "And I think I have as well." Cordelia helped the innkeeper's wife clear the empty mugs from the table.

"Agreed," Conroy said as he stood up from the table and stretched. He wobbled slightly and held the back of his chair for balance.

"You're all no fun. I'm sure there are others who are willing to continue tonight," Tallie said, slurring her words. She got up from the table and wandered over to a group sitting at a long table.

Cordelia walked back into the kitchen with mugs in hand. Elina was behind her with several emptied mugs as well. "Have the prices for your beds changed recently?" Cordelia asked as she set the mugs down near a sink.

In the kitchen there were two large stoves, though only

one seemed to be in use now. A man with graying hair had his sleeves rolled up as he stirred a wooden spoon in a large metal pot. Cordelia's stomach growled again. She had gotten so caught up in talking and drinking with the others she had forgotten to eat. At the same time, she had drunk so much that it felt as if there was no room for anything else in her stomach.

"I thought you were a familiar face," the woman said as she turned on the faucet and began cleaning. "The prices are the same, but unfortunately the beds are all accounted for this evening."

No comfortable bed. "It should have been my first priority when I came in. Any chance I could sleep in the hayloft outside?"

Elina cut in, "I have a camp set up across the road just outside. You're more than welcome to join me."

It wasn't obvious if Elina had drank as much as the rest of the group. Cordelia found herself struggling to recall. "That would be appreciated. Thank you." It wasn't ideal to wake up smelling like a horse anyway.

"I really am sorry, both of you. If you decide to change your minds, you are more than welcome to stay in the loft. Free of charge, of course. Not sure what kind of place we would turn into if we started charging for guests to sleep with the horses."

"It's no problem. I wouldn't have the coin for the room, and my camp is already set," Elina assured her.

Cordelia and Elina left the kitchen and passed through the great room once again. Victor was still asleep in his chair with his chin buried into his chest and arms crossed. Tallie was now sitting with a man and a woman at a table near the large stone fireplace. Tallie waved as she saw them reappear.

"Come back for another round?" she shouted.

"Not this time," Cordelia said and put a hand up. Tallie scoffed and turned away. The room spun ever so slightly when Cordelia had looked over to the hearth. She walked over to the table and shook Victor's shoulder. "Victor." There was no response. "Victor!" She shook the man a bit harder.

Victor snorted loudly and opened his eyes. "Cordelia." He stifled a yawn with the back of his massive hand. "Time to leave already? I am afraid the events of last night still have me a bit drunk. If you would like to start off, I can pick you up when I catch up."

Cordelia laughed to herself. "No, Victor. You have plenty of time to sleep. Did you rent a bed tonight? Do you need help getting there?"

Victor shook his head and pushed himself up from the table. Without saying a word, the man moved across the room. He bumped into another patron and gave a mumbled apology. The man rubbed his sleeve on his chin and waved Victor away as he tried to help. Victor then bumped into an empty chair and offered an apology just as equal. When he made it up the stairs and into one of the rooms along the balcony Cordelia turned to follow Elina outside.

The sky was completely black now, save for the streaks of light blues and greens of the Shield overhead. It took longer than she expected for her eyes to adjust as Cordelia walked out the door and toward the road. It was difficult to make out the shape of a canvas tent pitched among the trees of the forest as they crossed the dirt road.

"Normally I prefer to set up camp further from the road. There were so few traveling today, I figured I could risk it," Elina said as they walked through the dark forest toward the camp. "If anything were to happen, at least I'm right there in the inn anyway."

"Good thinking." Cordelia's eyes had begun to adjust to the darkness, but she still found it difficult avoiding the large roots they were walking over.

"Probably shouldn't need too much wood on that

tonight." Elina pointed to the remains of a small fire. "It's not terribly cold." she reached into her tent and pulled out a small metal box. She opened it and pulled a small coal from the sand within. "It's still got some heat," she said and stuck two fingers in her mouth. She grabbed a handful of small sticks and set them on top of the hot coal. It only took a few blows for the sticks to catch. She gave a satisfied nod and set some slightly larger sticks around the small flame. "We'll let that go and then add a few logs."

The alcohol had fully set in. Cordelia regretted drinking as much as she did. Her lack of sobriety put her on edge. She set down her pack and unstrapped her canteen from the side. She took a long drink in a feeble attempt to sober herself up.

Elina unbuckled the strap of her shoulder guard and tossed it into her tent. She began untying the knots that ran down the side of her leather armor. She wasn't preparing for a fight at least. Cordelia allowed herself to relax some.

"So, you're heading to East Edge to see a friend?" Elina placed the leather armor into her tent and sat down.

"Yes." Cordelia sat down opposite Elina. "I've got an old friend who lives out there. I like to visit him every now and then." She took another drink from her canteen.

"I'm actually heading to East Edge too. I normally like to keep my business to myself. Maybe I've had too much to drink."

"What's in East Edge for you?" Did she mean that? Was it that obvious that Cordelia was on edge? Maybe she hadn't relaxed as much as she thought she did.

"With all the raids, I figured some towns might want to hire some experienced fighters. It is an unfortunate situation, but I could use the coin. Credits if they have it."

"You mentioned earlier that the city could be more dangerous than the Perimeter, and you have experience fighting. Were you among the group of Humans who were selected for the City Guard?"

"No. There was a time when the thought had crossed my

70

mind. I grew up in the Ninth District, right along the gates to District Eight. There was never a lack of trouble for my family." Cordelia continued drinking from her canteen as she listened. That stew would have been more helpful than water. "My family owns a tannery. My father taught me and my two sisters the trade. It wasn't uncommon for our store to get robbed. Once we sold all we could in the Market District, we would spend the rest of the day searching for what was taken from us. My father would always leave his mark on our wares. It didn't take long to gain some fighting experience. After a while instead of helping sell our products, I would spend the entire day searching for our stolen goods."

Cordelia stared intently as Elina spoke. The small flames of the fire danced in her hazel eyes and made her pale skin seem brighter than it had when they were seated inside. Her short blond hair had been pushed back, but now framed her face as it fell forward.

"You say you travel to East Edge often? I don't see a blade on you. Are you not worried about traveling the roads alone?"

Cordelia rolled back her sleeves revealing two hidden blades on each forearm. She then stood up and lifted the back of her jacket revealing a short sword along her lower back. "I find it easier to travel if I keep things hidden. People tend to ask less questions if I look unassuming." She sat back down.

"Honestly, I thought you were just another traveler on the roads. So, you grew up in East Edge?"

"No, I—" Cordelia stopped herself. Anxiety began to well up inside her. "Well, yes. I guess technically I did."

"What does that mean?"

"I lived outside of the town." Cordelia shrugged. "It's just easier to say East Edge. Most people know where that is instead of the villages around it."

Elina's stone face was difficult to read. "I see." Had she believed her?

Thinking as quickly as the alcohol in her system would let

71

her, she changed the subject. "I've spent the past few years living in the city doing odd jobs for people who have the credits. I started off as a caravan guard. I didn't like that I wasn't in control of my schedule, so that didn't last more than a season."

"It seems we have that in common. I was hired by a merchant looking for a guard. When he saw that I was a woman, his interests changed." A blade flashed from nowhere into Elina's hand. "It didn't take long for him to realize I had little patience for what he had in mind." The blade disappeared. "Thankfully, we hadn't gotten too far from the city, so I just turned back."

"I see." Cordelia's eyes fixed onto the fire.

The fire between the two was popping and crackling with heat as the logs expanded. Embers rose up and became lost in the starry sky. The winds were calm, and the only other sound was an occasional owl hooting in the distance.

"Perhaps I will join you and Victor while traveling to East Edge."

"You certainly seem like you can handle yourself. If the attacks are increasing it would be smart to travel in a group."

"I believe Victor mentioned he would be leaving at dawn. If that is the case, and if he is able to rouse himself from tonight's drink in time, I will join the two of you." Elina got up. "I realize I never properly introduced myself. My name is Elina Tanveir."

"Cordelia Faucher."

"Good to have met you, Cordelia Faucher. I'm going to get some rest." Elina smiled and turned toward her tent.

"I think you've got the right idea," Cordelia said. She reached into her pack and pulled out a large cloak to wrap herself in. Using her pack as a pillow and the cloak as a blanket, she spread out next to the small fire as it crackled. The ground wasn't entirely soft, and there were some roots digging into her side. Focusing on the crackling of the fire, and not the roots, she felt sleep overcome her.

72

CHAPTER FIVE

The Scientist

Yesterday, Carter had wandered the plains beyond the Exterior Wall for the better part of the afternoon before finding a large oak to lie under. He tried to relax as he looked up into the blue midday sky, the sun's light reflected off the main Shield Generator over the city, but his mind had been racing. What did being Gaelcean's guard entail? He accepted a position he knew almost nothing about. Standing guard along the Exterior Wall was easy. The wall didn't go anywhere. *The wall didn't think it was in danger.* What had Gaelcean meant by that? Was the Council divided? He had always imagined the Council as a united group that worked together to improve the lives of everyone in the capital and the New Ring. Life in the capital had gotten tough lately, there was no mistaking that. Carter had heard from merchants and farmers that it had been a difficult year out in the New Ring, and that was without taking into account the attacks from beyond the Perimeter.

Now, he stood at the Fourth District gate that separated the Lower and Upper Districts. Observing the people that passed by. It had become more than second nature for him.

He wasn't on duty just yet this morning but waiting for someone. His thoughts had jumped between Gaelcean, Weleya, and his new position as a member of Gaelcean's personal guard. Everything about Gaelcean seemed genuine, even his concern for his own safety. Weleya was a tougher one to sort out. Their interaction had been short, and Carter found himself with more questions than information he could use to figure her out. He wouldn't waste today's opportunity to learn more about the strange woman.

He shrugged his shoulders to adjust the pack on his back and checked to see if his second pair of boots were still tied off to the side. People were beginning to fill the main street of the Fourth District. The sky was still darkened from the previous night. A shopkeeper and her assistant were carrying boxes to a standout in front of their shop. Each of the boxes were full of bolts of cloth. The wooden sign above the door had been carved to resemble a piece of fabric blowing in the wind. 'The Seamstress and The Tailor' was painted in white. The assistant dropped a piece of cloth on the stone-paved street and the woman shouted a curse at him and raised a fist over her head. The woman froze and her eyes widened when she noticed Carter watching them. She lowered the fist and smiled.

Would she have held back if anyone had taken notice, or had she been at the speech yesterday and recognized him? He wasn't wearing his City Guard armor. She would have had to have a good mind for faces if that was the case. It was most likely that any onlooker would have made her put her fist down. The boy picked up the fabric from the street and shook dirt from it and ran into the shop. The woman had looked away from Carter and occupied herself with the bits of fabric that were laid out on the stand.

A shadow moved out from a narrow side street.

Weleya crossed the street toward him, her movements fluid, yet there was intent. Her brown cloak was tossed behind her shoulders and exposed plate armor that covered her entire body with the exception of her hands and clean-shaven head. The slight smile seemed out of place on her hard face.

"Carter Gerro, I am glad you agreed to accept this position."

"Of course. As I said yesterday, it is an honor." Carter heard a scoff from behind him and turned. One of the Amboian Guards at the gate was looking in his direction. Maybe that shopkeeper had held back from hitting the boy because she had seen the Amboians at the gate. Was this new position going to his head already?

"Let's get inside and begin the process." Weleya turned toward the gate and one of the guards opened the wicket door that was a part of the gate. Carter followed behind and entered into the tunnel that led to the Upper Districts.

The tunnel was similar to those that led out to the New Ring. Although here there was a slight incline as it moved up toward the large wooden doors at the end of the tunnel. The walls were smooth tan stone, the floor made of bricks of the same. There was a slight hum coming from the two rows of tube lights that ran the length of the ceiling. No guards had been stationed along the path within, but Carter was certain there were rooms off the tunnel that contained any number of Amboians on duty. As the two continued onward Carter could feel the grade of the incline increasing, and the bricks that paved the floor slowly transitioned to steps.

"Have you heard that some of the citizens in the Lower District think that there are prison cells within the Exterior Wall?" Carter's voice echoed off the tunnel walls.

"Yes, I have heard. The fear of being locked away within the walls is useful when extracting information from some."

"I've never been to the dungeons below the city. The Amboian guards on duty usually do all the questioning whenever I had to bring someone into the barracks."

"It is a place I don't like spending my time in, if I can avoid it."

A silence filled the gap in conversation as Carter thought.

"I had always imagined the security that divided the two groups of districts would have been higher. This seems like any other tunnel within the Exterior Wall," Carter said. His voice continued to bounce off the sides of the tunnel as he spoke.

"It may seem that way, but there are measures in place that are unseen until they are needed."

"Like the security doors in the Exterior Wall?"

Weleya waited before replying. "Similar to that. The security measurements between the Lower and Upper Districts are a bit more involved than metal doors that seal the tunnel."

As they reached the top of the stone stairs two massive doors opened to the Upper Districts. It was difficult not to gasp, but he managed to hold some of his composure. Carter had hoped Weleya and the Amboians who were holding the doors hadn't seen his jaw drop once they were out of the tunnel.

"It *is* impressive," Weleya said and continued walking.

Carter stifled his amazement and fell in beside Weleya once more. So, she had noticed his reaction then.

The Upper District couldn't compare to anything Carter had seen before. The wide street they stood on was paved with white stone that glowed in the dim morning light. Vibrant green grass lined the street. There were trees! *Trees* within the capital. A variety of leafy trees as well as some with needles. A group of Amboians were walking through the shaded grassy area and crossed a small bridge that lie over a pond. They wore long elegant silk and velvet robes of varying shades of blues, greens, and purples. Even from this distance Carter could see the higher-quality craftsmanship of the Upper District.

Following closely behind the well-dressed Amboians was a group of hard-looking Knights. No, not Knights. Each seemed to wear their own unique armor. Each had a symbol in place of the Amboian crest on their chest plates. On one, a tree. Another had three angled lines in parallel. The third was the profile of the head of a wolf howling, or maybe a bear. One Amboian, a female Carter could tell from this distance, with the wolf-bear crest noticed Carter looking in their direction and nudged the other Guards. Something was said between them and they shook their heads. Had word spread already?

"The three Amboians in the front there are all members of the Council. Following them are members of their guard." Weleya nodded in the direction of the guards. They returned her nod and looked away.

"It's barely been a day. How many know of Gaelcean's offer?" Carter asked. The group of Amboians continued deeper into the small, forested area until their figures were too obscured by the thick trunks and foliage.

"The Council has known of Gaelcean's intentions to promote you for some time now. I imagine many within Central Amboy have heard rumors as well. Within the Upper Districts, I am not sure. There are many Humans who live in the Upper Districts so you may go unnoticed for some time."

"Those Amboians seem to regard you with some respect." Carter looked over toward the trees although he was sure he would no longer be able to see the group.

"I have known most of the members of the Council and their guards for a very long time. I have gained their respect, and in a very rare case, their trust." Weleya had seemed hesitant to speak more on that. What did it mean?

Carter continued to look around as they walked. "It's beautiful."

"It truly is. We must still press on. Maybe another day you can take the time to familiarize yourself with the Upper Districts. We are currently in the Eastern District. There are only four, North, South, East, and West, so it shouldn't be too difficult."

It only just hit Carter how *open* everything felt. There were no crowds of people shouting over each other. The air he breathed was clean and crisp as it filled his lungs. He could hear birds singing in the trees. Where he would have passed hundreds of people in the Lower Districts, he may have only seen twenty or thirty here so far. As they progressed down the bleached street, the trees and ponds became fewer, but even still, more than any in the Lower District. Which was none. Buildings became greater in number, but never clustered together sharing a wall between them.

The construction was a combination of metal, wood, and stone. Some walls of the buildings were entirely glass. The construction was exact, all hard lines and angles. Simple construction Carter thought, and yet it seemed so refined. Human children were running around and playing in a grassy patch in front of what must have been their family home. A building with an open front had tables and chairs set up where Human and Amboian alike were sitting, sharing meals and conversing. The open front of the building allowed Carter a glimpse inside. Food was being cooked behind a chest-high wooden wall and Human servers were speeding throughout the space delivering food and drink to tables, cleaning up leftovers from others, and taking an order here and there. The scent of cooked meat and fresh bread poured out of the store front.

In his amazement Carter realized he had let his guard down and snapped to attention.

"There isn't much need to be on guard down here," Weleya said. *Down* here. "Central Amboy, though, can be just as dangerous as the Lower Districts. Don't be a fool and give your trust to someone just because they're another Council Guard, even if you know without a doubt they will not betray you." Weleya had stopped walking and was staring directly into Carter's eyes. Her bright-orange irises burned into him as she waited for him to acknowledge what she had said. "The politics of the Council is just a game to some. Not all see the power they have." She turned her attention to a tall tower that loomed over them. "Maybe they do, and still enjoy it as a game."

The tall spire stood at the center of the Upper Districts, made of a blue-gray metal and the same white stone they walked on now. Near the top it split into two peaks, one taller than the other. Carter could see balconies here and there along the exterior. In some areas, the walls slid to the side revealing the interior of an Amboian's living quarters.

"Understood," Carter replied.

They approached yet another stone wall taller than the one they had just passed through moments ago. Before today, Carter never would have thought he would see the Upper Districts, let alone enter Central Amboy.

"How long have you been a Personal Guard to Gaelcean?" He thought that seemed an innocent enough question.

"A very long time. Since before your time."

Before his time? She couldn't have been more than a few years older than he. Was that her way of joking?

"I don't remember seeing you in training." He wouldn't have much more time.

"I was trained within Central Amboy." Weleya said nothing more and Carter had the feeling there wouldn't be anything more said on the matter.

Instead of the wooden gates Carter was accustomed to, they approached a large metal door that divided the Upper Districts and Central Amboy. Weleya walked over to a small terminal beside the door. She was fumbling with something in her hands. Carter tried to move to her side to glimpse what she was doing. A small hole opened up in the wall and Weleya stuck her forearm inside. Carter heard a series of mechanical whirs and then an agreeable beep from the terminal. The large metal door began to lift upward and the two walked inside.

"Remember what I said." Weleya removed her arm from the hole in the wall and turned to Carter. Her yellow-orange

79

eyes seemed to blaze. "Have caution, Carter Gerro."

The main room of Amboy Central seemed to extend upward without end. Carter's and Weleya's steps echoed on the white stone floor as they crossed the space. He could see railed walkways above that followed the curved walls of the massive structure. Here and there a walkway cut clear across to the other side. They weaved between groups of huddled Amboians. Carter had to quickly dodge out of the way of an Amboian rushing by with their hands full of papers and muttering to themselves. There were plenty of stares and surprised faces as they passed through. The rumors had spread, and now they saw the reality. Gaelcean had selected Carter Gerro as a personal guard. He realized all he could see were Amboians around him; maybe he and Weleya were the only Humans allowed in Central Amboy. He felt a need to remove himself from the open space of the entryway.

He was thankful that he got his wish. Weleya led him across the cavernous room and stopped in front of a door. Several like it lined the wall. Rows of buttons ran down the wall next to the door. All symbols that he couldn't recognize. Weleya pushed one that looked like the number seven with an extra horizontal line along the top and a circle around the base line. The doors opened to a small room and the two stepped in. *A speed lift, of course.* The small room shot upwards for some time and then stopped, doors opening. A male Amboian in a large white robe with two wide orange stripes down the front was about to enter the lift when he saw Carter. He had once thought Amboians incapable of showing expression, now he could see shock on this one's face.

"Councilor Noraem." Weleya gave a slight nod to the Amboian as he collected himself.

"W—weleya. Yes. Hello." Noraem glanced toward Carter then back to Weleya. "I had not realized he would be here so soon. I must admit I was taken aback." Noraem stepped to the side to allow them out of the lift. "I am sure I will see you in the Council Hall, Carter Gerro." Noraem didn't look in

Carter's direction as he stepped into the lift and the doors closed. The Amboians had become used to Weleya's presence over time and the other guards respected her. How long would it take for him to receive the same?

They walked down a hallway that followed the curve of the building. The walls to Carter's left were glass from floor to ceiling. He had to keep from stopping to gaze out across the city and beyond into the New Ring. The sun had made some progress now and was almost well above the horizon. The morning's gray gloom still hung over the Lower Districts and out into the New Ring. They passed several doors on their right until stopping at one. Weleya knocked three times, paused, and entered.

The room had white walls and a gray tiled floor. Black counter tops and gray cabinets lined the walls and there were two long tables in the center of the room that matched. Papers, books, and an assortment of mechanical objects in various states of repair covered the counters and tables. There were glass containers with colored fluids. Tubing connected some, while the contents of others were contained by themselves. A voice called from a room in the back, the Amboian speech was only noise to Carter, then a female Amboian came into the room.

Like most Amboians she was taller than him, and her skin was a vibrant blue and her eyes black. She wore a simple black jacket with black pants, and dark flats of a similar shade. Her jacket was unbuttoned, revealing the white shirt she wore underneath. An Amboian crest was pinned on her jacket.

"Oh, Weleya, I'm sorry I didn't realize you were—" The Amboian stopped. "Hello. You must be Carter Gerro."

"Yes ma'am."

"Please, no need for formalities." She smiled. "I am Paelle." It seemed Gaelcean wasn't the only Amboian capable of smiling.

Paelle walked over to the side of the room to a terminal at a desk. Next to the desk was a tall cylindrical glass pod. She sat down at the terminal and began typing and the front of the glass chamber slid open. Another Amboian, this one male, stepped out from the same back room that Paelle had appeared from. Carter didn't need any explanation to know that this was Paelle's personal guard. The Amboian gave a nod in Weleya and Carter's direction and stood along the wall near the entrance to the back room. It was only then that Carter noticed a third in the room, standing beside Paelle's desk. Had the Amboian remained still, Carter may have not noticed him. How was he able to remain so still that Carter hadn't seen him?

Paelle spoke as she typed, "I'll have to calibrate the scanner for a human. It should not take very long." She continued typing. Occasionally she stopped to point at the screen and mutter to herself.

"Paelle is a member of the Council." Weleya walked over to a table in the center of the room. She moved a large piece of metal and wires from a chair before taking a seat. "She is a member of the Science and Technology branch and represents them at most Council meetings. The Amboian by the doorway there is Kuril. The other over there is Baesin."

Kuril and Baesin nodded simultaneously as Carter looked at them. The two were almost identical in their matching black cloaks and almost-black armor. The hilt of their Amboian-style long swords stuck out over Kuril's left shoulder and Baesin's right. Every Amboian Carter had met had had dark eyes, but for some reason both Kuril's and Baesin's eyes seemed so black that they absorbed the light from the tubes that ran along the ceiling.

Carter pulled himself from their intense stare. "It is a pleasure to meet you, Councilor Paelle." He saluted.

Paelle stopped typing and got up from her chair. She leaned in to inspect the now-open pod. "I understand you're a soldier and all, but you do not have to be so formal with me. I find that if everyone were to speak plainly goals can be met much quicker." She turned toward Carter. "Everything is ready. I need you to strip down and get inside so we can scan you and enter your information into our system."

Carter set his pack on the table and, only hesitating for a moment, began undressing. He was standing in the room with only his underwear on now and realized how cold the air was. He walked over to the glass pod and inspected it. The glass cylinder was feet taller than him and was angled so that whoever was inside would be able to lie back comfortably. Well, however comfortable one could be in a glass tube.

"This design is much similar to the one you encountered upon entering the City Guard, I imagine. Only this is far more sophisticated." Carter could hear the pride in Paelle's voice.

"The armor I have now is just fine. I've hardly seen any serious action." Even when Carter had taken a full hit from a sword or heavy club, the armor hadn't taken a scratch.

"That is very well, but you will receive armor fit for a Council Guard, and we need to enter you into the systems within the Upper District, as well as Amboy Central. This will give you security clearance and access to almost the entire capital building. Come to think of it, you are probably the first Human to have this level of clearance." Paelle trailed off as she thought.

The room seemed to spin for a moment. "You don't have this level of clearance, Weleya?"

"I do. I have been Gaelcean's personal guard since the beginning." Weleya's expression was unreadable. Was this another strange joke?

"You'd have to be well over two hundred years old. That's impossible." Carter was astonished. She didn't look any older than he did. A very tenuous connection was slowly forming in the back of his mind.

"Two hundred and twenty-six, to be exact." A slight smile returned when Weleya finished speaking.

"Weleya is a Mark Eleven Android. The only left of her series actually. I keep insisting upon her getting proper upgrades, but she denies need for them every time." Paelle shook her head. "She was created specifically for the protection of Councilor Gaelcean. Her appearance was to be made to look as Human as possible to seem more approachable when Gaelcean was interacting with Humans."

With that, the connection had been completed in Carters mind. The full plate armor wasn't armor at all, that was her *skin*. The unnatural yellow-orange eyes. The slight tint of gray in her face and hands. *Her hands.* They were slightly cold when they had been introduced.

"An Android." Carter realized he was staring for a bit longer than seemed polite. "I had just thought you had some mechanical upgrades. I didn't realize how advanced Upper District tech was."

"Advanced, indeed. Now if you would please enter the chamber so we can run the scans. This is not the only thing on my agenda today." Paelle sat back down at the terminal.

Weleya was still leaning on the table. "Getting those upgrades would require down time that I don't have."

Paelle scowled at the screen, but it was surely meant for Weleya.

Carter stepped into the glass chamber and laid back again the padding. There was a quiet whirring as the glass slid closed. It was uncomfortably quiet inside the cylinder. Carter could hear his heartbeat and his blood pumping through his ears. Weleya was an Android. Carter was the first Human to gain access to Central Amboy. *And what other firsts?* Paelle was typing at the terminal to Carter's right and there was a soft hum. A grid of light washed over Carter from all directions. Sometimes the grid consisted of several beams, other times a single beam appeared and scanned a small section of his body. A thin metal arm appeared from the padding he was lying against. Tubing coiled around the mechanical arm and a sharp needle extended from the end. Carter took a deep breath and exhaled slowly as the needle entered his forearm. There was a loud clunking sound, and the tubes began filling with his blood. It lasted only a few seconds and then there was another clunk and the needle retracted from his arm. The mechanical arm disappeared back into the padding behind him.

Another set of arms appeared from the right side of the pads near his waist. The end of one contained a sharp blade, and the other had a small chip held between two metal fingers. The blade made an incision in his right forearm and the other inserted the chip. The blade retracted and was replaced by an open-ended cylinder. Carter's arm burned and his jaw clenched as the cylinder ran down the length of the incision. When he looked back down to his arm the incision was gone and the two mechanical arms were disappearing back from where they had come from.

Carter ran his left hand along the previously opened forearm. He could feel an ever so slight bump in his arm where the chip was now place. *A track? Identification?* There was a familiar whirring sound and Carter leaned forward and stepped out of the surgical chamber that held him. He immediately walked over to the table where he had folded his clothes and began redressing himself.

"That is that," Paelle said matter-of-factly and stood up from her chair.

Weleya stood as well. "I can take you to your quarters. I imagine your new armor will be there before we arrive." She walked toward the door that led into the hallway.

"What was the chip you put into my arm?" Carter said trying to mask the anger he felt.

He must not have done a good enough job; Paelle looked slightly annoyed at his questioning. "That *chip* will monitor your vitals, as well as grant you the security clearance you need to do your job. If you become injured or ill, a notification will be sent to the proper location and you will receive the aid you need."

Carter looked down at his arm again and ran his fingers across the small bump. Paelle walked over to him and held out a data pad. She pointed, quite forcefully, as she spoke, "Heart rate, blood pressure, oxygen levels, body temperature." She looked up from the screen. "Should I continue?"

"No, I understand." Carter stopped fingering his arm. "Thank you."

"I am sure I will be seeing you soon. Good day, Carter Gerro." Paelle turned and walked away, disappearing into the room in the back. Followed by Kuril. Baesin remained standing near the terminal; his gaze was enough for Carter to want to get out of the room as quickly as possible.

"Let's go, Carter, there is still plenty to do." Weleya opened the door and walked into the hallway; Carter grabbed his pack from the table and followed close behind.

Several floors below Paelle's labs, Carter followed Weleya down another curved hallway. She had told him that this floor and the one below were the personal guard's quarters. Two main hallways met in the center of this level of Amboy Central and other hallways branched off from those. White walls and white floors, the barracks was very plain. Weleya stopped at a door with more strange symbols on it, the Amboian numeric system. How long would it take to learn this new number system? He would have to start by learning the number on his door at least.

"Hold your forearm up to the scanner." Weleya pointed to a gray box that protruded from the wall next to the door and mimed holding her arm up to it. Carter mimicked Weleya and held his arm to the gray box. There was a satisfied beep and the door slid open.

As the two stepped inside the lights in the room turned on revealing more of the same white floor and walls. The small room contained a cot that Carter would fit on nicely. He set his pack on a white metal desk with a matching white chair.

"Storage is built into the walls." Weleya tapped a knuckle on the wall. A panel released from the others. She grabbed the edge and it slid out; there was enough room for more clothing than Carter had ever owned. "There is a washroom in the back as well," Weleya said as she crossed the small space. She touched the back wall of the room and a small blue circle appeared. She touched it again and the wall slid open, the lights in the washroom turned on as Weleya entered. "It is not much. After a time, you may receive more adequate quarters. Gaelcean wanted more for you, but he can't be seen playing favorites."

"I understand." Carter looked around his new room. It was more than he had had in the barracks in the Lower District. He was surprised to have an entire room to himself. Did all personal guard get their own space, or was it that none of the Amboians wished to share a space with a Human? None of it mattered now.

There was a knock and Carter turned toward the door. When he was only steps away the door slid open. The Amboian at the door jumped when he saw Carter.

"Carter Gerro," the Amboian said after clearing his throat. "Your new armor has just been finished." He pushed past Carter as he pulled a metal cart into the room. He mumbled to himself as he looked over several packages and boxes on the cart. "Ah! Here you are." The Amboian pulled a large metal chest from the bottom of the cart. With a grunt the Amboian heaved the chest onto Carter's desk. There was a loud metal clang as it hit the surface. Without another word the Amboian scuttled out of the room mumbling to himself. The door slid closed after he exited into the hallway.

The smooth dark-gray metal chest had no obvious latch to open. Carter reached out and felt around the exterior of the box, searching for a way to open it. Then the top of the chest split down the middle and opened outward. The light in the room bounced off the dark-gray chest plate inside. Removing the chest plate revealed the other pieces of his armor, all the same dark-gray metal.

"Impressive work," Carter said to himself as he gave the chest piece a once over. He undid the side latches of the armor and slid his torso inside. The latches closed shut automatically once he got it situated. The chest piece fit him perfectly and it felt as though he were only wearing a very rigid shirt.

"I would doubt that the other personal guards would stoop low enough to thievery, but I would keep that out of sight. They may not steal it for themselves, but some would gladly take a chance to make you look like a fool."

Carter nodded and closed the metal armor chest. He would only need minimal protection for now anyway. He looked around the room for a moment before deciding to put the chest in the bottom storage panel. Once the chest was situated, he slid the panel back into the wall. There was a barely audible click as the panel fit back into place among the others. Later he could put his personal belongings here as well.

"Now that that is taken care of, we should make our way to Gaelcean's quarters." The door slid open as Weleya approached it. "There are Council meetings every day. In some cases, there are many in one day." Carter followed Weleya out of the room. "During a Council meeting you are to remain silent. Personal guards are only allowed to attend out of tradition. Pay attention during the meetings, you never know what a Councilor might let slip. Even the most minor detail could prove useful in the future."

"Do the Councilors plot against one another often?" Carter followed Weleya out of the room. Instinct made him tap his hip where the weapon cylinder was tucked away.

"I doubt many will openly admit it." Weleya continued walking. "I mentioned that some treat their position as taking part in some game. Others take it far more seriously, for better and worse. Some of the Councilors have held their seats for hundreds of years, and they intend to keep it until they die."

The two stepped into a speed lift. When the doors closed Weleya pushed three buttons on the wall simultaneously. The lift lurched before speeding upward. To Gaelcean's quarters. Then Carter's first Council meeting.

CHAPTER SIX

A Job

Caleb sat at a small fountain in a courtyard in the Ninth District. The courtyard was lined with several small shops. A person who lived in the area could come here and buy everything from fresh baked goods to fine clothing. As fine as one could find in the Lower Districts, that is. Ana sat beside him to his left, one leg crossed over the other. Occasionally he saw one of her daggers flash out from her sleeve as she spun it in her hand. A man quickened his step as he passed by when he noticed Ana. It wasn't uncommon for a person to wear a weapon openly in the Lower Districts, especially one so close to the Eighth District. Many of the people who walked by going about their day carried a belt knife, sword of some kind, an axe here and there. When a weapon wasn't obvious there was surely a blade hidden up a sleeve, in a boot, or behind their back.

Lucas came into view in the gaps in the crowd. A wrinkled man was holding up a variety of jeweled necklaces in front of Lucas' face. Gaudy things with far too many gemstones in Caleb's opinion. Not that he had much say in what was fashionable. He looked down at his dark wool coat and travel-worn pants. The stones in the necklaces were most likely fakes, anyway. Lucas brought a hand to his chin as he thought for a moment and then pointed to something else on the man's small, wheeled stand. When the man turned to grab whatever it was that Lucas had pointed out, he turned around to look about the crowd.

Caleb turned to his right to try and spot Omar and Levi. He had to turn almost completely around until he saw the two of them seated at an iron wrought table. Both of them were enjoying a loaf of bread they had apparently found the time to purchase from the bakery in the building behind them. The scent of baked bread reached him from across the courtyard. Omar took a sizable bite out of the half loaf he had in his hand. Levi met Caleb's gaze and gave a nod. His half of the loaf remained untouched on the table.

He had been surprised to find Levi already packed and waiting for the others this morning. He hadn't said much since yesterday. Caleb returned Levi's nod before turning back around.

The wrinkled man at the jewelers' stand was now holding up an odd, silver-plated necklace. Caleb noticed Lucas' feigned interest again, hand on his chin with his other arm across his body.

He looked through the crowd for a sign of someone who might be giving them the drop. When he had received the fifty-credit transfer, there was also a message to wait at this fountain and face the direction of the Upper Districts. The massive gray-tan stone wall loomed in the distance. The lack of information put him on edge. Fifty credits was the most they had ever received prior to doing the actual job. If he estimated right, the payout at the end could be three times as much. They hadn't had such a well-paying job in some time; it was difficult to pass up. It wasn't like anyone would be fool enough to attack another during the day, in this crowd. Yet, he found himself watching the eyes and hands of anyone who passed in front of them. He needed to relax.

There was a man standing above a flock of people speaking. Caleb had to strain to hear what the man was saying. It didn't sound like he was preaching from the Church of Amboy's Salvation of Humanity. Over the din of the people moving through the courtyard Caleb thought he heard something about reaching the peak of Humanity by means of technological advancements. As the leathery-faced man spoke, he waved his mechanical arms about. His right arm had been completely replaced by a ruddy-looking prosthetic; its movements were much less fluid than those of his left arm. A much higher-quality enhancement was attached to his left arm at the elbow. The midday sun was glinting off the silvery metal as it waved about. He found it surprising that a good number of people had stopped to listen to the old man. If he were not waiting for the drop, he would have liked to get closer to get a better listen.

"Well, how much longer do we wait?" Ana threw her arms up and slapped her open palms against her legs. Apparently, her knife spinning was no longer keeping her interests.

"A bit longer." Caleb turned his attention back to the people in front of him. "Then we'll leave. Maybe find another job. The Church always needs help. It won't pay very well though."

"May the Shield protect us," Ana said sarcastically and sighed. Another dagger appeared from the sleeve of her coat. The light-blue coat she wore today still had its sleeves, unlike the other she had cut off. The coat sleeves hid her blades better than the loose sleeves of an undershirt. Her tan pants were tucked into boots that came up to her calves. The Ser'Delcea style of clothing was uncommon in the Lower Districts. Caleb thought for a moment that she should have worn something different to blend in. It was too late now though; they had left all of their packs at the room they had gotten at an inn.

His dark wool coat didn't flare at the waist like Ana's. His pants were a lighter brown compared to his coat. Almost the same color as Ana's tan pants. His boots didn't come to mid-calf. How she was able to move so quickly in those boots, he wasn't sure.

"I'd be careful speaking like that. We may not be in District Seven, but some might take offense to any negative speech toward the Church in the city."

"They're all a bunch of—" Ana began.

"Wait." Caleb held a hand out to stop her from continuing.

A bald woman was walking intently toward them through the crowd. Some women from Athanelle shaved the sides of their heads and wore the rest of their hair in long braids. Caleb couldn't remember seeing a woman who didn't have any hair at all. She wore a long brown cloak that covered her entire torso and stopped just below her knees. Once she got close enough to see, Caleb's surprise at her baldness was overtaken by his surprise at the color of her eyes. They looked like the sky at sunset when the sun hits the horizon. A sky ablaze.

Caleb noticed Lucas walking through the crowd behind the woman. The jeweler was shouting something after him. The wrinkled man didn't look happy at the loss of a possible sale. Caleb and Ana stood as she got closer. Lucas stopped a few paces behind. People moving through the crowd began shouting at Lucas as they pushed around him. He gave some a stern look to keep them moving.

"Hello." the woman's voice had a slight oddity to it. "You must be Caleb Fields, leader of the Amber Waves?"

"One of its leaders, yes. This is Ana Brooks."

"Caleb Fields. Ana Brooks. I am glad to have met you." She removed her hand from beneath her cloak and held out an envelope. He saw a flash of armor plating on her torso and forearm. A glimpse was all that was needed to tell it was Upper District craftsmanship. Lower District smithies and metal workers were talented, but there was no mistaking the quality of this woman's armor.

"That would mean Lucas Meadows is the man who followed me?" The woman's face looked like it had been carved from stone. "He is another leader of the Amber Waves, if my information is correct?"

The Amber Waves were well known in Homestead and other towns in the New Ring where they had chapters. Caleb knew that. Had their renown reached the Lower Districts as well? "Yes, that is correct." Caleb waved a hand at Lucas and he pushed the rest of the way toward them.

"This is all the information you will need." Once more she held out the envelope. "When the job is complete, inform the contact given. They will see to your payment. I wouldn't open that here. Once you have read it, destroy it."

Caleb took the envelope from the woman's hand. As he grabbed it, their fingers touched. The cool sensation of her skin remained on his even after he pulled away. He turned the sealed paper in his hands.

"Right." A message via data pad could have been traced. Information said aloud could be overheard by the wrong person. Paper could be burned. Caleb thumbed the wax seal that kept the paper folded shut.

"There will be more work after this. If it is deemed that you can meet our standards."

Before Caleb could respond the woman turned and began walking away in the direction that she had come from. The back of her cloak flowed in the breeze made by her brisk walk. The same metal armor covered her legs and feet.

Caleb looked at the folded paper in his hands. The blue wax seal was a symbol of a bird. A circle surrounded it.

"Something seemed off about her," Ana said without taking her gaze off the woman who was well off into the crowd.

From the corner of his eye Caleb saw Lucas nod. "I agree," Caleb said and turned and walked away from the fountain. Ana darted to his side and had to lengthen her stride to keep up with his and Lucas' pace. Caleb was so intent to get out of the crowd he had bumped into several people. He didn't pay attention to the shouts as he continued. Once they were out of the courtyard, they stepped into an empty side street. After waiting a moment he cracked the wax seal. Omar and Levi stepped into the street.

"Who was that?" Omar whispered when he got close.

"The armor she wore was no doubt made in the Upper Districts," Lucas said. Levi nodded in agreement.

So, they had seen it as well. Levi, from the opposite side of the courtyard.

"Any hint as to who we'll be working for?" Levi was looking at the paper in Caleb's hand. He unfolded it and a small black square fell out. He caught it just as it had fallen and read the contents of the message to himself.

Order a Spinneret at the Stamping Steed
Use Data Jumper at the terminal
Contact Voal District Nine

"The Stamping Steed," Ana read as she looked over Caleb's arm at the message.

"I know this place. It's in District Eight." Caleb handed the message to Ana so she could get a better look. He examined the black square that had been folded in the paper.

"A terminal. A data jumper," Ana muttered to herself. "Voal?" she said a bit too loudly. Her dark shoulder length curls bounced as she looked down both ends of the empty side street.

"There's still so little we know." Caleb looked at the data jumper in his hand.

The message had made its way to Levi. He only looked at it for a moment before pulling out a fire starter and lighting a corner of the message. The paper blackened and curled as the flames crawled up it.

"I think we were right about a gang making a move on another." Caleb shook his head. His thoughts raged like a river after winter's melt. He was familiar with data jumpers, the programs they held were normally automated after the user entered a run command.

"Okay." Lucas looked around for anyone unwanted ears. "What do we know?"

"Anyone familiar with an organization that uses a bird in a circle as their symbol?" Caleb showed them the broken seal he had removed from the paper.

The group all looked at it but was Levi who was first to respond. "It's difficult to be certain, but it looks like a dove." He paused. "Maybe a Widow's Dove?"

"What group uses a dove as their symbol?" Lucas questioned. This time genuinely bringing a hand to his chin as he thought.

"None that I can immediately recall," Omar replied.

New groups appeared all the time in the Lower Districts. Some of the well-known Upper District organizations were the Sickle of the Moon, the Airelleth Family, and the Jorogumo.

As if he had been reading Caleb's mind Lucas spoke up, "I can't think of any either, but going to a tavern in the Eighth District and ordering a *Spinneret* stinks of the Jorogumo."

"The Jorogumo?" Omar hissed. "Do we want to get involved with some group that has it out for the Jorogumo? If they found out ..."

"So, we don't get caught," Ana said as if it were obvious.

"Fifty credits up front." Lucas scoffed. He stepped away from the group and began pacing.

"Well, what do we know about the Jorogumo?" Ana reined the group back in.

"Last I knew they controlled most of the Third, Twelfth, and Eighth Districts," Levi said calmly. Caleb never would have guessed Levi had had a break down the day before. "Maybe these people don't want to be under the Jorogumo anymore?"

"That bald woman isn't from the Lower Districts," Caleb said.

"True. Maybe she plans on splintering the Jorogumo's control in the Lower Districts?"

"They're certainly number one in District Eight. When I was with the Church most of the people I helped had some sort of run-in with someone who had been paid by the Jorogumo. A shop owner getting beaten for not paying dues, sometimes just random acts of violence to keep people afraid." The look on Omar's face backed up his words enough. Caleb himself had had so many run-ins while in the Eighth with cutpurses and the like, that it had all seemed to blend together in his mind.

Lucas stopped pacing. "There are rumors that some Lower District Mayors are Jorogumo members." Everyone looked in his direction, but no one spoke. "Is this the first you've heard?" It was the first time Caleb had heard. None of the others spoke up. "Well." Lucas cleared his throat. "I guess it seems natural if you think on it. Why do they allow the attacks to continue? Either the Mayors are being paid off, or they're just as afraid as everyone else."

"I think we have all the information we need." Ana stepped forward. "I'll take the lead on this one. One person will be easier anyway. You all can stay nearby if things go to the Haze."

Caleb stood shocked. "No. That's not happening. Lucas or I will take this one. I don't want to risk any of you getting in over your heads. Besides, I got us into this."

"No one ever forces an Amber Waves member into a job. We chose to come along." Ana repeated the words every member knew. Levi and Omar nodded. Any of the Amber Waves chapter leaders, could never force a member into a job. "Besides what business would a fifty-year-old man have

97

with a bunch of gang members?"

"I'm not fifty," Caleb said with Lucas almost replying in unison.

"Ana has a point." Omar shrugged. "It has to be Levi or Ana. I'm too well known in District Eight from my time with the Church. And you and Lucas could be recognized if the right person saw you."

"Okay," Caleb conceded. "Take Levi with you at least. I'd rather two of you in there than one."

"I can handle this on my own." Ana's certainty was impossible to ignore.

"Ana will go in first," Lucas replied. "Order a drink at the bar." He turned to Levi, "Go in shortly after. Sit at a table so you can get a good view of the room. Omar, you wait outside near the entrance. Caleb and I will be nearby if things do get *Hazed.*" Lucas looked back to Ana. No one used that curse lightly.

Getting banished to the Haze was something that didn't happen often. Caleb had heard a rumor that a Council Member had been banished once.

"Sounds like a good plan." Ana had tried to hide the smile that appeared on her face. Caleb wished he were excited as Ana was; she jumped at every opportunity to fight it seemed. It suddenly felt as if dozens of eyes were watching them. Caleb looked up and down the narrow street, but other than their small group it had been empty.

CHAPTER SEVEN

An Old Friend

The sun in front of them was almost at its highest point in the sky as they traveled on the East Road. Cordelia sat in the back of Victor Aymin's wagon with Elina Tanveir. Victor sat at the front of the cart with the reins in hand. They made better time than Cordelia would have had she been walking by herself. At this pace they would be in East Edge before nightfall. She was surprised this morning to see Victor wide eyed and cheery considering the amount they had all drank the night before. She herself had a slight sensitivity to the brightness of the sun now, but her tinted glasses kept her eyes shielded enough. Even still Cordelia held a hand up to shade her eyes as she looked toward the sky. There was hardly a cloud in the sky currently, but Victor had mentioned a storm on the horizons. The Sky Watcher Victor had spoken to must have made a mistake, the bright-blue sky said enough. The sun glinted off of the surface of the Shield Generators. Without the aid of the reflecting sunlight the generators would be almost impossible to see from this distance. Elina didn't seem to be affected by last night's drinking either, or she was very good at not letting it show. Cordelia had helped Elina pack up the camp and prepared Victor's wagon for travel.

"I wouldn't mind stopping to stretch our legs and give the horses a rest," Victor said over his shoulder.

"That sounds good to me," Cordelia replied. She looked toward Elina, who hesitated for a moment and then nodded.

"If I remember correctly the forest opens ahead. We can pull off the road into the clearing."

Cordelia could tell by the sound of his voice that there was a large smile on Victor's face.

They had to travel a bit farther than Victor had remembered. Eventually they came upon a small grassy depression surrounded by trees. A pond toward the back of the green bowl was like glass. A large mossy oak leaned over the water, as if it were admiring its own reflection. The wagon slowed to a stop just off the dirt road and Victor climbed down and tended to the horses. He undid the straps that connected them to the wagon and hobbled them just a few feet away with a stake he drove into the ground.

Elina hopped down from the cart. "I'm going to have a look around. We haven't seen many on the road today, but this seems to be a well-used resting stop." She walked toward the nearby tree line with a hand resting on her sword.

She was right. The grass had been matted down in places from tents and sleeping rolls. There were scattered fire pits dug out throughout the grassy depression. *How did she notice that so quickly?* Cordelia felt slightly annoyed that she hadn't been as quick as Elina in noticing the subtle hints of past use. Her sense of things beyond the Exterior Wall was beginning to dull; maybe she had been spending too much time in the capital.

"We shouldn't need a fire, ourselves. We still have enough meat, cheese, and bread from the inn still," Cordelia said as she stretched her arms and back.

The innkeeper was kind enough to give them some food for the road, he had mentioned it was a gift in the spirit of the

Harvest's End celebrations which were beginning today in almost every town in the New Ring. Some towns would only take one day to celebrate, while others would spend several days feasting and drinking. Cordelia had been fortunate enough to spend a few days in a town outside of Athanelle to the North. Even though she had only passed through the small village once before, she was treated as if she had lived there her whole life.

East Edge would be celebrating today as well. They might be lucky enough to catch the end of today's festivities if they were back on the road soon. Cordelia looked down at the dried meat and cheese in her hands and felt a little guilty for wishing the gift had been a warm stew, or a thick slice of pork with potatoes. Her stomach growled and she bit off a piece of meat in response.

As if Victor had been reading her thoughts he turned around and said, "My wife makes the best squash soup, I look forward to it every holiday. Something about Harvest's End makes it extra special in my mind. You will have to try some!" His laugh was thunderous.

"I'll take you up on that offer." Cordelia smiled. Normally she tried to avoid traveling with others, but with the frequency of the attacks around the Perimeter, she was glad Victor had agreed to give her a ride out to East Edge. *What could be going on out there?*

Elina appeared from a different section of the woods than she had entered.

"Anything unusual?" Cordelia asked and held the gifted food out toward Victor and Elina.

"Just a couple more signs of some small camps." Elina took a bite of bread and washed it down with water from a flask she kept strung around her torso.

"This is a beautiful spot to stop for a break." The pride in Victor's voice made it sound as if it was crafted by his own hand.

"Not all the spots seem to have been used recently. Based

101

on the more recent camps that had been here, I'd guess a group of ten or fifteen. I believe they moved to the East. All seem to be traveling on foot." Elina's gaze was fixed on the trees surrounding the area.

"Traveling entertainers, hired for a nearby town's celebration most likely." Victor sounded sure of himself. "East Edge hires several music troops and entertainers each year. Once I saw a man and a woman *swallow* fire and blades."

Why would anyone swallow fire? And blades? Entertainers were strange people.

"Possibly," Elina said, still scanning the area.

Perhaps she was still feeling off from the drink, and maybe a bit annoyed at missing the signs of previous camps. Cordelia felt a wave of discomfort wash over her. "Wouldn't entertainers be traveling with carts? A group that size would have supplies for several days on the road."

"They likely would." Elina was still looking along the tree line. Was there something else she was seeing?

"We should get back on the road and get to East Edge." Cordelia's sudden change in tone noticeably affected her two traveling partners.

"You don't think?" Victor trailed off.

"Fifteen people from the Haze traveling in a group? Coordinating attacks on smaller towns?" Elina was looking directly at Cordelia now.

"I don't want to believe it, but I would rather be prepared for the worst, than be taken by surprise." Cordelia pushed past Victor and walked toward the horses. "We're probably half a day's travel behind them. If they are going to East Edge, we'll be too late by the time we get there. Victor, can we leave your cart here and ride the horses back?"

"I've only two, and we are three." Victor shrugged. He was visibly shaken.

"Elina and I will ride double, until we get to a town. Then we'll buy another or steal it if we have to." Cordelia handed the reins of one horse to Victor and looked toward Elina.

102

"How much riding experience do you have?"

"I have ridden before, but not much," Elina replied.

"It will have to do." Cordelia lifted herself up onto the bare horseback and held an arm out to Elina so she could pull herself up.

"Luckily, I keep a spare saddle in the cart." Victor said as he lifted up the riding bench of the cart and pulled out a single saddle with two small pouches on each side. Cordelia trotted the horse around while Victor got prepared. The brown horse seemed quick and light on its hooves, even with two riders. It was only moments later they were back on the dirt road. Cordelia thought she heard Elina let out a quiet yelp as the horse suddenly picked up speed. They kept a quick pace, but she was mindful not to push the horses too far. They would kill the horses if they didn't pace themselves. They alternated between a steady gallop and a trot to conserve the horses' energy.

The sun was almost setting as they crested a hill outside of East Edge. Of the major towns in the New Ring, East Edge wasn't the largest, but still considerable in size. Cordelia guessed there were several hundred permanent residents, and visitors came and went every day. Her main concern wasn't in the town itself, but a workshop outside of the town to the North. From up on the hill, she could see bonfires lit throughout the town for the festivities. She could hear the cheers and hollering even from up here. *Or were they fires set by attackers, and screams?*

Elina and Victor pulled up to her side each on their own horses. Shortly after setting out they came across a farm; luck had been on their side and the farmer agreed to sell one of his older work horses. It wasn't cheap but considering the circumstances she didn't have the time to try and get a better deal, and although she had mentioned stealing as an option, she couldn't bring herself to do it. She had used her data pad to transfer thirty credits to the man and gave him some coin to make up for the time it would take for the credit transfer this far out in the New Ring. He was kind enough to give them a saddle as well, for which Elina seemed grateful. Cordelia didn't mind riding without a saddle; she had had enough experience on horseback to tolerate it for the day's ride. Her body might say otherwise tomorrow. She massaged her thighs and knuckled her back.

"Everything seems as it should be from up here." Victor sounded relieved.

She wanted to believe him, and hoped she had just been overreacting, but she still didn't feel at ease. "I'm going to ride out to my friend's house. Once I see him for myself and know that everything is fine, I will meet back up with you in town."

"Yes, of course." Elina's eyes were scanning the town below as well.

"I can smell the feast already," Victor said. It felt as though he was trying to find some normalcy amongst all the excitement.

"I will meet up with you after," Cordelia repeated and heeled the sides of the horse and rode into the twilight.

Even with the day's ride, the horse still had plenty of energy. She was grateful for the generosity from the innkeeper this morning, from Victor for giving her a ride in his cart, lending her the horse, as well as the farmer who sold his own work horse. *I hope my luck hasn't run out.* It was difficult to push down the growing concern. She would know for certain once she found Jaeger Billet, hopefully unharmed.

Cordelia rode up to the house; there were no lights, or candles lit. Everything was quiet. She hopped off the horse before it had completely slowed and almost fell over as she ran to the door. She burst through the front door, her eyes had adjusted to the darkness since the sun had gone down, but she still couldn't see her friend.

"Jaeger!" she shouted, struggling to keep the fear out of her voice.

She ran through the main hallway and pushed into the

104

kitchen. The door swung wildly on its hinges as she stood in the empty room. From the kitchen windows she could see into the backyard and the workshop that lay just beyond the house. Light illuminated the windows. Cordelia thought she saw movement in the windows and felt relief. She moved across the room and out the back door into the yard. She tried to keep from sprinting as she approached the workshop.

Jaeger's workshop had always been impressive; he built almost everything himself. What he couldn't do himself he learned from others. There was a homemade forge and smithy, an electronics bench for working on his unfinished projects and refurbishing old tech found in the Haze. Above was a loft, a massive bookshelf that ran the length of it and it was completely filled. Jaeger's hand-drawn designs were scattered across tables, as well as loose papers with Jaeger's scrawling hand. More unfinished projects. She moved to the back of the building looking for any sign of the old man. As she rounded the corner, she finally felt complete comfort.

Her old friend was hunched over a workbench. His gray hair spilled out from underneath a dark knit cap. His short dark stubble was speckled with gray as well. A dirty white shirt and tan overalls were his usual workshop attire. He was well over twice her age. A lifetime spent in the workshop and scavenging the Haze had made Jaeger Billet a strong and formidable man. Metal parts were spread across the workbench. Pistons and pipes, electronics boards with loose wires in a tangled mess, and a strange reflective fabric.

"Jaeger."

The man looked up from his work and removed his protective goggles and smiled. His green eyes shimmered in the light of the workshop. "Well, this is a wonderful surprise. I thought you weren't going to be here for at least a few more days." He set his tools down and walked toward her, arms spread out.

The sudden rush of relief almost made Cordelia forget

why she had been worried only moments before. She pushed herself from the embrace. "Have there been any attacks today? Raiding parties or anything?"

A somber look crossed Jaeger's face. "Thankfully, none today. None in the past couple days as far as I know."

"While on the road we came across signs that a large group had been moving this way. Ten, maybe fifteen. With all the attacks on the smaller villages, I thought maybe ..." She could feel her emotions rising but steadied herself.

"I see, I see." Jaeger nodded and put a hand on her shoulder. "Everything is fine, Cordelia. I am fine."

"Did the town hire any traveling entertainers that may have arrived earlier today for the festivities?" Cordelia walked over and sat down at a table in the middle of the workshop. She moved some papers out of the way and stacked them to the side.

"There have been some that arrived today. You really think the raiding parties would attack a larger town like East Edge?" Jaeger sat down across from her and pushed a stack of books out of the way and moved some tools to the side. He pulled out a white cylinder and put it between his lips. As he inhaled a light on the end of the cylinder turned orange, as he exhaled thin wisps of vapor left his mouth.

"These past few attacks are the first reports of them actually killing people isn't it?" Now that things were calming down Cordelia could feel the soreness in her legs and back even more.

"As far as I know, yes." Jaeger leaned back, still puffing on the vapor stick. The fire in the forge crackled in the silence.

"Have they met with any resistance at all?" It was unlikely, but she needed all the information her friend could give.

"In those small villages, there's no town guard. What are farmers going to do against them?" Jaeger shrugged. "I've been sitting in on town council meetings. They have been sending word to Homestead, as well as the capital, to send soldiers to East Edge. Last I heard the Homestead leaders were wrapped up in their own issues, corruption, weak harvest in that area again." He got quiet as he thought.

"I can't imagine the Amboians sending soldiers out here." She paused. "Things have been getting worse in the city. So many people forcing themselves into the Lower Districts, overpopulation is driving people mad. A Diplomatic Council member actually gave a public speech and visited some of the districts. When has that ever happened?"

"Not in a very long time."

"I'm going out into the Haze tomorrow for a scavenge job." She hesitated. "I was also going to visit Mountain Station."

"Good. You haven't been out there in quite some time. I think you'd be a sight for sore eyes." Jaeger stood up and put the white stick back into his pocket. He walked over to a different workbench than the one he was working at before and reached underneath it. He grunted as he picked up a large chest and set it onto the table. It fell with a heavy thud and some books and papers fell to the floor. Jaeger fumbled with a lock for a moment. Cordelia heard a solid click and a squeaking of the metal hinges as the chest opened.

"I've improved your suit and breathing apparatus. It has gained some extra weight in the process, but the oxygen recycling system will be more efficient, giving you an extra ..." Jaeger thought. "Two hours? Perhaps?"

Cordelia stood up and hurried around the table to see what Jaeger had made for her. She reached in and picked up the dark-gray suit. The protective suit was lightweight, but sturdy, perfect for protecting against the caustic Haze and allowing her to move with relative ease. The helmet attached to a seal at the neck of the suit and was the same color. She slid it onto her head, the large oval visor allowed her to see with ease. It was just slightly too roomy, but that wasn't a major concern.

"Now, look at this." Jaeger picked up a small black box, there were several square buttons along the top. He pressed one and it turned red. Lights around the visor lit up, making it much easier to see in the dim light of the workshop. "And this!" The excitement in Jaeger's voice was building as he continued to press buttons on the box. The room seemed to get just slightly darker, but Cordelia didn't see any major differences.

"I get the lights, but what is this?" she asked.

"Take off the helmet and see for yourself." Jaeger was practically beaming with excitement. The visor had been clear before, but now matched the gray color of the rest of the suit. "I may have been lucky enough to come across a discarded Knight's helmet, and reverse engineered some of their tech." He *was* beaming.

"*Come across*, huh?"

Jaeger laughed and began putting the suit back in the box. "That's enough for now, I can show you the rest of the features tomorrow before you leave."

Cordelia placed the helmet back into the large box and Jaeger locked it up. Grunting again as he picked it up, he shuffled over to the workbench and slid it back into its place. He stood up and stretched his back and wiped his brow.

"Let me go inside and wash up, then we can walk into town and you can fill me in on the past few months of your life." He put a solid arm around her shoulders and the two walked out of the shop and into the dark night, toward the house.

The fires that lined the great town square of East Edge provided plenty of light. Smaller electric lights on poles were placed around the square as well. Jaeger was developing an electrical system for the town that ran off the energy from the sun. He had apparently learned it from old books he had found while scavenging in the Haze.

108

The warmth from the fires was welcome. The nights would only be getting cooler as time when on. East Edge had spared no expense for this year's Harvest's End celebration. Vendors were walking throughout the square selling cooked meats on skewers and fresh bread. A group of musicians stood at the top of the wide stone steps that led up to the town hall. There were several stringed instruments and small drums that hung at the side with the aid of a strap over the shoulder. A young boy was hopping around the group as he played the flute. A man in his middle years walked past the table they were seated at as he juggled six brightly colored balls. With a quick movement of his wrist six became eight, and the man didn't miss a step as he passed by. His yellow coat had orange stripes slashing across it, and his blue pants flared at the knee. It was almost too much to look at.

"I thought I was going to have to fight my way to the ale cart over there," Victor said as he sat heavily on the bench across from Cordelia. He easily carried five full mugs in his massive hands. "Lucky for us I delivered grain for Mistress Elwhin!" Victor tossed his head back as his laughter rose above the din of the festivities.

"Now, now, Victor." Lillianna patted her husband's forearm and laughed along with him. Her laugh sounded like a field mouse in comparison. Victor rested a hand on Lillianna's and with the other wiped a tear from his eye. The two of them together could have brightened the darkest room as soon as they entered.

"What shall we drink to?" Victor passed the drinks around the table. "If we didn't have such wonderful music, I would suggest we sing a song."

"Probably for the best. I'm not much of a singer myself." Jaeger smiled as he took a mug from Victor.

"I believe everyone has the talent," Victor said as he passed a mug to Cordelia. "Kynn, my eldest. He thought he couldn't sing. He is even better than myself!"

"I don't know about that, Pa." Kynn buried his face in his

109

mug as it reddened. Which caused yet another boisterous laugh from Victor. His laughter was infectious, and it didn't take much longer for the entire table to get swept up in it, even Kynn.

Cordelia guessed Kynn Aymin was only a few years younger than she. His shoulder-length dark hair matched his parents and his deep blue eyes seemed to have been taken from Lillianna. The resemblance was uncanny. There would never be a doubt he was Lillianna and Victor's son. Victor and Lillianna had two other children, a boy, and a girl much younger than Kynn. Cordelia had yet to meet them.

"Let me see if we can get the attention of one of these vendors. The smell alone could take care of my hunger," Jaeger said looking around. He spotted a man carrying an arm load of skewered meats. Cordelia could see the steam rising into the cool night. A slight breeze brought the scent toward her. The last thing she had eaten was the dried meat from the innkeeper near midday. Jaeger paid the man in coin, which brought a smile to his face. Coin was more appreciated out here. Each of them received a skewer the length of Cordelia's forearm packed with chicken, lamb, beef, and pork. The beef and pork gave off a smoky scent that made Cordelia's mouth water instantly, and the lamb and chicken looked to have been heavily seasoned and cooked on a hot skillet.

"Thank you, Jaeger," Kynn said with a mouthful. "We will have to send you home with some leftover food from our family meal."

Victor nodded with a mouthful of meat and gave his son a pat on the back.

"How kind, Kynn. We would gladly send you off with some food." Lillianna's smile made her eyes close almost entirely.

"That would be greatly appreciated," Jaeger replied once he had finished swallowing. He immediately went back in for another bite.

Hours ago, Cordelia had been worried one of her best

110

friends had been murdered, and now they were drinking good ale, eating delicious food, and listening to gleeful music. Maybe that campsite had just been travelers on the road. It could have been the group at the top of the town hall steps. Cordelia felt a pit in her stomach and set her food down. Although there was plenty of meat still left on the skewer, she was no longer hungry.

"Cordelia." The concern in Lillianna's voice brought the table's attention. "What's the matter, dear?"

Cordelia felt the pit grow larger. She didn't want to spoil the mood.

"I'm not sure." She let out a long sigh. She lowered her voice before she continued, "I was so sure when we crested that hill, we would see East Edge in flames."

Kynn coughed into his mug and ale splashed onto his face. Lillianna pulled a rag from a pocket and handed it to her son to wipe his face, and Kynn murmured a thanks.

"I was worried as well, to be honest." Victor sighed as well. "I had told Lillianna as soon as I arrived home. Everything seemed fine and I didn't want to frighten the children, so I kept it between us."

"I see." Cordelia trailed off and looked at Kynn. He had finished drying off his face and was looking around the table in confusion.

"Not to worry, Cordelia," Victor assured her. "I meant the young ones. Kynn can handle it. He should know."

Cordelia and Victor told the table what they had come across along the road, filling in the blanks where the other might have left out a detail. Kynn's eyebrows continued to rise as the story went on. Jaeger had pulled out his vapor stick and puffed on it as he listened. He seemed to be staring through the center of the table as he rubbed his scruffy chin. Lillianna appeared as though she were listening to them talk about the weather during their travels. Victor must have told her enough that this was no surprise.

"Perhaps there are several groups in the New Ring, and

111

this was a sort of gathering to report to one another," Jaeger said, still staring through the table. The white cylinder bounced between his lips as he spoke. The scent of lavender from the vapor mixed with the spice and smoke of the skewers making Cordelia's stomach churn.

"The town leaders should be informed. Better for them to be aware of it, even if they don't believe," Cordelia said. She picked up her mug to take a drink, but she got as far as bringing it near her lips. She stared into the dark liquid before setting the mug down with a sigh. "Jaeger you have been sitting in on some of their meetings. Maybe they will take it more seriously from you, than me."

Jaeger nodded; wisps of vapor floated out with each breath. Hardly anyone used vapor sticks anymore. Jaeger had said it was more of a physical habit, than an addiction to the plant based liquid inside. "I'll see about talking to them tomorrow. Might be difficult with all the festivities. I'll have to get to them before they get too much drink in them." Jaeger attempted a laugh, but he shook his head and sighed. "With all the reports, and now the more recent attack on the Meadows farm, they have to take it seriously."

"I will go with you when you speak with them." Victor's seriousness matched his usual cheer. It was almost startling, but a smile quickly reappeared on his face. "There is nothing to do about it now, though. No need to worry about it now. Let us enjoy this!" He held up his mug to the table and everyone joined him. "To Harvest's End!"

The table echoed Victor's cheer and they drank. When she finished Cordelia found herself staring into the empty mug. She knew she wasn't overreacting. Living in the capital may have dulled her senses when she was in the New Ring, but she trusted her instinct. It was all she could act on for now. Until she returned to Mountain Station. Until she returned home.

CHAPTER EIGHT

The Beginnings of a Web

Ana sat on a stool at the bar of the Stamping Steed. The air in the cramped room was heavy with body odor and stale alcohol. Taverns and inns in the Eighth District were notorious for trouble. Patrons didn't have to be drunk to begin a brawl. It wouldn't take long if someone's luck had been too consistent with dice or playing Twelve. The sound of the dice game being played behind her wasn't making her anxious now, though. It was the unknown. Ana had learned to respect the unknown from her time sailing with her parents on the Great Sea. Even the most skilled Sky Watcher was capable of making an error, and the waters weren't always clear as well-made glass.

The door behind her opened and she heard a new patron sit at a table behind her. Levi. He would have a good view of the room if anything went wrong. The Stamping Steed wasn't much of a tavern, or maybe there were rooms upstairs as well. Ana couldn't see stairs from where she was sitting at the bar and didn't remember seeing any when she walked in. A tavern then. A sickly-looking woman appeared from behind the counter; dirt covered her face. She walked in the direction of the table where Levi had sat.

"Anything for the young man?" The woman's voice reminded Ana of scraping barnacles off the hull of her father's ship, the Sea's Bane. When her mother's ship, Wind Seeker, came in it was more of the same. It wasn't how she expected to spend her first year as a member of their crews.

"Spiced wine, if you have it." Levi's voice was calm. Ana had to strain to hear it. He seemed collected in most scenarios. He would make an excellent ship captain.

A gaunt old man slapped a hand on the bar. "What will it be? You've been sittin' here far too long to not have ordered somethin'."

Ana leaned in toward the man and lowered her voice, "I'll take a Spinneret."

His sunken eyes flicked wide and the thin man's eyebrows raised up along his forehead before returning back to their original place. "I see," he said flatly. He turned his back to her.

Ana began to think of her attack — or possibly escape — plan, until he turned around with two bottles and a small glass in hand. A clear liquid was poured into the glass, and he pulled a cork from a bottle and carefully poured a single drop into the glass. He moved his wrist ever so slightly as the drop left the bottle. As the two liquids met the droplet formed a gray teardrop with a slightly hooked tip. Without word of payment, he turned his back again and began cleaning glasses.

Unsure what to do next, Ana remained seated and picked up the glass to get a better look at the creation.

"A work of art, but I'll be impressed if a person of your size can handle even half of that." A broad-shouldered man in a brown tunic sat beside Ana at the bar. He must have been one of the men dicing at the table. What little hair he had left was pulled back into a long black tail. His mustache covered his upper lip and was slicked down the sides of his mouth to his chin. He was also lacking a few teeth.

114

"Is that so?" Ana had no trouble acting tough, she was from Ser'Delcea after all. The man sat and stared at her. She had to fight to keep her cheeks from reddening. Maybe she was out of practice.

"Come." The man got up and moved towards the tavern door. While following the man Ana glanced over to Levi and flashed five fingers followed by one. *Wait before following us out.* Omar would be outside as well. He would pursue once he saw her leave with the man. Although Caleb and Lucas said they would be nearby, Ana figured that most likely meant they would be right outside as well.

As they exited the Stamping Steed into the twilight, the narrow street was mostly empty. A dog whimpered where it lay by the door. Ana could count every rib along its side. She looked up and down the dimly lit street and saw Omar leaning against some wooden crates a few buildings down. His iron-capped staff was in the crook of his arm. No one would give a man of Omar's size any trouble even if he wasn't holding a weapon. If only they knew he was once a member of the Church.

The man turned left along the side of the building and Ana quickened her step to keep up. She checked the hidden blades up her sleeves and shook her ankle to be sure the other blade was there as well. They turned once more into an alley that ran along the side of the Stamping Steed. It was difficult to see in the low light. She was surprised the man's broad shoulders allowed him to walk through without turning sideways. Before entering the alleyway, she heard footsteps behind her. She hoped they were familiar and thought for a moment to turn around just to be sure but didn't want to take her eyes off the man in front of her. He didn't seem to be carrying a blade of any kind, but if he landed one good punch on her she would go down. *Like I'd give him the opportunity.* Just before reaching the end of the alley the man stopped and felt along the wall of the Stamping Steed. After some fumbling with the wooden slats of the building, he found what he was looking for and put both hands under the wooden boards. With a grunt he lifted, and a part of the wall came away. It looked as if a shipwright had forgotten to repair the hull of a ship.

"You've got five minutes. I'll wait out here. None of my business what you've got to do with the Jorogumo." The man set the wooden boards aside and stood with his arms across his chest. Ana nodded before stepping into the hole in the side of the building.

As she entered lights that ran along the floor of the narrow passageway lit up. Had she been inches taller, she would have had to hunch over as she moved through the space. The size of the room at the end of the narrow passage was about the size of a captain's quarters on a modest ship. Wooden tables lined the walls, all covered in papers and files. Maps of the Lower Districts covered the walls to the point where wood was almost unseen. To her right was a desk with a terminal with a keyboard. She hurried over and pulled a chair close to the keys as she sat down.

Technology like the lights that lit up the passage and the terminal she was seated at now were fairly uncommon in Ser'Delcea. Ana would wait at the docks every morning for the first merchant ships to arrive. Getting first pick allowed her to get her hands on tech from across the sea. The scarcity of tech in her hometown was what drove her interests in it. She would spend most of her free days taking apart broken data pads, music boxes, and any other junk the merchants had brought over. They had considered it junk anyway. To Ana it was an opportunity to learn something she wouldn't likely be able to in Ser'Delcea.

When she had been removed from both her parents' ships, she had opened a small tech shop in her family's home on the coast. Business wasn't very good, but occasionally a local would come in with a question about something they had bought without knowing what it was, or someone had broken something they didn't know how to properly use. It

116

was a good way to make some money while her parents were out at sea.

Ana rested her hands on the keyboard. The black screen had three blinking white dots in the center. A signal that the machine was waiting for operator instruction. Ana reached in her pocket and pulled out the data jumper, turning it over in her hand as she examined it. There was no obvious point at which the jumper would connect to a terminal. She carefully pulled at what seemed to be a cover and the black rectangle came apart revealing an exposed data chip. Ana inserted the jumper into the open slot on the front of the terminal and the three dots began spinning around each other. An electrical humming began coming from inside the machine and as it went on became slightly louder, as if struggling.

Ana drummed her fingers impatiently as the three dots raced around on the screen. Finally, a text window appeared:

RUN? Y/N

"Simple enough," Ana murmured to herself, and hit the "Y" key and then "RETURN".

Once again, the electrical humming began only louder this time it seemed. Text windows and images were appearing and disappearing with only seconds for Ana to catch any information herself. She caught what seemed to be design schematics for human augmentations, maps for Districts Eight, Seven, Nine, Twelve, Three, and Four. Pictures of Lower District leaders with their personal information. Ana caught bits of information here and there as the documents on the Lower District Mayors appeared. Some read approved, on others there were indications of uncertainty.

A loud knock came from behind Ana. "Time's almost up," the large man bellowed down the passageway.

She wasn't sure how much longer the jumper needed to

run its process but decided she could wait it out if needed. The man seemed uninterested in gang activities. How long would his disinterest outweigh his patience? It would be difficult for him to move through the passageway. That could buy her more time.

Text boxes and images were continuing to come into and out of existence. As if the machine could sense her urgency, a text window appeared:

PROCESS COMPLETE.

Ana let out a sigh and removed the data jumper, reconnected the two pieces, and stuffed it back into her pocket. She stood and pushed the chair back in place and looked around the room once more. Without hesitation she pulled out her own data pad and used its scanning function to get images of the maps on the walls. As she walked along the tables the device scanned the paper documents and recreated them into electronic text files. She took one last look around the room before she turned toward the passageway and walked back out into the alley.

"Ah, there you are." The large man was leaning against the side of the Stamping Steed, arms still folded across his chest.

"Thank you. That'll be everything for me." Ana turned down the alley trying to keep a normal walking pace.

"Well hold on now." The man grunted as he put the wooden wall back in place. "What about the payment? We don't allow you to use our establishment for your schemes for free!"

Ana turned back toward the man. "Payment? What payment?" She could easily outmaneuver him had they been in an open area. Here in the narrow alley, she would find it difficult to put distance between herself and him. The man turned toward her. Ana retreated backward keeping her eyes on him.

"I told Berrick last time he was here." The man was getting increasingly angry. Even in the low light she could see his face reddening. "Payment. Every. Time!"

He laced his fingers together and brought his large fists up above his head. Ana instinctively rolled backward. A gust of wind from the man's swing was the only thing she felt, thankfully. She flung an arm in his direction and one of the hidden blades flew from her sleeve and sunk into his left shoulder. The man roared as he pulled the blade out and threw it to the ground. He lunged at her again with his fists raised. Again, Ana rolled backward. She pulled two daggers from beneath her coat as she came back to her feet. She was ready to throw herself at the man, but he was grasping at his throat. A terrible rasping sound bounced off the walls of the alley. Blood began dripping from his mouth as he continued to grasp what Ana could now see was an arrow shaft in his throat. She turned around to see Levi standing in the alley behind her.

"You could have hit me!" she shouted as she turned toward her companion. There was a loud thud as the large man's body hit the dirt and stone behind her.

"He was at least three heads taller than you. I could have hit him from over ten times the distance. Are you alright?"

"I'm fine. Where are the others?" The two walked out of the alley.

Omar appeared in the street ahead of them. "I was about to run in once I heard the shouting. Levi insisted he take the shot." He leaned on his staff. "I probably wouldn't have been much use in that narrow space anyway."

Footsteps rang on the paving stones. The three of them turned to see Caleb and Lucas come running from down the street. It seemed no one else had heard what had happened. In the Eighth District it was more likely someone had heard but didn't care to get involved.

"Everything okay?" Lucas sounded winded. Caleb was breathing heavily through his nose.

"That woman who gave us the drop didn't mention they would ask for payment." Ana tried to keep the heat out of her voice, but it was difficult.

"I see." Caleb looked past them. "If we were in any other District, I would suggest we take the time to hide the body. I don't think it will matter here."

"The barkeep knows Ana was the last person with the man when he was alive," Levi said.

Ana felt a tinge of concern rising. She hated the unknown. "Well, the owners of the Stamping Steed work with the Jorogumo, often enough that they didn't seem to make too much of a fuss about me ordering that drink. The barkeep seemed surprised for a moment, but that was it. Maybe they will just assume something went wrong and the Jorogumo had to make an example out of him or something."

"True. It's not likely they will go after you if they think you're working with the Jorogumo." Caleb stroked his beard as he spoke. "We can't worry about that too much now anyway. We need to find this Voal."

"One more thing." The group stopped walking away. "That guy mentioned a man named Berrick who usually shows up. Might be a good name to keep in mind." Ana shrugged.

"Good thinking," Omar said. "We should run that name by the contact when we find him. Might be useful."

The walk out of the Eighth District was a quiet one. Everyone kept their guard up. Walking through the Eighth District during the day was bad enough. Levi walked the street with an arrow already knocked. How did he move so effortlessly with that absurdly long bow? Omar used his staff as walking stick. It could be readied at any moment. Caleb and Lucas were the only ones who seemed unconcerned. They both had their swords unclasped in their sheaths. Maybe there was some concern. When they had almost reached the archway between Eight and Nine three men stepped out of an alley in front of them. There were more footsteps behind.

"Out for a stroll in the night, are we?" a gruff voice called out to them.

"We don't want any trouble," Caleb said putting a hand on the hilt of his sword. Ana heard the string of Levi's bow go taut.

"There won't be any if you just give us some coin."

Ana could see moonlight glint off of the weapons the men and women were carrying. She turned to get a look of the people behind her and noticed Omar had already turned around. Everything about Omar seemed calm and collected. A trap waiting to spring. Three in front and four behind. They were outnumbered. *This might be fun.* Ana strained to keep a smile from sliding across her face. It wasn't that she liked hurting people or killing. It was the rush she enjoyed. It was like sailing during a rough storm and coming out with the full crew and ship on the other side.

"No coin on us," Lucas spoke this time. "Why don't you just let us go on our way."

Ana heard the gruff-voiced man sigh. "Kill them."

As Ana flung her remaining hidden blade in the direction of a woman rushing toward her, she realized she had left her other blade back in the alley. It sunk into the woman's left eye and her momentum brought her body into a jumble on the stone. She pulled her daggers from her coat and turned toward a man who was moving toward her. She rounded the body on the ground to put some distance between her and the man. The dark street was filled with the sound of metal on metal. The twang of arrows being loosed. The cracking of bone. The man stopped his approach and began to back away. It was then Ana realized she had been smiling. She laughed as she ran toward the man. Omar's staff was a blur as it clubbed the man in the back of the head.

"He was mine."

"I'm sure you could have handled him." Omar wiped the end of his staff on the man's cloak. "I'd rather you didn't take the risk."

"Let me guess," Ana sighed. "Some sort of Church belief that's been ground into your head?"

Omar shook his head and chuckled.

"Everyone alright?" Lucas walked over; his sword dripped red.

"We're okay," Ana replied. "You might want to clean that off before it's ruined."

Lucas bent down and cleaned the blade off on one of the bodies in the street.

"If everyone is okay, we should get out of here now." Caleb had a cut along the right side of his face. His beard was matted down with blood.

"You're bleeding, Caleb." Ana reached toward his face, but he brushed her hand away.

"I'll be okay. I've got some water left in my canteen. I can clean up before we pass through the archway, so the guards don't stop to ask us questions."

The rest of the walk through the Eighth District was uneventful and when they had passed through the gateway between Eight and Nine Ana informed the group of everything that had happened in the hidden room. The files, the maps, the depth of data that was pulled from the terminal, and the quick haul of information she was able to get.

"Good thinking, Ana." Caleb sounded proud. "Very good."

"Now to find this Voal and get our payment." Lucas reminded everyone that the job wasn't yet completed.

"Indeed," Omar said, leaning on his staff. "I would like to look through what you were able to find. From what you described it sounds like Lucas was right."

"This could be true. Let's worry about that after we drop

122

this data jumper," Caleb said.

"And get our payment," Lucas finished.

The information from the drop told them Voal was in District Nine, but it didn't say where. Caleb suggested they return to the fountain where the drop had been made and scout around from there. It wouldn't be as dangerous to walk around the Ninth District at night as long as they kept their wits about them. The courtyard with the fountain was empty except for a single person.

"Who's there?" Ana readied a dagger in her left hand. Caleb held a cautioning hand out toward her.

"Why, I am Voal." The man smiled.

CHAPTER NINE

Contact

L ucas stared at the man who introduced himself as
Voal. He was slender and tall, younger than Lucas, but
not by much. Tufts of his dark hair stuck out in every
direction from his head. The short scruffy facial hair
showed he hadn't shaved. He had either just woken up or
hadn't cleaned up in sometime. His fine gray coat was
buttoned to the neck and he had gray pants to match. Both
been recently cleaned and pressed. He may not have taken
care of himself, but he did seem to take care of his clothing.
Or someone had. Behind his black-rimmed glasses his blue
eyes seemed to shine in the dim light of the night.

"I am aware that the initial plan was for you to find me. It
seems my assistant forgot to include *where* that would actually
be." Voal stepped closer to them. "My assistant is a good
man, if a bit distracted at times. You will meet him shortly."
He continued to approach. Lucas tightened his grip on the
hilt of his sword. Out of the corner of his eye he saw Ana
reach into her coat.

"Is that so?" Caleb replied. Had he relaxed some? Lucas
remained focused, two paces between them and he could

land a solid hit. He wasn't about to be tricked by some bedraggled man in a fancy gray suit. His eyes bounced back and forth between the man, and the streets and alleys surrounding the courtyard. They may be out of the Eighth District, but that wouldn't mean that there wouldn't be trouble here in the Ninth.

"Yes. If you would follow me you can inform me of what you have discovered, and then I can see to the rest of your payment." Without waiting for a reply, the man walked between them and continued down the nearly empty street. Caleb looked at Lucas with raised eyebrows and gave a slight shrug and followed behind the man. Ana, Levi, and Omar followed as well.

Lucas searched the courtyard once again. He let out a sigh and murmured, "Let's see about that payment."

He kept to the back of the group and with each scan of the street around them, he stopped for a moment on Voal. Caleb was walking at the front alongside the strange man. He seemed at ease; Lucas knew better. He could hear them speaking to each other, but he remained focus was on their surroundings. Lucas picked up his pace to walk beside Omar. "What do you think?" He kept his voice low.

"It does seem odd, but the woman who gave the drop was odd as well." Omar paused. "They could also have been tracking that data jumper considering what we might have found."

"Could be. Then why even have us try to find him in the first place?" Lucas thought he saw Voal turn his attention to the two of them as they whispered.

"Maybe the tracking was insurance."

Voal led the group down the narrower side streets, occasionally stopping to look around. Sometimes when they stopped the man would murmur something to himself before picking a direction to continue onward. At times it seemed he was picking a direction at random. Was he crazy? Lucas turned to look down the dark street behind them. It was empty. Eventually Voal stopped at a store front and approached the door.

The two-story stone building seemed like any other on the street, a large tan canvas awning covering the area in front of the store. The windows were boarded up and a sign out front gave information detailing a construction timeline and an estimated grand opening date.

Voal unlocked the door and stepped inside. He turned to hold the door open while he motioned the others to come in. "Quickly now." He waved his free arm toward Lucas and the others.

The plainness of the interior matched the outside. Several rows of shelves lined the center of the room. All were empty and covered in a thick layer of dust. Two wooden tables toward the back of the store were bare and chairs had been overturned and placed atop each table. The thick layer of dust had covered everything, save for a path on the floor where they currently walked. As they passed through the room, they added their own footprints to those that had passed through before. *Four. Maybe five people.* Once Voal reached the far end of the room he unlocked another wooden door.

The steps to the cellar creaked under his weight as he began descending. "Don't mind the store. As you can imagine we must keep up appearances," he said over his shoulder as he continued down the stairs, again not waiting to see if anyone was even following.

Caleb followed first, then Ana, Levi, Omar, and Lucas brought up the rear. He grabbed a chair off of one of the tables and propped it against the door to keep it from closing. *Just in case.* He waited for a moment to be sure that the weight of the chair would keep the door open. Once he was certain, he turned down the stairs to catch up with the rest of the group. Lucas reached the bottom of the staircase and turned into the cellar just as Voal was pushing a shelf along the far wall.

The air in the dark room was cool and slightly damp. A

large metal door appeared in the space that the shelf had occupied. Voal pulled something from his coat pocket. Lucas' hand instinctively went to the hilt of his sword. There was a beep and a loud metal clunk. The door disappeared sideways into the wall and Voal entered. The others followed behind. Lucas' knuckle ached as he let go of his sword. Had he been gripping so hard? He sighed and moved toward the doorway.

Warm light filled the new room and it seemed to have much more frequent use. Two rows of three wooden desks were in the center of the room. The terminals at each desk seemed to be of differing age. A man and a woman worked at their own terminal; neither looked up when the group entered the room. A third man was standing over a table along the side of the room looking over paperwork; he let out an occasional frustrated sigh. This man turned to acknowledge the newcomers.

"Howlen, meet the Amber Waves Company." Voal extended an arm as if performing a trick.

"Well only some of us." Caleb approached with an outstretched hand.

"Howlen Norre."

Lucas thought Howlen looked like he could have been a baker or butcher in Homestead. His horseshoe of brown hair and flush cheeks gave him a welcoming appearance. No. He didn't know this man. He wasn't in Homestead. He was in an odd basement doing jobs for people who had it out for one of the most dangerous Families in the Upper District.

Howlen continued to shake Caleb's hand as he spoke. "It's good to finally meet you. Being so close to District Eight, your names have come across my desk for some time." Voal shot a look to Howlen.

"Yes, well." Voal cleared his throat. "We will transfer the funds once we see the quality of information you have gotten for us." He held his hand out, palm up.

Ana handed over the data jumper, and he immediately walked over to the woman typing at one of the terminals. She didn't notice Voal until he was practically standing on top of her. She held her hand up to receive the black rectangle without looking away from her screen. One hand continued to type even with the absence of the other. As soon as the data jumper landed in her hand the woman plugged it in and immediately returned to typing. She had actually begun to work faster, it seemed.

"We will sift through the data in the coming days. In the meantime, we have another job for you if you are willing." Voal held out a folded paper with the same wax seal as before. A bird surrounded by a single circle.

Caleb took the paper from Voal. "It will depend on the job." He turned to his companions and met eyes with Lucas.

The work would be good, Caleb, but what are we getting into here? They had known each other long enough to get a good idea what the other was thinking without needing to say much. Caleb shrugged with his eyebrows.

"What I can tell you right away is that you will need to decide tonight. There is a supply train heading to Port Amboy tomorrow. This job would see that you be on it." Urgency bubbled up as Voal spoke.

"What do we think?" Caleb wasn't just looking at Lucas this time. No one was ever forced to take a job; the question was given to each member equally. Ana was the first to answer that she would go, Levi almost immediately after, and then Omar nodded without saying a word. Caleb was looking back at Lucas now.

"Some more information would be ideal." Lucas saw some relief cross his friend's face as he spoke.

"Yes. Very well." Voal pushed his glasses up the bridge of his nose and ran a hand through his hair. The dark tangles seemed to be tame for a moment. As he spoke, they began to rise back up. "After you enter Port Amboy you will be collecting information from the locals. We need you to probe the people and see how they feel about their lives. What are they upset about? Do they have needs they feel aren't being

128

met? What gang-related activity has been occurring?" Lucas was sure everyone had caught Voal's attempt to slip that last part in.

"I want to ask a question." Ana stepped forward.

"I cannot say whether I will be able to answer fully, but you may ask." Voal crossed his arms and his face hardened again. How patient was this man?

"Do you think the Upper District Families are setting lines within the Lower Districts?" Straight to the point. Ana was never one to be behind the cart on most things. Lucas had always thought that had been her best trait. She was also good with those daggers, of course.

"*Setting lines.*" Voal paused. "You are somewhat correct. Rather, it is certainly a possibility." There was nothing more. It was clear that was all he had to say.

Ana gave a nod of acceptance and stepped back, leaning against the table that had Howlen swimming in papers. Howlen had been muttering to himself the whole time. Grabbing a paper, looking for a moment and then tossing it to the side with a scoff. It seemed as though he was making two piles. The one he was scoffing papers into seemed much larger than the other.

"Based on what I've seen so far," the woman at the terminal spoke without looking away from her screen. "I'd say this was a success. Six hundred credits easily. Certainly, more once we've gone through everything."

Six hundred credits. Lucas managed to still himself. He thought he had heard a gasp from Levi or Ana. Omar was shaking his head with a smile.

"Excellent." Voal clapped his hands together and grabbed a credit reader off his desk. Turning to Caleb he held it out with a smile. Caleb pulled his data pad out and held it to the reader. Voal tapped the screen and with a sound of satisfaction he set the reader back down on his desk. "The credits will be available immediately. We know you take your work seriously and you have done well, so we wouldn't want

129

to keep the transfer held up."

Lucas shot a glance at Caleb. *An immediate transfer of six hundred credits?* If Lucas had used that same reader to transfer ten credits to Caleb, he would be lucky to have it tomorrow morning.

"Once the data you have brought us has been completely looked through you should expect a second payment." Voal was still smiling.

"Thank you," Caleb said as he put his data pad back under his cloak.

"I believe it will be us who are thanking you in the end, Caleb Fields." Voal pushed his glasses up once more. "We will be thanking all of you." He turned to Lucas and smiled.

As the group exited the store front Voal said his goodbyes and closed the door on them with a soft clunk of the locks. The five stood in the dark street of the Ninth District. The silence of the night felt like a heavy blanket.

"As per usual ten percent of what we've made goes to the Amber Waves account. The rest we'll split evenly amongst ourselves. With a little extra toward Ana," Caleb added after a look from her.

"What about this new job?" Levi asked and looked up and down the street. If anyone was out this late, they would have more than unwanted ears to worry about.

Caleb broke the wax seal on the folded paper. Five small pieces of paper fell as the sheet unfolded. He managed to catch all but two, which Omar grabbed before they fell to the paved street. Omar brought his open palm closer to his face to see in the darkness.

"Well?" Ana sounded anxious. Did the girl never tire?

"Tickets for the train to Port Amboy." Omar held his hand out toward Ana. Her face lit up as soon as she saw the tickets. Although she wouldn't be returning to her home across the Great Sea, Port Amboy would be the closest thing.

"It's all here," Caleb said. "We take the train and ask the people of the port how their lives are." Caleb held the paper

130

out to Ana. "We'll be posing as construction workers. I heard they are expanding the harbors out there."

"Voal seemed to forget that part," Lucas grumbled. Although, it would help them get past the station security. The Knights guarded the train stations as heavily as they did the Upper District Gates. Lucas and Caleb had stowed away once. Barely.

"It will help us get through security." Caleb had been thinking the same thing. Lucas and Caleb were becoming the same person it seemed. "Let's get back to the inn. We could all use some rest." Caleb was right. Lucas could feel exhaustion overcoming him. His shoulders ached from the fight with those would-be thieves.

A muffled beeping came from the pocket inside Lucas' coat. The beeping the data pads made could be one of the most annoying sounds. He thought he had disabled all notifications. Lucas reached inside his coat and took the flat square screen out. Tapping the clear screen twice woke the device up. As it booted up the clear glass became opaque, and a notification appeared. He knew why the pad had given him an alert even though he had shut them off. He had received a message from his younger brother, Fredrick, out on the Perimeter:

URGENT. FARM ATTACKED. FAMILY EMERGENCY.

A numbness came over him. His legs felt like old oaks that had planted roots into the stone street centuries ago. He felt a chill but sweat beaded and slid down his brow and his back. Then rage. Both of his hands were clenched into tight fists, his knuckles hurt.

"Are you okay, Lucas?"

He realized everyone was staring at him when Caleb

131

asked the question. "Family emergency. I have to go. Do the job without me."

Without saying another word, he turned, and he began walking off. He had only kept himself from running for a few paces and then broke out into a full sprint. He thought he heard Caleb yell something, but he kept on. Caleb would let him handle this himself, and they didn't chase after him. Unfortunately, the fastest way to the East Gate would be back through the Eighth District.

Lucas slowed himself to a brisk walk as he approached the archway between the Ninth and Eighth District. The two guards who had been stationed before had been replaced by another two. Thankfully both Human. Any Amboians might have given him a difficult time. He approached the archway and didn't slow his pace any further.

"Hold up." A female guard stuck a spear out to block Lucas' path.

"Myra, we just saw this man pass through with his friends." The other guard, a male, stepped forward from the archway.

"Passing back and forth between the Eighth District this late at night? Suspicions aside, it would be too dangerous to travel alone at night." The woman had withdrawn her weapon but hadn't moved from her spot.

He wanted to push past them and continue on but didn't want to risk spending a night in a holding cell. "I received word from my family in the New Ring. Their farm was attacked. One of the raids from the Haze I suspect. I need to get to them as quickly as possible."

"I see." The woman stepped back. "Ronald, grab Trint and Liam." The other guard walked back into the archway and entered through a metal door. "Ronald and I will escort you through the Eighth. If you are telling the truth I'd see you make it to your family. If not, then we'll find some Amboians to question you."

Lucas nodded.

The guard reappeared with two others with him. Myra turned to them as they walked out of the archway. "Trint. Liam. Take our post for a moment. Ronald and I are going to take this man through the Eighth. We'll relieve you when we get back." The two men saluted, closed fist to chest and fell into place.

The man named Ronald paled when Myra had mentioned they would be taking him through the Eighth District. Lucas would have preferred to sneak through by himself. Perhaps the presence of the City Guard might keep any cutpurses at bay.

"Thank you." Lucas looked at the both of them and then passed through the archway. The two City Guards followed closely behind. They really did seem like an escort.

"This is madness, Myra." Ronald's whisper wasn't much of a whisper. The man was genuinely concerned.

"We keep a quick pace and continue onward. When we make it to the next archway, we'll take the lift up and return along the wall. I don't want to be in this place any longer than you, Ronald." She seemed as though she could handle herself. Lucas was concern that Ronald would run away at the first sign of trouble. Lucas had heard the training program from the City Guard had been especially difficult on Humans. How did this man make it through?

"Thank you both for putting yourself at risk to help me through. You're very brave." Maybe that would settle Ronald's nerves. Myra didn't need it that was certain.

"Yes, of course." Myra quickened her pace to catch up to Lucas. "Let's keep our wits about us. I hope you are good with that sword."

He had been about to reply that he was more than capable, and then recalled the run-in with the group that attacked them only moments ago. He hoped scavengers had removed the bodies for them. It was a nasty thought, but the less fortunate in the Lower Districts would take what they could from those they found. Even worse, in some cases they

133

didn't stop at stealing their belongings. Food was difficult to find for some.

"We should stick to one of the smaller side streets. That might keep us better hidden from those who might mean us harm," Lucas said. *And keep us away from the bodies.*

"The space in the main street is better for fighting with spears," Ronald replied quickly, his voice shaking. Lucas' attempt to comfort him had failed. In any other district there would be plenty of space in the main street. In the Forgotten District structures had pushed out into the street and had been stacked on top of each other with no regard. Buildings of all styles were built as needed.

"A side street would be better," Myra said. Lucas heard a strange metal on metal sound and turned to see Myra's spear disappear and, in a flash, it became a short sword. Upper District technology. A person could hide any number of weapons on themselves with that. Maybe he could...*No.* These two were helping him. Another time he might be able to sneak into a barracks and try to steal one for himself.

The three turned off the main street and then turned again onto a smaller street that ran parallel to the main. They kept a quick pace down the dimly lit street with swords at the ready. The only sound Lucas could hear was his own breathing and their footsteps on the stone paved street. Each time they reached an intersection He held up a hand to signal them to stop. He looked around each corner and when it was safe, they would continue onward. Even though Lucas wasn't a member of the City Guard who outranked them, the two still listened. He was thankful for that. He didn't need some hothead looking for a fight. If they came across a group like Lucas had seen earlier, they would have to run.

"Movement up ahead," Myra whispered from behind him. The group stopped. Lucas strained in the low light but was unable to see what the guard had. He was breathing heavier than he expected.

"I didn't see. What was it?" Lucas said. He still strained

his eyes. He forced them to see something, but in the darkness all he could see was the walls of the buildings that lined the street and refuse that had been scattered about.

"I'm not sure. Could have been a dog or something." Ronald had seen the movement too. He was crouched down on the opposite side of the street. Not that it was very far from where Lucas and Myra were. Five people could barely stand abreast on these narrow streets.

"We wait a moment, then continue forward. You two take the lead, I'll watch our backs. My eyes aren't what they used to be." Lucas hated to admit it. He knew better than to let his pride get in the way of their safety. He could bring up the rear. That he could do.

Time passed slowly as they waited. Minutes passed. There was no other sign of movement. Lucas felt a tap on the shoulder.

Myra stalked down one side of the street with Lucas behind. Ronald walked along the other side. They moved slowly toward the spot where the guards had seen the shadows move. Lucas walked sidestep so he was able to look around them. Myra and Ronald were intent on the street ahead. Their pace slowed further when they got close. Lucas had almost toppled over Myra when he didn't see her stop and crouch. There was a quiet scuffle of boots on pavement before he steadied himself.

"You really can't see, can you?" Myra sounded annoyed. Or did she pity him? No one need pity Lucas Meadows. He had just been watching their backs like he said he would!

"I'm fine. Too focused on what might be happening behind us," Lucas said.

"Must have been a dog or something," Ronald whispered.

Lucas heard something cut through the air and metal ringing on metal. An arrow bounced off Ronald's chest and clattered to the ground.

Myra shoved Lucas to his feet. "Run, man!" They sprinted back the way they came. "On to the main street.

We're not that far from the next barracks. "We'll cut back onto the main street and continue on."

On to the main street? With archers in the windows? That would get them killed. "No. We cut deeper into the side streets and make our way around them. Then we can get back on the main when we're closer to the archway." Lucas didn't hear any arguments. Arrows clattered on the pavement around them. He stopped at the next corner and checked the street. It was clear. They pushed deeper into the maze-like side streets of the Forgotten District.

"This is madness."

Lucas heard Ronald over the sound of his own breathing. He took them as straight as he could in the direction of the Exterior Wall. *If only there were an exterior gate in this district.*

After taking a few oddly angled streets that seemed to connect to others at random, He started bringing them back to parallel with the main street that cut down the middle of the district. They hadn't heard anyone chasing after them. Others could be in front to cut them off. He slowed down but kept them at a good pace. Maybe they could get ahead of the attackers before they cut them off. He no longer bothered stopping to check the other streets that cut their path. It was reckless, but every second he wasted was time that kept him from getting out into the New Ring.

"There's the District wall up ahead. Let's get out of these narrows," Myra called from behind.

Lucas turned left down a street. He could see the wider street at the end and was relieved that this had been a more direct route back. When they got to the mouth of the street they stopped. He looked back toward the direction of the attackers. It was empty. He looked down the opposite end. Two guards were stationed at the archway that led into the Seventh District.

"We should be safe now," Ronald whispered as he looked toward the archway. The three stepped out and began walking toward the guards.

"Myra? Ronald? Aren't you posted on the opposite arch tonight?" a short man with a neatly trimmed beard called out as they approached.

"Kiell." Myra saluted. Kiell returned a salute. "That's correct. This man needed to get through the district. We chose to escort him. Liam and Trint are on our posts until we return." Myra spoke between ragged breaths. Lucas was breathing heavier than he had been before.

"I see." Kiell looked at Lucas. The man had a hard stare. "What was so dire that you needed to get through the Eighth during the night? That's a fool's task."

"Emergency on my family's farm out in the New Ring."

Kiell nodded. "Run into any trouble?"

"We were attacked just off the main street, about halfway through the district." Myra gestured back the way they had come. "Ronald and I are going to take the wall back across to avoid any more attacks."

"Sounds g—" Kiell was cut off as a hulking Amboian guard stepped out from the archway. "Captain Aireen." The guards all saluted, fist to chest, and lowered their heads to the Captain.

The Captain stepped out into the group. Lucas could see his black eyes behind the visor of his helmet. He must have been a head and a half taller than Lucas. Captain Aireen looked him over, "Lucas Meadows, leader of the Amber Waves, unable to make it through the Eighth District on his own?" The other guards looked at Lucas. It seemed even Amboians knew of the Amber Waves now. Was this Captain always stationed here?

"I'm only one of the leaders," Lucas said. He didn't bother to speak respectfully. "And I never asked them to escort me. They insisted. You've got some well-trained soldiers here." That wasn't meant for the Amboian, he wanted the others to know his thanks.

Captain Aireen grunted, "Go see to your family, Meadows." Aireen looked to Ronald and Myra. "You two are coming with me. We're going to root out some rats."

Lucas turned to Myra and Ronald. "Thank you, again." Now he pitied them. The two nodded back. He hoped they would make it through to the other side. With an Amboian with them their odds were better at least. Lucas turned and walked into the Holy District.

He needed a horse, a fast horse.

CHAPTER TEN

Into the Haze

C ordelia pulled the thick wool blanket off her and rolled out of bed. She had slept well even though the bed was barely large enough for her to lie comfortably. She stretched her arms above her head and let out a groan. There was a dull aching in her back and her thighs were sore from riding yesterday.

Jaeger was surely already downstairs in the kitchen cooking breakfast for the two of them. He would travel with her to the Perimeter and then return to the workshop to continue on one of his many projects. She pulled her shirt over her head and tossed it onto the unmade bed. She would tidy up the room before she left. He had already done so much by letting her stay here over the years. Doing her part to keep his home clean was the very least she could do. She stood up and walked over to the wooden dresser on the other side of the small room.

From her pack she pulled a slim-fitting long-sleeve shirt and pants. She would have preferred her usual dark-green jacket and looser traveling pants, but with her Haze suit she needed something that would keep from bunching up underneath. She pulled the shirt down over her head and pulled her long red hair out from the neck hole, only struggling slightly. Maybe she *would* cut it soon. After pulling the tight-fitting pants up around her waist she sat down at an old oak dresser. She looked into the mirror and began braiding her long hair. She wrapped the loose braid into a bun near the back of her head. She hoped there would be enough room in the helmet. She could always braid it again if needed. Her pale skin had become slightly sun tanned. Except her cheeks. Her cheeks always seemed to redden under the sun no matter how she protected herself. Freckles were scattered about her cheeks and there were even a few along her forehead. She had heard stories of people who got sick from too much sun exposure. She would have to be more careful.

As she stood up from the dresser, she grabbed her pack. She walked over to the bed and set the pack down and began rummaging around for a pair of wool socks. They always treated her feet well on long trips. After finding a black pair, she picked up the shirt she had slept in and tossed it into her pack. She slid her pack under the bed and fixed the sheets and wool blanket, making it seem as though it had never been slept in. Cordelia picked her boots up from the floor near the end of the bed and turned to leave the room.

As she walked down the creaky wooden stairs into the hallway outside the kitchen, she heard Jaeger call out to greet her good morning. If anyone had ever tried to sneak into Jaeger's house, it would let him know. She replied as she let the kitchen door swing shut behind her.

Jaeger was setting two plates of ham, eggs, and toast on the table. He turned from the table to grab a kettle from the stove and brought it over as Cordelia sat down. Jaeger loved lavender tea. He always made them each a cup, even if Cordelia had never come to enjoy the taste. He reached across the small wooden table and filled Cordelia's cup with hot water. Steam danced up from the surface and into the cool air of the kitchen.

"Thank you for breakfast. You didn't have to do this. I had planned on eating while we walked out."

Jaeger waved his free hand at her. "No problem at all. I figured you could use a warm meal before you head out into that forsaken fog." He filled his own cup and set the kettle down on a square piece of fabric in between them. He removed the lid off a small porcelain jar and picked up a small metal sphere from beside it. Attached to the sphere was a thin chain. Sliding a clasp along its equator opened it up. Jaeger spooned some dried lavender buds into it and closed it back up. He reached across the table and dipped the sphere into Cordelia's steaming mug a few times before attaching it to the edge of the mug with a small hook.

"What do you think about that?" Jaeger smiled. "Pretty handy!" He chuckled to himself as he sat back down in his chair and began doing the same for his own drink.

Cordelia looked into her mug at the curious metal strainer. Dark tendrils crept from the strainer as the clear water mixed with the buds. Rolling and reaching, until the entire cup was a deep brown.

"You haven't gone beyond the Perimeter some time." Jaeger was looking at her when she lifted her gaze from her tea. "They will appreciate it, Cordelia." He paused for a moment. "And it is okay to be afraid, of course."

"I'm not afraid of the Haze." The last time she had been frightened by the Haze was when she was a young girl. That was a long time ago now. "You are right though. It has been some time."

"Have I ever told you about the first time I went into the Haze?" Jaeger took a sip from his mug and smiled. "I must have been twelve, or maybe thirteen." Cordelia took a sip from her mug as well and listened as her old friend spoke. "My family didn't always live in the New Ring. As far as I've been told my great-grandfather brought his family into the New Ring to escape the Haze. You could imagine his

141

frustration when his sons and their friends began mounting expeditions back into the place he had tried to save them from." Jaeger chuckled again. "People back then had all kinds of names for them; Mist Seekers, Gloomers, there were dozens. Haze Walkers was the name that stuck. They were the first." He paused his story to sip from his mug again. "As far as I know, you may very well be the last." He smiled over his mug at her.

"You're still a Haze Walker, Jaeger." She smiled back.

He shook his head. "I haven't been into the Haze in well over a decade, maybe more." He scratched his chin as he thought. "Well, let's not let our food get cold now."

She used her toast to break open the yellow of the egg. She dipped the toast in the runny yolk a few times before forking a piece of ham on to it. Jaeger had shown her that when she was younger and now she found herself doing it almost reflexively. The two of them enjoyed their breakfast in silence.

When they were both finished Cordelia cleaned up while Jaeger poured more lavender tea into a canteen for the both of them. Once the kitchen was cleaned, they both exited the house and walked toward the workshop.

Last night, after walking with Jaeger back to his house, Cordelia went back into town to return Victor's horse to him. It would be a walk out to the Perimeter this morning. She hadn't seen Elina since she had left Victor and her on top of the hill outside of East Edge the night before. She hoped she might get the chance to see them when she returned.

Thinking about Victor and his family made Cordelia think about the food they had eaten at the festival last night. As they walked into the workshop, she felt a dull grumble in her stomach, even though they had just eaten moments earlier. Jaeger looked over his shoulder as he grabbed his pack and laughed. "Good thing I brought us some cheese and bread."

Jaeger pulled the same metal chest from beneath one of the work benches and pulled out the suit he had made for

Her. The one-piece jumper had a zipper in the back for the wearer to step into, and once closed up, fabric of the same material of the suit enclosed it to ensure a tight seal. The helmet itself connected to a gasket on the neck, completing the internal system that would protect Cordelia from the harsh environment of the Haze. There was no need to wear the full suit in the New Ring; Cordelia kept the helmet off for now and left the top rolled down to her waist and tied the long sleeves around herself. As they left the workshop very faint blues began peeking up in the sky. It was only a short walk to the Perimeter from the workshop. The real journey began once she stepped beyond the safety of the Shield.

As they approached the dimly glowing Perimeter Wall Cordelia could better see the blues, greens, and sometimes purples of the shield that kept the Haze at bay. The Haze immediately outside the Perimeter was the most dangerous. As she moved out, the elevation would increase, and the Haze became less dense and less dangerous. Once she breached the Haze line in the mountains, she could finish the trip without her suit. Her grandmother, Theresa, had told her that the Haze settled as time went on. There had even been a time when it had covered the mountains they had grown up on. The last time Cordelia had made the journey home she was in the Haze for a large majority of the trip. She had finally breached out of it an hour's hike from the Station's outer fences. The Mountain Station and the outposts that were in the higher elevations were lucky. During her trips with the Deep Scout teams Cordelia had visited some outposts which were still covered in the Haze. Those outposts were entirely underground. Most of the inhabitants were born, lived, and died without ever leaving the safety of their subterranean shelter. She shuddered at the idea. To never be able to feel a cool breeze on a hot day, the sun on her skin, or birds singing in the trees. Terrible.

Cordelia and Jaeger reached the edge of the New Ring and set their packs down. She took the small blade that was

143

usually hidden along her lower back and strapped it to her right thigh. Her other knives would have to remain behind. The chances of seeing another person while she was in the Haze was extremely low, but it was better to be prepared. Jaeger handed her a piece of dried meat and tore off a piece of bread for her. While she was in the Haze, she wouldn't be able to remove her suit, so the next time she would be able to eat would be when she breached in the mountains.

"How many days you think?" Jaeger asked after swallowing. He took a sip of tea from the canteen and held it out to her.

She waved the canteen away and Jaeger shrugged. "Two days in the Haze most likely. Then another half day or so to the Station." That seemed about right to her. Jaeger offered a different canteen this time. She tipped her head back and cool water washed the meat and bread from her mouth as she drank.

"That reminds me." Jaeger began digging around in his pack. "I made an addition to your suit this morning. Not sure why I didn't think of it before." He held up a small water skin. "You just wear it like a pack, see? Put your arms through these straps, and we'll bring the hose up to your helmet." He held the hose up to his mouth and pretended to drink. "We'll have to use some adhesive paper to keep it attached for now, but I can make a more refined version later."

Water would be important in the Haze. She had once come across a small lake and noticed the Haze hung over the water without penetrating the surface. She went deep enough to get her helmeted head beneath the water and was surprised to see small fish swimming about. It had been said that almost nothing could survive in the Haze, but these fish had managed to live underneath the water. Initially she had thought it a sign that the water was safe to drink. It was also possible that the fish had adapted to the environment, and if she had drunk it would have been as if she were drinking the

144

Haze itself.

Jaeger helped her get her arms through the shoulder straps. She tightened them and connected the two ends of another strap across her chest and tightened that one as well. He zipped the back of the suit and handed her the hose. "I'll take care of that." Jaeger came around with a roll of his adhesive paper.

Such strange things her friend created. It made a terrible sound as he pulled a length of it off the roll. Strands of brown tacky goo stretched as he pulled. It reminded her of sappy bark. He placed the hose along the jawline of the inside of the helmet and placed pieces of the sticky paper along the hose. "I guess it was a good thing this helmet ended up being a little roomy," he said as he looked over his work. "Well, let's see how this looks." He handed the helmet back to Cordelia.

She placed the helmet over her head. There was a metal-on-metal sound as the neck and helmet met, and the seal was made. Along the left side of the jaw line was a fabricated hole where the air in the pack-like tank on the exterior of the suit was pumped in. There was a barely audible humming as the suit filled. The air tank was small enough that it wouldn't impede her movement. She hardly noticed its presence. The internal water skin felt cool on her back. The water would soon heat up as her body warmed it, but warm water was better than none.

Jaeger explained the functions of each button on her left forearm. Four in total; one to activate the lights on the helmet, one to darken the visor, another to seal the suit off from the tank if there was a rupture in the hose, the last one enabled a display on the helmet visor that informed her of the oxygen level in the tank as well as the integrity of the suit.

Jaeger put his pack back on. "That should be about it." Although he seemed calm, she could sense his worry. "I'll keep your things in your room. When do you expect you'll be heading back this way?"

145

She thought for a moment. "Seven or eight days." Then after a pause she added. "Ten at the most, hopefully. I don't plan on spending too much time up there."

"Alright, be careful and keep your wits about you. Those raids are happening, for whatever reason, and you don't know what's going on out there right now." He had given up trying to hide his concern now.

She put a gloved hand on his shoulder. "I'll be careful. I learned from the best." She flashed a wry smile at him. She hoped he could see her through the visor.

"I guess I did pretty well." He returned a smile. Cordelia let her hand drop from his shoulder and turned away.

It only took a few steps before she passed through the Perimeter and out into the Haze. Although she couldn't feel anything through the suit, she felt a tingling sensation pass over her body. She turned around and looked back from where she had just been. She could only make out a very faint silhouette of her friend as he was walking away. Cordelia took a deep breath and continued through the thick fog.

CHAPTER ELEVEN

Information

O mar Cross walked beside Caleb as they moved through the packed streets of District Seven, the Holy District. Levi and Ana were following behind them. Ana mentioned what ships they might see at Port Amboy and boasted how her father's ships were the fastest. Or was it her mother's ship? Omar tried to keep his thoughts on the current job but found himself worrying about Lucas.

Lucas had left them the night before without saying much other than there was an emergency with his family. Omar had never met any of others' families. All he had known about Lucas' was that they lived out near the Perimeter, which likely meant they were victims of the attacks from the Haze that everyone seemed to be talking about.

It seemed that each time they had heard someone talking about attacks near the Perimeter the story changed, first the attacks hadn't been coordinated at all, then there was talk that it was a systematic attack, some said the attacks were only rumors. The number of attackers ranged from two to over thirty in some cases. The only similarity in what he had heard was that it seemed that their intentions were supply raids and there were no instances of violence. Several small villages had been attacked, but it seemed as though the Council paid it no mind. They probably wouldn't until it affected the capital itself.

Omar glanced over to Caleb and could see his friend was also deep in thought. "He'll be okay, Caleb. Lucas will send a message once he's got some information, or we'll all just reconnect back here once the job is done."

Caleb smiled, but it disappeared as soon as he looked forward again. "Lucas can certainly handle himself. I was just thinking about these attacks, and if things continue what we might be able to do. It's been sometime since the entire company banded together. After this we should gather everyone we can and consider moving out toward East Edge."

"I agree. For now, let's get to the supply train."

As they entered the main square of the Holy District, its namesake came into view. The massive gray stone church rose above every other rooftop in the square. Steps cut from the same stone as the building led up to three wooden arched doors, the central door was twenty feet tall at the point of the arch and the other two were eighteen feet in height with the same arched shape as the middle. The nave of the church rose up into the sky and had a bell tower at the top covered by a shallow pointed roof. The bells were silent currently, but within the hour one of the young members of the Church would be walking up the many wooden stairs to pull the ropes that made them sing. Two aisles ran down the sides of the church, with angled roofs that met the outer walls of the nave about halfway.

Above the large central door was a decorative stained glass window depicting a scene of Amboians with outstretched arms reaching down toward a group of humans in yellow clouds. Rays of sunlight surrounded the Amboians. There were two smaller stained-glass windows above the other doors, one depicting a scene where a Human and Amboian were greeting each other and another showing several Amboians standing in Council robes.

Omar knew of the other stained windows that ran down the sides of the building, and he knew the story they told. He had to learn every parable of the Salvation of Humanity while he was a member of the Church of Amboy. It started with the Old World Conflicts that led to mass casualties and the near total destruction of the world and ended with the Amboians coming from above to save what Humans they could by creating the Perimeter and sheltering them from the Haze.

They continued through the main square of the district and turned down the street that led to the outer gate, and the Seventh District supply depot where the train would be stationed. The crowds thinned near the Holy District gate. Not many merchants or travelers entered through this gate to begin with, but even fewer were present now due to the celebrations throughout the New Ring.

Caleb handed a ticket for the train to each of them as they approached the security leading to the depot. Four Amboian City Guards stood at the walled entrance. The massive stone building that jutted from the Exterior Wall towered over them.

"Hello Guardsmen," Caleb greeted the Amboians. He received a grunt in reply. "We're part of the construction team heading to Port Amboy this morning." He held out his ticket. One of the guards took it from his hand and looked it over.

"Caleb Fields?" The Amboian looked at the other guards. Omar had heard they were capable of speaking with their minds. That seemed ridiculous. "It has been so peaceful that mercenaries are now taking up construction work. You Humans should be thankful."

Mercenaries? Omar looked at Caleb. He remained an example of calm. Is that what everyone thought they were?

149

Maybe by definition the Amber Waves were a mercenary group. Omar felt a stinging in his stomach.

"Peaceful, indeed. May we pass? I wouldn't want to be late for our first job." Caleb took the ticket back as the guard handed it to him.

Omar stepped up and handed his ticket to the same guard. Ana and Levi did the same. In minutes they were on the other side of security and walking up to the large train depot. Shirtless men were hauling crates and canvas bags from carts in front and bringing them through the open bay doors.

"The guards knew you by name?" Omar kept his voice low. "They might be ignorant enough to think times are quiet enough for mercenaries to pick up new lines of work, but I doubt most Humans will." Now he had referred to himself as a mercenary. He would have to be sure to correct that.

"Perhaps the other Chapters have been working as hard as we have. It's been sometime since I've made contact with Homestead."

"Maybe we should plan to meet up with Lucas in Homestead after the job? Might be easier to meet back up out there." Omar looked back to Levi and Ana for their opinion. The two of them were too busy in their own conversation. Levi's curved bow stave made for an odd looking walking stick. Omar was never sure how Levi had the strength to bring that bow to a full draw. He had tried once and found it to be surprisingly easy, but he was wildly inaccurate with it. Caleb still wore his sword. Everyone seemed to wear some type of blade openly. Omar preferred his staff. The staff was less messy.

"I don't think going to Homestead would be needed." Caleb jumped right on the idea and snuffed it out.

Omar had never been to Homestead. Lucas and Caleb didn't seem to like talking about their home. There must have been something keeping them from returning.

"I have to be honest, Caleb." Omar spoke quietly again,

"With how recognizable we're becoming, this job is getting more risky."

"Should have known better when they offered so much for the payment. We don't need to continue further after this one."

Omar wanted to believe that, but he had a feeling that once they began working for this new Upper District family, it would be tough getting out. If they could meet with that bald woman again, maybe that might help.

Caleb approached a shirtless man standing at the back of a cart. "We've been hired to help out at the Port. Can you point us in the right direction?"

The man grunted as he slung two canvas bags over his wide shoulders. "You're looking for Garrith. Grab something from the cart and follow me." He huffed as he turned around.

Omar slid his staff behind his back under the straps of his pack. He did the same as the man and hoisted two of the bags over his shoulders. They were heavier than he was expecting, and it took him a moment to manage the weight. The others grabbed what they could, and they all followed him inside. The man shouted across the room to a group and jerked his head in the direction of Omar and the others. The shirtless man continued walking toward the back of the building.

One man walked out from the group; he was a head taller than Omar and heavier. He had a thick beard and his wavy brown hair fell around his head. White teeth appeared from within his hairy face as he approached with an outstretched hand. His deep voice boomed as he spoke, "I heard we were pickin' up some stragglers this mornin'. I'm Garrith Payn." Garrith acknowledged them as he repeated their names when they introduced themselves.

"We were hired to work at the Port," Caleb said as he set down the crate he was holding and held out the work papers Voal had given them the night before.

151

Garrith looked at the papers and then his eyes scanned from Caleb, then to Omar, and back. "If I'm not mistaken, you're Caleb Fields. Amber Waves hired out in the port? I've been managing this station since before you were a member of the Church, Omar Cross. I certainly recognize you."

"That's correct," Caleb said briefly and took the papers back from Garrith as he handed them back. Caleb shot a look at Omar. They *were* becoming recognizable.

"I'm actually no longer officially with the Church. I joined the Amber Waves a few years back. I'm afraid even with all my time in District Seven, I can't place you." Omar was genuinely surprised he wasn't familiar with the man; he knew a majority of those that spent their time in this district. The initiates of the Church of Amboy spent their first five years working only within District Seven.

"You can set that stuff in an open supply car at the back of the room. We'll be headin' off soon, so get yourselves sorted." Garrith's long wavy hair bobbed back and forth as he turned away and walked back toward the group he had come from.

The back of the room was connected to a tunnel system that ran within the outer wall. The loop of track ran within the Exterior Wall of the city, as well as below it in some areas. Omar had seen the train passing through the New Ring as it made its trips, but he had never been aboard it himself. It was like nothing else in the Lower Districts; the dark blue-gray of the metal that made each cart had the unmistakable craftsmanship of the Upper Districts. Where a cart had wheels, here there was nothing. The train hovered above the flat metal track. He could hear a dim humming.

"Frictionless tracks mean the train can travel faster and more efficiently." Caleb sighed as he set the crate down next to the train car. "I only rode this thing once . . . well stowed away on it once, with Lucas." He rubbed the back of his bald head as he nervously looked around.

"I've heard this thing can make it to the Perimeter in an

152

hour," Ana said as she looked the train over.

"That's probably about right," Caleb responded and stepped into the open car. "Start handing me that stuff so we can get into one of the passenger cars and see about gathering information."

Omar stepped into the car and set the two canvas bags down next to some that looked similar to what he had. He turned to grab another bag from Levi and set that one down as well. As he was standing in the car the thought of the nothingness between it and the track made him uneasy. There was almost a feeling similar to a boat in a lake on a calm day. He stepped back down onto the platform and walked with the others toward what they thought was the front of the train where the passenger cars would be located.

They passed by several cars that looked much like the one they put their supplies in, until they came to those that differed. While still made of the same blue-gray metal, the passenger cars were lined with long windows that ran down the sides of the train.

Inside were rows of seats that ran down the length of the train. Four seats in a group were facing each other, and in others two seats faced the backs of the two in front of them. Men and women were moving throughout the train car, some stuffing bags in the storage above the seats. Others were busy finding a place to sit. Those who were already seated seemed to be sleeping or chatting among themselves. They walked by three of the passenger cars until Caleb had decided on one and stepped through the open doorway and the others followed behind.

Omar sat down next to Caleb, while Ana and Levi sat across from them. After a moment of silence while waiting for a large group to pass by and others to settle in their seats, Caleb spoke in a hushed tone, "Once we're off, we won't have much time. I'll head two cars back, Levi, you head in the opposite direction. Try and find a talkative group and pick up whatever you can. I'm willing to bet there will be some

153

passengers left standing, so once we get up, our seats will be taken quickly. Omar and Ana, see what you can learn from the two that take our spots."

Just as Caleb had finished speaking Omar caught a portion of a conversation between two men walking past, something about orders and to follow them to the exact plan. He and Levi shared a look, and Levi nodded. Without a word Levi got up from his seat and fell into the group of passengers looking for a spot in the next car.

Ana scoffed. "They could have been talking about construction plans."

"It's a start," Caleb said and got up to move in the opposite direction. He struggled against the line of passengers for a moment, but slowly made his way.

"Chance finds us all," Omar said matter-of-factly as he moved to the seat across from Ana.

"I understand we're in the Holy District, Omar, but please spare me the sermon."

He hadn't realized he had referenced the Salvation; maybe being in District Seven was bringing up old memories. He hadn't renounced the Church entirely; in his eyes it was a clean departure, and he was still friendly with most of the members he had known during his time there.

He had been nervous the first time he took a job from them but was relieved when they were met warmly. Not that what they did for the Church really were *jobs*, it was more like charity work to maintain the peace in the District and boost renown for Amber Waves. It didn't hurt to be in good favor with the Church. Omar wondered now if they had done too much work. *Recognized twice in one day, and such a short period of time!*

As he was finishing his thought a woman and man took the recently emptied seats in their group. The woman's dark hair was tied into a long braid that was draped over her shoulder, while the sides of her head were shaved. A style worn in Athanelle, if Omar remembered correctly. Her slightly dirty tank top showed off her toned arms.

"You're still drunk aren't you, Isaac?" The woman glared at the man as he slouched into the seat across from her.

"I...well yeah. I might be."

The smell of alcohol emanated from the man. He looked across to Ana. Her lips compressed into a wry smile that she seemed to struggle to keep from stretching across her face.

"Pardon my friend, he seems to have forgotten we had a job to do today. My name is Ellowen."

"Omar Cross. This is Ana Brooks."

"I'm sure your friend isn't the only one on this train in that condition. These jobs can really take a toll," Ana said.

"Oh, were you a part of the crew that worked on that last job in Athanelle?" Ellowen leaned back into her seat and pulled a deck of cards from a pocket on her baggy pants. "I heard the foreman was an idiot and the whole thing got Hazed." After she spoke, she looked at them as if to study their reactions.

"Not me, no. I'm originally from Port Amboy. I lived through a bit of the construction that expanded the city."

"I see." Ellowen began shuffling her deck of cards.

He found it difficult to read the woman. He had no idea if she even believed Ana. He was a bit annoyed she had jumped right into telling some fake background story. They had used their real names, there was no need. She never had the patience to just let others give information, always jumping into a situation headfirst. Usually brandishing one of those daggers, or *two*. The man next to Omar let out a hiccup and a groan.

"I'd have Isaac introduce himself, but I don't see that happening." She stopped shuffling the cards and shook her head. Then she leaned forward and rested her forearms on her thighs. "There's no way you're going to be ready to work when we get there. You're going to cost us another day's wage." Once she noticed Omar and Ana's eyes on her, she sat back and continued shuffling her cards.

155

Isaac had a gray cap pulled down over his eyes and his long dirty blond hair was sticking out haphazardly underneath it. Brown scruff covered his jaw and upper lip. He looked sickly pale. His brown jacket looked as though it had been slept in several times over.

"Don't judge him," Ellowen said curtly. "He's had it rough and we're all the other has got. He and I take care of each other. We have since we were kids growing up in the Lower Districts."

"No judgement here," Omar said and held his hands up.

"I leave that to the Generators of the Shield," Ana said sarcastically.

The Generators were among the highest members of the Church. The High Generator sat at the top. In their eyes only the Amboians were above them, as they had saved Humanity from the wrath of the Haze.

"Oh, the Church of Amboy. Yes." Ellowen rolled her eyes. "How the few keep the many suppressed."

A smile flashed on Ana's face again. There was a chance she really did dislike the organization. Once he had left the Church it had never really been brought up. He was never one to talk about it and Lucas or Caleb never asked about it. When Levi joined the Company, he hadn't spoken to anyone for some time and had never acted one way or the other toward Omar's past.

"They do what they can for those they can help." He tried not to sound defensive, but the way Ellowen looked at him, he guessed it came out that way.

"Well enough of that anyway. No need to get into a religious debate with people you might end up working side by side with." There was a short silence. "Do you two like to play Twelve?" She held up the deck.

"I've only ever played in bars and taverns for credits." Ana tried to seem nonchalant. Omar had to keep from groaning and shaking his head.

Ellowen let out a sharp laugh. "I bet you do." She pulled

156

the folding table up from between the seats between her and Ana. She began dealing out four cards between the two of them and then twelve face down radially. Omar had never been good at Twelve. Most of the people who played used loaded decks anyway. An extra Councilor card or not enough of the Lower District cards.

"How about instead of credits, we bet information." A shadow seemed to cross Ellowen's face. "Loser of each hand tells a bit about themselves."

"Information has always been more valuable in my eyes anyway," she said as she picked up her cards. That smile was going to get stuck on her face.

"I am very curious what Omar Cross and Ana Brooks of the Amber Waves Company are doing taking construction jobs in Port Amboy." Ellowen's smile stretched across her face. Omar shot a glance at Ana, who only rolled her eyes again. "That *was* Caleb Fields who I saw you with earlier, was it not?" Ellowen looked at her hand and seemed to ignore everything else.

Ana sighed. "Haze it all."

Ellowen let out a sharp laugh again and smiled, her dark eyes looking at him over her hand of cards.

There were two loud sirens and the train accelerated smoothly. That makes three times.

Chance finds us all.

Caleb had barely found a seat before the train picked up speed. He guessed the passenger car he had settled on was almost near the supply cars. The two women who sat across from him had been asleep since he sat down. They both wore tattered clothing and dirt covered their skin. Wide-brimmed hats were pulled down to cover their faces. The man next to Caleb was carving something. The man's thick fingers worked quickly has he carved small dots into a wooden cube. The man blew on the wooden square and inspected his work. He

157

tossed it onto the small table. Five. The man nodded to himself and picked it up. He tossed it again. Five. Three more times he tossed the dice and five came up. He noticed Caleb looking at him.

"Looking to lose some coin, friend?" He pulled out four more dice from the inside pocket of his worn leather jacket. "I've got my own set here."

"I think I'll pass, thanks."

Caleb turned his attention to the seats to his right. Two women were quietly speaking to each other. When one of them noticed him, Caleb smiled. The woman smiled back and the other turned to face him. The second woman rolled her eyes and turned away. The first woman smiled once more before being pulled back into conversation. Years ago, Caleb might have asked her to dance at the Harvest's End celebration. It had been a long time since he had celebrated the season.

He was about to try to get some information from the dicing man when his ear caught two men speaking to his right just in front of the two women. The men had opted to turn their chairs away from the women. Not uncommon. Caleb caught their hushed voices and leaned forward in his chair slightly.

He could only hear a few words that were spoken. A new tavern opening up near the northern construction site, wages being cut, and something about leaving the Lower Districts to move to Port Amboy permanently. Apparently, they both had families in the Lower Districts and this construction in Port Amboy would be going on for some time. Not like some other job in Athanelle. Whatever that meant. Caleb made note of it in his mind anyway. You never knew what bit of information could prove useful later. He let out a sigh and sat back in his seat. There wouldn't be much time left at the rate the train was traveling. He might as well just enjoy the ride.

Green plains filled the long windows of the passenger car when the train emerged from the underground track. Faces of those who tried to sneak into the underground tunnel flashed by. They would never make it into the hole in the ground before the doors closed. Some would still try. Most would get injured. Those few who made it into the tunnels would have to sneak into the depot, at night if they were smart, and then get by the guarded wall outside the depot if they wanted to get into the Lower District. Maybe the Amber Waves could help smuggle people in? *No. That would never work.* People who were coming in would never have the coin to make it worth it. On top of that it would only add to the overpopulation in the Lower Districts.

There wasn't much of a forest between the capital and Port Amboy. Caleb could see maple and pine in the distance. Some tall oak, as well. The greenery of the New Ring was a welcome change from the dingy grays, tans, and browns of the stone and wooden Lower District. He hoped the others were doing better than Caleb was at collecting information. At least he could enjoy the scenery.

"Longest docks ever been built in the Port. Any port!" The thin man sitting across from Levi was too well dressed to be a worker. His deep blue jacket was of fine wool and his pants matched. The man's white under shirt was of a softer fabric and button to the neck with a high collar. His dark hair had been slicked back with an oil that Levi could smell all too easily. Levi had placed him as one of the men responsible for overseeing the construction. The man hadn't made it difficult. "Just you see, boy. Of course, the docks aren't complete now. Of course. How long did you say you'd be staying in the Port?"

"As long as there's work," Levi replied. Which wasn't a lie. As soon as the Amber Waves' job was done, they would leave.

"Tough to tell under that jacket of yours, young man, but I see your shoulders. You've been in construction for some time, yes?" The woman seated next to the man was either his wife or business partner. Perhaps both. She wore a green dress finer than the man's. A color of the sunlight coming through a canopy of leaves. The nearly transparent sleeves were more voluminous than the dress that seemed to hug the woman's body. Such an odd fashion was likely common in the Upper District. Her black hair was neatly organized at the back of her head. A white lace net kept in place.

"Not very long." Again, not a lie. He had kept it simple. The more he fabricated, the more he would have to remember. Not that remembering was difficult for him. It was just easier this way.

"What does a young man need a walking stick for?" The man gestured to Levi's unstrung bow.

"Helps when I'm traveling." This style of longbow was extremely uncommon; very few recognized it for what it was when it was unstrung. He had been surprised to find it in the Market District, and he paid more than he would have liked. It reminded him of the one his father had taught him to make. Levi suppressed a shudder and focused back on the couple.

"A well-traveled, young man then?" The woman had a very practiced way about how she spoke.

"It's good for a boy like yourself to get out and have some experiences before he settles down." The man patted the woman's arm. She smiled at him. "Of course. You had better be careful out in the New Ring. These rumors of attacks. I hope they *are* only rumors."

A man with a square face and unkempt hair looked over the back of the seat the man was in. "Rumors?" His harsh voice startled the couple. "They aren't rumors. Those poor farmers out there in the east are losing crop and family, alike. They lose crop, we all lose crop. Don't tell me you missed the Diplomats' speech? Those New Ring farmers are our foundation." The man stood up and leaned in to continue but was cut off by another voice.

160

"That was just the Diplomat trying to put a bandage on our woes in the Lower District. There's no trouble in the New Ring. It's just a made-up distraction for us."

Levi couldn't see the owner of the other voice. He *could* see how nervous the couple had become. As soon as the second man had finished speaking others began to give their own opinions on the current events. Passengers argued back and forth. Some began to shout at each other. Levi tightened his grip on his bow..

He raised his voice enough so that those immediately near could hear him. "I believe the reports." He was sure to say reports. Not rumors. "A friend of mine, his family's farm was attacked. Just out near East Edge." He didn't need to hear it from Lucas when he ran off the night before. That was a simple connection to make.

There was no response. The square-faced man disappeared back into his seat.

The man in the suit cleared his throat. "I am deeply sorry. I didn't mean anything by what I said."

Levi nodded.

The car filled with the lowered murmurings of conversation. Nothing else was said between Levi and the couple for the rest of the ride out to Port Amboy. The woman had picked a hole into the cuff of her green sleeve.

CHAPTER TWELVE

Something Lost, Something Gained

While Lucas was leaving the city the previous night, the guards stationed at the East Gate had seemed as if they were about ready to bring him in for interrogation, even though it wasn't uncommon for travelers to come and go at all hours. If Myra and Ronald would have been able to come with him, he would have had an easier time getting through. He hoped they made it back through the Eighth District unharmed.

Once in the New Ring he stopped at the first farm he could find. He had sneaked inside the stable trying not to think of who he was stealing from. Whoever owned the horses had taken great care of them. He was thankful for that. He looked over the animals and decided on one that was mostly brown with white hair on its front legs that came to its knees. He had saddled the horse as quickly as he could without startling it. It had taken some time for the horse to relax around him. He had even found himself talking to it at one point. Why had he been talking to an animal? The stress must have gotten to him. As he situated himself in the saddle the horse began trotting in place. Lucas had hoped that this was a sign that the horse had been in the stable for some time and was ready to move.

They had only stopped once during the night so Lucas could get his bearings and to let Vym rest for a moment—the horse needed a name and Vym seemed to be a good one. He wasn't sure as to why, he just felt the horse needed a name. He and Vym stopped at a grassy patch in the forest and drank from a small pond with a large oak tree bending so far over it that it almost seemed ready to fall in.

They had ridden through the entire night and the sun was now just past its midday peak. They crested a hill and East Edge came into view. Lucas' destination was slightly south of the large village though, he tapped his heels into Vym's sides, and the mare sprang into action and they began descending down the hill.

His brother, Fredrick Meadows, operated one of the larger farms that provided for East Edge and a few other villages along the Perimeter. The success of the farm wasn't solely due to the hard work from Fredrick. His wife Edith and their three sons; Ben, Dion, and Owain worked the farm as well. Ben was the eldest and would one day take his father's place running the farm. Dion and Owain were twins, not much younger than Ben. Lucas' fond thoughts of his family soured in his head as he was reminded of the reason for his visit. He tried to keep himself from running through the possibilities of what had happened, but he was sure that someone had been hurt. He only hoped that was the extent of it.

He didn't slow Vym's pace or avoid cutting through the harvested fields surrounding the farmhouse and storage barn. Soil and plant matter kicked up as Vym's hooves tore across the open field. He brought her to a trot at the front porch of the house and leaped off of Vym's back. Edith came out to greet him before his feet reached the steps leading to the front door.

"Oh, Lucas." Her eyes were puffy and her cheeks slightly

163

damp. "I am so glad you are here." She wrapped her arms around him and began to sob.

Lucas felt a mass in his throat and was barely able to speak, "Fredrick?..." Tears welled up in his eyes.

"I wish it were me, brother." A voice came from the open door. Fredrick was only three years older than Lucas, but now he looked as though it could have been a decade. His brown hair seemed grayer now and he looked as though he hadn't slept or eaten in days. "Please, come in. We need to talk." Fredrick was holding back tears as well it seemed.

Edith put a kettle on while Lucas and Fredrick sat at a solid oak table in a room off the kitchen. He remembered helping Fredrick with the table after his brother had built their home.

The ceiling above them creaked.

"I don't know what to say to them." Fredrick looked down at the table. "Their brother is dead, and I don't know what to say to them." He put his head in his hands.

"What happened?"

Edith walked into the room with a tray of steaming mugs. "I'm sure you have heard of the attacks." She set the tray down on the center of the table and placed a mug of tea in front of each of them.

Lucas grabbed the mug and tried to bring a smile to his face as he looked at Edith. The tea smelled of lavender and honey. A staple out here near East Edge. *I'd rather it was ale.* He took a sip and waited for either of them to continue.

Edith cleared her throat. "Harvest had just ended, preparations for the Harvest's End Festival were finished. It was going to be such a wonderful day. I woke up that morning...and..." She took a deep breath and tears rolled down her cheeks.

"Ben was murdered that night." Fredrick spoke plainly, as if he were talking about next season's crops. Lucas felt a sudden chill and took a sip of the warm tea. He sat and waited. "We think three or four of them came here and

164

forced him to let them into the storage barn. There's not much missing. It seems they went in, took what they could carry, murdered our son...and left." Fredrick's knuckles were white as he gripped the mug in his hands. Edith reached a hand out to put on Fredrick's forearm. He flinched at her touch and relaxed as he looked up to his wife.

"I see." It was all Lucas could think to say. He paused. "Has anyone been in the storage house since he—Since Ben was killed in there?"

Fredrick sighed. "It happened in the yard; we think. That's where we found him. Elina has been the only one to go inside. We couldn't bring ourselves to go in." Fredrick looked into his mug. "My son was murdered. The next day they continued the festivities as if nothing happened." His knuckles went white again. "Most of them went off to East Edge to celebrate. I guess they thought they'd be doing us a kindness."

"Elina?" Lucas took the opportunity to shift the focus from Ben's murder. Was he as bad as the rest for doing so?

"After the attack, the village leaders met, and we decided to send for help from East Edge. They couldn't spare any of their few town guards, but travelers and mercenaries have been appearing all over the Eastern Perimeter since the attacks have increased. We hired Elina as protection if...if they come back." Fredrick looked up at the ceiling. Whatever Dion and Owain were doing up there, it sounded as if they were about to crash through the floor and onto the table.

Lucas almost admonished his brother for hiring strangers to protect what was theirs. Then he remembered himself and held his tongue. The last thing he wanted to be was a hypocrite. "I can send word to the Amber Waves members in Homestead. Last I knew there were at least sixty living in the area. They could come to East Edge and hold watch over the Eastern Perimeter."

"How could anyone out here afford that?" Fredrick was exasperated. "We could barely afford to hire Elina. She took half pay and even refused a room in the house. She stays in a small camp near the storage building."

Lucas thought for a moment; surely his brothers and sisters in the Amber Waves would understand the situation and forgo pay to protect the New Ring. He didn't want to use his position as a founder to sway the members. He might make an exception in this case. He had to get a message to Caleb, and to the chapter in Homestead. "I'd like to meet Elina. I have questions for her regarding what happened." Lucas stood up and began walking to the back door that led to the yard between the house and the storage building but stopped short. He felt that lump in his throat again and he turned to his brother and Edith.

"Where is my nephew buried? I would like to pay my respects as well."

Fredrick's gaze went through Lucas and into the yard. "They always used to lie in the tall grass beyond the farm, we thought it the best place for him. We planted a white-bark tree to mark him." He turned back to stare into the mug he hadn't taken a drink from.

Lucas stepped out into the yard and closed the door behind him.

Next to the tall storage building was a canvas tent and small cook fire. A large pack was leaned against the side of the building, and another smaller pack was next to the open flaps of a canvas tent. A horse was hobbled on the other side of the tent, grazing on the grass in front of it. As he approached the horse looked in his direction and a woman in leather armor stood up from her cook fire. Her hand hovered over the sword at her side.

"I'm Lucas Meadows, Fredrick's younger brother." He held his hands away from his sword belt and slowly stepped forward. "I wanted to ask you some questions."

"Of course." The woman relaxed. Not entirely though. Her blond hair came down to her jaw line and framed her face. Her face was hard, but there was beauty in her features.

Her hazel eyes stared back at him. "I am Elina Tanveir." She held out a welcoming hand.

Lucas shook it. "Lucas Meadows. Elina Tanveir, hm? Tanveir. A name like that, you must be from the capital."

"Correct. I come from tanners and leather workers. Armor, saddles, boots, that sort." Elina put a hand to her chest as she spoke.

"Your own work?" He pointed to her armor and then to the leather packs near the tent.

"The packs are mine, yes. The armor, my father's work." Pride welled up through her solid demeanor. Only slightly.

"About my nephew. Did you learn anything from going inside the storage building?"

She stared at him for a moment. "There were clear signs of a struggle between two, maybe three, people near the tables along the room. A wash hose was strung about the floor, and after a look there was a small amount of dried blood on a portion of the hose. It seems someone had been strangled with it."

"Ben?" The word was a whisper being carried out of his mouth.

"I don't think so. The bod—" Elina cleared her throat. "Your nephew's body didn't have any marks along his neck as far as the medical report mentions. Your nephew was found with a short blade in his ribcage. I can continue if you would like."

"I believe he was able to separate one of the members of this raiding party and attempted to strangle him with the wash hose. Your nephew had markings from the hose on the palms of his hands and fingers. During the fight he was stabbed and left to die. His body was found in the yard just over there." Elina pointed toward the house.

He had almost made it to get help. The lump was back in Lucas' throat.

"He was murdered but didn't die without a fight left in him. Your nephew was a brave young man."

Ben was murdered.

Lucas cleared his throat in an attempt to rid the lump. "Anything else? Have you spoken to Doc Tymbers? He would have been the one to write up a medical report."

"I'm afraid the doctor was one of the other villagers in the town who was murdered."

"I see." Doctor Tymbers had been there for every one of his nephews' births.

"The raiding party didn't take much. I imagine others will be back. During my travels here I came upon what seemed to be an old encampment along the Sun Road. My guess is there are still fifteen to twenty within the New Ring. There could be others out along the Perimeter within the Haze as well. I don't doubt they have some kind of settlement or camp nearby. What I don't understand is how they manage to survive out there."

"Protective suits, masks, breathing tanks," Lucas listed as he looked out beyond the fields and toward the looming yellow murk. It was taller than the outer wall of Amboy city. Hundreds of feet of thick, deadly smoke.

"You've seen them?" Elina stepped closer to him; he could feel her eyes on him.

"No. Only their equipment. This was maybe thirty years ago. There are some within the city who call themselves Haze Walkers. Fools who travel back and forth between here and there. Scavengers, eccentrics . . . fools." Lucas turned to look at Elina. Her tough exterior was beginning to show some cracks.

"Have these Haze Walkers made some kind of deal with those that live out there?"

"I've heard rumors that they have an agreement not to do each other harm, but who knows. Maybe they trade in information as well as technology and other supplies. Food perhaps too."

"You're saying these people who attacked your family could be Haze Walkers as well?"

168

"It is possible, but it doesn't matter. Whether they originate in the Haze, the New Ring, or the Council itself, someone has harmed my family and is harming others. I must learn as much as I can about what is happening." Lucas eyed small camp. "You seem as though you can handle yourself. I know my brother has hired you to help protect the farm, but I would also like to ask for your help."

The woman crossed her arms and nodded. "Of course."

"I'm heading to East Edge to gather more information. I need to contact my friends in the Amber Waves for aid. I'm not sure how well we'll be able to pay you if you decide to help us." Caleb and the others would finish that other job. Lucas could give some of his cut to Elina for helping him here.

Elina held up a hand. "I'm not worried about payment. Fredrick and Edith have given me enough already." She turned from him and moved toward the larger of the two packs. She pulled a water skin from it and slung it across her torso. She tightened her sword belt at her waist and looked her armor over before turning her attention back to Lucas and nodded.

"Good." He sighed. "I just need to pay respects to my nephew first."

Lucas had held back in the house, but now he let the tears come. When he had found out that his brother and Edith were going to have Ben, he stayed with them through the last months of Edith's pregnancy. That had turned into him staying for the first year of his nephew's life. Lucas had helped with the farm, and with Ben. After he left, he tried to visit as often as he could, but it wasn't common for jobs to take him near East Edge. Maybe he should have lived a life like Fredrick had. Who might he be now? *No. No point in thinking like that.* He had his own people he was responsible for now.

There was a rustling in the tall grass behind him. Lucas unbuckled the clasp that held his sword in its sheath. A gust of wind passed through. He waited and listened. The rustling came again, this time closer. He turned to see where the sound was coming from and let himself relax. He wiped the tears from his face.

"Alright, boys, come on out."

Two identical boys emerged from the tall grass; the legs of their pants stained green.

"How'd you know it was us, Uncle Luc?" Dion asked. He shook head and bits of grass fell from his long brown hair.

"He probably heard you trip on that rock. I always tell you; you need to watch your footing." Owain brushed at his pants in an attempt to remove the grass stain.

"It will take some time to get those stains out, boys."

"These stains?" Dion asked as he pulled as his pant legs. "These are old. Ma and Pa gave up once we kept ruining the clothes we got from East Edge."

"We haven't ruined *all* of our clothes," Owain added. "Is that a new sword?"

"No. Same one I've had since you saw me last." Lucas felt that lump in his throat again. How long had it been since he had visited? The two seemed so much older than fourteen.

"When are you going to teach us how to use a sword?" Dion asked. He let out a grunt as Owain elbowed him.

"Why would I—" Lucas began. "Oh, I see."

"We had *planned* on waiting to ask, but I guess it's too late now." Owain glared at his brother.

"If I were to teach you how to use a sword, I don't think I'd be in good favor with your parents. Besides, I remember you two being better than me with a bow." His nephews lit up at the compliment.

"We are!" they both shouted in unison.

"It's just that," Owain began. "We thought if we knew how to protect ourselves…"

"I understand you want to protect your Ma and Pa."

170

Lucas stepped closer and put a hand on each of their shoulders. "If I taught you, I would always be worried about you boys getting into some unnecessary fight." He sighed. "That said, your skills with the bow are enough. I don't need you two running into trouble all throughout the New Ring." The two shot a wry smile at each other. Lucas laughed.

"Alright, Uncle Luc. We'll stick to the bow." Dion stepped back.

"One day we'll join the Amber Waves. Then you'll have to teach us!" Owain smiled up at him.

"That won't be anytime soon, if I have any say in it." Lucas smiled. That lump in his throat grew.

A gust of wind rushed across the fields from the east; the white-bark sapling bent in the wind and sprang back in its absence.

CHAPTER THIRTEEN

Port Amboy

L evi waited beneath the roof of the open platform that
covered the length of Port Amboy Station. The shade
was welcome in the late afternoon heat. The train had
only been at the station for a few minutes and was
already bustling with activity.

It was difficult to see anything in the throng of passengers
and workers moving to and from the train cars. Men and
women were loading horse-drawn carts with supplies from
the train, while others would grab a box or sack and walk into
the port town. He stepped up onto a stone wall and looked
out on the crowd for familiar faces but couldn't see Ana or
any of the others. After searching a bit longer, he turned his
attention away from the packed platform and out over the
town below.

He could see out across the red tiled roofs of Port
Amboy. Sunlight reflected off the gray-blue water of the
Great Sea; it stretched for miles until it disappeared on the
horizon. Fishing boats speckled the water and ships of all
builds and sizes moved in and out of port. On the other side
of the Great Sea was Ser'Delcea, and beyond that the

172

Perimeter Shield held the Haze at bay. Far past Amboy in the northeast, along the massive river Athanellekil, was the town of Athanelle. The mouth of the Athanellekil was split by a large island and beyond that were several smaller islands.

He wasn't sure all the islands had names, or if they were even populated. The largest was home to the Tou'sani people. A very long time ago the Tou'sani traded in Port Amboy, but a wall had been built around the island and the Tou'sani closed their ports. He had heard stories that an illness had taken over the island and the Amboians built the wall around it to keep the sickness from spreading. There were also rumors that the Tou'sani people wouldn't accept Amboian rule, so they constructed the wall themselves to keep others out. Ana said her great-grandfather had been one of the last to trade with the Tou'sani. The timing didn't add up though.

Levi looked over the crowd around the platform. Still no sign of a familiar face. He turned his attention back to the town. Stone-paved streets sloped down from the station and disappeared into the mass of stone and wood buildings. The streets were packed with people. Even this far away from the capital it was overcrowded. Cart handlers shouted from their seats at those who wouldn't move out of their way. Children ran through the crowds as they chased each other. Men and women with fishing poles twice the length of Levi's arm span walked in the direction of the docks and talked among themselves. The fishermen and women wore wide-brimmed hats and flowing shirts. Their pants were bunched and tied at the calf. They wore no shoes. The loose clothing allowed them to sit under the sun all day comfortably. He suddenly became aware of the sweat that slicked his back.

He could see the new construction at the coastline. He could make out the shapes of workers moving about, dockworkers hauling wooden planks, carts being wheeled here and there. He could almost hear the sounds of hammers driving in nails over the din of the train platform. *The construction area would be a good place to start asking questions.*

173

Workers fell into conversation while they went about their tasks. Especially unhappy workers.

As he waited on the platform, he heard talk about a foreman on another job who didn't know what she was doing. Something about wasting supplies and extending the job's timeline another week. Another week of work that most of the workers hadn't been paid for yet. He hoped that the discontent from the train might spread to the docks. He could use that to his advantage.

"You can head down to the docks first if you'd like, Levi."

Levi turned around and saw Caleb's bald head and bearded face looking up at him from the platform. Ana and Omar were standing behind him talking to each other. Levi heard something about a terrible hand and chance. "I think that would be best." He stepped down from the stone wall. "I'll see what I can learn about the hierarchy of the job site and maybe find out who's in charge."

A tanned woman with a shaved head save for a dark braid walked behind Omar and Ana. As she passed, Levi noticed her place a hand on Ana's shoulder and smile. Ana didn't acknowledge the woman but rolled her eyes. Omar turned his head to the woman and smiled. She let out a sharp laugh and pushed a disheveled man along with her.

"Who was that?" Caleb asked as he watched the woman walk down the stone steps toward the town.

"No one," Ana said angrily.

"Ellowen, we met her on the train. She has worked several of these construction jobs, so we thought we could get some information from her. She ended up getting more from us." Omar rubbed the back of his head and stared off into the direction Ellowen had left in. "She had recognized you, Caleb, then assumed we were members of the Amber Waves. She was curious why we took a construction job."

Caleb shook his head. "I remember a time when the average person couldn't even remember the Company's

174

name. I believe those days are coming to an end." He seemed tired. Perhaps he was worried about Lucas but would be fine—he could handle himself.

Levi opened his mouth to reassure Caleb, but Omar spoke first. "She said she grew up in District Eight, so it was more likely that she would be familiar with Amber Waves members."

"What did she learn from you, and how was she so convincing?" Caleb crossed his arms, and his brows furrowed.

"Well," Ana began. "she suggested we play Twelve—"

"Gambling." Caleb sighed. "You left it up to *chance*?"

Omar smiled. Not the kind of chance the Church preached of.

"She must have cheated!" Ana protested. "I've never seen anyone get a Full Council in five turns." Her face reddened. Was she getting angry, or embarrassed for having admitted she had been beaten?

Before Caleb could respond, Levi stepped in to bring the focus back to this woman. "What does she know?"

"She knows my name and Omar's. Yours too, Levi. Obviously, she recognized *you*." Ana glared at Caleb.

"What else?" Levi asked. He had to keep the focus on the woman.

"She knows we're working construction, but I told her it was because jobs were becoming harder to find." Ana let out a long sigh.

"That's it, then?" Levi could see Caleb relax.

"That's it."

Caleb turned his attention out toward the town. Levi could see the thoughts rolling in his head, the plans forming. Caleb rubbed his bald head with a hand and then brought it down to stroke his beard.

"Here's what we'll do." Caleb turned back toward the three of them. "Levi, I know I said you could go to the docks, but I want Ana down there. Her experience will be useful."

175

Ana nodded in response.

"Levi, I want you to follow this Ellowen. I want to know who she is, where she goes, and who she talks to. Ana says she knows your name, but—" Caleb looked to Omar and Ana. "—does she know what you look like?"

"She could have seen us talking to Levi just then, but who knows," Omar said.

"Let's assume she didn't, and won't remember seeing you just now," Caleb continued. "Omar will come with me to the Amber Waves chapter here in town, and then tonight we will all meet there."

Before any answer could have been given, Levi vaulted over the stone wall and searched the crowd along the street for a braid-topped head. She couldn't have gotten far. His task was all that was important now. Among the crowd he saw several braided hair styles, but not the shaved sides indicative of the Athanelle style. He moved through the crowd as he searched. He had to dart out of the way of a few horse-drawn carts and almost knocked a fruit stand over. Between the shouts of the old man behind the fruit stand, and Levi's rushed apology, he saw who he was looking for. After tossing a few apples back onto the stand, he turned away from the yelling man and started after the woman.

As they moved away from the station the crowds thinned slightly. That helped him keep track of her. Although, if she had turned around, she would easily see him. He kept his distance and hoped that he wouldn't be seen. It was then that he realized the rough-looking man who was at the platform wasn't with her now. The man had seemed ill; perhaps he made his way to a doctor after leaving the train. Wherever the man was it didn't matter now, he had to keep his focus on the woman with the braid.

It was easy enough to keep her in sight as she moved through the crowd and turned down side streets. It was only after the third side street they had taken that she had quickened her pace. *Was I seen? Did the thinner crowds allow her to*

176

move at a more comfortable pace?

His thoughts were answered as she darted down a narrow alley between two store fronts. Levi sprinted toward the alley and turned to enter. As he rounded the corner a woven basket flew toward him. He brought up his bow and knocked the basket aside. He was glad it had been mostly empty. Some half-eaten fruits spilled onto the stone-paved alley. As the basket was knocked out of the way Levi continued after the woman. The alley he ran down was just wide enough for him to fit. Her braid bounced on her back as she ran; she seemed to have no issue as she moved through the tight space. At the end of the alley, she turned left.

Levi followed onto a street that was mostly empty. She had begun to slow her pace. Was she tired already? Levi cradled his bow in one arm and tucked it tight to his side as he ran. With a clear street he would be able to catch her shortly. He opened his stride. The sounds of his boots hitting the stone bounced off the buildings he streamed past. Signs hung over doorways. He was only able to catch a few as he continued the chase; a bundle of herbs in a woven basket indicated a healer of some kind, a sign that read The Mizzenmast could have been a tavern, and a hammer and anvil indicated a smithy. The lack of a heavy scent of a forge meant they must have sold finished works and received orders.

Just as it seemed he was closing the gap, the woman turned down another alley. Fortunately, this was more spacious than the previous and Levi was able to keep his pace without bumping arms or legs on the stone walls beside him. His bow occasionally scraped the stone sides of the buildings. He tried to keep from grimacing too much at the thought of it becoming damaged.

A wall blocked the end, but the woman cleared it without struggle. She leaped from one side of the alley to the other, and then toward the dead-end wall, and pulled herself up. She had made it look easy enough. Levi threw his bow like a spear

177

over the top of the wall. Trying to mimic her movements, he pushed off one wall and threw himself forward. His hands found the top edge and his body slammed into it, forcing air from his lungs. He pulled himself up. It wasn't a wall, but the top of another building. He picked up his bow and coughed. His quarry was running along the roof he was now standing on. When she reached the edge, she jumped across the gap to the next roof.

The day's heat seemed to double up on the red-tiled roofs. It took several strides for Levi to find comfortable footing. Again, just from seeing it done once, he crossed the gap and continued his pursuit. Running and jumping along the same path that the woman was taking helped Levi close the distance between them once again. The pair were running along rooftops of buildings that followed the slope of the land down toward the harbor in the distance. Sometimes a jump from one tiled roof to the next was as simple as extending a stride, while others required a vault up to a higher roof, or a step down to a lower. Levi had found his rhythm and almost removed the distance between them. If he threw his bow toward her legs, he might be able to knock her off balance. It was possible that that would cause her to fall down to the stone-paved streets below. That wouldn't work. He needed to question her.

The space between buildings they were approaching was much further than he had crossed previously. He threw himself down and rolled to a stop to avoid falling. He heard the woman let out a grunt as she threw herself out across the gap. It must have been close to twenty feet. He watched as her body cleared the space and her outstretched hands grabbed hold of the roof on the other side. She effortlessly pulled herself up and turned to look in Levi's direction. Her shoulders rose and fell rapidly; her tanned skin glistened with sweat. She put her hands on her hips and smiled at him before turning away. She opened a wooden hatch on the roof and disappeared within.

Once he had gotten down off the roof, Levi spent the rest of the day searching the immediate area around the building the woman had entered. The main street that the building was on was like any other in the town: lined with stores, taverns, inns, and homes.

He set himself within view of the front of the building the woman had disappeared into. He could see who was coming and going. From the time he had been there the only person to enter it had been the woman through the roof top hatch. The buildings on this street were all right up against one another; if there was a different way into the building it was on the opposite side along the street that ran parallel to where Levi was now. At least he knew where she had entered. He had thought about scaling the side of the building. It was possible that others were inside.

If she was that agile, she could also be a good fighter. he didn't like his odds of making it to the roof and then getting in and out of the building safely. A sign hung out into the street from above the entrance he had been watching; it was a wood carving of a long-legged spider, with white lines along the sides of its body. Six white spots covered its abdomen. Above that, a sign read The Six-spotted Fisher. No, Levi wouldn't enter that building alone.

Ellowen closed the hatch above her, and nearly fell to the floor below. Her arms and legs were burning and sweat stung the cuts that covered her palms. *That jump could have killed me. Fool!* She took a deep breath and let it out slowly.

The windowless attic was dark and smelled like rotting wood. After collecting herself, she took a step toward where she thought the staircase was. Her fourth step found air and then fell hard on the staircase. Her momentum almost took her down the entire flight of stairs. She grabbed the wooden rail that ran the length of the staircase. Her legs and arms screamed at her once more. She gritted her teeth and forced down a groan. Light washed over her as the door below opened.

A woman much older than Ellowen looked up into the attic at her with a scowl on her face. The lines in her face were deep. Her long white hair was pulled up into an unkempt bun. Loose bits of hair spread wildly. "Well?"

"They took the bait," she said between breaths.

"Good. Now come down and let me have a look at you." A thin smile split the woman's face.

Even though the air was much cooler inside, sweat beaded on Ellowen's skin.

The Shipwright's Daughter was a modest tavern. Omar was surprised when his boots hadn't stuck to the floor when he and Caleb walked in, and none of the floorboards creaked when they crossed the room. Allegra Sovoso kept the place clean. A dozen or so square tables filled the main room. Dark stained oak boards covered the lower half of the walls and the stone that reached to the ceiling had been painted white. The glass in the windows of the room were mostly clear as well. Allegra had called out to the two of them immediately when they entered. This time their recognition was expected.

Allegra was the leader of the Amber Waves Chapter in Port Amboy. She ran her business and her portion of the Amber Waves all in the same building. At first Omar had thought it odd. She was ambitious, though and after he had gotten to know her, the way she ran things was fitting.

The people who lived in the port knew the Shipwright's Daughter was a place they could get a drink after a day's work and not have to worry about getting into a fight. At this time of day though most would still be down at the docks, or out on the sea. When they arrived here the worst that might happen to them would be losing a day's wage at a game of dice or Twelve.

Omar fought down the urge to cringe at the thought of

the game. He should have stopped Ana before she had gotten ahead of herself. He wondered how she was faring down at the docks. Making up a fake identity was even less likely to work for her here. It wasn't Ser'Delcea, but Omar was willing to bet she wouldn't go unrecognized in Port Amboy for long.

Allegra hollered to a young woman behind the bar before she sat down. She seemed startled when Allegra called out to her, and then shocked when Allegra had said she was taking a break and that she needed the woman to take over for a moment.

Most of Allegra's long wavy black hair flowed over her shoulders and down the front her of chest, almost into her lap, the rest she had tossed behind her as she sat down. Her brown jacket flared out near the waist in the fashion of Ser'Delcea. The long sleeves had been rolled up to her forearms. The top buttons of her undershirt were unbuttoned. Omar only glanced for a second. Then he noticed she was looking at him. He felt his face become warm.

"They may be celebrating Harvest's End throughout the New Ring, but the days don't seem to be getting any cooler yet." Allegra smiled at him. He felt like a fool smiling back.

"Give a few more days. I'm no Sky Watcher, but it'll cool down soon enough." Caleb took a drink from a tall metal mug. Unaware of their exchange. "I'd even put a few coins on it."

"You would?" Allegra raised an eyebrow and smiled again. She was beautiful.

Omar took a drink to keep from staring. He had first met Allegra when they had last come to Port Amboy, before sailing to Ser'Delcea to help Ana's father with some missing shipments. Allegra had had this same effect on him that time too. Did she know? She must have, the way she smiled like that.

"Well, maybe not." Caleb laughed. "Like I said, I'm no Sky Watcher."

"I'm not even sure they know what they're doing." She took a drink from her mug and set it on the table, then wiped her mouth with the back of her hand. "So, what can you tell me about this job you've taken? I'll help out any way I can, of course."

They didn't need to worry about unwanted ears here in the tavern. Omar mostly saw Amber Waves members at the tables around them currently. Still, he noticed Caleb lean in a bit closer.

"We've been given a job from some new Upper District group. Weren't sure exactly who they are, but they might be a new Family."

"They're going after the Jorogumo." The words just fell out of Omar's mouth. Allegra's eyes widened at the words. *Why did I say that?*

"What have you gotten yourselves into?" Although Allegra had regained her composure, there was concern in her voice.

"I've been asking myself the same thing." Caleb shook his head. "After this we're out."

If we can get out. Normally one didn't just stop their involvement with an Upper District Family. There was one way, but no one preferred that option. "We're here in the Port to see if there has been any unusual activity lately. Any trouble with gangs from the capital?" Omar found himself regaining some composure. He almost found himself angry with the woman for making him act like such a fool. Although, it wasn't her fault he found her so beautiful.

"Gang activity?" Allegra paused while she took another drink. "We would have picked up on anything like that I'd imagine. Someone would have reported something to us. Honestly, we've taken over guarding most of the western areas of the Port. The Spears of the Sea mostly work in the east now. It's possible something could have slipped through if it were to happen over there."

"Not surprising considering they're all washed-up

sailors," Caleb said into his mug before taking a drink.

"They're not all thieves and cutthroats. Some just weren't fit for life on the Great Sea," Allegra replied.

"Maybe the Amber Waves could take over entirely," Omar suggested. *If anyone could manage it, she could.* He sighed internally. He felt like a young boy fawning over a girl he had seen across a District Square.

"Might be useful to take a walk around that area tonight, if Levi or Ana haven't found themselves there already." Caleb ran a hand through his beard as he spoke.

"We could also go-" Omar was cut off as the door to the tavern opened. Ana walked in with Levi behind her. Levi's hands were wrapped in bandages.

Ana looked around the room. Her face lit up when she saw them sitting at the table near the center of the room. "Allegra!" Ana strode forward and nodded to the few Amber Waves members scattered among the tables. Levi acknowledged them as well. It was unlikely he knew any of them, he was merely being polite.

"Ana Brooks." Allegra stood up from the table and faced the two as they approached. Ana held out a hand to greet Allegra, but she slapped it out of the way and pulled Ana in for an embrace. Allegra was several heads taller than Ana. She was almost as tall as Omar himself. Ana patted the taller woman on the lower back a few times and pushed away.

"It's good to see you." Ana adjusted her jacket and glanced down her sleeves as she stepped back.

"You must be Levi." This time Allegra held out a hand. "Allegra Sovoso."

"Yes. Nice to meet you, Allegra."

"Any luck down at the docks, Ana?" Caleb asked when she sat down next to Allegra. Levi grabbed a chair from an empty table nearby and brought it over to theirs.

"Most of the dockworkers were talking about the previous job in Athanelle. Apparently, those who were in charge Hazed the entire job. A series of bridges were

183

supposed to be constructed across the Athanellekil. They wanted to use the few small patches of land as anchoring points for the construction. Funds for supplies had gone missing, as well the supplies. Now a bridge barely reaches into the river. The job has been put on hold until further notice."

"They wanted to build a bridge across the entire Athanellekil?" Allegra shook her head. "Missing supplies or no, it's no wonder the job was a failure. Even at narrow sections to the northeast of Athanelle it's still miles wide!"

"What a feat to undertake." Caleb seemed genuinely impressed.

Omar wasn't sure what to think. It seemed a bit extravagant. Ships could make trips across the Athanellekil perfectly fine. What was the need for a bridge? The woman covering the tavern for Allegra came to the table and set down a wooden tray with five tall mugs on it. Condensed droplets of water slid down the sides of the metal mugs. Foam capped the tops. Allegra also brewed a good ale. Omar reached for one and immediately took a large gulp.

"I also learned some information about that Ellowen woman," Ana said as she set down her own mug.

"*What?*" Caleb snapped. He had set his mug down a bit too hard and some of his drink spilled onto the table. The woman who had brought the drinks over jumped at Caleb's outburst.

"You wouldn't happen to have spice wine, would you?" Levi said as he looked at his mug.

"She has information on us. It only seemed reasonable to try and get some on her!" Ana's eyes were as sharp as her blades.

The woman pulled the empty tray from the table, "I–I can go see. I think we—"

"You were supposed see if there was anything that could lead us to the Jorogumo," Caleb said in hushed tones.

The woman standing next to him almost dropped the tray

when she heard mention of the Family.

"There's a small cask of wine in the back storage. I've been saving it. I think this seems as good a time as any." Allegra glanced between Ana and Caleb. Her smile was slightly different than before.

"The workers are unhappy with the previous job. I tried to ask more about the people who were in charge and they told me the Athanelle town council received funds from the capital for the construction, but then they were cut off. That's all I kept hearing." Ana managed to take the heat from her voice. "I'm guessing the capital ran out of funds to continue the job. I also heard about a weak harvest this year in the New Ring."

Caleb sighed. "That could be useful. What did you learn about this woman?"

"Not much." Ana shrugged. "A lot of the workers at the docks knew her by name and the description I gave. She was in Athanelle, but no one knew exactly what her position was. Before that she had worked on a few jobs in the Lower District."

"Well hopefully you didn't bring unnecessary attention to yourself to get that information." Caleb rubbed a hand from his forehead to the back of his bald head.

"Actually," Levi spoke up. "I think getting information on her might be helpful. I followed her through the town. She entered a tavern called The Six-Spotted Fisher." The woman returned with a mug for Levi. He looked into it and smiled. He took a sip and nodded to himself. "The Six-Spotted Fisher is a spider, if you didn't know."

Omar felt a pit open up in his stomach. Although he had never seen it himself, there were rumors that some in the Lower Districts received tattoos of spiders to show their connection to the Jorogumo. It had become a sort of unofficial symbol for the Family in the Lower Districts.

"Where is the tavern? How far did you have to follow her?" Caleb had leaned into the table once again.

"She ran shortly after I started tailing her. We ended up near the eastern part of town." Levi took another drink from his mug.

Omar looked across the table to Allegra. She had been watching the conversation unfold but was no longer smiling. "Do you know this tavern, Allegra?"

"They opened a few months back. They aren't too far into the eastern side of the town, so we asked if they wanted the Amber Waves to help out in keeping the place in order. The old woman I spoke to said she would be alright. I didn't see any muscle in the place though. Gave me an uneasy feeling, to be honest. Could just be the conversation though."

"What's more interesting, it was almost as if she was letting me chase her. Like she was leading me to the place. She leaped across an entire street and entered through a hatch on the roof. Just before she did though she looked back to see if I was still there."

Everyone at the table was staring at Levi.

Ana was the first to speak. "She was on the rooftops? Where were you?"

"On the rooftops," Levi said matter-of-factly.

"Pardon, what?" Allegra was smiling again. Omar wanted to as well, but it wasn't because of what Levi had said.

"I wanted to catch her to question her." Levi held up his bow. There were a few rough-looking marks near the ends. "I didn't want her to fall from the rooftops. She jumped to the roof of the Fisher. There was no way I was going to make that jump." He looked at them flatly as he spoke.

"Well." Caleb looked stunned. "Can it be coincidence?"

"Don't even say it, Omar," Ana said.

"Say what? Oh." He hadn't even been thinking about the Salvation now. Ana seemed to mention it more than he did. "I guess it's a good thing you ended up asking about her then."

Ana was beaming as she set down her mug.

"Well, Allegra, do you know anything else about this

186

tavern, or the old woman who you met there?" Caleb asked.

Allegra shrugged. "Not much else. I can ask the Amber Wave members. Some of them have been taking longer patrols and could have been in that part of town." Allegra looked around the room and called out to a man sitting at a tall stool at the bar. "Tomas! Join us for a moment."

The man turned from the bar and nodded. He reached over the bar top and refilled his mug from a tapped barrel.

"Tomas. If you need another round, just ask me." A woman swatted his back with a rag as he stepped away from the bar.

Tomas had a few years on Omar. He had a high hairline, and his black hair was tied back into a long tail. He had a thick black beard that could rival Caleb's. Tomas' had been shaved to match the angles of his face. He wore a hard expression, but his deep brown eyes seemed warm. The plate armor he wore was scratched and dented in some areas. He carried a long sword at one side of his hip and a short sword at the other.

"What'll it be Allegra?" Tomas said as he pulled up a chair for himself. He nodded to the group as he sat down. "Caleb Fields. It's an honor to finally meet you." Now that he was closer Omar could see the lines at the corners of his eyes. Maybe the man had more than a few years on Omar.

"You were among the group that did patrols toward the eastern end of the Port these past few days. Have you heard anything about that new tavern that just opened, The Six-Spotted Fisher?" Allegra's demeanor had changed completely. She was now Allegra Sovoso, Amber Waves Chapter Head. Not Allegra Sovoso, tavernkeeper.

Tomas nodded as he swallowed the drink he had taken. "That old woman could rust my armor just by looking at it. Shield protect me." He took another drink.

Omar was beginning to wonder how much of this was going to turn into tavern hearsay. Had the man had too much to drink?

"A fight had broken out, someone outside the tavern was shouting for the Spears. We decided to haul ourselves over there. Probably out of the Spears territory anyway." There was a bit of sting in the way Tomas spoke of the Spears. "A man told us there was a group dicing. One of them didn't like the way the dice fell, no surprise, and pulled a knife. When we got inside the place was silent. We found the man at a table near the back. Someone had cut his throat." The table had fallen silent as well. "Once we started asking questions everyone bunged up. That old woman told us there wasn't a problem anymore and we could leave." Tomas shook his head. "So, we left. Nothing else to do." He put his mug to his mouth and tipped it back. As he set it back onto the table it made a hollow sound.

"Had they hired anyone to watch over the place?" Caleb asked.

"None of them looked like hired muscle. My guess, one from that group that was dicing cut the man's throat when he saw the blade and the others didn't want to turn them over." Tomas shrugged and looked into his empty mug as if he had forgotten he had just emptied it.

"I'm not sure what to make of all of this." Caleb was staring across the room toward one of the windows that looked out toward the Great Sea. "We need more information. We can't just assume these people are tied to the Jorogumo because they have a tavern named after a spider."

"Dock spiders are common." Allegra nodded. "You see them all the time making webs near the surface of the water to catch bugs as they spawn. I never knew they had a name."

Caleb looked around the table. "None of us can go to gather more information. Tomas and his patrol would be too obvious. Ellowen knows who *we* are." Caleb gestured to himself, Omar, Levi, and Ana. "Allegra is too well known in the Port. Are there any others who might be able to get inside and gather information for us?"

"I'm sure there is someone who is willing to do so. None

of the Amber Waves in the Port. Our numbers may not be high, but we are all well known." Allegra looked to Tomas, who nodded. "Give me the night and I will find someone trustworthy."

CHAPTER FOURTEEN

Memories of an Old World

C ordelia had searched four dilapidated buildings since
she had reached the ruins half a day's walk from the
Perimeter. Nothing of value had turned up yet. There
wouldn't be much daylight left; she had to make a
decision about whether or not to move on. If it could even be
considered daylight. Hardly any of the light from the blazing
sun in the sky reached the surface below through the murky
fog around her.

"Like anyone in the capital would even know the worth
of any of these things," Cordelia said, and picked up a chair
to sit down to rest. Normally she would come to these ruins
and grab the first thing she saw and head back into the New
Ring.

The Council's Reclamation crews hadn't made it this far
into the ruins yet; that made it good for scavenging. She
thought it was a shame that the Amboian Reclamation crews
destroyed any evidence of the Old World. She had heard they
took any useful materials or objects of interest back to the
capital, but once there was nothing left to indicate the past
inhabitants, terraforming equipment came through and

shaped the land according to the plans of the Council. *How would they know what is and isn't important?*

The machines and terraforming technology were advanced; the equipment reverted the land back to its former state. Once the terraforming was completed, the floating Shield Generators in the sky would move outward to expand the border between the New Ring and the Haze. With the continued expansion eastward, there were more reports of people from within the Haze, coming into the New Ring for supplies. *And more recently the murders.*

Cordelia had been stalling. She hadn't been home to Mountain Station in almost a year. She hadn't even planned on going home, but she needed answers. Her grandmother, Theresa Faucher, was one of the Elders at the station. Perhaps she would have the answers Cordelia was looking for. She sighed, put her hands on her knees, and reluctantly stood up.

The dusty room around her must have been some family's dining area. There were several wooden chairs in various conditions. The one she had been sitting on was the only one with four solid legs. Aside from the thick layer of dust and broken glass here and there, the table looked as though it was ready for the previous owners to come into the room to sit down for a family meal. Six table settings were out: plates, forks, spoons, and knives. There were four tall glass cups and two stemmed wine glasses among the place settings, some broken and some seemingly untouched.

She struggled to keep her mind from imagining the family preparing for their evening together, unaware of what was to come. She turned away from the table to a cabinet and wiped the dust off the glass to get a look inside. As she pulled on the metal knob to open the cabinet, the entire door separated away, rusted hinges and all. She set the door to the side to get a look at the decorative plates and cups inside. It took a moment to find a piece that hadn't been cracked or broken, but eventually she found a small plate that would fit into one

191

of the larger pockets on the exterior of her suit.

The plate was made of a white porcelain. Flowers with interwoven stems decorated the edge of the plate. The deeper center of the plate was a painted scene of a cottage with a small stream flowing by. The cottage was almost entirely shrouded with plants and vines, most of which she had never seen. This would do; she put the plate in a pocket on her thigh and sealed it up before she moved out of the room toward the front of the house.

As she passed through the room adjacent to the dining area, she thought she saw movement in the street through a blown-out wall that barely resembled where two windows used to be. She immediately pushed her body against the crumbling wall and stilled herself. Yes, she had seen three dark shadows close to the ground moving between the burnt-out metal husks in the cracked street. She tried to listen for any sound coming from beyond the ruined house. All she could hear was her shallow breath and the steady rhythm of her own heartbeat. Her breath fogged the glass of her visor. She counted a slow fifteen before crouching on the balls of her feet and peered over the crumbling wall.

Beyond the busted porch that ran along the front of the house there were metal frames lining the street. A single large crack in the pavement ran the length of the street. Tall grass and leafy plants grew within the space made by the crack. There were no shadowy figures in sight. Slowly and still crouched, Cordelia moved back the way she came through the house hoping to find an exit in the rear of the building. She passed back through the dining area and carefully pushed open the swinging door that led to the kitchen. Once beyond she held the door with both hands and gingerly closed it to keep it from swinging wildly.

The kitchen almost reminded her of Jaeger's. A small table was pushed against the wall with two undisturbed chairs and an empty vase sat atop the table. Cabinets and cupboards lined the walls; there was a stove and a cold box. Much like

Jaeger's home there was a door that led from the kitchen out into the backyard.

She continued to crouch as she moved toward the door. She carefully twisted the knob, hoping the rusty hinges didn't keep the door completely shut. Dread filled her as the exact opposite happened. The rotted door frame gave way, and the door began to fall outward down the stairs leading to the backyard. She tried to grab the other edge of the door with her free hand, but barely caught it as it fell into the metal railing along the cement stairs.

As the door came into contact with the railing a loud metal ringing reverberated out into the waste. Without waiting to listen for a sign she let go of the door and leaned back into the kitchen to grab the vase that was on the table. She almost fell down the cement stairs as she bounded into the backyard. As she crossed the space behind the house the yellow fog revealed that it was fenced in. She threw the vase to her left into an adjacent yard as hard as she could and then threw herself into the fence hoping her weight would be enough to break through the old wood. The fence gave almost no resistance as her body slammed into it and gave way. Before she even hit the ground, she sprang up and began running through the yard, toward the back of the next ruined home. There was a sound of glass smashing behind her. *The vase.* She hoped it was enough to give her some time to enter the building in front of her.

She skipped the entire staircase she leapt onto the wooden back porch. Her first footfall brought her right through the porch and into the space below. Cordelia rolled onto her stomach and peered out through the lattice of the back porch. She strained her eyes looking through the yellow murk. Her heavy breathing fogged up her visor again. She would have to mention this to Jaeger. She closed her eyes and took a deep breath, held it, and then slowly let it out. She fought back a gasp as she opened her eyes.

The hole she had made in the fence was being occupied

by a four-legged animal, like a large dog. The Haze made it difficult to make out the details of the animal. If it *was* a dog, there was something wrong with it. Instead of fur, its skin seemed to be made of rough scale plates. It lifted its head up to the air, and then began inspecting the broken fence. The animal had a blocky head and massive shoulders. Its forelegs were twice the thickness of the rear legs. It paced around the space before it turned back in the direction in came from. There was a deep ragged howl nearby. Then a similar one not far off.

She cursed and rolled back over to the opening in the porch that she had slipped through. She pulled herself up through it and stepped over a broken wall into the building. As she stepped inside a pain shot up her leg and fell to the ground. *The plate.* She quickly checked the integrity of her suit from the outside with her hands, and then remembered the black box on her left forearm. Pushing a button loaded the heads-up display:

Oxygen remaining: 14 hours.

Suit Integrity:

Internal Environment: Compromised.

Suit Exterior: Uncompromised.

Heart Rate: 156 BPM.

After her heart rate was measured a message appeared: Take it easy, kid.

Jaeger.

Cordelia laughed to herself as she tried to ignore the pain in her leg. The plate must have shattered and stabbed through the lining of the pocket and into her leg. The seal on the pocket held. The exterior of the suit was fine. As long as the seal of the pocket held, she would be okay. Relatively okay. She had no idea how much, or if, she was bleeding and she couldn't check until she got out of the Haze, or into a safe house. It would take her well into the night to get out of the Haze. She was going to have to locate one of the safe houses in the area. If they were even still in use, and if they would even accept her. Cordelia had used a safe house in the area years ago; she guessed it was another ten or fifteen miles to the northeast.

She gently patted her thigh to try and get a sense of the damage she had done. She could feel the mostly whole plate in her pocket. Two pieces several inches long moved about as she patted the pocket. Pain shot up and down her leg as her hand brushed a shard of the plate. There must have been two inches sticking out, and a good amount inside her thigh. Taking another deep breath, she stood up and tried to still herself. She let the breath out and looked around the room, keeping most of her weight on her left leg.

The room she was in must have been some kind of study. A large solid desk was to her left. An assortment of things covered the surface of the desk. A model of a ship made from some kind of metal. A stone carving of an animal made her shiver. She picked up a clear square box.

Inside was a white ball with brown lacing around it. Writing had covered the entire ball. With the shards of her previous scavenging attempt jingling in her pocket and sticking out of her leg, she decided to hold on to this plastic box. Fortunately for her, there was a metal cane on the floor near what she assumed used to be a doorway, now a large arch of splintered wood. She picked it up and supported herself with it as she slowly moved down the hall toward a closed door that would take her to the rooms in the front of the house. Again, she carefully turned the knob this time expecting it to either not open or fall right out as had happened previously. The hinges of the door cried out as she slowly pushed it open. She hoped it wasn't as loud as it seemed. There was no front of the house. The door opened up to the space that once was a building, now a pile of stone, wood, and metal.

She looked out, another street. Skeletons of houses lined it; more metal frames were in the street as well. No dogs with scales. Sitting down first, she slowly lowered herself onto the rubble and gingerly navigated the terrain. A few times she had mistrusted a piece of rubble or board of wood and almost fell, but she made her way to the street and crouched against one of the more solid metal objects. She took a moment to look around and listen for any signs of those dogs again. She was alone, for now. By her best judgment she would have to move down the street parallel to the street she originally saw the dogs. In the same direction they had been heading. Pushing against the side of the metal frame, she got to her feet and crossed to the other side of the street and began walking in the direction she hoped would take her closer to the safe house. If it was still there. If they would accept her.

Even with the assistance from the cane she had found and moving her right leg as little as possible as she walked, the pain had begun to spread up and down Cordelia's leg. The murk around her had gotten much darker. The sun must have begun to set. She could hardly see further than twenty or so feet ahead of her. There hadn't been any sign of those dogs, she was thankful for that. She could turn on the lights that lined the visor of her helmet but didn't want to risk being seen by anyone or anything that may be nearby in the Haze. Her injury had put behind her planned schedule. She could have been out of the Haze by now and camped in the mountains for the night. At this point she would have to settle for the safe house once she found it and, hopefully, she would make it to Mountain Station tomorrow before the sun had set.

It was going to be difficult to find the markers that led to the safe house as the visibility was decreasing. Some of her surroundings looked familiar, hopefully she could trust her memory. As she walked through the town there were fewer buildings that seemed like homes. These were square, box-like, buildings made of stone, with flat roofs. If she was correct the building, she was looking for was only a few miles down the road. Theresa told her in the Old World people would visit this place to store their coin and any valuables they owned. In the basement was a vault that had been turned into a shelter. She had used it years ago when she first left Mountain Station and made her journey down to the New Ring.

As she walked the mostly empty, cracked streets, the looming shadow of a large building came into view. Cordelia imagined the gray dingy stone that the two-story building was constructed from was once a bright white. Surprisingly, only one of the six massive stone pillars had been reduced to debris. Almost none of the windows of the building had glass in their frames. The dense fog around her muffled her steps on the stone as she walked up the broad steps to the large wooden doors. If the doors were still intact someone must have been here recently.

She put her weight into the solid wooden door, and it only fought back slightly as it swung open. Tables and chairs were tossed here and there throughout the room. Ropes and metal poles were piled in a tangled mess in the corner of the cavernous room. At the far end was a long wooden counter. Frames made from the same red-brown wood stuck up from the surface. If this place had held valuables perhaps that kept visitors from accessing what wasn't theirs.

She moved toward the back, beyond the tables to a door that would take her down into the basement. She flipped a switch on the wall at the top of the staircase, but no lights turned on. If this safe house was still in use, someone would have been maintaining it. She hit the button on the black box attached to her forearm that activated the lights on her helmet.

White paint was peeling off the walls of the stairway. The wooden handrails were broken in several places, but the stone steps were still intact. As Cordelia slowly made her way down the steps, she noticed several sets of footprints in the dust. Whoever had been here hadn't kept up with the standards that she had remembered. Why let the lights go to waste? At the first landing she turned left and continued down the stairs.

She was cautious as she moved, due to her injured leg, as well as what might be waiting for her in the basement. Halfway down she unsheathed the short blade at her hip. Not everyone who knew about these places would be friendly. She would rather no one be here at all, than someone who pretended to be a friend. Before she could get into the room that contained the entrance to the safe house, she had to pass through a smaller room that would vent out any of the Haze.

An average-looking door opened up to a metal door. Cordelia struggled to slide it to the side, but she did. When she finally slid the door shut lights along the floor of the chamber lit up. She stumbled to a terminal on the wall and began entering the commands to vent the space so she could continue onward. There was a loud metal sound followed by the whir of the vent system drawing out the Haze that had followed her into the chamber. If she had been able to get the door open sooner, she wouldn't have had to wait as long as she did. Once the yellow poison was clear from the space, she released the locks on the door on the opposite side and pulled it open. There was a pressure in her ears as she stepped from the chamber and into the next room.

Skinny metal cabinets with sliding drawers lined this new room. The drawers of some cabinets were pulled out entirely, their contents spilled onto the floor. Piles of unrecognizable papers had long since decayed. There were two rooms on each side of the main room. Cordelia could imagine workers moving about the space, checking files, organizing coin for the people of the towns in the area. All unassuming, going about a normal day. *Stop. Focus.*

At the back of the room was a massive circular door with a large, spoked wheel. The wheel itself opened the vault at one point, she had been told. Now all one had to do to enter the safe house on the other side was push a button on the intercom and ask to be let in. If no one was in the safe house currently, an access panel could be used to open the door from the outside. She limped up to the intercom on the side of the door and pushed the button.

"Hello?" She could hear the exhaustion in her own voice. "Is anyone there?" She waited for a response. If she had just entered without asking first, and someone was inside they may get startled, and someone could get hurt. *I would most likely get hurt.*

Time seemed to drag. Eventually there was a voice from the other side.

"Yes, hello?" It was a woman's voice, older than Cordelia.

"I'm hurt. Will you please open the door?" She leaned against the intercom. Exhaustion had set in fully.

Another long pause. "I-I don't know. Who are you? I don't know that I can let you in."

"Please. I'm not going to hurt you. I need the medical supplies in the safe house and some rest. Then I'll be on my way." She was going to get in one way or another. She was running out of patience.

"You still haven't told me who you are. Maybe you should just move along."

Her mouth felt dry. "There's an access panel out here. I'm going to open the door from the outside and come in. I'm not going to hurt you. I just need to take care of a cut on my leg."

"*What?*" the woman snapped. "Don't you come in here!"

She almost fell onto the ground as she crouched. Along the floor there was a small metal hole in the wall for ventilation. She pulled the slatted cover off and reached inside. She grabbed a handheld terminal from inside the vent and carefully pulled it out. Wires led from the terminal into the vent, through the wall, to the terminal on the other side that would release the locks and open the door. She punched in the code and there was a loud metal noise as the locks released from the door. She slid the handheld back into the vent and replaced the cover. As the door swung open she stood up and looked inside.

The room was completely empty. It was lit by two rows of overhead lights. There were bunk beds along the right wall and cabinets along the left. Walls had been put in place toward the back of the room to divide it. If it was as she remembered there was a room where she could bathe and get the medical supplies she needed. She took a step into the room but stopped. She almost fell over as an old woman appeared from the back room with a long rifle in her hands.

She was a head shorter than Cordelia. The wool of her red jacket looked rough, and her dark pants were worn as well. Her brown leather flats had coins Cordelia didn't recognize slipped into slits near the toes. Dark eyes were fixed, and her thin lips were compressed flat. The wrinkles on her forehead were accentuated by her furrowed brow. Long white hair fell loosely around her shoulders.

"Now look here." The woman's voice was as solid as the stone walls around them. "I don't appreciate someone barging in on me like that. You better just turn around and leave."

The room spun as she tried to work some moisture into her mouth to speak. "I just need some medical supplies. Please."

"I don't have anything for you. Now *leave.*"

She looked at the rifle in the woman's hands. Where did she find a rifle? "There's no way you even have bullets for that weapon." A throbbing began in her head. "My...My grandmother told me ammunition was almost as valuable as clean water." *Water.* Wetting her mouth seemed impossible.

"Your grandmother sounds like a smart person." The old woman looked her up and down. "You're right though, bullets are extremely rare. I don't want to have to waste one on some fool who doesn't know when they're not welcome. You still haven't told me your name, girl."

200

Before the room went completely sideways and her vision went black, she thought she saw the old woman rushing toward her.

"Cordelia Faucher."

There was a quiet hum coming from the tube lighting that ran along the ceiling. As she tried to sit up, the room spun slightly, and her head throbbed. Cordelia reached a hand up to the side of her head and found a small bump.

"Good thing you had that helmet on. Even with that, bouncing your head off these stone floors couldn't have felt too good." The old woman was standing at a small electric stove with her back to her. *The suit.* Cordelia sat up and threw the blankets to the side. Her pants had been removed and a large bandage was wrapped around her right thigh.

"Where are my things?" Her voice sounded hoarse.

"I put all of your belongings on the bed above you." The woman turned around and had a bowl in her hand. "You need to eat something, girl. You're dehydrated, and you lost quite a bit of blood even with that ceramic stopping the wound up. What are you doing out here? Some fool girl running about in the Fog like this." The woman shook her head as she sat down and handed her the bowl.

A deep brown broth filled the bowl. The scent of vegetables and meat wafted up to her nose. She hadn't eaten since she left Jaeger at the Perimeter. She spoke between spoonfuls of stew. "How long was I out?"

"Not even a thank you." The woman scoffed. "For the food, or for taking that plate out of your leg."

Her face grew warm, and not because of the stew. She stopped eating. "I'm sorry." She looked up at the old woman. "Thank you. I'm not sure what would have happened to me had you not helped me."

"Forget it." She waved a hand. "Eat. Then tell me what it is you're doing out here and where you're headed."

201

Cordelia made the contents of the bowl quickly disappear and then drank down the rest of the broth that remained.

"I was scavenging for a job, but I'm actually headed to Mountain Station. Do you know it?"

The woman scoffed. "Do I know it…Of course I know it. I know your grandmother too, girl." Cordelia only looked at her. "I know Theresa, and I've met your mother once or twice. Well, to say I *know* your grandmother might be a stretch. Her and I have been in contact for a long time, but I have never physically *met* her." She moved her hands about as she spoke. She was older than Cordelia's mother, but not as old as her grandmother.

"My mother…" She trailed off as she looked into the emptied bowl and then back toward the woman. "You've been in contact with my grandmother?"

"Yes, yes. I tend to the safe houses around Tunnel Outpost and Mountain Station. Whenever I locate a Deep Scout team, I give them information to pass along to Theresa. If supply teams need to visit or if work must be done to maintain them." She looked around the room they were sitting in now. "This is one of the better-kept safe houses around here. You were lucky."

"It's the only one I know of in the area." She looked into the empty bowl again. *My mother and my grandmother.* "You haven't told me your name yet."

"Hm? Oh, yes. I am Deona." She smiled.

"It is nice to meet you, Deona, and thank you again." Cordelia smiled back.

"Nonsense, child. What was I to do once I heard your family name?" The woman tossed a hand again. "I wouldn't be able to show my face to the Deep Scout teams knowing I had let a Faucher die out in the Fog." The woman laughed.

Cordelia chuckled to herself. Then she remembered. "Has my grandmother said anything about why our people have been coming from beyond the Ha—the Fog and attacking towns?"

Deona stopped laughing at the mention of the attacks and her face became as solid as a rock. "*Our people?* Those fools are not *our people*. They are lost." She sighed. "The numbers in the Outposts have increased. We aren't able to support everyone like we used to. Mountain Station is filled to the security walls."

"What Outposts remain? Why are they leaving?" Cordelia realized she was gripping the bowl in her hands a bit too hard and set it on the bed next to her.

"As far as I know, Ruins Outpost to the North, Tunnel Outpost not far from here, and Lake Outpost to the South, where your mother has taken charge recently. Other than that, many of the outposts have fallen into disarray." Deona rubbed her temples. "It's chaos."

"The attacks. They weren't orders from Mountain Station then?" She felt relieved. The only way she imagined that an order like that would come from Mountain Station was if her grandmother had been removed from the Elders Circle, or worse, dead.

"Of course not." Deona stopped rubbing her temples, but kept her eyes closed. "Some fool from one of the smaller Outposts nearby, started a coup and rallied several others behind him. They've been traveling from settlement to settlement gathering people and resources." She finally opened her eyes again.

Cordelia tried to stand but her head still felt foggy and there was still a dull pain in her leg. Deona helped her sit back onto the bed. "Does my grandmother know?"

"She is aware and is trying to move the Circle to do something about it, but there are some in Mountain Station who would rather sit back until the problem is at their feet, rather than take action. Fools."

"And my mother is leading Lake Outpost now?"

"Yes. She relocated there years ago. How long have you been gone, Cordelia?" It was the first time she actually used her name. Those dark eyes were locked onto her again.

"How long?" Cordelia thought. "Five? Six years, maybe?" *How long had it been?*

"I see. A lot has changed, but a lot has stayed the same." Deona took the bowl from the bed and stood up. "You will head to Mountain Station then?" She asked as she walked back over to the electric cook top and spooned more stew into the bowl.

"Yes. As soon as I can. When is first light?" Cordelia was actually able to stand up this time. She grabbed her pants off the top bunk.

"Five hours from now. It is smart to wait until then." The woman leaned against the counter and began eating from the bowl. "I can send you off with something for the pain, but it will be difficult with that suit." She nodded her head as she spoke. "That is a nice suit you have there. Better than the clunkers we have. Benefits of living beyond the border I guess."

"A friend made it for me. From *their* technology." Cordelia didn't have to say who 'they' were, it was understood she was speaking about the Amboians.

Deona nodded again while spooning more soup into her mouth.

Cordelia grabbed her suit and turned the leg inside out to inspect the tear in the pocket lining; it had been patched already. "I guess I need to thank you once more," Cordelia said, holding Deona's work.

"Again, nothing, but you are welcome." Deona set the bowl down. "That wound on your leg wouldn't have been as bad, but I think when you first opened the pocket some of the Fog got into it. Then when the plate broke the Fog spread into the leg and affected the wound. You're lucky you didn't lose your leg."

Deona was right. She hadn't even thought of that, it was no wonder the pain had been so intense. She had been far enough from the border that the intensity of the Haze was diminished but could still do damage to exposed skin.

"I saw, something, in the H—the Fog," she began. Inside the Perimeter they called it the Haze, but out here it was the Fog. "They looked like large dogs, covered in scales, or something. There were three of them, but only one had followed me."

"Followed you? Here?" Worry crossed Deona's face.

"No, not here. Just a short time after they heard me. I hid though and it moved on."

"You *hid* from one of those things? No one hides from those Fog Hounds."

"So, they *are* dogs? Fog Hounds?" Cordelia put her suit back up on the top bunk and sat in the chair next to the bed.

"Everyone has a different name for them, Stone Dogs, Fog Beast. There are many." Deona's pointer finger tapped her other open palm with each name. "Doesn't matter what you call those things, all that matters is that you stay clear of them. I've only ever seen one up close, and that's because it was already dead." She turned around and took the pot of stew off the cook top and set her bowl in a deep metal sink. She turned around and dragged another chair to sit next to Cordelia, a small table at her left stood between them.

Deona sat back in her chair and sighed. "Their skin is as hard as stone, hence the name, I couldn't pierce it with a sharpened blade. I would have tried testing a bullet on it, but I wasn't sure that there weren't others in the area, and I couldn't bring myself to use a bullet. I have no idea where they came from, but a few years ago there were some rumors of packs of wolves roaming the Fog. No one took it seriously. How could any animal survive out there?" Another sigh. It was an odd thing to talk about. Beasts in the fog.

"The reports of supply caravans being attacked were the only proof anyone needed. A young man returned to Mountain Station from Tunnel Outpost, babbling about wolves in the Fog, and how everyone was dead. They just thought he had been separated from the team and was frightened. Then he showed them the remains of his team.

205

He had dragged the bodies, or what was left, on a sled he had made from tree branches. He kept saying he couldn't leave them behind for the beasts."

Cordelia didn't know what to say. Was the Fog diminishing enough to allow animals to survive? It definitely hadn't harmed her as much as it would have a few years ago, or so she was told. Her grandmother told her that when she was a child she and a friend were running in the mountains, admittedly where they shouldn't have been, and her friend fell from an outcrop and into the Fog below. Later a team was sent down to recover the body, but there wasn't much to recover. The Fog had dissolved a majority of the girl. There were some skeletal remains with muscle and sinew still attached. The girl hadn't been in the Fog for more than half an hour, but it was enough to almost destroy her completely.

"I have to get to my grandmother." Cordelia stood up and carefully tested her weight on her leg again. Deona had done excellent work. "I need to understand what's been going on and help if I can. If there has been a division in our people, we have to do something about it before more people get hurt."

"You can't leave now child." Deona stood up as well. "It's still hours before sun up, and if you saw what you saw, you didn't escape them. They have likely been following you since your encounter." She stepped closer. "They are smart, these beasts. They move in packs, exhaust their prey, and attack."

"I limped for *fifteen miles*, with a shard sticking out of my leg and a cane to support me. If they didn't attack me then, I think I'll be okay." Cordelia was putting her legs through the pants of her suit. Carefully. "You said you have pain medicine I could use?"

"Everyone is a fool!" Deona threw her hands in the air and walked into the back room. She came back only minutes later while Cordelia was attempting to seal the back of the suit up as best she could by herself. "Take two of these pills now. They should last until you reach the Fog Horizon, then take two more if you need to. From there you should only need one or two tomorrow. If the pain continues have the doctors at the Station take a look at you."

"Thank you, Deona." Cordelia stopped and looked into the woman's dark eyes. "I would likely be dead if not for you."

"You are welcome, Cordelia Faucher." A thin smile stretched across the woman's face. "Give Theresa and the other Elders my regards."

There was a solid metal noise as the locks engaged on the massive door behind her. Cordelia hit the switch on her forearm to bring up the suit's system information:

Oxygen remaining: 6 hours.

Suit Integrity:

Internal Environment: Compromised

Suit Exterior: Uncompromised

Heart Rate: 78 BPM

Even with Deona's patch job on the suit she didn't trust opening the sealed pocket again. With a good pace she could get up the mountain and out of the Haze before running out of oxygen. She found herself thanking Jaeger for increasing the oxygen capacity in her tank. She activated the lights on her helmet and began moving toward the stairs.

CHAPTER FIFTEEN

The Council

C ouncilor Ruintael's voice was becoming more recognizable to Carter's ears. "What of the attacks on the Eastern Perimeter?" He was a member of the Military Branch. "Is there any confirmation that these attackers are coming from beyond the Perimeter?"

"Most of the reports are from the victims. There have been descriptions of what sound like rudimentary breathing apparatuses worn by the attackers." That was Gaelcean responding. Carter could pick his voice out the easiest.

He ran a finger over the bump behind his left ear and glanced over to where Paelle was seated among the rest of the Council. She had described how the translating device worked while she was fitting the implant beneath his skin. Between her complex explanation of the device's function, and the feeling of her tools working within the side of his numbed head, he had found it difficult to absorb the information *and* comprehend it all. Afterward, Weleya had simplified how it worked for him; it was a real-time translating device that was connected to the part of his brain that processed auditory information.

Carter pulled himself back into the conversation as Gaelcean was finishing a thought. "...We should be prepared to send aid if needed." There were a series of mumbles, and a few groans.

Several Amboians were seated in metal high-backed chairs around a large ring-shaped table. Each represented various branches of the Council they belonged to. The Council hadn't yet been fully explained to Carter in its entirety. He had come to understand that there were several branches: Diplomatic, Military, Science and Technology, Agriculture and Industry, and Finance. No other branch seemed of higher position than another, and in many cases, there seemed to be some overlap. Of these branches in the Council there were at least one representative at each meeting, and sometimes several from one branch outnumbered the combined members of the other branches. Who was in attendance and how many from each group always varied. Within those groups, Carter had come to assume the eldest was the leader, but this wasn't always the case. For example, Paelle seemed to do most of the speaking for the Science and Technology Branch and had been present at every meeting Carter had been to so far. Other than the seven Councilors present, there were several Council Guards stationed around the circumference of the room behind their respective Councilor.

The large oval-shaped room had a tall domed ceiling. On the opposite side of the room from Carter, a large glass window began at the floor and followed the curvature up some twenty or so feet. He could see out across the Upper District, over the Lower District and out into the New Ring. There were hardly any clouds in the sky this afternoon, but the midday sun wasn't felt in the cool Council Hall. Smooth, floors met dark blue-gray walls. Banners were layered in concentric arcs around the domed ceiling.

Weleya had explained that when an Amboian was selected to sit on the Council, a banner was raised in the Hall to

209

represent their place among its members. Some Amboians had been members of the Council for quite some time it had seemed. There were banners that were old and tattered while others seemed to have been put up recently. Carter knew the Amboian lifespan was much longer than a Human, but it seemed rude to directly asked the age of any members of the Council.

Gaelcean's banner had been easy to pick out after Weleya had described it to him the first time they had entered the Hall. It was one of the more tattered banners among the few at the top of the domed room. He didn't need to look up to see it now. The symbol was solid in his memory. The banner itself was a dark green, that reminded him of the forests that were out in the New Ring. A white circle surrounded a light pinkish-brown bird, with light-gray wings. The wings were speckled with a few black spots, and its tail feathers were long and tapered toward the end.

Carter felt a pang of guilt for letting his mind wander, but there was hardly any reason for him to be on full guard here up in the Council Hall. As if she knew his mind had wandered, Weleya made a sound in her throat that brought Carter back. *Do androids even need to clear their throats?*

"Our yields from this harvest will not meet demands as is." Gurae, a member of Agriculture and Industry, looked at several data pads strewn out on the table as he spoke. "I do not see how we could send extra aid to these...*victims*." Carter almost became angry at the sophistication of the translator allowing him to hear the skepticism in the Councilor's voice. To him it didn't matter whether or not these attackers were from this side of the Perimeter or the other, people were being murdered, and villages pillaged. Something had to be done about it.

He wasn't the only one in the room to pick up on Gurae's skepticism. An old Amboian seated next to Gurae put a hand on his and brought his attention away from the information on his data pads. Carter could hear the age in Aecar's voice as

210

she spoke, "Perhaps we can send a trusted member out to the Perimeter to collect information for us, so we can have some certainty." Carter was still learning to read the Amboians, and for a moment it was almost as if Gurae's face had darkened. Whether it was out of anger or embarrassment was difficult to tell.

Gaelcean turned around in his chair to face Carter who was standing behind him and smiled. Reading the other Amboians may have been tough for him, but he had spent enough of the past few days with Gaelcean to get a good understanding of the Amboian's unspoken words. Out of the corner of his eye he could see Weleya to his right, who was also looking at him. Then he realized several of the Council members that were seated at the large circular table were looking in his direction.

"Gaelcean if you want to send your Human out beyond the walls on the Council's behalf, I *will* have to speak out against it." This was another member of the Military Council, Rylae. He was the younger of the two military representatives. Rylae hadn't been afraid to express his lack of trust in Carter. It was likely extended to all Humans, and surely extended beyond a lack of trust. Before Carter had joined the City Guard, he felt enmity between Humans and Amboians. He became increasingly aware of it as he found himself rising to his current position.

Rylae was reminiscent of the Knight who had trained Carter. He was tall even for an Amboian, and while every Amboian had dark eyes, Rylae's seemed darker than most. His cerulean skin lacked the signs of age that Ruintael and Aecar and Gaelcean's had shown. Carter had thought Gaelcean had no signs of his age until he met younger Amboians like Rylae and Paelle and Gurae. It had become clear who the elders were.

Ruintael and Gaelcean responded at the same time, and Gaelcean held an open hand to his fellow Councilor and nodded. Ruintael nodded in response and began again. "If we

211

must send someone to confirm the events of the Perimeter, why not send Weleya?" The eyes of the room shifted toward her, even Carter glanced over. Weleya's face looked like it was carved from stone. Did she ever feel worried or uncertain?

"Weleya must stay in the capital with me, as will Carter. I am confident in either of their abilities, but I cannot have my personal security running around the New Ring collecting information for us." Standing behind Gaelcean made it difficult to see his face. Carter could hear his smile as he spoke. He always seemed to keep his composure.

"While we are on the matter of those that live beyond our Perimeter." Council member Maecell leaned in as she spoke and looked toward Rylae and Ruintael. "Is there any news from your forward scouting teams?" Carter wasn't exactly sure what Maecell's official position on the council was. From the meetings Carter had been present for he believed she was a member of the Financial Branch.

"Reports come in slowly." Ruintael was scrolling through data pads. "In the South, they are still mapping the freshwater lakes that were discovered. The western scouts have yet to find an end to the Great Sea, but their reports are slightly worrisome." Ruintael looked up from his data pad to Gaelcean and glanced at Carter.

Gaelcean pulled a small device from his coat sleeve and pressed a button on it twice. There was a rushing sound in Carter's ears, then silence, then his hearing returned. Now when the Council members spoke all Carter could hear was the complex Amboian language. It had been decided during the first meeting that he had been present for, that there were somethings that he couldn't know. There was a word, a sound really, that Carter had heard enough to know it meant Human, or that it related to Humanity.

Beneath the table in front of him Carter saw Gaelcean's hand slide into a sleeve and once again his ears filled with a rushing sound. His hearing returned as Gaelcean began to speak. "I believe with our current situation at hand, worrying about these reports does not take precedence. However, if there is a *cetraeptus* in the water, we should not let an *ursaemont* take our full attention. What did the scout's report say exactly?" There were a few nods and noises of agreement after Gaelcean spoke. Carter wondered for a moment if the translator was having trouble with some of the words had been used. *Maybe there was no direct translation?* He would have to ask about these creatures another time.

Ruintael looked at his data pad again before speaking. "Several large metal objects breached the waters off the coast. They surfaced for a moment and then returned below. The scouts think they may have been inspecting them, but it is possible it was coincidental, and they were not seen. The environmental hazard at that distance is less present, but still obscures sight at range." The environmental hazard Ruintael spoke of was the Haze. Aside from Gaelcean, the council members always seemed to avoid acknowledging it whenever possible.

"Is it possible that these metal ships are related to the groups we know of that reside to the east?" Maecell still leaned forward as she spoke. She didn't seem concerned, but genuinely curious.

Gurae had lost interest and was scrolling through data pads again, while Aecar listened as intently. Carter had a hard time reading Paelle's expression. Rylae's seemed one of anger. His lips compressed flat, and his jaw clenched.

"We cannot be certain, but none of those settlements seem to have the means to make such ships. The scouts made note of the location on their maps and continued further west along the northern coast. They should be starting the return trip and arrive before the snows impede their travel." Ruintael's tone dismissed any further discussion.

"I look forward to the full report. Although, I believe we have more pressing matters to focus on." Gaelcean feigned hitting the device and turned to Carter. He gave a small nod in reply and Gaelcean continued. "I think we should prepare to assist the Perimeter villages and towns who need our help. They cannot protect themselves, and if we refuse to, we will lose their support."

There were a series of murmurs; it was clear there was no consensus. Finally, Ruintael spoke. "It is my understanding that East Edge has one of the larger town guards of the settlements beyond the walls. Even still, they are surely not properly trained and require assistance. Perhaps we could pull resources from some of the other settlements and direct them toward the Eastern Perimeter, led by some of the Knights of Amboy of course."

"Waste *our* Knights on..." The words shot of out Rylae, until his eyes fell on Carter again. "I do not see the point of sending valuable soldiers to deal with what seems to be a handful of brigands."

Ruintael looked at Rylae in a way that Carter guessed was either disappointment or anger, perhaps a combination of the two.

"Let us see what the inquiry into the reports of the attacks reveal. Then we can make a measured decision on how to react." Maecell took the time to acknowledge the other six Council members in the room as she spoke. All returned equal attention. Even Gurae looked up from his data pads when Maecell spoke.

There was a summation of actions that needed to be addressed before the next Council meeting and Gaelcean called for an official end to the session. Some members wasted no time leaving, while others took time to speak to each other. As Gaelcean stood he motioned to Carter and Weleya to follow him. The three walked across the room toward Rylae and Ruintael, who were gathering their things from the table.

"I was wondering if the two of you had a moment to speak." Carter and Weleya stood on either side of Gaelcean as he addressed Ruintael and Rylae. It was merely formality. Carter couldn't imagine a Council meeting getting so heated

214

that any of the personal guard would need to get involved. He wouldn't want to find himself in combat against Ruintael or Rylae's personal guard. *Council Guards fighting in the Hall?* He would have laughed at the thought if the two other Council Guards had not approached.

Zaenin and Oralaen had augmentations much like Weleya, but unlike her and Carter they were Amboian. *Was Weleya considered Human to them?* Zaenin and Oralaen were as physically opposite as two Amboians could appear. Zaenin was slender and short, for an Amboian, only a few inches taller than Carter. She had ornate plate armor on her entire body up to the pale blue skin of her neck and head. On her breastplate was Rylae's crest. The profile of the head of some roaring long-toothed beast. Maybe this was the *ursaemont* Gaelcean had mentioned. Oralaen easily stood two feet taller than Carter. He wore the same plate armor as Zaenin. His armor lacked a crest, but a large pin kept his cloak pinned around his broad shoulders; a shield with two swords crossed behind. His blue-violet face was also expressionless and hard. Weleya had mentioned Zaenin and Oralaen had mark fourteen modifications, or so she believed. He wasn't sure what the differences were with each new generation of android. Perhaps it had something to do with the quality of the technology that ran the augmentations.

The chip behind his ear and the one in his arm were of the latest generation. Was he technically an android now? The thought hadn't occurred to him until now. He wasn't sure how to feel about it. He pushed the thoughts aside for the time being.

"Of course, Gaelcean." Ruintael gave his full attention, but Rylae continued to gather his things. Oralaen followed behind Ruintael's left as he approached.

"I wanted to speak a bit more on the extent of what we can do about these attacks on the Perimeter," Gaelcean said.

Rylae scoffed and stopped organizing his things. He stood and approached them. "Let us not speak of the absurdity of this any longer. I feel enough council time has been wasted today." Zaenin stepped forward and stood to his right. Carter didn't have to look to know that Gaelcean had kept his composure; the Amboian was unbreakable.

Ruintael shook his head slightly and let out a breath through the slits of his nose.

"Rylae, I have always appreciated your ability to stand behind your conviction so strongly." As Gaelcean spoke, a smile beginning to spread across Rylae's face. "I only wish you would focus your indomitable will in other areas."

"Rylae, see that our things are returned to the branch quarters. I will speak with Gaelcean a moment and be with you shortly." Ruintael didn't look at Rylae as he spoke, and it seemed there was no need. Rylae nodded and turned to gather his things. Zaenin shadowed him as they left. Even the fluidity of her leaving the room seemed threatening.

"I have been his mentor for half of his time, yet I feel he grasps a fraction of what I teach." If an Amboian could appear beside themselves, Ruintael seemed to begin to show the slightest hint of it. His stoicism quickly returned. "What would you like to speak of, Gaelcean?"

"If we must send aid to the Eastern Perimeter, I would like to know what thoughts you might have on the matter."

"I do not know their exact numbers, but East Edge is one of the larger settlements in the New Ring. Their own town guard should be enough protection for the surrounding area. If needed, Humans from Athanelle and Homestead could be moved to bolster the towns and villages." Ruintael didn't speak with the same heat as Rylae did about the matter, but Carter noticed that he mentioned only sending Humans. Not the Knights or even Amboian City Guard.

"I see. You are also against sending aid from the capital itself then?"

"Yes. For the time being." There was a pause, then Ruintael added. "If there is need for more, of course we cannot let anyone go on without. We must look after all we

216

are tasked with protecting." At that Ruintael looked to Carter and nodded.

"Indeed." Gaelcean held a handout for Ruintael, who immediately received it. Their hands grasped the other's wrist, while the free hand clasped the other on the shoulder. Carter had seen this many times before when Amboians were saying their goodbyes.

"Until next we meet, Gaelcean. Shield protect us."

"Shield protect us, Ruintael."

Carter and Weleya followed Gaelcean out of the Council Hall. The short hallway was lined with speed lifts. They stopped at the first available lift and Gaelcean pressed three buttons in unison that would take them to the floor where his quarters were. To Carter's left he heard a door open and saw Maecell give a slight nod in their direction. Her personal guard enter the room before her and then gestured for her to follow after he looked around. *Gaegan was his name*, Carter thought. His light-blue skin was wrinkled slightly, and his eyes seemed a touch more gray than black. He may have been old for an Amboian, but Carter could only guess at the modifications that the guard had undergone that would allow him to protect his Councilor.

"She says she took that modest room as her quarters for the view." Gaelcean smiled in return and lowered his voice. "I believe she has gotten too old to go any further than the distance between the Hall and that room." He shook his head as they stepped into the open doors of the lift.

"Everything must rest." Carter hadn't even meant to say it out loud. Gaelcean looked over his shoulder and nodded.

The three were standing shoulder to shoulder looking out of the lift as the doors closed. Carter felt his insides shift upwards as the lift sped downward. He would have to get used to that sooner than later. Symbols flashed on a screen to the right, and above the door as they sped past floors of

Amboy Central.

"Unfortunately, neither of you shall be resting just yet."
Gaelcean sounded almost apologetic. "Weleya, has there been
any news from our friends in the Port?"

"Nothing yet. They most likely arrived early today or
yesterday. If their previous work set a standard, I trust they
will not return empty-handed."

"Excellent. In the meantime, I have some more work for
you in the Lower District. Another possible thread to pluck."

Carter had gotten use to the two of them speaking this
way; if there was anything that he needed to know they would
have told him.

"While Weleya is running errands for me, you will stay by
my side, Carter. I may have you bring your things to my
chambers so you can make yourself more available to me if
the need arises. I have several spare rooms you may make
your own."

Nothing else was said as the lift traveled downward. The
doors opened to Gaelcean's floor where his entire living and
work area was contained. Gaelcean and Weleya stepped out
while Carter remained behind. Gaelcean gave instructions on
how to return and sent him off.

The lift doors opened once again to the Council Security
floor where Carter and many of the other security members
of his rank lived. All Amboian or technologically augmented
Amboian. Carter walked down the gray hallway avoiding all
the dark eyes that seemed to lock onto him. He stopped at
the gray door that muscle memory brought him to. It slid
open to a windowless room.

Although he had been here several days now it looked as
though no one had ever moved in. He tapped the wall and it
slid outward into the room. Three long-sleeve shirts, two
short sleeve, and three pairs of dark-brown pants. He picked
up his clothing and put everything into his pack. He tied his
extra pair of boots to the pack and tossed it on his back. He
lifted the chest that contained his armor from the storage

space. He was still surprised by how light it was. He looked around the room. There was nothing else. He turned to exit the room and looked back before the door closed. He muttered under his breath about sending it all to the Haze. Not as quietly as he had thought as two passing Amboians had a hitch in their step. He paid them no mind and continued back to the lift that would bring him above all of the judging eyes.

CHAPTER SIXTEEN

Homecoming

T he wind that passed through the mountains was calm. The Haze Horizon was only a few feet below where Cordelia sat on a rocky outcrop. It churned like a soil-ridden lake. Far off in the distance she could see the soft blue-green glow of the Shield rising out of the Haze. From this distance she could barely make out the shine of the Shield Generators.

She twisted the cap off the small vial Deona gave her and shook the vial over her opened hand. Two small blue pills tumbled out. They had done their job. She hadn't felt any pain from the injury to her leg the entire day. It had been a concern at first, not being able to feel the pain had made her think she had been about to lose consciousness.

As she continued through the early morning and began the long hike into the mountains, she found her rhythm. She fell into a trance-like state as one booted foot fell in front of the other. Before she had realized it, she had breached the surface of the Haze and the sun had begun to set. What little light was left from the sun wouldn't last. She still had to hike a few more miles before reaching the outer fences of

Mountain Station. Her home.

Cordelia stood up. She twisted her torso and stretched her arms up over her head. She let out a long sigh as she picked up her helmet off the rocky ground next to her. She turned away from the Haze and the Shield in the distance and began to walk up the trail behind her. She had been surprised how easy she found hiking the mountain. *Could be the pain killers.* Crisp cool air filled her lungs. Her suit was unzipped to the waist and the sleeves tied around to keep them out of the way as she hiked. Carrying the helmet was a bit of an annoyance, but it was better than wearing it. She had tucked the encased ball into the folds of her suit, so she didn't have to carry that as well.

The long journey up the mountain had given her time to think about what she was going to ask her grandmother. Why was this group attacking the Perimeter villages and towns? How did it come to this? What are their numbers?

"Who is that out there?" A shout from the trees ahead of her pulled her from her thoughts. Instinctively she fell to the rocky path at her feet and shuffled into the trees. "I've already seen you! Come on out!" Twigs snapped as the owner of the voice began moving closer.

If there *had* been a division of some kind this person might not be friendly. "My name is Cordelia Faucher! Theresa Faucher is my grandmother!" She shouted as she leaned her back against a tree and readied her short blade. There was no response. The footsteps continued closer. "Who are you?" Maybe she shouldn't have announced herself. Short blade at the ready, Cordelia leapt out from behind the tree and lunged toward the person facing her. She grabbed the long barrel of a rifle in one hand and pushed it up and away from her as she brought the edge of her blade to the throat of the person.

"Cordelia, it *is* you!" the man yelped. "Take it easy."

She pulled the blade away from the neck of the man almost as immediately as she had brought it there. He was slightly taller than her. The sunlight that found its way through the trees behind her was enough to make out his warm brown eyes. A short-trimmed beard covered the strong jaw she remembered. His dark hair was kept back under a very old-looking cap. He brought his long rifle to his shoulder and smiled.

"Landon?" Cordelia smiled when she recognized her childhood friend. "I didn't hurt you, did I? I wasn't sure if…" She trailed off. She still wasn't sure of the situation; maybe he had gotten caught up in whatever trouble had been going on.

"I'm fine. I wasn't sure if you were actually who you said you were." His laugh was reassuring. "It's been what? Five or six years? I'm surprised to see you up here."

"Yeah, that's about right." As much as she wanted to catch up with an old friend, now wasn't the time. "Can you take me to my grandmother? It's important that I see her right away."

Landon stared back; seconds felt like hours.

"Of course. You've heard of the rebellion." He let out a long sigh. He seemed lost in thought as he turned away and began walking. She followed. He looked over his shoulder as he spoke. "Unfortunate circumstances, but really is nice to see you after these years."

Landon Williams was only a few years older than Cordelia. That beard that he had grown made it seem much more than that. When she had decided to leave Mountain Station, Landon had joined the scouting teams. As kids they had both talked of joining the Mountain Station Scouts and Sentries together.

Landon hadn't only stuck with his plan, but quickly moved up the ranks. He now was responsible for multiple Deep Scout teams.

"Sounds about right." Cordelia chuckled.

"I imagine you'd probably have a few teams of your own right now. That, or you'd be sitting in with the Elders and running this place." If Landon had turned around, he would have seen her roll her eyes. Even though he wouldn't have noticed, she quickly regained her composure. Just in case. They weren't kids anymore and she wasn't going to let his prodding get to her.

"My mother may have left to lead at Lake Outpost, but that doesn't immediately make me next in line for a seat with the Elders." *Although.* If things were anything like they had been before she had left, a person had good odds of being elected if they had the last name of any of the families who had founded Mountain Station. *If there's a Founding Family among the Elders, things must be in good hands.* Or something like that. She had heard it all the time growing up.

"So, you've heard about the rebellion, and Frances leaving the Station to lead Lake Outpost. Who have you been in contact with since you left?"

"I met one of the safe house caretakers during my travels."

Landon stopped walking and turned toward her. "Who was it?"

She felt a tingling up her spine and her hand reflexively went toward the blade at her hip again. "A woman named Deona." She returned his icy stare.

Landon relaxed as soon as he heard the name. "Deona is a good woman. I'm glad you found her and not someone else. Lines have been drawn, but it's too early to tell who's on which side."

"Who's responsible for the raids on the other side?" The other side, not the New Ring. Not up here.

"I only know what the Deep Scouts bring back, and that's usually what they hear from other teams." He gave a small shrug before he turned and continued the hike up the trail.

The two hiked in silence until Landon spoke up again. He seemed hesitant. The Deep Scouts were normally taken on their word when they gave reports, had that changed?

"I'm not even sure where to begin." Another pause. "There was a failed coup at Tunnel Outpost. They thought that we should organize the Scouts and Sentries into an army of sorts." Landon let out a loud grunt as he hoisted himself up onto a boulder at the base of a rock face. "Apparently, they wanted to strike at the settlements on the other side." He stretched a hand down to Cordelia as he continued. "Like I said, they failed. So, they left Tunnel Outpost. I've heard reports they took over a few safe houses west of Tunnel Outpost."

On top of the rock face Cordelia took a moment to gather herself. The safe houses these attackers occupied would put them right between Tunnel Outpost and East Edge. "Are there any reports on their numbers? When I was making my way east, I found a camp that suggested there were fifteen or so that were on the other side."

The ground began to level off and the trail became more dirt than rock. The path allowed Cordelia to walk beside Landon now. She lengthened her stride to catch up to him.

"I've heard anywhere from fifty to seventy, and that doesn't include those who aren't a part of the raiding parties." He stared off into the distance.

Seventy.

Cordelia tripped on a tree root that crossed the path. Landon snapped from his trance to grab her forearm and their pace was kept. "Seventy, not including those who aren't in the raiding parties. How certain are you of what you've heard regarding their plans to attack?"

"I'm not. Sometimes a story about a wolf pup, becomes a story about a pack."

"The pack exists, I'm sure. I have heard some rumors on my side of things too." She cringed at saying *my side* and hoped Landon hadn't picked up any deeper meaning. He nodded in reply.

She hadn't been expecting a huge welcoming upon her return, though shortly after being let through the outer defenses there were greetings coming from the simple wooden houses that made up the outermost parts of Mountain Station. At first she had assumed the warm

224

welcomes were for Landon's return from scouting. The occasional gasp followed by a comment on how much time had passed since they had last spoke, had proven otherwise. There were comments that she had seemed to have grown up so much it was a wonder how they must have appeared to her. All of the commotion didn't cause Landon to slow their pace. All the while he remained polite and returned the greetings from the crowd.

"Not much seems to have changed since I left." Cordelia returned a wave as she walked beside Landon along a dirt and pine needle path between the small wooden houses.

Once the livable space inside the station had been used up and the Haze had receded down to the lower elevations, houses began popping up around the underground bunker. As time went on and the houses and other buildings that had been constructed farther from the station received less attention. There was an odd trade-off between safety in numbers and scarcity of resources. District Eight flashed into Cordelia's thoughts for a moment. She pushed it away. She was no longer in the capital, she was home.

"Up here, not much, no. I'd be willing to bet the Outposts might think otherwise."

As they continued to walk, the number of houses and other small buildings began increasing, though not by much. The quality of the construction had improved since entering the outer fence. On the surface Mountain Station would be comparable to any of the larger villages within the New Ring. Nothing to the scale of a town like Homestead, or even East Edge. However, if the subterranean metal labyrinth of what was the original Mountain Station were included, this settlement would match a town like East Edge.

Just ahead of them, two massive metal doors were swung outward from a square opening in the side of the mountain. Within the square opening was a smaller metal door that led to the main hallway of the Station.

As Cordelia stepped into the hallway behind Landon their

footsteps echoed on the metal floor. The weather up in the mountains had been significantly cooler than within the New Ring, and now walking down these narrow hallways made her shiver and untied her sleeves from her waist and shrugged them on.

"The Elders should be in dining hall now." Landon slipped into a doorway and Cordelia pressed herself against the cool wall as they let a leathery-faced man walk by. He gave a grumble in thanks as he passed. "They've been meeting almost every day to discuss what should be done, if anything."

If anything? She almost grabbed Landon's arm in anger, only stopping herself once her hand had moved. Reacting before she knew the full story wouldn't help her here.

They stopped here and there to answer many of the same questions they had received when they had passed through the outer fences. Some had thought that Landon had found Cordelia wandering in the Haze. Did they think she had survived in the Haze alone for this long? For a moment she felt anger creeping up. If they knew what she had accomplished by herself this far.

The narrow hallway opened up into a large room filled with tables of varying sizes, materials, and styles. Along the left side of the room was a receiving line for meals; a metal counter space with square-shaped wells allowed for the kitchen staff to drop trays of food along the line. On the other side of the receiving line several of the workers were moving about the space with steaming pots and tossing used pans and utensils into a deep metal sink with a running faucet. Judging by the smells they were preparing some sort of stew for dinner tonight. Her stomach groaned as the scent spread through the room.

"Have you eaten today?" A small smile was spreading across Landon's face. Her stomach must have been louder than she thought.

"I'm fine." There was a pause. "For now." Cordelia tried

not to smile back. She couldn't help but feel a sense of comfort being here.

Only one table was occupied at the moment. Seven Elders sat at a large rectangular table at the back of the room. One on either end, and five on one side facing the room so she could make out all their faces.

On the leftmost end from Cordelia's point of view sat Arnold Reed; sparse gray hair covered the top of his head while the rest of his short hair was combed neatly. He leaned forward in his chair with arms folded on the table in front of him. His blue eyes watched the conversation intently as he listened. There was Rene Harris, her long black hair flowing behind her as she sat with eyes closed seemingly asleep. Even when it seemed like Rene was miles off, she was absorbing everything. Samuel Greene was hurriedly writing in a large leather-bound book, head down, showing the top of his tan bald head. Occasionally stopping to stroke his brown beard with one hand while the other tapped his pen on the table. Once her eyes fell on the person seated at the center, she smiled. The woman stared right back at her with a warm smile on her face, as well.

"Everyone's attention for a moment." Her grandmother's voice carried across the room and even the movement in the kitchen had ceased. They returned to their work once they realized they weren't the ones being spoken to. Theresa Faucher put her hands on the table and stood up. For a woman who was well into her eighties she carried herself as if she were decades younger. "My granddaughter has come to visit us." She moved out from behind the wooden table and moved toward Cordelia with open arms.

"It is so good to see you again, grandmother," Cordelia said as the two embraced. Theresa was shorter than she remembered. Her long gray hair was woven into a braid that extended past her waist.

"I'm glad you've come. We can catch up afterward, but right now I'm afraid we could use your assistance on a matter." Lines led from the corners of her eyes as she smiled. Theresa's deep green eyes were almost identical to her own. There was another saying Cordelia struggled to remember from her childhood, something about all Fauchers having the same trustworthy green eyes. Or was it commanding green eyes?

Before she could say another word, her grandmother had a firm grip on her wrist and was walking her toward the table she had just come from. Cordelia turned back toward Landon, who was shrugging and trying very hard to keep a smile from his face. *It was probably commanding eyes.*

"You all remembered my granddaughter, Cordelia, of course," Theresa half said to the table as she pulled up a chair opposite the one she had been sitting in before. Once Cordelia was settled in her chair Theresa took her seat on the other side of the table from her. The way the seating was arranged she felt like she was on trial, rather than someone who was being asked to give assistance.

"You look well, child." Rene's eyes opened for a moment while she spoke and smiled.

"Indeed! Very well. You must tell me all about your travels on the other side when you have some time." Samuel had a kind smile and a soothing voice. Cordelia returned all of their welcomes with all the politeness she could find, maybe even overdoing it a bit in some cases.

Theresa cut in before any of the others could speak again. "Where to begin? During one of the Gatherings, many months ago, a new representative from Tunnel Outpost arrived to speak on their behalf. This was this first I had ever met the man, Dimitri Endano. He was very demanding and dominated the meeting for the first day. He was adamant that the other Outposts who had met certain standard be raised to the same level as Mountain Station. He believed that Tunnel Outpost had reached these standards he set. That wasn't surprising." There were scoffs in agreement from the table. Rene shook her head, eyes still closed. "He also believed that

228

Tunnel Outpost should start training some of their Scout and Sentry members into more of an offensive direction." Theresa took her time with her words as she spoke.

"The fool man wanted to start an army." Samuel was shaking his head, his long beard trailing behind his movements.

"It certainly seemed so." Theresa sighed. "There was clear disagreement. Not one other representative, or member of this group stood with his ideas. If anything, I would have thought there would have been support from the Ruins Outpost. The Amboian border has been encroaching upon them as much as it has the Tunnel."

"You should have seen the way your mother reacted, Cordelia." Arnold's blue eyes seemed to shine as he spoke. "She was about to knock sense into him as if he was a child, and not a man in his middle years." He chuckled.

"My mother was here?" Cordelia looked to Theresa.

"Yes, Frances was here. It seems she's not only taken charge of the operation of Lake Outpost but sees to representing it at the Gatherings." The pride in Theresa's voice was undoubted.

"What happened after that? How many days did the Gathering meet?" Cordelia could ask about her mother later, right now she needed more information on this Dimitri Endano and his followers.

The proud look on Theresa's face dissolved as she recalled. "Dimitri was present for the two days that followed. He didn't have any outbursts like the first day and didn't try to control the focus of the meeting. When we asked for information regarding current population at Tunnel Outpost, he gave it. We asked if they were meeting their quotas on food and other necessities, and he talked for a moment about projections he had made. Based on his data, Tunnel Outpost, and the surrounding smaller settlements would be at risk of starvation by the year's end."

"They never could manage to get their hydroponic farms

229

to produce the maximum yield." Cordelia looked to her right at Selene Moore. Her hair had more silver than Cordelia remembered and there seemed to be more lines around her eyes. Once a member joined the Elders they retired from their previous roles at the station. That didn't seem to stop Selene from thinking from the perspective the position she once held.

"Dimitri stressed it was more than that." Theresa picked up right as Selene finished. That was the way they all spoke, one after another as if they all shared the same thoughts. "While the parallel tunnels they settled in provide them safety, it seems they are beginning to run out of space. Dimitri suggested a portion of the population be moved here. While we are certainly the most well off of all of the settlements, I'm sure you saw we have our own limitations on space as well."

"You should have seen the way the Ruins Outpost responded to that. Hah!" Arnold hit his fist into an open palm.

"There was a *fight?*" Cordelia couldn't contain her shock. There had been times at the Gatherings where voices were raised, but there was never violence.

"Of course not!" Theresa snapped at Arnold. "Arnold, you have always had a knack for embellishment."

A wry smile appeared on Arnold's face. A vision of the two, decades younger and speaking as close friends flashed into Cordelia's imagination. She had to strain to stifle a laugh.

"No, there was no fight, but I imagine there could have been." Arnold folded his forearms and leaned forward onto the table once more.

"If we don't mind." Rene opened her eyes and sat forward. "I could summarize the events leading up to the division and the attacks. I believe the kitchen is about ready to serve the first round of dinner, and I must admit I am rather hungry." There were murmurs of agreement from the table. Cordelia's stomach reminded her how hungry she was

230

herself. "Yes, well then. We found out that Dimitri had been operating unofficially as the representative for Tunnel Outpost. We had only found out when the actual representative had shown up days after the final meeting for that Gathering. Dimitri had somehow intercepted the invitation to the Gathering and altered the dates before sending it on. We then found out from the true representative that he had been trying to do the same at Tunnel Outpost, and when he couldn't get the Elders there to see things his way he left with a number of people."

Theresa broken in once more, "Since then, we believe he has continued to increase his numbers by visiting smaller settlements in the area. Knowing how tough it can be for those that actually live within the Fog, I can understand why some would follow him." Theresa laced her fingers together and brought her hands to her chin. "That brings us to you. What have you seen while you've been living within the Amboians' borders?"

All the eyes shifted to Cordelia. Even Rene was listening intently. She wanted to avoid using words that made it sound like they weren't on the same side, as she had before when talking to Landon. The Elders might not read into it the way she thought they might, but she still took her time and chose her words carefully. "I had always heard rumors of raiding parties hitting villages along the Peri- the Amboian border." She looked around the table. There seemed to be no acknowledgment of her correction that she could see. "However, within the past few weeks the number of raids seem to have increased, and even more recently there were murders. A village just south of a town called East Edge. I've heard there were three or four killed. I never got the chance to visit on my way here. I plan on finding out what I can when I go back though."

She wasn't sure how the Elders would react to her mentioning the raids. In the beginning it had been a priority to find out which settlement had been the cause of the raids

231

and those that carried them out had been reprimanded. As time went on less attention was paid. Some would rather it not be mentioned, and those that acknowledged the events only did so half-heartedly.

"Terrible, just terrible." Rene shook her head.

"What else, Cordelia?" Theresa's laced hands clenched.

"During my travel to East Edge, I came upon what may have been an old encampment. I can't be sure that it was these raiding parties, but if it was there seemed to be about fifteen of them moving together." She pictured the grassy depression where they had stopped to rest. She hoped Victor and Elina were safe. "A traveling companion of mine lives in East Edge, and another was heading to the village that had been attacked to offer her services."

She continued to think for a moment while the Elders spoke among themselves. She waited as long as she could manage before speaking again. "Do we know how many Dimitri has gathered?"

"Landon and his Deep Scouts have given us some insight, but we can't be certain." Samuel was looking through his leather-bound book as a bony finger glided across the pages.

"We should assume the worst." Theresa unclenched her hands, and they became fists as she put them on the table. "Reports say seventy, but I'm willing to bet the numbers are closer to one hundred. One hundred able-bodied men and women, who are following him and believe in his talk of forming an army."

"There are also those who are too old, or too young to fight. Those who choose not to fight. The numbers only increase." Samuel closed his book and rested his hands on the leather cover.

"When do you plan to leave us again, Cordelia?" It was only a simple question from her grandmother, but she felt a pang of guilt. "There is much we need you to learn for us, and we would ask that you return as soon as possible, or perhaps we could send another with you to return to us."

232

"I had hoped to stay for a few days, but with all that is happening and the uncertainty of everything. I should leave as soon as possible. I'm not sure when I'll be returning here again. Once I've learned what I can, it may be useful to have someone who can return with that information."

Theresa looked past her granddaughter's head to the man still standing on the opposite side of the room. "Landon? I'm sure you've heard our discussion. What do you think?"

Cordelia turned in her chair as Landon walked toward them.

"If I wasn't in charge of the teams, I'd offer to go myself." He stood next to her. She had to crane her neck to look up at him. "There's a Deep Scout team returning tomorrow. Andreas Martinez is among them. If I'm not able to go, he'll be the next best choice."

"That settles it then." Theresa stood up to signal an end to the conversation. "There isn't much daylight left, and dinner will be served any moment now. Tomorrow when the Deep Scout team arrives inform Andreas of his duties and see that he is able to rest. The day after that Cordelia and Andreas will make for the border. There is still much we do not know and the sooner we do the better."

"Knowing Andreas, he may not need the day to rest. In fact, I'm sure he'll be willing to head right back out shortly after their return." Landon stood feet apart, both hands resting on the wooden stock of his long rifle that was pointed into the floor.

"I don't doubt your Scouts but be sure that he understands what's at hand before we send anyone running off." Theresa rounded the table and put a hand on Landon's shoulder.

The sound of a bell ringing came from the kitchen, and a worker hurried over to a box on the wall. With a press of a button their voice carried throughout the station, as well as out of the loudspeakers at the entrance of the station, informing everyone that the first dinner shift was being

233

served and the second would be served shortly after.

Landon left the dining hall after he mentioned doing another round along the outer fence and that he needed to check on the guard posts. Samuel said he would take his food in his rooms, and that there was much to think on. The other Elders moved to the serving line to get their dinner.

After getting their meal, Cordelia and Theresa sat at a small table along the side of the room. Between mouthfuls, Cordelia told her grandmother everything she could remember about the past few years of her life. Her grandmother smiled and nodded while she ate her own meal, and occasionally asked a question or two. Cordelia needed a shower, and the thought of getting to sleep in a nice comfortable bed kept springing up in the back of her mind, but all that could wait. If there was any chance she would be leaving tomorrow, she wanted to make sure she had as much time as possible with the woman who helped raise her.

CHAPTER SEVENTEEN

Smoke Rising

It had been two days since Lucas sent an emergency message to the Amber Waves chapter in Homestead, and only one day since their reply. Five members from Homestead would be arriving tomorrow. Five. Lucas and Caleb had started The Amber Waves Company in Homestead almost twenty years ago. They had the largest number of garrisoned members. He rarely used his status in the Company to command others, but now he wished he had. With the reports of attacks increasing several had been hired or asked to offer protection in smaller towns in the east and north within the New Ring. *Five members, only five!*

"Five is better than none," Elina said.

Lucas hadn't realized he had been muttering aloud. He had almost forgotten that Elina was beside him. They had been walking around East Edge all morning so he could think. There had to be another way to get more members to East Edge soon. If he knew he would have received such little help, he would have just sent word to Caleb and the others in Port Amboy, if they were still even there. They could be back in the capital for all he knew. Maybe he should have sent word to Caleb anyway. It didn't matter now though, Lucas had to make do with what he had. If there was going to be an attack here in East Edge, there were preparations to be made. Lucas and Elina rounded a corner and turned onto one of the main streets.

Even in the early morning the town buzzed with activity. Cart drivers forced their way through the small crowds. A produce vendor had a stall set up outside his store front. The man yelled above the bustle in an attempt to pull in customers. Some of the traveling entertainers who were hired for the Harvest End festival had apparently stuck around. A man played a harp while a woman danced and sang. The tune sounded sad to Lucas, but the words he was able to hear as they passed seemed to tell a happier story. Something about finding a lost love or reuniting anyway.

"...Even if there were that many in the area surrounding the town, I would think someone would have reported seeing them move. Unless they are moving in smaller groups to these encampments. Small groups and constantly moving camp, that might explain it."

He hadn't even realized he stopped listening to Elina. All this frustration must have been getting to him. "What was that, again?" He glanced over to Elina, who was as stone faced as always. Annoyance peeked out for a moment in her eyes.

"The areas I've been scouting. Each time I find traces of an encampment the numbers vary. It seems as if there are anywhere from fifteen to twenty-five total."

She had turned out to be very resourceful. He found her taking care of tasks without him needing to ask. When they arrived, she had found rooms for them in an inn near the center of town, a place called the Old Oak. There was a massive oak tree that stood well above the second floor of the building where Lucas' room was. He hadn't spent much time in the place though. He needed to move so he could think. Elina's tracking skills had been useful as well. Before

236

they had met at his brother Fredrick's farm, she had already been scouting the forest around the town and found several places where she believed the raiders had been camped out.

Why did they stay in within the Perimeter so long? If they had been stealing food and supplies it would be difficult to constantly move all of it around without horses or wagons, and Elina hadn't seen sign of either. Unless they immediately fled into the Haze to drop off what they had managed to take. Word of the raids had increased since he had come to East Edge. It was difficult to discern which information was being repeated and exaggerated. He trusted the information Elina had given him. That was what he would have go on.

"Was there any sort of pattern to where they were camping or which villages they were hitting?" He regretted not lowering his voice a little as an old woman gave him a look that would have startled him if he hadn't been on guard. Everyone seemed to be talking about the attacks, maybe lowering his voice wouldn't make a difference.

"A pattern?" Elina scanned the long street as she spoke. As if she expected the raiders to appear from the crowd in front of them. "The encampments I found were mostly between East Edge and the Perimeter, occasionally there have been some on to the west outside of the town. Even still the camps seem to be clustered to the northeast."

Lucas felt a lump in his throat and coughed to attempt to clear it before he spoke. "They're staying away from East Edge, while they hit the villages in the surrounding area." The pieces struggled to slide into place in his head. "We'll assume the worst and say they have thirty people total. East Edge has more than that in the town guard, but they're spread thin. Five members are arriving tomorrow from Homestead. I don't like the numbers, but maybe if we can catch the raiders while they're camped out, we could get the upper hand."

They were reaching the end of the main street and were almost to the north end of town. Lucas stopped and walked toward a bench in the shade of a few trees but didn't sit down.

"Even if we could find out where they are, we can't pull the guard from the town. Even if we had the authority to do so, it would leave the town defenseless." Elina was standing in the shade as well, looking back down the street.

"Right, their numbers could be split to avoid an ambush." Lucas felt his hands clench into fists and took a deep breath. That lump was still in his throat.

He opened his mouth to continue his thought but was cut off by a loud boom to the south. The street in front of them turned into a massive panic as people ran from the sound. There were shouts of another attack. People were pushed past each other to find safety. Elina had been right to be wary. A woman snatched up a small boy and tossed him over her shoulder as she ran. Elina ran in the direction that the sound had come from. *An explosion of some kind.* Smoke was billowing up into the sky to the south. Lucas had taken one step to follow her when there was a second blast to the east and then behind them to the north immediately after.

"This way!" Lucas shouted to Elina over the panic of the crowd.

He turned back toward the closest explosion without looking to see if she had followed or even heard. He fought his way through people running from the explosion as he pushed to the north. Smoke was beginning to rise above the rooftops in front of him to the left. The crowd thinned as they moved closer to the column of smoke. He slowed to a jog as he moved into an alley on the side of the street, Elina close behind.

The alley opened up to a street perpendicular to the main street they had just been running down. There was no one in sight. Sounds of panic spread throughout the town. A dog was eating from an overturned cart, fruits and vegetables spilled out across the street. Down the opposite end of the street.

"Get back," he rasped and pushed Elina against the

wooden exterior of a building. He turned his head and peeked over his shoulder into the street. Elina had proved to be an excellent scout. He had hoped her skills in a fight were as good.

Three people in dark-brown full body suits ran out of an alley and into the street. They were coming right toward them. Each had a mask pulled down from their faces, tubes ran from the mask around to their backs which connected to their breathing tanks. The woman out in front of them was shouting about meeting up with the others. A man behind her was cackling as he ran and almost skipping. The third man seemed to quicken his pace to catch up with the woman leading them. In the distance a bell rang out.

"There are three of them." Lucas turned to the stone-faced Elina. She had both hands on the hilt of her long sword and stood ready. "Wait for them to pass and we'll get them from behind. There's one lagging a bit. I'll go for him first, then we take the others."

He turned back toward the street. The footsteps were getting closer, and the man was still laughing as they ran. Two blurred shapes moved past the alley and Lucas darted into the street as a third came into view. The cackling man fell to the stones as Lucas' body slammed into his. He brought his sword to the man's chest and pushed his blade into the man's ribcage. A quick death. Instinct took over as he pulled the sword from the man and faced the two others that ran in the street. They hadn't yet realized what had happened. A dagger appeared in Elina's hand and she threw it toward the two. The only sound from the man Lucas had brought to the ground was a bloody gurgle. *Maybe not so quick.* The other man had turned just as the dagger hit him in the chest. It clattered to the street as a hand went up to where the blade had made contact.

Elina yelled as she charged the two. Her long sword raked upward across the man's torso and before he had even begun to fall, she turned her hips and brought her sword around and

239

down into the woman's shoulder. She kicked the woman as she pulled her sword from the massive wound. She readied her sword again and rounded on the man whose chest she had just opened, but he didn't move.

Lucas' heart pounded in his ears and the bell tolled in the distance.

Taking a deep breath Lucas sheathed his sword on his hip. "That was impressive. You handle that sword as if it were half the size."

"Do you think she was in charge of these two? It seemed so." She wiped her sword on the woman's baggy brown suit before she returned it to its place on her back. She crouched down and began to go through the pockets on the outside of the suit.

"She could have been." Lucas was still having trouble catching his breath. "We should be quick about this. We can assume there were at least three at each of the blast sites. The woman had said something about meeting up with the rest of them. Maybe ten in total then?" He walked beside Elina to look over her shoulder. Blood was pouring from the wound in the woman's shoulder. It filled the spaces between the stones that had been laid on the street, a shocked expression frozen on her face.

"Unless the explosions were meant to push everyone in the town to the west, where they would meet the rest of them. Three explosions. South, east and north." Elina stood up and was looking through some papers she pulled from a pocket inside the woman's suit. Columns of smoke were now towering up into the sky.

"We won't make it to the other two sites in time to catch whoever set off the blasts. We should head west and keep an eye out for any of the town guard on the way."

"Look at this." She held out a tattered piece of paper. On it was a crude map of the town and surrounding forests. There was a mark on the map nearby where they were in the town, and two others. Each indicating a location where an explosion had happened moments ago.

"Anything else?" Lucas folded the paper and slid it into the inside pocket of his coat.

"This could be a rank or something." Elina pushed the woman to her side with a boot and pointed to a patch on her left shoulder. She pulled a dagger out from her own sleeve and bent down to cut the patch off of the woman's suit. *Ana and Elina would get along well.* She looked at it for a moment and then handed it to him. In the center of the circular blue patch were two silver arches that were outlined by a darker square.

"Could be. I'm not familiar with this symbol at all." Lucas put it in the same pocket with the folded map. "We should get moving. We'll stick to the alleys and try to avoid any more of this if we can." He gestured at the bodies as he spoke.

"Agreed." She turned and began running down the alley that they had just jumped out from. Within a few strides Lucas was right behind her. Elina's short blond hair trailed behind her as she ran.

The two moved between side streets and alleys to avoid the main roads. The bell was still ringing. They had come across two of the town guard as they made their way west. The guards had almost attacked them as they moved out of the alley. After a moment of explanation, they lowered their weapons. He showed them the map Elina had found and told the guardsmen they believed the real attack was to the west. He had tried convincing them to come with him and Elina, but they had orders to go to the town hall to protect the town's council. There was no convincing them otherwise, so they continued on.

Elina dropped back and was running side by side with Lucas. "Do you think they had the right idea?" She hardly seemed out of breath after all this running and the fight. It was impressive.

"It would make sense for them to go after the town's council. If they can hold the town hall this might make things a bit more complicated." Lucas spoke between breaths as he

241

ran. "We could continue heading to the west side of town, and from there come back around. If they are going to the townhall, we could catch them from behind." He was almost panting at this point. He would have to get a hold of himself if he was going to keep this up.

They were almost to the edge of town when they heard shouting coming from an adjacent street. Elina had rounded in the direction of the shout without slowing her pace. He followed, but with less grace. Peering out from around the corner of a stone building, he could see a woman on her knees in the street surrounded by three people. All of them were wearing the same dark suits with tubes running to the tanks on their backs.

"We don't have time for this! We have orders," a fair-skinned woman with a long black braid shouted at a thin man who grabbed at the woman on her knees.

The thin man shoved the black-haired woman away. "You go on then! I'll handle Dimitri when I see him." His voice sounded like gravel.

The woman walked over to a darker-skinned man with short brown hair and talked to him for a moment, then he spoke to the thin man. The distance was too far for Lucas to hear what was being said, but the thin man tried to shove the other man. His attempt to push the other man away failed as he bounced back.

"You can go on too, Jonas! Take Annika and Will to Dimitri. I've got other things to attend to." The thin man reached for the woman again.

The man called Jonas clubbed the thin man on the back of the head with two interlaced fists. The woman got up and ran in the direction that Lucas was observing from. He ducked back behind the corner of the building.

"There's a woman running this way. She looks like one of the townspeople though. If she doesn't see us, let her run by." He spoke in hushed tones. Moments later the woman passed by screaming.

242

Lucas peered around the corner again and the woman with the braid was kicking the unconscious thin man on the ground.

"Enough, Annika. Let's get moving. Rinn will come to in a while and he can meet up with everyone then." She kicked the man once more before the two ran toward the town center. Lucas counted to ten until he stepped out into the street and trotted toward the thin man.

"We should tie him up and bring him somewhere to question later," Elina said as she passed Lucas and moved toward the body.

"That's a good idea. If I had my pack with me, we could have tied him up with some rope. We'll have to look quickly for something, but if we can't find anything we should move on." He started toward a store front when he heard the sound of fabric ripping. He turned to see Elina cutting the man's bulky suit into strips. "Good thinking."

Once the thin man's feet and hands were bound and a gag placed in his mouth, Lucas carried him into a store front and set him down at a table.

"Would be better to put him out with the garbage." Elina spat on the floor.

"This will do for now. Let's get moving." They ran out of the store and Lucas turned in the direction that the others ran off in.

The town center was a large square space with fountains and statues of local leaders and Amboians. Large white stone lined the usual tan stone that made up the square and streets themselves. A few trees dotted the edge. Other than that, there wasn't much cover. On the steps of a large brick building with a dark tiled roof stood a man in one of the suits. From this distance all Lucas could see was that the man had a dark-brown beard and hair to match that was kept up in a bun behind his head. The torso of his suit had been folded and tied around his waist. He wore a dirty-looking gray shirt. On the steps below him were three people on their knees with hands tied. A mass of townspeople was gathered—corralled really—at the bottom of the steps. All along the outside of the mass of people were more suited attackers. It was then that Lucas noticed a pile of bodies. All wore the armor of the town guard.

"I can barely hear what he's saying. We should try to move closer." Elina crouched up ahead of him and darted behind an overturned produce stall. She darted from overturned stall, to stall, to tree trunk, and anything else she could use for cover. Lucas was one step behind until they were close enough to hear the man at the top of the steps.

"...Is under our control now. Don't step out of line and you will not be harmed. I mean to find a place for my people to live safely, and to accomplish this I will do whatever it takes."

The man continued to speak to the crowd, but Lucas' attention was caught by movement behind the man. Past the top of the steps there were four massive white columns that supported a balcony above that was normally used by the town leaders for speeches. Among the columns was a member of the town guard. The guard slowly moved toward the back of the man giving the speech. He lunged forward with a pike in hand. The man turned around and pulled something from his waistline. There was a loud crack and the guard fell; their momentum sent them tumbling down the steps below. The crowd had simultaneously hunched over. Some tried to run but were grabbed or knocked to the ground by one of the attackers.

"What *was* that?" Elina, still crouched, turned to him. Her stoic exterior had been shattered. "I couldn't see what he did, but that sound. He killed that guard with a *sound?*"

He was as confused as she was. "The guard ran toward him, and he pulled something from his waist. It looked like a small gray piece of metal." He brought his attention back to the steps. The man named Jonas from before now stood next to the man as he continued his speech. "I'm guessing that's

Dimitri, the man we heard them talking about in the street just before."

"I was thinking the same. Whatever that weapon is, it's beyond both of us."

Lucas scanned the crowd of people, counting the dark suited figures as he went. "There can't be more than twenty of them, including those two on top of the steps." He turned away and looked about the square behind them. "I don't think they managed to gather the entire town here. There must be others hiding out."

There was another loud cracking sound. Lucas turned around to see what had happened. Dimitri was standing over the body of one of the people who had been bound and on their knees. He then side stepped in front of another and held that metal object out toward their head. He appeared to be speaking to the person on their knees. The person yelled something Lucas couldn't hear. Then another crack sound.

This time he could see something that looked like a flash of fire out of the metal object. Screams erupted from the crowd, but no one tried to run this time. The body slumped in a heap where Dimitri's feet would have been if he hadn't side stepped to the final person on their knees. This time when he brought the metal object to the person's head, they threw themselves to the ground and grabbed at Dimitri's feet. Lucas thought he could hear the faint sound of sobbing.

"Did you see that flash of fire?" Elina didn't take her eyes off the scene that was unfolding before them.

"I did. We need to leave the square and search for anyone who may have avoided being rounded up." Lucas started moving back the way they came from.

"So, we wait it out until the other members of Amber Waves arrive? How will we get word to them that this has happened?" she whispered as they quietly hurried down an empty side street.

"There's a road that follows a river from Farmer's Lake in Homestead. They'll be arriving from that direction. Tonight, we'll get out of town and wait for them on the road. If we're lucky we can meet up with them before they get too close to the town." Lucas was all but running again at this point. "We should see about getting the horses and our belongings from the Old Oak before we get out." Any extra time spent in East Edge would be a risk. He wasn't sure if they would get a chance to get their things once they left. Vym was stabled at the Old Oak along with Elina's horse.

"We should bring that man we tied up. We can question him." Anger surfaced in Elina's voice. She was right, and Lucas had several questions for the thin man.

CHAPTER EIGHTEEN

To East Edge

Gaelcean looked away from the screen of his terminal and across his curved desk to where Carter was standing against the wall. "You are familiar with bears and mountain cats, correct?"

"Of course." Carter shifted his feet. "The *ursaemont* is a combination of the two?" The thought almost made his head spin. A beast with the agility of a cat and strength of a bear. And they were used as mounts in battle!

"In some ways, yes. That is accurate." Gaelcean turned back to his work. When he wasn't in the Hall for a Council meeting, he was meeting with other Councilors in his quarters, or at his terminal. Carter was curious what it was that Gaelcean worked at all day. It was not his place to ask, but he did pick up on a few things from meetings. The intricacies of politics made Carter's head spin most of the time. He was content being a guard.

The room was silent for some time, which he didn't mind. He was surprised at how comfortable he had become around Gaelcean and even living in Amboy Central. It had only been a few days since he crossed into the Upper District for the first time. There was still much to learn about the Council. It seemed every time he thought he had a grasp on which council member represented which branch, something new would be said to make him think otherwise.

There had been almost thirty council members seated around the large ring-shaped table yesterday. He hadn't once wished to have his old post on top of the outer wall back, but that meeting had come close. All the talk of misuse of funds, a possible food shortage in the coming seasons, delays on construction throughout the New Ring. It was all too much to keep track of.

"When Weleya returns from the Lower Districts we sh—" Gaelcean was cut off as the large wooden doors to his offices were thrown open. An exhausted Amboian adjusted his dark-red coat and tidied himself as he approached Gaelcean's desk.

"There is no need for that, Carter. What is the meaning of this?"

He hadn't even realized he had his spear in his hand and that he had nearly stepped between Gaelcean and the Amboian who had entered. He pressed the button on his spear, and it retracted back into a small cylinder that he placed into the leather pocket on his waist belt.

The flustered Amboian took a moment to catch his breath before he spoke. "T—there's been an attack. The Eastern Perimeter." He sucked in air and put his hands on his knees. "I apologize for my appearance and for entering unannounced." When the Amboian stood his serenity returned.

"An attack?" Gaelcean stood up and moved toward the door that had just been thrown open moments before. Carter was immediately at his side. "Has an emergency meeting been called? Tell me all you know as we walk." The Amboian glanced at Carter and then back to Gaelcean. "He will hear what you have to say as well."

The three moved down the hall to the speed lifts at a

248

brisk walk. They reached the lifts just as the doors opened. It was packed with Amboian Council members. They spoke among themselves about the attack. Some noticed Carter and stopped speaking. Gaelcean paid it no mind as they stepped inside. Once the others in the lift heard Gaelcean speaking freely of the attack, their own conversations resumed.

When the doors opened again, they were in the long hallway that led to the Council Hall. There had never been this many councilors coming to sit in the Hall. The hallway itself was so crowded he had to force his way through so Gaelcean could reach the opened doors of the Hall. His pushing was met with anger and shouts, but once they saw Gaelcean, he didn't have to try as hard to make room for them. The Hall itself had been rearranged at some point. The ring-shaped table was gone and in its place there were rows of seats.

Each row was taller than the one before it, which allowed those seated behind to see clearly. The curved rows ran down both sides of the oval-shaped room. A long table was covered in data pads and loose papers. Most of the seats were filled, but there were still plenty of movement. Councilors were pushing toward the table to add their opinion to whatever was being said. At one end of the table stood Ruintael and Paelle. After a quick look for any other familiar faces, he saw Maecell and Gurae seated in the first row of high-backed chairs speaking to each other. Behind them Rylae was seated with arms folded glaring out into the room as two Amboians were speaking on either side of him. His face was twisted with what Carter could guess was anger.

Gaelcean stepped into the center of the room near the table and spoke with his hands cupped around his mouth, "Let us all take our seats! Some order is needed here! Order!"

Paelle ushered those around her to some seats nearby. Ruintael stood at the table still and gave orders to those around to take their seats. After some murmurs and shouts all had found their seats. While they took their seats, personal guards lined up along the walls. Carter looked for a spot that would still allow him to see and hear what was happening. It was only after he settled in among the others that he realized he stood next to Zaenin.

"It seems your kind cannot keep from slaughtering each other." There was almost a metallic quality to her voice. "I hear that hordes of Humans appeared from beyond the Perimeter and used some sort of explosive to bring a town to rubble."

Carter tried to keep the heat from his voice. "Let's see what the Council has to say."

"If we go to war, I hope Rylae leads us. I want to be the first to cross metal with these invaders." Zaenin buzzed with excitement.

Gaelcean and Ruintael stood in the center of the room and once there was silence Ruintael spoke. "Midday yesterday there was an attack in the town called East Edge, along the Perimeter." Whispers spread among the council. "I will speak!" Ruintael shouted and the room quickly fell silent. "We received word through the emergency channels this morning. Only one of their town leaders remains. The others were killed by the man who leads these attackers. He murdered them on the steps of their town hall. A display for the people it may seem."

"What do we know of these attackers?" a familiar voice said. The curvature of the seats kept Carter from seeing who was speaking. "Are there any demands? Do they plan on taking the Perimeter for themselves?"

Ruintael held up a data pad. "No demands. It seems they intend to control the town. They are led by a man who goes by the name Dimitri," he said as he set the data pad down. "They will most likely use this attack to test our response. Perhaps there is yet another attack coming. It is in all of our interests to send a battalion of Knights to stop this madness." There were a few cheers and shouts of agreement. Some shook their heads, others only sat and listened.

"I would advise a different approach," Gaelcean addressed the entire room.

"What would you have us do, Gaelcean?" Ruintael rounded the table.

"I do agree with General Ruintael." Now it was General and not Councilor Ruintael. Something different each time, Carter noted. "We shall send a battalion of Knights, but I will lead them." The room exploded. Ruintael stood with arms crossed. "I *will* lead them!" Gaelcean shouted over the uproar. "I do not intend to bring more violence to this town! I will meet with this Dimitri, and we will come to a peaceful solution." The room was still abuzz, but it had seemed to quiet down.

"I see." Ruintael rounded the table once more and looked over the papers spread out across its surface. "Take them down the Sun Road. Then split the forces to surround the town. Our numbers will give us the upper hand."

"I will bring my personal guard, Carter Gerro. He will be my second in command."

The room had burst into an uproar once more. Faces of all the shades of blue were looking toward him and shouting.

Carter felt an elbow in his side. "You will be second in command of the Knights of Amboy." Zaenin scoffed, and then leaned in closer. A soft hum emanated from her body. "If Gaelcean is harmed in the slightest, it will fall on you. If we lose him, I would not return to the capital."

"Your love for Humanity blinds you!" A single voice rose above the commotion. Rylae joined Ruintael and Gaelcean in the center of the room. "You will bring the Knights east, but then what? Enter the town and speak with these *Humans*?" The word seemed like a curse coming from him. "We allowed you to have your guard, but this is too much." Carter noticed a few glances in his direction from the Council.

"If we meet them with violence, there will be no coming back." Gaelcean appeared serene, but fire was behind his words. "I will not let anyone, including *you*, bring us into another war with Humanity." Murmurs and whispers still floated among the rows of high-backed chairs. "It was many years ago, Rylae, but I know you recall First Contact. The war that followed? How many did we lose, because of rash reactions? How many?" This was the closest to a shout that Carter had ever heard from Gaelcean.

"Indeed. There were many casualties." Ruintael put a hand on each of the Councilors' shoulders. "I know a several of us were present. We would not want to bring that upon ourselves again." He stepped away and turned to look across the room. "Gaelcean will lead the Knights to East Edge. He will speak with their leader. I trust Gaelcean will find a solution that will avoid further conflict."

Rylae forced a nod and returned to his seat. Gaelcean walked over to Ruintael and the two did the same sort of handshake Carter had seen them do before. Grasping each other by the wrist and placing an open hand on the other's shoulder.

"I will make plans to leave immediately. Ruintael will ready the Knights and we will make for East Edge." There was collective agreement through nods and cheers. It didn't seem that all agreed with the decision, but once Ruintael and Gaelcean had come to an agreement no others voiced an opinion otherwise.

"I can have the Knights outside the Exterior Walls and ready for your command before you arrive," Ruintael said.

"No," Gaelcean addressed the room again. "The Knights will make formation in the Upper District and we will march through the Lower Districts. There must be no room for denial that we will protect those who live beneath the Shield."

After Gaelcean had finished speaking the Hall began to clear out. This was Gaelcean's responsibility now and there were other matters to attend to for many of the Council. Carter matched Gaelcean's pace as they left the room and made for the speed lifts. Instead of getting into the first open lift, they waited for an empty one. A few of the Councilors and their guard tried to step in as well, but Gaelcean held out a hand to stop them and let the doors close.

"There has not been a full Council in… Well, I'm not exactly sure, but it has been a long time." Gaelcean shook his head. "This is what it takes from them to do their duties. Most only sat and listened. They do not care what will happen either way."

"Should we have sent for Weleya?" Carter asked. He had hoped his nerves hadn't shown in his voice. He was second in command to the Knights of Amboy. He was helping Gaelcean lead the Knights to possible war. No. It wouldn't be war. Gaelcean would find a solution.

"No, she has her own duties to attend to. I would not say more important, but they are of importance as well."

"I see." He paused. "The Council dislikes that a Human is your personal guard."

Gaelcean was silent for a moment. "Yes. Some have made it very clear. I try to impress upon them the importance of our species working together to survive, but they do not see it that way. Some see Humanity as a sort of child to be taken care of. Some see Humanity as tools, and others would wish them gone entirely." He must have noticed Carter's reaction. He spoke quickly, "Do not worry about the last. They are so few that they have hardly any say. During the war after First Contact some saw it as a means to remove Humanity from this planet, but I pressed peace and a resolution was made. I'm sure you are familiar with the tellings of the Church of Amboy."

In truth he had never stepped foot inside the large stone building in District Seven, but he had heard some parts of the Salvation of Humanity from preachers on the streets. The Amboians had saved Humanity from the Haze and gave them shelter beneath the Shield.

"Rylae would have humanity removed given the chance, I'm sure." As soon as the words left his mouth he immediately regretted it. Perhaps he was becoming too

253

comfortable around Gaelcean.

"I do not think so. He does not like how you have come up in our world, but he does not wish Humanity erased." The lift doors opened to Gaelcean's floor and he hurriedly stepped into the room.

Once inside he crossed the room and began typing on his terminal. "I must send a message to Weleya. Ready your things and we will leave to meet the Knights in the Upper District."

Carter's room was off of Gaelcean's main office. It was a reasonably sized space with a large window that let plenty of light in. He walked over to his bed and pulled the large metal chest from underneath it. He hadn't had to wear his complete armor set before today. He hoped after this he wouldn't have to wear it again any time soon. A blue light pulsed around the chest. There was a single beep followed by a click and the chest opened on its own revealing the contents. Carter pulled the matte-gray metal chest piece from its container and held it to his torso. Once the armor made contact with his shirt it automatically extended to encompass his entire torso. When he placed a pauldron on his shoulder it attached itself seamlessly to the amour that covered him. Piece by piece he connected everything until he was covered from neck to toe in armor. When he moved the armor moved as if it were a second skin. The weight was barely noticeable. He would have been worried how well it would protect him if Weleya hadn't showed him the strength of it by sparring with him with practice swords.

Stepping back into the room he didn't see Gaelcean at his desk but standing by the door waiting. He was no longer in one of his many long coats, he wore armor similar to what the Knights of Amboy might wear. Only Gaelcean's was more ornate, the silver armor was trimmed with gold and on the breastplate was his crest. That bird with elongated tail feathers. The breast plate appeared to be his only armor. A dark-grey cloak covered most of him, but he wore his usual pants with a crease pressed down the sides, and deep blue long sleeves covered his arms to the wrist.

"If you are ready," Gaelcean said and turned to leave the room.

As Gaelcean and Carter approached the Knights of Amboy battalion one Knight stepped out. "Command of this battalion has been given to Diplomat Gaelcean!"
When the Knight stepped back into formation the entire battalion spoke in unison. "For Gaelcean! For Amboy!"

There were footsteps behind him and as he turned, he had to keep from pulling out his spear again reflexively. A man was leading two massive horses toward them. No, they only resembled horses. Each had long curved horns protruding from the sides of their heads, like a bull.

"Thank you, Therodil," Gaelcean said as he took the reins from the man.

"Of course, Gaelcean. Paelle has done wonders with this most recent batch of *boveqq*." The man wiped his hands on a dirty apron. "That is the term, yes?"

"These are not exactly the same, but yes, very close to *boveqq*." Gaelcean pulled himself up onto the beast's back.

Therodil handed the other reins to Carter and smiled before turning and walking away. He had ridden a horse before, and this animal seemed to resemble a horse in a way. He put one foot in a stirrup and pulled himself up onto its back. The beast shook its head and let out what sounded like a low growl.

"Therodil Airelleth tends to the animals that Paelle engineers. These seem to be the best." Gaelcean patted the neck of his mount. "We must make haste to East Edge." Gaelcean heeled the sides of his *boveqq* and trotted forward. "You all know what we must do. I am glad for your service, but I hope it will not be needed. We will march hard and arrive in East Edge before these attackers cause further harm

255

to those we must protect." As he spoke, he moved through the rows of Knights. Carter followed close behind him trying not to focus on the dark eyes glaring up at him. The Knights of Amboy were proud. They were the best of what the City Guard had to offer. Carter had heard that most of the Amboians who train to become a Knight die during their training, whether it be in combat or from exhaustion. To them, he had skipped several steps to get where he was now.

They marched down through a tunnel and into the Lower Districts. Gaelcean wanted the people to see them ride out to East Edge, but Carter wasn't expecting what met them when they exited the other side of the tunnel.

The wide street was packed full of cheering people all pushing against Knights that lined the street to allow them through. There were shouts of praise for Gaelcean and the Council. Carter thought he had heard his own name a few times. He was probably imagining things. A sea of cheering faces was all that he saw as they passed through District Three toward the outer gate. As they made their way, the Knights who had been keeping the crowd back, fell into formation behind them. The result was a mass of cheering people that followed them out to the gates. Perhaps Gaelcean was right, there was a possibility that Humans and Amboians could work together.

"Carter Gerro!" a voice shouted from the crowd near the Exterior Gates.

Maybe he hadn't been imagining things. He looked in the direction the shout had come from. Two familiar faces were looking back at him. Myra and Ronald stood in the crowd. Each had a closed fist to their chest in salute. Ronald had been wounded during a patrol. He had a long cut across his face and now wore a dark eye patch. Carter brought a fist to his chest and nodded in their direction.

He rode through the Exterior Wall at Gaelcean's side, and an entire battalion of Knights at their back.

CHAPTER NINETEEN

Another Thread to Pluck

The Market Square of District Twelve expanded outward ahead of Weleya as she stood at the southern entrance to the square. Vendors with their carts and stalls surrounded her. Those who didn't sell from carts had decorative rugs laid out. Some were covered with pottery and wooden bowls of a variety of shapes and sizes. If there was something that could be bought or sold in the Lower Districts, it could be found here.

A weaver approached Weleya and tried to sell her a knit hat. The older man said something in regard to the cooler weather being here before they all knew it and that she looked like she could use a hat. She had hoped that if she had ignored the man he would move on, but he continued to push hats and scarfs until she turned to face him. It could have been that she stood half a head above him, or the look that she gave him, but chances were it was her eyes that made him speed off. The man glanced over his shoulder once before he picked up his pace and disappeared into the crowd.

Paelle had offered to install a modification that would allow hair to grow naturally on her head, but Weleya preferred her current look. Bald women weren't common. Bald women with orange eyes even less. Maybe one day she would adopt the style of the women from Athanelle.

Blending into a group of people had its own benefits. She had found that the benefits of being recognizable outweighed the opposite. Days before Gaelcean's speech she had entered the Lower Districts for the first time in a long time. A *very* long time. Once she was seen on stage with Gaelcean the rumors of the orange-eyed Upper District mercenary changed to the orange-eyed Council guard. When it was thought that she was a mercenary hired by some Upper District Family, she found that people gave information rather freely. There were some who took longer to break, but they all did eventually. Now that it was known who she truly was, it wasn't as simple. Weleya rubbed a hand across the top of her head. If she had ever wanted to change her appearance a day in Paelle's lab would take care of that for her.

It had angered her that she wasn't informed of their departure until she had heard from people moving through the crowd. She had heard Carter forced the Council to let him take the Knights East, some said Gaelcean was only going as a formality, the most absurd she had heard was Gaelcean and tens of thousands of Knights were on the move. Impossible. She didn't need to be present to have a good idea of what had gone down in the emergency Council meeting that had no doubt taken place before their departure. Gaelcean could see the pieces of everything around him and always had a way to make the situation work in his favor. Ruintael would have supported him, but he also couldn't let it happen without at least feigning an argument. Rylae would have put up an argument for himself to lead the Knights, but that would only result in more deaths, mostly Human. The analysis occurred in Weleya's head in a fraction of the time it would take for a Human.

The modifications made to her sensory processing allowed her to cut out background noise and focus in on the mass of people around her. Her eyes scanned the crowd. She transitioned her focus from groups to individuals. The mechanical apertures in her eyes whirred as she changed the magnification of her vision. Through the years, her experience with her ocular upgrades became second nature and she rarely paid attention to the information that floated in the air next to those she locked in on. The information was never more than an estimated age, height, weight, and any obvious physical traits she could see. Occasionally she added her own entries into the system's data base. It was useful to keep a log on the numerous individuals in the Lower District.

Even now when she analyzed some of the people walking by information about them appeared that she hadn't recalled. An old man who had information about a gang that use to be in the Upper District decades ago was all but hunched over as he shuffled by. A woman who had been marked as an informant for another Council member stood at a stall holding up a gold necklace with several large white and blue stones around it. A group of four young adults by a store front had streams of information around them. She had recognized them without the information this time though. They had all been hired by the Jorogumo at one time or another. One of the boys with long shaggy black hair saw her staring at them. He hit the others to get their attention and they all ran down an alley away from her. She was about to follow them into the alley when a voice caught her attention.

Far down the Market Square a man was standing on a box. His leathery face and white hair stood slightly above the crowd that had gathered around him. As he spoke, he gesticulated with two mechanical arms. From where she was, she could hear enough of what he was saying to know that this was the man she had been searching for. She needed him to see her, so she moved through the crowd toward him.

"...Is our destiny! We have been given the means to live well beyond the expectancies of our ancestors." The man spoke and the group that had stopped to hear him listened intently. So much so that Weleya had to force herself into the throng of people a bit harder than she expected. There were some grunts and curses as she moved, but once those around her acknowledged who she was there were apologies, and even bows in some cases.

"Put your eyes upon me, brothers and sisters! I am well into my ninety-sixth year, and here I am standing, talking to you all!" The man continued to move his mechanical appendages as he spoke.

The prosthetic on his right arm started at his shoulder and was made of a low-quality metal. The pock-marked metal casings on the outside were a likely indicator of the quality of the hardware inside them. It did seem as though it had enough articulation in the shoulder and elbow to allow a full range of motion, but that stopped at the wrist. The motion of his right hand seemed encumbered; two thick metal fingers extended from the palm and a third extended outward acting as a thumb. It was standard work one would find in the Lower District.

His right arm was of a much higher quality and the modifications began below the elbow. It was most likely purchased from an Upper District seller. Upper District works weren't necessarily illegal in the Lower Districts, but it did seem to cause trouble for those who bought and sold them. His left hand was fully articulated, and more care had gone into making it resemble an organic hand. If the metal had been covered by a synthetic skin it may be difficult to see it for what it truly was.

There had been an increasing number of reports of some new group starting up in the Third District. The previous reports had mentioned men and woman with augmentations lecturing to anyone in the streets who would listen. She hadn't thought it was much to be concerned about, but looking at the crowd around this man, she could see there was more to this than what Voal and the others had mentioned. Maybe she should have had the Amber Waves look into this instead of going to Port Amboy. If she had, she would be with Gaelcean right now.

"Ah!" The man looked directly at her now. Exactly what she wanted. "We are graced by the presence of the peak of Humanity." The less articulate arm spread out across the gathering to his right, while the other pointed in her direction. The crowd around her stepped away as much as those around them would allow. "Now if only young Carter Gerro were here. We could see the full spectrum of the great work done by our leaders. Leaders who pick and choose who receives their awesome gifts! All of you should be allowed to live healthy and long lives regardless of your trade, or wealth. The Technological Society for Human Advancement would allow any and all to improve themselves. *If* we were given a position of power!" A low murmur spread throughout the crowd.

"I have some questions for you." Now that she was out of the crowd, she could also see that both of his legs from the knee down weren't organic.

"Yes, of course." A kind smile appeared on his face. "Remember what I have told you today, brothers and sisters! Look upon Weleya, personal guard to Diplomatic Councilor Gaelcean. Look upon myself. Look upon those around you who are hurt, or sick. How many do you know?" A few sparse cheers came from the crowd behind her as the man hopped down from the wooden box. His legs seemed to be of the same quality as his left arm. She needed to find out how he had gotten them. There was no manufacturer in the Third District whose work could match these.

"Why don't you walk with me. I will answer any questions of yours that I can. I would hope you may answer some of mine as well. My name is Davil Coram." Davil folded his hands behind his back and began walking through the crowd.

Weleya updated her internal log with his name and notes on her visual assessment of his upgrades. She was sure he had said he was ninety-six years old, but even with the work that had been done to his body he moved like a man decades

261

younger. He would have had to undergo an intense surgery to acquire the necessary internal augmentations to achieve that.

Rows of stalls and carts lined the perimeter of the Market Square, and more rows were present inward from the outermost. In the center was a large plaza. She followed Davil through the crowd and into the open plaza. Children were chasing each other and playing a game that involved kicking a ball into a net supported by two large tree branches.

"The Amboians have given Humanity the chance to flourish and rise up from the ashes of the Old World." He nodded in the direction of the children. "The Church of Amboy tells us how we were saved, but it seems they do have a tendency to leave some information out."

Out of the corner of her eye Weleya could see him look in her direction. To study her reaction, no doubt. She knew more than anyone what had happened those centuries ago. She had been there. What did this man think he knew that she didn't?

"You aren't wrong." She would have to give him some slack before she pulled back. "The Church was born during the final years of the wars that proceeded shortly after the First Contact. A way to show Humanity that the Amboians were there to aid them, not harm them."

"Indeed. I know the power of words more than most. Words only go so far, especially when the stories are so old there is no one living to remember their origins." He let out a soft laugh and looked in her direction again. "Well almost no one."

"I wanted to ask about your group. You must understand the Council will take interest in any new organizations that amass a following in the Lower Districts." They had reached the other side of the plaza and stepped back into the crowd. As they moved through people made way for them.

"Of course, of course." He smiled to those who passed by and greeted him. It was clear now they had made room for him in the crowd as much as they had for her. "It was only recently that our little group decided on a name. Personally, I think it's too much. Too long." He shook his head.

"What is your end goal?" Weleya scanned those who acknowledged him. Nothing of importance appeared.

"If you listened to my speech, which I'm sure you did, it should be quite clear." Davil continued to nod and smile as they walked. Some even came out of the crowd to thank him for the work he was doing; he gave them as much acknowledgment as the others. "I want the best for Humanity. There are clearly issues throughout the city. Overcrowding, starvation, criminal organizations stretch beyond the Forgotten District." He shook his head again. "Terrible. Terrible times we are living in. It clearly could be better."

"You believe if everyone had a longer life there would be no overcrowding? No starvation? Obsolescence exists for a reason." She didn't enjoy antagonizing people this way, but frustration could sometimes make people say things they didn't intend to. What would get a reaction out of him?

He continued speaking as if he hadn't heard. "To make sure this technology will be available to all we must educate the masses on how they work, how they are made. Education is important. A strong mind is just as important as a strong body. We will need to rebuild the Third District to support the need for the parts. This will create jobs!" Excitement was filling his voice as he went on. Weleya wasn't sure if he was aware of his surroundings as he spoke. He was entirely enthralled in his thoughts. "People will need to be hired to upgrade the factories, to work the factories, to educate those who receive their improvements. Do you see?" He had finally stopped talking and turned to her. His deep brown eyes stared into hers.

"I do see. If only it were that simple. You are no doubt an intelligent man, but you must see that it is more complex than that. To educa—"

"Well yes, yes. Of course, it won't be easy!" He waved a

263

hand and continued walking. It didn't faze her though, there would be more chances to puncture holes in his armor. If she was lucky, something useful would come out then.

The two continued to walk and Davil continued to lecture on the importance of access to higher forms of technology. Better methods of farming in the New Ring would lead to higher yields, that would solve the impending starvation he believed was upon them.

He wasn't far off. There had been several proposed methods of action to bring advanced technology to the farms closer to the city as a test group before allowing all farms access to it. It was decided that the possible negatives outweighed the positives.

If the Lower Districts would be allowed to share the medical services that were available in the Upper Districts, the quality of life would improve immensely for those who lived around them. That was obvious too, but was he assuming the Upper Districts had better health services? The certainty in his voice led her to believe he knew more than he was letting on. He never stayed on one topic for very long. Maybe he would reveal too much if he did.

As they entered the Third District the smell of the factories filled the air, and the temperature seemed to increase slightly. Davil had something to say about every building, store front, and vendor they passed as they walked down the wide main street of the district. This blacksmith made equipment for the farms just outside the outer walls of the city. That store specialized in replacement parts for one of the factories just down the street. Multiple generations of a family all lived in one small house wedged between an electrician's shop and a factory that mass produced parts of modular homes in the Upper District. Any time Davil spoke about a business or store that only produced something for the Upper District there was a tinge of anger in his voice. He was able to maintain his composure, but Weleya had noticed.

Davil stopped at a tall and narrow stone and wood

building between two more just like it. A metal sign above the front door read: The Technological Society for Human Advancement. He motioned for her to follow him and opened the large wooden door. Voices were coming from a room at the end of the dimly lit hallway they were now standing in. Davil closed the door behind Weleya as she stepped in. Two closed doors were on the left of the hallway. A stairway to the right went up to the second floor.

"Come, come. You can meet our members and see for yourself that we are no threat to the Council."

He walked past the first door on his left but stopped at the second and turned the handle. It seemed to be locked. Before she had caught up to him, he looked back with a smile and continued to the end of the hall. "We have a guest!" Davil announced as he entered the room that was just as dimly lit as the hallway had been. Weleya opened the apertures of her eyes, allowing her to see in the low light. The room appeared almost as bright as if they had been standing outside in the sun.

There were several people seated around a metal table. A man in the corner of the room had gasped when he saw her. The two men on either side of him elbowed him almost simultaneously. A man seated at the table had tried to casually cover up some documents that were laid out and others shut off data pads they had been looking at. Without low-light vision it may have gone unnoticed. She made a note for each person seated at the table, and those who attempted to cover up whatever it was that they had been discussing before she entered. Everyone in the room had had some sort of visible mechanical prosthetic. There would be some internal enhancements as well.

"There is no need to worry." Davil held up his hands. "As I said, Weleya is here as a guest. The Council has taken some interest in us." His reassurance didn't seem to calm anyone in the room.

"The Council hasn't officially taken interest. I am here

265

because *I* have interest." She stepped over to the table and scanned what she could see. Blueprints for equipment, some sort of planned curriculum for an electronics class, nothing of major interest. A list of names caught her eye. A woman seated at the table grabbed it before she could get a decent scan.

"If you have any questions. We will answer them. We *will not* have you going through our things!" The woman spat angrily as she spoke, and it twisted her aging features. Her gray hair was braided into a crown around her head.

"Now, now, Allinda." Davil attempted to maintain his air of calm as he stepped next to Weleya. "There is no need to be so rash."

Allinda looked up at her, then Davil, then back to her. "Yes, I forget myself."

None of the names were of any note to Weleya. She logged them anyway. "Thank you, Allinda." Weleya turned and looked around the room. Other than the table and chairs in the center, there was no other furniture. Electric lights lined the walls, a lack of power keeping them from generating their full luminosity. Wallpaper had been used to decorate the room, someone had recently removed it carelessly and scraps were still here and there.

"It isn't much yet, but this is where we meet. Rooms upstairs are used for lectures and hands on training. The third and fourth floor are mostly bedrooms. Many members of the Society live and work from this building." Davil put his arms around a young woman and man. "I would offer you some hospitality, but I must be honest, I don't know the extent of your improvements." He had removed himself from the woman and man and stepped closer. He was looking her over and wringing his hands.

"That won't be necessary." Weleya closed the distance between them before he could.

He almost lost his footing as he stepped back. "I see." Embarrassment covered his face and his cheeks reddened. He

266

ushered Weleya back down the hallway they had come from. "Would you like to see the classrooms upstairs? We are currently teaching some of the younger students how to wire up a rudimentary alarm system."

Taking her following as an affirmation, Davil walked briskly back down the hallway and rounded the banister at the bottom of the stairs. "Some of our students' families own their own shops, you see. The alarm they will make will create a high-pitched frequency when tripped, not lethal, but in some cases enough to scare criminals away." At the top of the stairs Davil turned left.

The hallway was similar to the one below, at the top of the stairs was a larger room. Along the hallway were three more rooms. Light was coming in from a window at the opposite end which allowed Weleya to relax her ocular apertures. She turned around to face Davil, who had moved closer than he had been before. He inspected the parts of her arms that weren't covered by her brown cloak. He almost jumped backward when he noticed she was staring at him.

"Let me show you the projects the students are working on." He entered the room at the top of the stairs and motioned for her to come in. "We let the more advanced students spend their free time in here. All of them are working on individual projects under the supervision of a mentor. There are some very promising pieces in here." He moved from table to table. In some cases, it was obvious what the students were attempting. Others seemed half finished or without direction.

A helmet that took inspiration from a Knight of Amboy's helmet stood out from the other objects scattered about the room. A Knight wouldn't be able fit their head into this. *The student who made this must have been an older boy.* A shallow V-shaped visor covered the front and along the jawline were two small cylinders. Upon further inspection she found they could be unscrewed from the mask, and as she removed one a small amount of pressure was released. She scanned the

267

helmet and created a new entry for it. The attention to design was impressive and the quality of metal was almost reminiscent of Upper District work. The inside of the helmet was mostly loose wires and exposed circuits.

"Please do be careful with that one," Davil said hurriedly behind her. "Young Cayle would be truly heartbroken if anything would happen to that." She set it down and turned around. Davil was walking toward her hands folded behind his back. "You see, Cayle came to us from the Eastern Perimeter. He came to us some few weeks ago but showed great promise. He wouldn't say where he was from or what his family's line of work was, but it is clear he knows what he is doing. I'm saddened to say that his town was one of those that were attacked by those who have been coming from the Haze. Young Cayle lost his entire family during an attack."

"He is certainly talented, and intelligent. I would like to meet him." Weleya finished her entry on Cayle and turned back to look at the helmet. "He is attempting to recreate the suits worn by those from the Haze?"

"Yes, I believe so." Davil was now almost right beside her. "I worry he means to go back and possibly run off into the Haze for revenge. I don't know what to say to him, but I will support his interests and perhaps something positive will come."

Weleya felt something pull at her cloak and rounded on Davil. Her right hand clenched into a fist and upon closing two small pieces of metal extended between her first and second finger, and her third and fourth. Electricity arced between the two small rods and when she connected with Davil's chest he convulsed for a moment before grabbing at her arm and yanking it away.

The pressure from his grip was unexpected and she was barely able to pull her arm free. His hand had left scour marks in her forearm. She lunged toward him. He vaulted a table to his left effortlessly and landed on the other side. He reached behind him and picked up a long metal rod. The rod

268

swung outward at her. At this distance, from the opposite side of the table it wasn't long enough to reach. Davil swung the rod again and as it reached the apex of the swing, it broke up and had become whip-like. Electricity crackled as it was flung in her direction and arced across her body as it wrapped around her right arm. The smell of burning circuitry filled the air. Then the crackling stopped.

Davil cursed at the weapon's failure and dropped it has he ran toward the door. A fine blade extended from Weleya's left forearm and she raked it across the metal that ensnared her right. The blade cut through it as if it were a delicate fabric.

She caught Davil as he reached the closed door. She tackled him through it into the hallway on the other side. Shouts came from downstairs and footsteps were at the bottom of the stairway. She wouldn't make it out if any of the others could give her as tough a time as he had. She was sure if she didn't make it out, they wouldn't leave her in one piece either. She brought a fist down into Davil's throat and there was a crunch. He grabbed at his throat and rasped. There was a terrible wheezing sound as air barely made it through his collapsing throat. Shouts and curses filled the hallway as a group of men and women reached the top of the staircase. Weleya darted toward the other end of the hall and threw herself through the window.

Tumbling downward, she forced her feet beneath her just as they met the tan paving stones of the street. She was up and moving down the street and away from shouts and curses behind her. She glanced back twice and saw no one following her. Just to be safe she cut into the first opening between two buildings she saw and made her way through the narrow alley. She moved from side street to alley until she was far enough away to return to one of the main streets.

Once out onto the wide street she turned in the direction of an Upper District Gate. As she moved, she simultaneously scanned her surroundings and organized the data she had just collected.

It was clear Davil had gained access to Upper District technology, but how? It was possible that he had some connections in the Upper District or was from the Upper District himself and posing otherwise. The second seemed less likely.

Still, no one followed behind her.

No suspicious movement from the alley to her left either. Were they reverse engineering technology and then teaching it to their students? They were allowing them to make weapons and armor. There must be more members in the Lower Districts, more boarding houses like the one she had just left.

Gaelcean wouldn't likely return for weeks, she had to get word to him. They had both suspected for some time that the Families in the Upper District had control of the smaller gangs in the Lower. The Amber Waves had confirmed that with the information they had found in that tavern. The Technology Society for Human Advancement could be another front. That seemed very likely. Those in the Lower District who meant to improve their situation without getting involved in crime could be taken advantage of in other ways. Davil could be a high-ranking Jorogumo member. The others who were at the table as well. Weleya pulled up the list of names that she had scanned. Nothing obvious. Staying in the Lower Districts without letting things cool off could bring more trouble, but Weleya wasn't done. Voal needed this information, and he could also get an emergency message to Gaelcean without going through the usual channels. She moved back into an alley and made her way toward District Nine.

CHAPTER TWENTY

Patterns in the Web

Caleb's thoughts were an encumbrance at times. Earlier in the day the train arrived in Port Amboy and brought news of the attack on East Edge, as well as Gaelcean leaving the city with an army of Knights. *An army of Knights seemed the only appropriate way to describe it.* He had heard anywhere from a thousand to twenty thousand Knights walked right out the Eastern Gate. The most ridiculous reports were that they were being led by a Human. A member of Gaelcean's personal guard. Caleb had heard one of the City Guard had been promoted to some sort of higher rank, but a Human would never be that involved with the Council. It was impossible. Voal might have some answers. They had to move quickly. They needed to get to East Edge. He needed to get to Lucas.

Ana and Levi had agreed to stay in Port Amboy with Allegra and the other Amber Waves, while they continued to gather information. He realized he hadn't checked to see if Omar had been following him since he had gotten off the train at the station in the Ninth District. He stopped to turn around and felt a solid mass bump into him. He *had* been following him. He grabbed onto Omar's shoulder to keep himself from falling over. Luckily, he had grabbed hold of him as well.

"I wasn't expecting you to stop so suddenly," Omar said, slightly short of breath. "I thought you were going to run back to Voal's place once you set foot on the platform at the station."

"I know. I got caught up in my head. We need to get back to Voal." Caleb noticed a solemn look on his friend's face. "What is it?"

"We're all worried about Lucas, Caleb," Omar said.

"Come on." Caleb started walking again. This time he lessened his pace so Omar could keep up. "After we meet with Voal and tell him what we've learned, we'll head directly to East Edge. I don't plan on stopping or making camp along the way, but that doesn't mean you need to exhaust yourself either. If we're lucky we can make it there tomorrow night. Might be useful if we need to sneak into town."

"What exactly are we going to tell Voal?" Omar asked.

He wasn't exactly sure. They had had someone posted outside the Six-Spotted Fisher since Levi had seen Ellowen enter. The Amber Waves members in Port Amboy that had been patrolling the area had nothing new to report either. He hoped Allegra's eyes and ears outside of the Amber Waves would pick up on something.

Caleb had gotten impatient and gone in himself one night. He drank with some dock workers who told him what Ana had already learned. The construction was on time and the workers seemed pretty content with their work and their pay. The third day brought nothing of worth either. With the news of the attack on East Edge Caleb decided he and Omar should go find Lucas. Voal would have to take what they had, because Caleb needed to get out of the city.

"I think it would still be an odd coincidence that the old woman decided to name her tavern after a spider," Omar said from behind Caleb as they pushed through the crowded

272

street. There were gasps and grumbles as they made their way.

"That, I think, is the only bit of worthy information we'll have to bring," Caleb said. He hoped he was wrong. Maybe Voal could puzzle something out of it all.

"What do you make of Ellowen?" Omar asked.

Caleb could hear his hesitancy in mentioning the name. Was Omar still feeling guilty about letting her get the best of him and Ana? Maybe he had been too hard. He would need to apologize.

"It's not uncommon for some of the Families to employ workers of all trades." Caleb had thought he had lowered his voice, but the look he got from an old man that indicated otherwise. "We should stop talking about this until we get to where were going." How many others had heard what they had said? He needed to get a grip on himself before meeting with Voal. It was difficult to keep his mind from drifting to the east.

After a bit of walking around and back-tracking they found the abandoned store front that Voal had brought them to several days ago. The front door was locked and Voal hadn't given them a key to enter. Caleb pounded on the door twice before Omar grab his arm.

"There's no way they will hear someone knocking down there." He let go of his arm and stepped back. "There's got to be another entrance in the alley in the back or something." Omar looked up and down the street. "I don't see space to get behind the store fronts, we might need to find another street to get back there."

Caleb was about to send Omar off when the door opened enough for Voal to stick his messy-haired head out. Last time he had seen him the man looked as though he hadn't slept in days. His hair was still a curly mess, but he must have shaved this morning and he did look as though he had slept the night before.

"Your timing couldn't be any better. Please come in

273

before too many see you." Voal opened the door inward and urged the two of them inside. The door closed behind them and Voal locked it once more. "I am sure you have heard about the attack in East Edge." He moved between them and toward the stairs at the back of the dusty store.

"We have. I'm sure you can understand if our visit is only to tell you what we have learned and then leave." He followed Voal and matched his fast pace. "We must get to East Edge as soon as possible. Ana and Levi are still in Port Amboy collecting information."

"Yes, correct. Very good," Voal said as he led them down the stairs and into the basement once more. "I am aware that Lucas is in that area. Though, I'm not sure if he was present during the attack."

Caleb almost missed a step. "How do you know where Lucas is?"

Voal walked toward the back of the room and held out a small blue light. "The Amber Waves Company is important to us. We know more about your members than you may think." There was a beep followed by a heavy sound on the other side of the wall. A section of the wall in front of Voal slid to the left and disappeared into the wall beside it.

"How long?" Caleb tried to keep calm as he spoke.

"How long have we been tracking your organization?" Voal entered the room and walked over to a woman typing away at the terminal on her desk. He spoke to her as he passed, "Bring up the information they brought in last time. We'll add what they have brought us now." Voal turned around to look at him. "Once your chapter in Homestead reached thirty members, we sent a team out to watch your development and gather information. Gaelcean didn't believe you were a threat to the Council or himself, so you were added to low priority and occasionally we would check in on members of the Amber Waves. That isn't important now."

"Caleb. Omar. Welcome back. It is good to see you." Howlen Norre didn't look up as he spoke. The man seemed to have hardly moved from the place where he had been the previous time, the only difference now was that the stacks of documents he sorted through appeared to have tripled in height.

"*Gaelcean?* The Diplomatic Councilor?" Caleb's heart raced.

"It seems in the excitement; I have let too much slip." Voal took a deep breath and let it out slowly. It was as if it was the first time he had breathed since letting them inside. "Yes. I work for Councilor Gaelcean, and so, by proxy, you all do as well. That said, what do you have for us?"

Caleb had to work the moisture back into his mouth before he spoke. "Ana spent most of her time at the docks speaking to the workers. Omar and I checked in with the local Amber Waves chapter. Levi followed up on the only lead we seemed to have." What had he gotten them into?

"There was a woman on the train," Omar began. "She recognized Caleb and pieced together that the rest of us were Amber Waves."

Omar told Voal everything that had happened that first day and when he was finished, Caleb spoke about Ana's questioning the dock workers. They filled in the gaps where the other might have missed something. Voal listened and stared at the two of them. It wasn't clear if he was upset with the lack of information, or if he was just taking it all in.

Caleb opened his mouth to speak when Voal asked, "Did you get all of that, Deirdre?"

The woman seated at the terminal nodded. She never seemed to stop typing.

"Good. It is no coincidence this Ellowen woman brought you to the Six-Spotted Fisher. I imagine whoever is leading the Jorogumo in Port Amboy wanted you to find that place. But why?"

"They knew why we were there," Caleb said. Voal gave an affirming grunt. "Is it possible that Ellowen had informed her superiors that we had arrived *and* received word to let us tail her, from the time she left the platform to the time Levi found her?"

"Unlikely." Voal scrubbed his hands through his hair and sighed. "They must have known before you had left. Ellowen was most likely sent to follow you and lead you to the inn."

"What about the other man she was with?" Omar spoke up. "Levi said he just disappeared."

"Yes. The drunk. She may have been telling you the truth about him. We'll look through all the known Jorogumo associates from District Eight and see if their descriptions match what we have."

"If they knew our intentions before we—" Caleb was cut off when Voal put up a hand.

"That would be extremely unlikely, but I won't discount it entirely." Voal's eyes darted to the men and women at the terminals, and to Howlen who had a data pad in one hand and a stack of loose pages in the other. If any of them were even paying attention they made no sign of reacting to what was being said.

"Why though?" Omar asked. "Why let Levi find their place and then nothing?"

"Could be to send a message." Caleb ran a hand through his beard. "Now they know that we know they are in Port Amboy, and if it extends beyond that they have us thinking that ..."

"Caleb is right. We can't worry about this at the moment." Voal pulled out a credit reader and held an open hand out toward Caleb. "Let me pay you for what you have given us. As you can imagine there is much more to be done, but you must now go to East Edge."

Caleb handed Voal his data pad. "Thank you."

"You have given us more than you think. I'm transferring four hundred credits. This is the rest from the last job and some for the information you have given us now." He handed the data pad back and held out a small black rectangle. "When you get to East Edge, find Gaelcean and

276

give him this."

Caleb looked at the data jumper in his hand and then put it in the inside pocket of his coat. "I can do that, but that is it. We need t—"

The wall opposite the one Caleb and Omar entered through slid open and a bald woman with bright, oranges eyes entered the room. She stopped when she saw Caleb and Omar before she continued. "Things are not quite as we had thought," she said to Voal, and then turned to Caleb. "Caleb Fields, it is good to see you again."

That explains her Upper District connections. "You as well," Caleb said. "This is Omar Cross."

"I imagine Voal will update me on your findings in Port Amboy. I must speak with him. Alone, if you don't mind."

"We were just about to leave. I imagine we'll be seeing Gaelcean and the Knights soon." Before Caleb turned away, he thought he saw her glare at Voal.

"Could you give Gaelcean a message from me?" She stepped toward Caleb.

"Weleya." Voal tried to reach for her arm, but she rounded on him.

"You don't give me orders."

The words cut through Voal and he turned away to look at a terminal screen.

"'There was a closer connection than we originally had thought.' That will be enough for him to understand." Without waiting for his reply, she walked back over to Voal and spoke in hushed tones.

Caleb looked to Omar and motioned toward the basement space behind him. As they left the room the wall extended and sealed them off. Enough light was coming down from the open door at the top of the stairs to guide them through the room and back up to the empty store. Caleb held the door for Omar and then shut it behind them. Now to find Lucas.

"I am sorry I spoke to you that way," Weleya said to Voal after the entrance to the room had been sealed off. "There has been a development."

"There is no need to apologize," Voal said as he put away his data pad. "There is much going on right now and it is easy to be overwhelmed. These attacks from the Haze are coming at an inopportune time.

"I haven't spoken to Gaelcean since learning of the attack. I can only guess as to what he is thinking, but I imagine he is going to use this to further his plans."

Voal's expression changed. He was tapping his data pad with one finger, and she understood. She accessed the link to her own data pad that collected dust up in Gaelcean's rooms. A message from him appeared in her vision. *Possible breach in security. Uncertain, but we should be careful.*

She pretended to be lost in thought before speaking again. "We can't be sure what he will do. He should return within the week."

"Yes, I agree. For now, we have other things to focus on. There are several of our hired teams out collecting information. Come with me and I can show you what we have put together so far."

Voal walked over to the entrance that she had just come from. The two stepped into the room that Voal had used as his office for their network. Maps of the individual districts covered the walls, Lower and Upper. Each map had pictures of people of interest and small pieces of paper with names scribbled on them. Some of the pictures were District representatives and others, Weleya didn't recognize.

Voal fell into the chair behind his desk, he pushed the terminal screen to the side and motioned to Weleya to take the chair across from him. He ran his hands through his hair like always did while he thought, and then sighed.

As the hidden door slid into place and the lock engaged she felt comfortable speaking. "That group we thought was

278

going to be another technology-based religion, was actually a sort of school."

Voal stopped scrubbing his head. "A new school? That could be a positive thing for the Lower Districts."

"I wouldn't say so just yet. I think the man I met is their leader and he has Upper District connections. I met him in the Market Square preaching on a box to the crowd. He spoke about me as if I were some higher power." She shook her head. "I thought they *were* just a bunch of overzealous followers, until he took me to their school in the Third District. They have been teaching children how to work with higher tech. Some of the projects the students are working on are worrisome."

"I see. I will give it as much concern as I can allow right now." Voal tugged at his coat sleeves and folded his hands. "I'm not sure how much I have to spare to be honest."

"There are many gears in motion. There have always been." Weleya tried to comfort him. He would be fine once he was able to absorb and sort the information. *What had Caleb Fields and the others brought him?*

"It does seem that way."

"I can't say for certain that the Technological Society for Human Advancement is directly connected to the Jorogumo, but there may be some overlap in their goals. If an overlap exists, it could make their paths cross, if they haven't already. We should try to move this new school into a direction that would be beneficial to us."

"Yes, that would be good. Especially if they have students who can work with Upper District technology."

"I'm sending you a list of names I found, as well as some blueprints. Also, a rough schematic of a helmet one of the students was working on. I think that should take priority." Text and image scans appeared and disappeared from her vision as she spoke.

"Got them," Voal said, looking at his terminal screen. "The Amber Waves continue to produce, even if they didn't

279

seem to think so this time. The Jorogumo has a foothold in Port Amboy just as we thought. Unfortunately, it appears they know we are looking into them. It was wise to hire the work out to other groups, but it seems they made the connections sooner than we would have hoped." Another sigh. "Which leads me to say that which I had feared most since I began working with you and Gaelcean, it appears there is someone among my network who is in contact with the Jorogumo. Possibly worse."

"I see. Until Gaelcean returns I will sit in on Council meetings as his eyes and ears. Maintain contact with the hired individuals that are highest priority. Send payment and cease contact with anyone else. It might be used to send out some misinformation to those closest to you. I hope you find out who has betrayed your trust soon."

"I will. I can promise that much."

CHAPTER TWENTY-ONE

Gathering in the Night

The sun had set. Blue-green wisps danced across the surface of the Shield above. The night sky beyond the safety of the dome was a dark emptiness, save for the white shimmering dots that were scattered throughout. Caleb had learned how to travel using the stars a long time ago; it was simple if one knew what to look for. Seven stars made up the image in the sky he was tracking now. Some part of the Scythe was always visible in the night sky, but this time of year it hung over the eastern horizon. They had traveled at an exhausting pace using the constellation as a guide and were almost to East Edge. By his estimates they would arrive well into the night which would be a useful cover for their entrance. The difficult part would be finding Lucas once they were in the area. He was tempted to head straight to the Meadows family's farm but appearing in the small town in the middle of the night might seem suspicious. Especially when he considered everything that was going on.

Caleb walked with a hand on the hilt of his sword. Omar walked beside him with his iron-capped staff in his hand. The path ahead was lit by the moon enough to see a good distance ahead. A thick forest of needle-bearing trees, and oak surrounded them. That was far more concerning. Shadows from branches stretched out over the road like hands ready to pull an unsuspecting traveler into the shadow-filled growth. With the increasing raids and now the attack on East Edge no one dared travel, especially at night.

There was a snapping in the woods to their left. "Who's out there?" Caleb called out.

There was no reply and no more sound. Whoever had attacked East Edge may have sent scouts into the forest. Caleb half expected shadow-cloaked figures to rush out at any moment, but there was nothing. He squinted into the darkness.

"Could have been an animal of some kind," Omar said. They hadn't walked much farther when he stretched an arm out toward Caleb. He spoke without taking his eyes off the forest. "Wait. There *is* someone out there."

A sliver of moonlight found its way through the thick tree cover and Caleb thought he saw a glint of light. A face distorted by the low light playing tricks on his eyes. "I see you there. Moving behind that tree! Come out!"

Still silence, and then the shadowy figure began to move toward them. Whoever this man was, he was a giant. As he got closer, he seemed to only get taller. As they stepped out from the tree line, moonlight reflected off their silver armor.

"I am impressed. Had I not stepped on that dead branch I may have been able to follow you until you reached the edge of the forest." The Amboian stood at least two heads taller than Caleb. On his breast plate was a shield with two swords crossed behind it. A crest Caleb wasn't familiar with.

"You would have been better off wearing a cloak to cover that armor." Omar held his staff in the crook of his arm. Was this one of the Knights who traveled with Gaelcean and the others?

"My name is Laiere." The Amboian put a massive hand

to his chest. "Why are you traveling the Sun Road in the middle of the night?"

"We heard of the attack. We have a friend in the area, and we believe he may be in the town." Caleb stepped forward. Steel flashed as a long sword appeared in Laiere's hands.

"That is close enough." Laiere held the great sword with two hands. From tip to hilt the massive weapon would have matched Levi's height from shoulder to foot, Caleb thought. The weapon had been readied his sword as if it had been as light as a much smaller weapon.

"No need for that." Caleb held empty hands up. "We have a message for Gaelcean from Weleya. After we deliver that we mean to move into the town to find our friend, Lucas Meadows. That is all."

Laiere relaxed. "You have been given a message for Gaelcean? Why would you be trusted with this message?"

"We are members of the Amber Waves Company. We were hired by Weleya."

"Amber Waves." The sword disappeared from Laiere's hands. "There are Humans in our camp who claim to be members of the Amber Waves Company as well."

"How many?" Words couldn't come out fast enough for Caleb's thoughts. "Do you know their names? Are there any injured?"

"Do not worry." Laiere turned to walk down the dirt road. "I will take you to the camp and you will see for yourselves that your Amber Waves are fine."

Omar and Caleb exchanged a look and followed the Amboian down the road.

Laiere led them down the road until the forest began to open up and the moonlight filled the vast fields around them. In the distance down the hill lights from East Edge were visible. Laiere turned off the path and began moving through the trees. To their right in the grassy hills Caleb could see campfires and a sea of gray-green tents. In the center was a

283

much larger tent of the same color with two high peaks.

The rumors about the number of Knights Gaelcean had brought didn't seem far off. There must have been thousands of them among the camp. As they were led through the camp he could hear strange noises coming from inside some of the tents. It sounded like slurred growls and whistles. Did the Amboians bring animals to fight as well?

Caleb looked behind him to Omar and looked toward the tent where the noises had come from. Omar pointed to his ear and then around in a circle. Similar sounds could be heard throughout the camp. He had heard rumors that the Amboians had their own language that had been kept secret. He nearly reached for his sword when he remembered that that rumor was usually followed up by another that said that anyone who heard their language didn't live long afterward. As they approached the twin-peaked tent in the center of the camp six guards approached Laiere.

A Knight who wasn't much taller than Laiere stepped out from the other guards. "Who are these Humans you bring, Laiere?"

"They claim to be members of the Amber Waves Company." Laiere's response was stern. The air around the Knights seemed to thicken.

"And you believe them?" The Knight snarled as he spoke.

"I will take them inside. If they are Amber Waves the others will know. If they are not, then we can just interrogate them to find out if they are with the attackers in the town." Laiere didn't wait for a response from the Knight and pushed past him.

The interior walls of the tent were warm natural colors. Intricate carpets covered the ground. Braziers had been lit making the air inside the tent considerably warmer. Almost too warm. Beyond the carpeted floor with its decorative pillows for lounging, was a table where Amboians and several Humans were talking. Caleb recognized some, but once he saw Lucas he smiled.

"Lucas!" He pushed past Laiere, and immediately felt something pull him backward. A Knight at the table whirled around with a spear in both hands that wasn't there a moment before. The tip of the spear was nearly touched Caleb's neck. Had Laiere not pulled him back when he grabbed him, it would have easily gone through.

"Caelletan!" a voice said sternly from the table. "That is not necessary. These are allies of Lucas."

He looked around Caelletan once he felt Laiere let go of his cloak. A light-blue-skinned Amboian had been the one who had spoken. Dark-blue coat sleeves covered his arms, and a dark gray cloak was draped down his back. The cloak covered a breastplate with a familiar-looking bird on it. It all slammed into place when he recognized the bird from the wax seals. *So, this is Gaelcean.*

"Caleb." Lucas walked over and hugged him.

"I am glad you're safe, old friend," Caleb whispered.

"You'll have to fill me in on Port Amboy once this is all over." Lucas smiled. "Omar. I'm glad you are all here as well. Ana and Levi?"

"They stayed in Port Amboy to continue gathering information for us," Caleb replied, and followed Lucas as he took his place back at the table.

"It is nice to meet you in person, Caleb Fields." Gaelcean smiled as well. He wasn't sure he had ever seen an Amboian smile.

"You as well, Councilor Gaelcean."

"There is no need for formalities. You may call me Gaelcean." He gestured to a dark-skinned man in armor that almost resembled a Knight's. "This is Carter Gerro. He is a member of my personal guard."

Caleb reached across the table and held out a hand. "Good to meet you, Carter Gerro."

"Likewise," Carter replied shortly.

"Caleb, this is Elina." Lucas jerked his head to his right.

285

"She has been helping me since I got to my brother's farm."

"Elina, nice to meet you. Thank you for looking after my friend for me." A sadness overcame him as he remembered why Lucas had left in the first place. He leaned toward Lucas and lowered his voice. "You will have to fill me in your travels as well when we find the time." Lucas nodded in reply.

"Now that introductions are settled." Gaelcean waved everyone's focus back to the map that covered the table. "We have worked out a plan that we think will give us the best chance at avoiding further loss of life."

Caleb looked at the map of the town. Several groups of blue cubes were arranged in rows that arced along the hills to the west of the town. "The Knights will form to the west. I will lead a smaller group into the town." Gaelcean looked up from the map to address the table. "Myself, Carter, Laiere, and thirty Knights. Caelletan will lead the Knights in the west while Laiere is with me." He placed more blue cubes on the map to the east of town between it and the Perimeter wall. "Two groups of Knights will be stationed to the east. We believe there are more of their numbers beyond the Perimeter."

Once Gaelcean finished, Lucas placed a dull orange circle on the map near the northeast of town. "The Amber Waves will come from the north. We've gotten word that there is a small group of resistance fighters. Five members of the Amber Waves from Homestead sneaked into the town early this morning to attempt to locate them. We'll be meeting up with the Homestead group regardless at the northern end of the main town road."

"I'm sure the Knights outnumber these attackers from the Haze. Why not just push into the town?" Caleb asked.

"It is possible that if they see the Knights descending on the town, they will kill the townspeople. I intend to meet with their leader and find a peaceful solution. If the report of the resistance group is accurate, the Amber Waves will move through the town with them and neutralize any threats."

There was a pause. "I must stress that you use lethal methods only when absolutely needed." Gaelcean must have been the most soft-spoken Amboian he had ever heard.

Here they were, in a tent surrounded by Knights and listening to a joint battle plan from Lucas and a Diplomatic member of the Amboian Council. Yet, the way Gaelcean spoke was unusually comforting. As if East Edge hadn't been held captive by people from the Haze. It was as if Gaelcean knew everything would work out in their favor. The tent had fallen silent. A wind rustled the tent flaps. The faint sound of the Amboians speaking outside the tent floated in and was gone once the wind died down and the canvas settled.

"Once we have made terms, we must move quickly to restore order." Gaelcean stepped back from the map. "But that is not important now. It is getting late, and I still have some matters to attend to. You should all get some rest before tomorrow." Before anyone could responded he walked to the back of the tent followed by Carter, Laiere and Caelletan.

"Gaelcean?" Caleb asked.

The Amboian turned around. "Yes?"

"I have something for you, as well as a message from Weleya." Caleb stepped forward and held out the small black data jumper. Carter stepped into his path. His dark eyes were set on Caleb, and he radiated an air of intimidation that had taken him off guard.

"Thank you, Caleb." Gaelcean took the data jumper. "And the message?"

He fumbled for the words. "Weleya told me to tell you, 'There was a closer connection than you had previously thought'" *That was close enough.*

"I see." Gaelcean appeared to look past them all. "Thank you, again."

The night air was cool, almost unseasonably cool Caleb

thought. It would still be months until any significant snowfall. If a Sky Watcher were to tell him there would be snow tomorrow, he would have believed it. Seated in the opening of his small canvas tent, he looked around the campfire at those who were with him. Their involvement in this was entirely his fault. Guilt rose up inside him and he struggled to push it back.

"How have you been, Lucas?" Caleb asked, and Lucas turned from his conversation.

"I'm fine," He replied. Light from the fire danced on his features. Shadows seemed to fill the lines in his face, and he had bags under his eyes. Did his friend's hair seem grayer now than it had only days before?

"How are Fredrick and the family holding up?" Caleb could see a distant look in Lucas' eyes. He wished he could do more to comfort his friend. For now, talking would help.

"It's tough." Lucas sighed. "It is a tough situation. They're a strong bunch. Dion and Owain are holding up well. I think it hasn't really hit them yet. They want to join up with us." He chuckled. "That's not going to happen as long as I have any say, though."

"If there is anything we can do to help, Lucas," Omar said.

"Thank you, Omar. Thank you, all." A faint smile appeared on his face.

"So, who showed up from Homestead?" Caleb changed the subject.

"Do you remember Nattel Jassim?" Lucas raised an eyebrow. "He brought a young group from Homestead. He said they needed to prove themselves, said they were soft."

"He is a madman." Caleb shook his head. "All that talk of searching for his purpose in life, yet he runs headfirst into every conflict he can find."

"Purpose." Lucas scoffed. "He's a fan of embellishment. My guess, he was too much for any town guard to handle. That's why he joined us all those years ago."

"I don't think he's a madman. Maybe…" Omar trailed off. "Inspired?"

"Yes!" Lucas snapped his fingers.

Laughter erupted from the group and for a moment things seemed lighter than they had been in recent days. Caleb wiped a tear from his eye as he chuckled to himself. Lucas was no longer laughing. A darkness covered his face, one that the fire's light couldn't remove.

"There's something you haven't told us, isn't there?" Caleb asked.

Lucas looked up into the night sky before he spoke again. Caleb reflexively looked up as well, as if the answers to whatever troubled Lucas would be found in the starry sky over them. "Yes. Elina and I were in the town when the initial attack began."

"Oh, Haze," Omar whispered. A curse like that coming from a man like him held weight, and Caleb could feel it.

"There were three explosions. Distractions, we think, to cause chaos and confusion while the attackers made their way to the town hall. They…"

"What, Lucas?" Caleb leaned forward.

"They have some kind of weapon. I don't know what it is. After Elina and I saw one of them murder the town council we fled town, to wait for Jassim and the others to arrive." Lucas shook his head.

"What did you see?"

"There was a loud sound and a flash from this small object he held in his hand." He took a deep breath. "It was a bloody mess, Caleb. I've never seen anything like it. We came to the Amboian camp and convinced Laiere to send a message to Gaelcean. If I knew I would end up helping him with the battle plan…"

A sound and a flash?

"Did Gaelcean say anything about this weapon?" Omar asked.

"If he has any idea of what it is, I couldn't tell." Lucas

shrugged. Even that seemed to exhaust him.

Caleb wanted to change the subject; they could talk about this weapon later. Maybe Gaelcean had a plan to deal with it. "What do you think of Carter Gerro?"

"He seems like a smart man. He keeps quiet and observes. He takes his role as Gaelcean's guard seriously." Lucas poked the fire with a stick.

"I remember him from my time in the city," Elina spoke up. Caleb had almost forgotten she was there. "He had helped us find a thief who had stolen from our family. This was years ago; I think he and the other guards had just been allowed to patrol the Lower Districts."

"From patrol duty to Council guard." Caleb shook his head. "He must be an excellent solider. It will be interesting to see how he handles himself tomorrow if it comes to it." The words fell out of his mouth, and he immediately regretted it. Solemn faces looked back at him from everyone around the fire. He *would* ensure that nothing happened to those he cared about.

CHAPTER TWENTY-TWO

The Streets of East Edge

Cordelia looked into the yellow murk as she stood in the early morning light. If she were back up in the mountains, she might be able to see the very first tendrils of sunlight. She and Andreas sat just inside the Perimeter Shield. She guessed Andreas was years younger than she, but Landon wasn't wrong when he said he was one of the best Deep Scouts. He had kept right up with her and barely tired at the pace she kept. She had offered to let him rest a day at Mountain Station before they left, but once he heard of their mission, he had gathered his gear and asked when they were leaving.

She opened the small satchel her grandmother had given her to carry supplies and pulled out the small container that kept her pain medicine. She popped the last pill into her mouth. These pills that Deona had given her had done their job. Her body was tired, and her muscles ached, but there was no pain in her leg from the wound. She placed the container back into the satchel and saw the white ball encased in plastic.

Samuel had said it was called a *baseball,* and it was used in some Old World game. Now it seemed completely irrelevant with everything that had come to light since she had left the capital over a week ago. She had gone through the trouble of getting it, so it seemed a waste not to see it through. She rubbed her thigh where the plate had punctured her skin. The wound hadn't slowed her yet. She hoped her body could hold out a bit longer.

"These people beyond the Fog use close-combat weapons, right?" Andreas was packing his Haze suit away. His long rifle was slung across his back and he had a short blade at his hip.

"I have never seen a rifle or pistol of any kind during the time I've spent here." Cordelia stood up and stretched. A wind blew across the grassy fields. She was glad to be out of that suit. She would still have to grab her things from Jaeger's place. The long-sleeve shirt she wore now was travel-worn and need a wash. She wanted her traveling jacket and her loose fitting, but comfortable pants. "Swords, spears, axes. Expect a lot of the same."

"Do you think Dimitri's people brought any rifles, or anything?" Andreas didn't look up from his pack as he zipped it shut and stood up.

"If he did, they can't have many. We should assume he does." She checked the short blade she had at her hip and looked out across the field in front of them.

At first, she thought it was the low light of the morning that was tricking her vision. Her eyes strained as she squinted to see across the field. A mass of dark silhouettes moved across the green in the direction of the town.

"Andreas." Cordelia began a crouched run. "They are already here." There was a soft thump and then she heard Andreas running behind her.

"What do you want to do?" he whispered as they stalked through the tall grass.

"I have a friend who lives on the edge of town not far from here. We need to go to him first and then we'll move into the town. We need to find Dimitri and speak with him."

She wasn't sure if the pounding in her chest was from exhaustion or fear. She thought they would have had more time.

She counted as they moved, when the number reach forty, she gave up counting and stopped moving. "I counted forty. They don't seem to be moving in the direction of Jaeger's place, but that doesn't mean they haven't sent any people to him."

"There's also more over there." Andreas pointed in the direction behind Cordelia, and she turned. Throughout the field, a surge of brown and gray Haze suits was charging toward the town. In the distance a dull cheer began to cry out. It had begun.

"We need to run. Now!"

Cordelia threw her helmet and the bag that her grandmother had given her into the grass and began sprinting toward the direction of Jaeger's home. She hoped none of the attackers would look behind them and see her. Andreas caught up quickly and matched her pace. His rifle bounced on his back as he took long strides beside her. Cordelia heard the sounds of metal on metal ringing out in the field. Voices shouted. She looked behind her to her left and saw a massive group in silver armor mixing with the brown and gray suits of Dimitri's followers. Had the Amboians actually come to East Edge?

Jaeger's workshop and house came into view. Most of the suits had gone toward the town it seemed. She couldn't see anyone in the yard or any movement in the buildings from here. Jaeger might just be getting up now. A gray suit rounded the corner of the workshop followed by two others. She wasn't going to make up the distance in time. They would be inside the house before she was even close to the workshop. Her friend was going to die. Jaeger was going to d—.

There was a loud crack, and a ringing in her ears. She turned around to see Andreas on one knee and his rifle sight raised to his eye. She whipped back to look toward the workshop. One of the gray suits was bent over looking at something she couldn't see and the other was looking in their direction.

"Thank you, Andreas," she whispered.

She sprinted toward the workshop and heard another shot ring out. A red mist erupted from a masked head before the body fell to the ground. Cordelia could feel the blood pumping in her ears. Her lungs burned as she gasped for air. Her legs were moving without thought, one reached out ahead of the other. She covered the space between where she had been and the workshop in an instant. She was on top of the third suited person and her blade was pushed up into their skull. She hadn't even remembered unsheathing it. There was a wet gurgle as she pulled the blade out. She thought about removing the masks that were still on the faces of the attackers, but she stopped herself. There was a chance that she had known one of the people who she had just killed.

She heard footsteps behind her and spun around blade ready as Andreas stepped out of the tall grass.

"It's okay. It's okay," he said as he held up his hands. His rifle was slung over his back again. "I was barely able to hit the second shot. I tried to get the third, but I couldn't risk hitting you."

"It's fine, Andreas." She was panting. "I owe you."

There was the sound of a door opening to her left and Jaeger appeared from the workshop. "They're back," he said, looking at the bodies in his yard. "They came by the other day and asked me to make weapons and armor for them. I think they would have killed me, had I refused."

Cordelia wrapped her arms around the old man. "I am glad you are safe, Jaeger."

"Thanks to you, and...?" Jaeger said over her head.

"Andreas. Andreas Martinez." Andreas was looking out across the field and toward the town. "They would have

294

heard those shots, but I don't see any movement in this direction. It looks like that mass is too caught up in the fighting. Some have made it into the town."

"Martinez. It's good to see a Faucher and a Martinez working together," Jaeger said stepping back from the hug. "There are people in the town who had formed a resistance group, find them. I can handle myself."

"No, I'll go." She turned to Andreas who was still looking out toward the town. "Stay here with Jaeger, keep him safe." Andreas didn't say anything, he only continued to keep an eye on their surroundings.

The streets of the town were silent. In the distance Cordelia thought she could hear cheering. Or was it screaming? She shuddered. She needed to get to Dimitri and talk to him. There had to be a better way. A group of Haze suits crossed the street ahead of her and she slid into a doorway. She peered out and could see the last of them head into an alley. She stayed close to the side of the street along the buildings and moved in the direction they had gone. She unsheathed her blade and readied it as she rounded the corner. The alley was empty. They must have continued down the next street. As she slowly moved through the cramped space, she wondered how so many of them had gotten through so quickly.

At the end of the alley Cordelia stuck her head out enough to see into the wide street. This must have been the main road that led to the town center. If she remembered right the town hall was at the other end of the plaza in the town center. The group of Haze suits was walking down the street; their guard was down. There was no way she would be able to handle them all, but she could follow them. They might lead her to Dimitri.

As she stepped out into the street, she heard movement behind her and brought her blade around just in time to redirect a long sword that swung near her head. Cordelia stepped to the side and brought her blade to the woman's neck. Her short blond hair framed her handsome face, and intense hazel eyes stared back.

"Elina?" Cordelia stepped back from the woman and cursed. "I could have *killed* you!" A group of men and woman ran up from behind her with swords and bows at the ready.

"I don't know about that," Elina said, almost laughing. "It's okay. I know this woman."

"Good. More people to add to our numbers." A bald man with a thick black beard approached her. "I'm Caleb Fields of the Amber Waves."

"Cordelia Faucher." She shook his hand. "The Amber Waves don't have an East Edge chapter, if I remember right. It's fortunate you are all here."

"It's more than coincidence." A man with olive skin and graying dirty blond hair walked toward her and Elina. He was about to open his mouth to say something else, but his attention shifted to the street behind her. The man groaned and readied his sword. "Ready yourselves!"

Cordelia turned to see the group of Haze suits running toward them.

Arrows flew overhead and brown and gray suits hit the stone-paved streets as they found their targets. Cordelia braced herself as the suits closed in on them. A blur rushed past her. Elina. Then there was a wave of people moving on both sides her. She fell in with them. She may not be able to do much with the injury still so fresh, but she wouldn't stand by as the others fought. The two groups crashed into one another. The street was filled with shouts. One moment she was stepping out of the way of a swinging sword or club, and at the next opening she was driving her blade into the chest of an unmasked man. A look of surprise was cemented on his face as he dropped. If she hadn't been so focused on her survival, she would have been sick right there. She spun around to see Elina's sword cut clean through the leg of a suit that charged at her. The person stood for a moment before they fell screaming as they clutched at the bloody stump where their leg had been. Elina disappeared into the frenzy once more.

A tall dark-skinned man swung an iron-capped staff into the head of a masked suit beside her. There was a loud crack as the staff made contact. The man turned to her and nodded. He then turned away from her and held his staff out in front of him.

The crowded melee was hot, and the stench of blood filled the air around her. Cordelia stayed on the balls of her feet and looked around for an opening or an attacker moving toward her. It was then she had realized the fighting had stopped. It had felt like an eternity had passed. Cordelia took a deep breath in and slowly let it out as she looked around the street. Most of the suits were no longer moving. Those that were lay groaning. She wiped her blade clean before sheathing it and walked over to Elina.

"Are you hurt?"

"No." Elina didn't even seem winded. She still held her long sword in both hands and was looking further down the street. "More could be coming. We should keep moving."

"I agree. We should make for the town center and try to avoid any more of this. Is anyone hurt?" Caleb looked at the bodies as he spoke, and then to his companions. A few of the men and women had cuts and small lumps that would be bruised soon. None seemed terribly injured.

"We should try to take as many as we can." A man with a strong jaw stepped beside Caleb. His waist-long black hair was woven into an intricate braid. Sweat glistened on his pale skin and a long pink scar ran down the side of his face from his hairline to his jaw.

"Jassim, you are going to get yourself killed being so reckless." The olive-skinned man with the graying hair slapped Jassim on the back. The two men laughed. Caleb shook his head. Cordelia thought she heard him mutter something about a madman.

"We should keep moving." Elina didn't look back as she continued down the street, long sword still in hand. Caleb looked at the group of men and women who stood around him and nodded.

"I had hoped when I returned to East Edge you would still be here." Cordelia matched Elina's trot as they moved down the street.

"I am glad you are here as well. Although the circumstances are not ideal." She scanned store fronts and alleys. They stopped every few paces to avoid coming upon another group of suits.

"I counted well over forty charging into the town from the east." A cat darted out of an alley as they approached it. Cordelia had almost struck out at the sound but lowered her blade once the cat ran across to another space between two buildings.

"The east?" Elina stopped moving at met Cordelia's eyes.

She fumbled for an explanation. Suspicion was clear on Elina's face. "I heard of the attack on the town. I had to return to make sure my friend was okay." The knot in her stomach unwound. If she continued to slip more and more, soon she would have to tell Elina the truth. The fighting wasn't the only reason she needed to keep her guard up, but it seemed it was distracting her from shrouding her intentions. Her lie seemed to have worked for now, but she couldn't be certain.

"The town center isn't much farther." The olive-skinned man stopped beside Elina. The others had caught up as well "The resistance fighters should be just about making it to the southern side of the square. Gaelcean and the others should be entering the square from the West as well."

"Gaelcean? The Amboian Diplomat is here?"

"Him and an entire battalion of Knights." Jassim smiled. "The Knights have spread around the town. If they made it to their positions, they might have kept a good number of the attackers out."

"He means to meet with—" Cordelia caught herself. "With their leader?"

"Yes," The olive-skinned man said. "We're creating diversions, so Gaelcean's group can make it to the town center with as little trouble as possible. We should keep moving to stick to that plan."

"Lucas is right," Caleb said and began moving again. "Let's go."

"I would like to join Gaelcean when he meets with the leader."

Caleb almost tripped over his own feet as Cordelia spoke. "What?" He rounded on her once he regained his balance. "Why do you want to meet with the leader of these Haze settlers?"

"I have questions that he may have the answers to."

"We all have questions, Cordelia," Elina said while still scanning the street.

"I *will* meet with him." She didn't break eye contact with Caleb. She could feel everyone's eyes on her. How could she get into that meeting without giving too much away? Lucas eyed her intently. She couldn't bring herself to look toward Elina.

Finally, Caleb spoke, "We will have to make it there first."

It was all that was said, and they began moving again.

They had avoided almost all the groups of Haze suits moving through the streets, all but one. Jassim had pressed that there was no way to avoid the situation ending in bloodshed, but he had charged out of the group swinging his long sword. He had taken down two suits before the rest had realized. Cordelia and the others had reached him only seconds after, and when the fighting was over Jassim was the only one who had been injured. A diagonal cut stretched from his left shoulder to his ribcage on the other side.

"It's nothing. I'm fine." Jassim's long braid swung as he shook his head. One of the Amber Waves members stepped toward him. She ignored his protests and forced him to lie

299

down on the side of the street. The rest of the group formed a circle around the two and kept watch. Cordelia looked up and down the street and didn't see anything of note. She turned her attention back to Jassim and the woman.

"If that gets an infection, you will not be fine. I need to look at that." The short woman's brown hair had been neatly braided and wrapped around the crown of her head. She set down the longbow she was carrying and opened a small satchel at her side and pulled out a small draw string pouch. "You're lucky it isn't too deep." She poured a white powder from the pouch along the wound. The wound sizzled like meat cooking on a hot stove top. Jassim clenched his jaw.

"Thank you, Sendene." Jassim's thanks came through gritted teeth as the wound stopped making that awful sound. She thought for a moment she had actually seen smoke rise from the cut.

"Cauterroot powder is only a temporary fix. That will need to be properly looked at once we are back at camp." Sendene pulled the drawstring closed and tucked the pouch back into the small satchel at her side. As she stood, she checked the string of her bow and nodded to herself. The cut that had been across Jassim's chest was now a painful-looking red valley, but the bleeding had stopped.

"Are you going to be okay to keep moving Jassim?" Lucas asked as he held out a hand to the man still lying on the paved street. Jassim grabbed Lucas' hand. Not even a grunt came from him as he was lifted to his feet. "Alright then. We should try to avoid any further combat." Lucas shot a quick look to Jassim, but then looked to the others.

"Let's hope this hasn't set us back. Gaelcean's team is most likely to the town square now."

The group kept tight to the sides of the buildings and hid in alleyways and entrances of shops when a mass of suits walked past a connecting street ahead. It seemed as they got closer to their destination the number of attackers they saw had increased. Cordelia had tried to keep a count in her head but gave up when keeping low took precedence. She still hadn't come up with a plan to convince the others, let alone Gaelcean, that she needed to be in that room when they spoke with Dimitri. They had been able to hear sounds of fighting throughout the town as they moved closer to the center. Now the town had fallen silent. The Haze had come to East Edge.

CHAPTER TWENTY-THREE

A Kind of Diplomacy

Carter and Gaelcean were flanked on both sides by two rows of Amboian Knights much like when they had toured the Lower Districts. That felt like another lifetime, even though it had only been almost two weeks ago. He marched in front of Gaelcean, with Laiere behind. Laiere had argued that he should lead in front of Gaelcean, but that position was reserved for the personal guard. Normally that would have gone to Weleya as she had seniority over Carter, but in her absence, he would lead and Laiere would follow.

Carter's thoughts drifted from the wide street and the smaller side streets around them. He wondered where Weleya was and what took precedence over removing invaders from the Haze from a Perimeter settlement. Perhaps it was more that, if Carter and Weleya were here with Gaelcean, who would be trusted to inform him of what was happening while they were gone. Paelle was a possibility, but she seemed too far removed from Gaelcean within the Hall.

The late morning sun was reflecting off the silver armor of the Knights around him and the massive, long swords on their backs. Each held a shorter sword—a long sword in any Human's hands—at the ready as they marched through the wide street that would lead to the town center. Carter was wearing his own matte-gray armor of the same material, which was surprisingly cool even in the direct sunlight. This was the first time he had worn the entire set that protected his body. Paelle had almost bragged at the construction, *it was the best combination of light-weight protective material.*

The wooden and stone buildings that lined the gray stone-paved street were empty. He had suggested they use the side streets to avoid as much risk to Gaelcean's life as possible; out here they were exposed. All it would take was one arrow and their plan would fall apart. *Gaelcean's death could even cause the entire capital to fall apart.* His suggestion was heard but wasn't held with very high consideration. Gaelcean had mentioned the need for them to make their presence known as much as when they had left the capital. *Those who live along the Perimeter, must see that we stand with them. A strong force will make an impact on their understanding that we are here for them. For all of them.*

At first he had thought Gaelcean meant all in the Perimeter, but now marching through the streets, the words took new meaning. He had hoped to avoid fighting. Almost as if Chance was reading his thoughts, a small number of people in brown, gray, and dark-green body suits rushed out from a side street. Some wore masks that covered their entire faces, with tubes running from the front or side of the mask to tanks that were on their hips or backs. They carried clubs with metal hammered into them and chipped blades of all lengths. One of them was swinging a long wooden pole that had a long, curved blade on one end.

The Knights sprang into action and quickly surrounded the attackers, moving as if they were half their size. Short and long swords flowed through the air. The Amboians cut down the futile surprise attack without any of them taking an injury. Only the one attacker remained. The two-handed long pole

303

with the curved blade swung wildly.

Unable to see any definite features, Carter was unsure if the short-haired slender-looking figure was a man or a woman. The unknown fighter stood with their weapon out in front of them, keeping the Knights at bay. A Knight lunged in with a sword and the fighter used the curved blade to redirect the sword away and brought the blunt end of the pole up into the Knight's visor. The pole slid off the rounded surface of the helmet, but the blow did make the Knight stagger back for a moment while he regained his footing. The fighter followed through the motion of the failed blow to the face and rolled to the side while spinning the pole, blocking away another attack.

Gaelcean watched intently as two Knights approached this time from opposite sides. "It is inspiring to see so much fight in one person alone. We will be lucky if the others are not this determined."

A Knight swung a long sword at the legs of the fighter. They jumped in the air and upon landing slashed the wicked blade downward and knocked the sword from the hands of the Knight. They followed up by letting go of the long pole with one hand and letting it spin diagonally around their torso catching it back in front of them as they blocked an attack from the other Knight.

"Impressive," Gaelcean said, still watching intently. Carter thought he heard a snarl from Laiere.

It had seemed that the melee could have continued on like this, until a Knight rushed in and was able to slash at the back of the legs of the remaining attacker. As they dropped to a knee, they were still able to redirect an attack from the Knight who had retrieved his sword. The Knight who was able to finally land a hit swung about and cut across their back tearing the green-gray suit. They let out a cry that was only slightly muffed by their mask and fell to the ground dropping the weapon. The Knight approached the injured fighter and kicked away the pole.

Gaelcean called out, "Hold!" He approached. "If you could remove your mask. I'd like to ask you some questions."

From where Carter was standing, he could only make out a muffled voice. What was said didn't sound agreeable. Gaelcean motioned to the Knight who had been about to make the killing blow; instead, they removed the mask from the fighter.

The sun-tanned woman looked up at Gaelcean with dark eyes, as if they themselves were weapons she could harm with. Her dark hair was almost shaved to nothing.

"What is your name?" Gaelcean asked. "I would like to avoid as much loss of life as possible. Skills in combat are not the requirement to avoid that, but you *have* fought well."

The woman glared up at Gaelcean. "You wish to avoid loss of life?" She spat blood at Gaelcean's feet. "I find that contradicts my people's current situation." Her voice sounded slightly hoarse and gravelly. Carter wondered if a lifetime in the Haze had done that to her voice, or if she had been born with it.

"That is something I am here to discuss with your leader, or whoever is in charge of the assault on those who are under my protection." Gaelcean's tone didn't change. A calm pond, on a windless day. "I would very much like to know your name."

"Rosalynn Greene." She still didn't take her eyes off Gaelcean. Carter was unsure how she hadn't passed out from the wounds she had received. "Who are you?"

"I am Gaelcean, Amboian Diplomat and a member of the Diplomatic Council in Central Amboy."

Carter could hear the smile in Gaelcean's voice appear as he spoke.

"Gaelcean, Amboian Diplomat, you say you want to avoid loss of life." Rosalynn's eyes began to flutter. "I doubt that will be possible today." Her body fell to the side in a heap. Carter could see now how much blood she had lost. The left leg of her suit was covered in dark-red blood, and all

305

down her back looked the same.

"Laiere," Gaelcean called without looking away from Rosalynn lying at his feet. "Take this woman back to the camps immediately. See she is given treatment. When she recovers, I will speak with her."

Laiere snared again, but before Gaelcean had finished speaking he lifted the woman off the street and began a full sprint back in the direction they had come.

Gaelcean turned toward Carter. "I mean to keep my word, Carter Gerro. I will avoid loss of life if possible."

With the combat over, the group returned to formation. A Knight who Carter didn't recognize took Laiere's place.

The group had picked up the pace of their march toward the town center. Carter hoped the Amber Waves had found the resistance fighters. The three groups were to enter the square as if the captors were expecting a delegation; the Knights would hold back anyone who tried to stop them. Carter and Gaelcean were to continue on toward the town hall. The resistance and the Amber Waves were to move toward the town hall as well and meet up with the Knights to stand guard while Gaelcean met with the leader of the assault. Carter thought it impossible that they would be able to make it to the top of the large stone steps without a fight. To his surprise they weren't met with conflict, but a man who stood at the top of the steps began shouting orders, and a mass of people in those same suits surrounded the steps.

Those who weren't wearing the suits began crying out. Carter could hear shouts of, 'Shield protect us!' and 'Amboy protect us!' He also thought he heard shouts for the Amber Waves and the resistance once their group moved into the square as well. The resistance moved toward the mass of people being held in the square while the Amber Waves and Gaelcean's group walked around the eastern and western paths. They met at the base of the stone steps that led up to the town hall. Only a few of those steps were between the assaulting force and their own. The shouts from the town's people had stopped and the entire square fell silent as the two groups stood facing each other. After a quick count, Carter guessed there were about one hundred men and women standing on those steps looking down at them.

Gaelcean broke the silence first. He only needed to raise his voice slightly for it to be carried throughout the square. "I am Gaelcean. I am here as a representative of the Diplomatic Branch of the Council of Amboy. I stand here to speak with the leader of this attack on those who are under the protection of the Council of Amboy. I mean to resolve this terrible event peacefully."

A bald man with umber skin stepped out from the columns at the top of the steps. "Well, I am Jonas!" The man held his arms out as he walked to the edge of the top step. "I represent the people who took your town!" The man's bray-like laugh echoed through the square.

Gaelcean opened his mouth to speak, but another man stepped beside Jonas and spoke, "My name is Dimitri Endano. I agree with you, Gaelcean." He had struggled with the name, but at least he seemed more reasonable than Jonas. "Come and speak with us. Let him through." The men and women on the steps parted. Was he the one who was really in charge? Jonas seemed to listen to him as well. Maybe this Dimitri was a second in command, or some sort of advisor?

"I think it is not unreasonable for me to bring my personal guard, Carter Gerro." Gaelcean motioned a hand to Carter who was standing behind him and to his left. "As well as two of the Knights." Two Knights who were standing behind Carter stepped forward.

"Of course." Dimitri nodded and motioned them to approach.

"I would also like to sit in on this meeting!" a voice shouted to Carters left and a fair-skinned woman stepped forward. She removed the dark fabric that had been covering her head and her long red hair flowed out. "My name is Cordelia Faucher, and I have some questions for you Dimitri

Endano."

Dimitri's face was expressionless. Jonas had just barely kept his jaw from falling. He glanced toward Dimitri. Whoever this woman was, she made them uncomfortable.

"Yes, yes of course. Cordelia Faucher." Dimitri seemed to struggle with her name as much as he had Gaelcean's. Jonas leaned in to speak to Dimitri, but he shoved him away.

Without waiting for word, the red-haired woman walked up the steps toward them. Carter noticed a few faces among Dimitri's forces looked at the woman nervously, and just as many others avoided eye contact.

Another voice from the crowd called out, "I won't allow Cordelia to attend without her own guard." Cordelia stopped on a step to turn around.

Carter looked to his left and saw the tall blond woman who he had met with the Amber Waves in the camp the night before. Elina was her name if he remembered right. Was Cordelia a high-ranking member of the Amber Waves? What did they have to do with the attack on East Edge? There was no chapter in East Edge that Carter knew of, unless they were going to use this as some means to create one. Carter shook his head. The mercenary group would use any opportunity to better their position in the New Ring. Next, they would want a branch in the Lower Districts. They had done good work in the past keeping the people safe, when the city guard couldn't, but they were becoming very close to any other power-hungry organization in the capital. Cordelia nodded to Elina, and the two continued up the steps.

Carter looked toward Gaelcean, who was studying the women walking up the steps. "Come, Carter. I believe this meeting will be far more enlightening than I had previously thought."

Carter and Gaelcean, Dimitri and Jonas, and Cordelia sat a solid oak table in the center of a large rectangular room. This was once the room where the East Edge council would meet. A smaller town's council was modeled after The

Council. Each member was tasked with focusing on one need or another.

Now the five people sitting at the table were meeting to discuss their own wants and desires. East Edge was merely a host. Standing behind Carter and Gaelcean were the two Knights who followed them in. Carter had insisted on standing with the Knights, but Gaelcean insisted sit at the table. Elina leaned against the mantle of the cold fireplace. It wouldn't be long before there would have to be a regular fire to keep the chill of winter off those who sat in this room. Behind Jonas and Dimitri stood a hard-faced man and a woman with her black hair in a braid. Her piercing blue eyes seemed to look right through Carter when they made eye contact, and her fair skin seemed to glow in the light from the overhead lamps that lit the room.

Dimitri waved a hand to the man and he turned to a table beside him and picked up a wooden tray that had a tall glass pitcher and several glass cups. "If we had alcohol, we would offer it to you, but it seems all we could find in the building was water on short notice." He nodded to the man as he set the tray down on the table next to him and lifted the glass pitcher to fill the glasses. He passed one to each seated at the table. "I appreciate your willingness to speak with us, Gaelcean. I'm sure we will come upon a solution that benefits *all* parties involved." With that last he held out a glass to Cordelia. She didn't take her eyes off him as she took the glass from his hand and set it down on the table in front of her.

Carter had seen Gaelcean in the Council Hall enough to know he would be in his element and in the end would have Jonas and Dimitri submitting to his demands. What they would be, he was eager to learn.

"Thank you, Dimitri." Gaelcean accepted the drink with a slight smile but didn't drink. "Now which of you leads this group from beyond the Perimeter?" Gaelcean folded his hands and set them on the table. A picture of serenity.

"That would be me," Jonas said after downing several mouthfuls of water. He wiped his mouth with his hand. "The way I see it. You're the outsiders here, and we've only taken back what was stolen from us." He was too confident though, and that would most likely be his downfall.

"I would ask you to explain why you feel that way." Gaelcean looked toward Jonas and the man's face reddened slightly.

"Why?" He put two clenched fists down on the table. "Your kind are the reason our people live in that forsaken poison cloud!" He slammed his fists down. Some of the water spilled from Gaelcean's cup. A wet ring formed around his own glass as well.

"We are expanding the Perimeter as fast as our resources allow. What are the coordinates of your settlement? We can give you a projection of when you will be included among those under our protection."

Jonas' face went crimson as Gaelcean responded. Dimitri sat shaking his head.

"You know well enough what I mean." The man's anger was cutting through as he spoke. "No human is alive today to give a personal account, but everyone knows the stories. Your kind dropped this Fog on us when your ship appeared in the sky all those years ago."

Carter looked to Gaelcean, but the Diplomat was expressionless. The stories from the Old World taught that the civilizations that existed then were enveloped in a war that engulfed the entire planet, which led to its destruction. Cordelia looked at Jonas with disbelief. Dimitri was still locked in on Gaelcean.

"I can imagine the stories that your Elders tell." Gaelcean began and stood up. He walked about the room as he spoke. "I have heard some of them myself over the years. My species created humanity. My species made the Haze—the Fog as you call it beyond the Perimeter—to keep Humanity under control. Many, many things." Gaelcean stopped and looked

310

toward Jonas again. "I can assure you none of those stories are truth." Gaelcean actually sighed before continuing. "What is truth. . .we had been watching your planet for quite some time. We were concerned at your constant warmongering. The Humans who inhabited this planet were destroying it. Destroying something so unique." Gaelcean set his hands on the table and leaned in. "When the wars reached their climax, we intervened. To save what little of Humanity we could."

"Then why do your Reclamation Crews destroy the Old World as you expand?" Cordelia sat with her arms folded. "Your crews are destroying whatever little remains of the past. You remove what you deem important, but how would *you* know what is important in our history?"

Who was this woman? Carter had never thought about what remnants of civilization existed beyond the Perimeter. He had thought when the Perimeter expanded, the lands that were added to the New Ring looked as untouched as those he had seen during his time atop the Exterior Wall.

"Indeed." Gaelcean had almost seemed shaken slightly, but he quickly recovered his calm exterior. "It was decided that in order to avoid the events of the past, we would take it upon ourselves to guide Humanity in a direction that would ensure the safety of this planet."

"Who knows what important parts of Humanity's history have been lost." Cordelia didn't move as she spoke. "There are things out there that have significance to our people. How can the Amboians pick and choose what remains?"

Jonas opened his mouth to speak, but Dimitri nudged him and shook his head.

It was Gaelcean that responded. "You have made a good point, Cordelia Faucher." He studied her. The Amboian looked as though he was learning the history of her own life from looking at her face. "I would like to speak to you on this matter another time. Not that I do not see the importance, only that I believe our current situation takes priority."

Cordelia nodded and she let out a sigh.

"Jonas, in the ideal situation for you, what would be the result of our meeting today?" Gaelcean asked.

"This town remains under our control. The farmlands in the surrounding area are also ours. The recent harvest will go to our people in the Fog. Anyone who wishes to stay can stay, but we run the town. We don't answer to your *Council.*" He counted each demand on a finger. He listed them out as if they were rehearsed.

"I see." Gaelcean walked the room and ended standing between Carter and Jonas seated at the table. "I think we can come to a compromise that will meet both our desires. Those who you have brought with you can stay in the town. We will expand the town to shelter all the new citizens. Any of your people who still live in the Haze will be welcome as well. However." Gaelcean paused before continuing. "I cannot allow East Edge to leave the control of The Coun—"

Jonas slammed the table. For the first time that Carter had seen, Gaelcean appeared angry. If Gaelcean could be angry that is, impatient might be a more accurate description.

"No!" Jonas' fist pounded the table once more. "I decide how it will be. I do! When I—"

If Carter had blinked, he probably would have missed it. Gaelcean grabbed the back of the man's head and slammed it into the table so his jaw caught the edge. There was a crunch and a terrible gurgling as Jonas tried to breathe through bones and blood. His body fell to the floor twitching. The hard-faced man and the black-haired woman moved toward Dimitri, and where Jonas was lying on the floor. Elina pulled Cordelia's chair back and it made a loud scraping sound on the wooden floor. She had pulled a dagger from nowhere and was pointing it out toward the room. At same time Carter had stood up and moved to put himself between Gaelcean and the others, but Gaelcean held a hand out and everyone stopped moving in the room. The two Knights flanked the group on either side. The only sound was fading bubbling from Jonas on the floor.

312

"As I have said many times today." Gaelcean adjusted the long sleeves of his blue coat. "I *wish* to avoid loss of life." He walked back to his seat and sat down. Carter was frozen where he was standing. Still trying to process what had just happened. What *had* just happened? Gaelcean motioned for Carter to sit back down and he did. Cordelia was wide-eyed looking from the seat where Jonas had just been and then to Gaelcean. She pushed Elina out of the way and fell into her seat back at the table.

Gaelcean took a sip from the glass of water and set it back on the table. "Now, Dimitri. Would you like to come to a solution that will benefit *all* parties involved?"

CHAPTER TWENTY-FOUR

Among the Crowd

The square in the center of East Edge was packed with residents, and those who had sacked the town and sought to control it. Cordelia stood in the crowd with Elina and the members of the Amber Waves. Gaelcean stood at the top of the stone steps with Carter at one side and Dimitri at the other. Behind them were the Knights of Amboy. He was making a speech to the massive crowd, but she was only half paying attention. Images of Jonas' head being pushed into the table flashed in her mind. Her positioning at the table had spared her from seeing what Gaelcean had done, but the sounds that came from him as he lay on the floor painted a horrible picture in her mind. Jonas' jaw shattered into his throat, as he lay on the floor. The image flashed again and again. She couldn't stop herself from shivering, even in the late afternoon sun. She had never met him before today; she didn't even know which outpost he was from. She thought she saw the twin silver arches of Tunnel Outpost on his shoulder patch. It all seemed a blur now.

"I'm still processing it as well," Elina said in a low voice beside her. "A diplomatic member of The Council nonetheless…"

"I've heard things about some of the Councilors." Caleb's voice startled her. She had almost forgotten there was a crowd of people around them. "Had it been one of *them*, I'd believe it. Had I heard Gaelcean had done it from anyone other than you two, I wouldn't. Seeing the way you all came out from the townhall, I believe it. Even Carter Gerro looks stunned up there."

She looked up at Carter. An after image of shock still covered his face. He seemed to be looking off into the distance, as if he could see the farm fields beyond the buildings in the town.

"The Council always gets their way," Jassim rasped. "Always." He let out a ragged cough.

"You should have gone to the camps after the fighting stopped, Jassim," Caleb whispered. "Lucas, would you take him now?" Cordelia felt bodies shuffling behind her and heard Lucas asking for people to make way.

She had heard that some of the attackers had been captured and brought back to the camps. She would have to visit them to question those who were captured.

"It is important that we work together." Gaelcean's voice carried over the crowd. She had to force herself to listen to the words. "We must work together to ensure the survival of Humanity and the Amboians. Only together can we survive." There was a mixture of cheering and cursing from the crowd.

"Send them back to the Haze!" a booming voice shouted. She immediately recognized that voice. She stood on her toes to see over the crowd in the direction that it came from. "They killed my family! They killed them in my own home!" She had to look away as she recognized the round-faced man. The smile that once stretched across his face was replaced by anger and hatred. Shouts from the crowd rose up after that, this time most all were angry.

"This will never work," Caleb said. "Oil and water will

315

mix when shaken up. Once they settle, there's a clear separation."

"Do you believe killing *their* families, the ones that *they* love, will bring yours back?" Gaelcean looked in the direction the shout had come from. "Can you point out the one in this crowd who committed the murder? If you are able to do that without a doubt in your mind, justice may yet be found. If you cannot, you must move forward." There was a murmur through the crowd. Could Gaelcean actually convince all these people who had been fighting to unite? "I will stay and see the reconstruction and expansion of East Edge. I will be here to assist in the appointment of new officials and in setting up the infrastructure to get aid to those still beyond the Perimeter." The murmurs in the crowd seemed to be shifting to acceptance, but there was still an occasional shout and curse from some individuals. Cordelia got back on her toes to see if her once traveling companion, Victor, was still in the crowd, but she couldn't see him.

Cordelia looked to Dimitri. His eyes were downcast. He had been defeated. The chance to question him about why he did what he was doing was taken from her when Gaelcean took control. What was the point of letting Jonas pretend to play the part? Was Dimitri truly the one in control?

"Together!" Gaelcean tried ending on a high note. "Together we will move forward and put this terrible event behind us." A majority of the crowd cheered at that. How quickly they had all forgotten and wanted to move on. It made little sense to her. She looked up at Gaelcean. He was staring directly back at her. She felt as though she was going to be sick.

The Humans that had been a part of the attack from the Haze were quickly detained and brought into the Town Hall for questioning. More Knights had entered the town as well and were stationed throughout the square. They pulled anyone in a Haze suit from the crowd. Cordelia was lucky she had left hers with Jaeger and Andreas. She would have to get back there soon to let them know everything had passed, and about the new East Edge. Elina and Caleb walked beside her. Caleb shifted between running his fingers through his beard and rubbing his bald head. The three had been walking laps around the square talking the events of the attack over and discussing the future of East Edge.

"Lucas and I have been talking about it for some time." He rubbed his head this time. "I think we should set up a permanent Amber Waves chapter in East Edge. Now more than ever. I don't see Gaelcean's peace holding very long. He and the Knights can't stay here forever, and if they're going to continue to bring more people from the Haze in..." He trailed off and then stepped out in front of them. "Dimitri looked at you as if he knew you, or at least recognized your name. How is that possible?"

Cordelia tripped on an upturned paving stone. Elina grabbed her arm to steady her. It would have to come out eventually. She looked at Caleb and Elina directly as she spoke; she didn't want to leave any room for speculation as to what her relationship to Dimitri was. Before she spoke, she looked around to make sure there were no Knights within earshot. "I was born up in the mountains above the Haze. Mountain Station. I have never met Dimitri or any of those with him, that I have seen so far. He knew my name, because my family is one of several who founded the station as a way to protect their families during the wars that took place in the Old World." Caleb's face went hard. Cordelia thought she saw Elina's eyes widen for a moment, but she couldn't be sure. "I was tasked with gathering information to better understand his motives. I can't make it any clearer that he doesn't represent all of those who live beyond the Haze." She waited for one of the two to respond, but they only stared at her.

"I see." Caleb's expression didn't change.

317

"I knew there was something peculiar about you, Cordelia." Elina sighed. "I haven't known you long, but I believe you. If you had intended to cause harm, there were plenty of opportunities where you could have."

"You both fought with the Amber Waves. For now, that is good enough for me." Caleb still seemed cold. Cold was acceptable considering what she had just told him.

And as if she hadn't just told him she was originally from the Haze, Caleb continued where he had left off. "When we do settle the new chapter," he began walking again and Cordelia and Elina did as well, "I would like you to head it, Elina. You helped Lucas when he arrived, and he has only said positive things about you. You would be tasked with recruiting members in the area and seeing that they are trained and taken care of. They will be your family, our family." Caleb smiled and then caught himself. The coldness returned slightly. "That is, if you accept the position."

"I had planned on asking Lucas if I could accompany you all when you left East Edge, so I consider this a step up from that. I accept your offer, Caleb Fields."

"Excellent!" Caleb clasped a hand on Elina's shoulder. "Of course, Cordelia, you are welcome to join if Elina believes you meet her standards."

"Oh." Cordelia was caught off guard again but managed to keep her feet under her. "Actually, I had thought about joining the Amber Waves a few years ago when I was doing jobs in the Lower Districts. I appreciate the offer, but right now I have my matters I need to see to."

"Ah, yes," Caleb said all too knowingly. "I had almost forgotten already. Maybe it's because you have spent time in the New Ring and in the City, but I would never have guessed you were from a Haze settlement."

Cordelia looked around them to see if anyone had heard. No one was running to get a Knight, that she could see.

"I left as soon my grandmother would allow." She managed to speak without looking around the crowd. "I

318

never thought I'd stay up there. People have always left their settlements for what they thought was a better life under the Shield. You'd be surprised how easy it is to slip in and out of the Perimeter. The outer gates of the City on the other hand." She actually felt like laughing, and to her surprise Caleb *did* laugh.

"I've had plenty of issues with the city guard as well." He continued to laugh and ran a hand through his thick black beard.

Ahead of them in the square she saw Victor. He had two men in Haze suits by the backs of their necks and was shoving them in the direction of a group of Knights who were processing other suited humans. "These two were trying to sneak out of the square to the east." Victor lifted them up off the ground slightly before throwing them down to the hard stone. "If you Knights can't catch them all I'd be more than happy to help out." He meant more than rounding up the rest of Dimitri's followers in the square. He had a point though, there surely were some attackers who had slipped off.

"That won't be necessary." A Knight pulled up the two who had been thrown to the ground. "You all will be allowed to leave the square once these Humans have been questioned and processed." What would they do with those who they deemed unfit to join the town?

"Victor, I—" Cordelia began, but she wasn't sure what she was trying to say.

"Cordelia. Elina." Anger melted away from Victor's face once he recognized them. "I am glad to see friendly faces, especially at a time like this." His eyes glistened with unshed tears.

"If there is anything we can do for you, Victor, don't hesitate to ask," Elina said as she patted him on his massive shoulder. "I will be staying in East Edge for the foreseeable future."

"Good." He sniffed and drew himself up. "It is good to have friends nearby." He looked toward the group being questioned by the Knights and then back toward them. "Let's move away from this spot." The four of them stepped back toward the center of the square and Victor dropped down onto a bench. The wooden creaked under his weight. Cordelia sat down next to him while Elina and Caleb stood. "So, you will be staying in East Edge. Why is that?"

"She's going to be leading the new chapter of the Amber Waves." Caleb stepped forward and held out a hand. "Caleb Fields. I'm sorry for your loss, Victor."

"Caleb Fields." Victor shook his hand. "Victor Aymin. Amber Waves, hm? I thought I heard people shouting something about your mercenaries."

"We'd prefer not to be labeled as mercenaries," Caleb corrected delicately.

Victor waved a hand. "You helped recover my town from the hands of *that man*. I don't care what you call yourselves." Caleb folded his arms across his chest and nodded.

"I'll be around for a time as well, Victor." Cordelia tried to console the once-jolly man sitting beside her, but she wasn't sure what to say or do to return him to what she had remembered only days before.

"Thank you. Thank you all." Victor put his hands on his knees and stood up with a grunt. "I'm going to walk around for a bit more. Maybe I can do something to help out."

Cordelia thought she knew what he meant and looked to Elina, who shook her head and put a cautioning hand in her direction.

"We'll see each other again soon, Victor." Elina gave a slight smile. He smiled back, but the corners of his mouth barely lifted.

Behind Caleb, Gaelcean and Carter moved through the crowd with a group of Knights. "I'm going to go check on my friend Jaeger. He lives to the East just outside of town, if you need a place to stay tonight," Cordelia said to Elina and then turned to Caleb. "The Amber Waves are welcome to set up camp near the house and are welcome to a hot meal as well."

"Thank you, Cordelia," Elina said. Caleb nodded his thanks.

She turned and pushed her way through the crowd. The Knights had said they would be releasing people soon, but if those two that Victor had caught had been able to slip out, then she could as well.

"I thought I might find Cordelia Faucher with the two of you." A voice came from behind Caleb, and he turned to see Gaelcean and Carter, as well as several Knights. This was only the second time Caleb had spoken to the Amboian Diplomat. If the story he had heard was true, he would have to be more cautious around him. Not that he had planned on giving Gaelcean a reason to harm him; it was unlikely the Amboian would do anything of the sort in the crowded square.

"She was here a moment ago. I'm sure she will turn up again." Elina was a block of ice. Her arms were folded across her chest and Caleb noticed her knuckles were white. *Fear or anger?*

"I see." A small smile appeared on Gaelcean's face. He turned to Caleb. "It would have been fortunate to find Cordelia with you, Caleb, so I could speak with both of you at once. Still, I would like to speak with you now, if you have the time."

Caleb looked around at the square, still full of people. It didn't seem like anyone was going anywhere else soon. Perhaps Gaelcean was being polite, but there wasn't much of a choice.

"Of course." Caleb collected himself. It was unlikely Gaelcean wanted to speak about the weather, or anything of that sort. This was official business of some kind. "Regarding the Amber Waves and the work we've done with Weleya, I imagine?" He kept his voice low enough for those immediately around just in case secrecy was still needed. The

321

Knights were a few paces away. If they heard they made no show of it.

"Yes, that is correct." Gaelcean nodded. He laced his fingers together and held his hands down near his waist. "Firstly, I would like to thank you for the work you have done for us. We took a chance trusting you without knowing much more than hearsay and what little information Voal had collected. Weleya is a good judge of character. I hold her opinion of others highly. After your first meeting with her, she felt you and your companions would be a perfect fit for the job."

"Thank you, sir." Caleb couldn't help but fill with pride. He basked in thanks for a job well done.

"There is something more I wish you to do for me." Gaelcean's smile faded. A grave look crossed his face before he recovered. "I fear you may have only uncovered the surface of a much larger problem at hand." His fingers unlaced and he brought a hand to his chin as he spoke. "If what Weleya has told me—what your team has recently discovered—then it seems we may need to make some *adjustments* to Weleya's team."

Caleb could imagine it now. The facade of wholesome the Diplomat had cracks in it. He must have been unable to hide his reaction, because Gaelcean was quick to continue.

"Of course, we must do the proper investigative work. It would be a shame to accuse the wrong individuals. It is important we find them and learn what we can from them before it is too late."

Caleb waited to respond. If he didn't speak Gaelcean might reveal a bit more.

"I plan to stay here no longer than a month. Less, perhaps." His smile returned. "I would hope that you and your companions would accompany me on the return to the capital once everything here is in order."

"I'll speak with them tonight and bring word to you tomorrow. Would it be best to come to the Town Hall, or

322

will you be staying in the camps during your time here?"

"No need to seek me out. I have no doubt I will be able to find you. Until then, Caleb Fields." Gaelcean gave a nod to Elina and turned away. Carter gave a nod to them before turning away as well. The Knights followed close behind the two of them.

"I saw him give a speech a very long time ago, when I was just a boy." Caleb watched the Amboian pass through the crowd. "He has a very convincing way about him. It worries me." Once again he felt he would be asking his family to get involved in something that was much larger than them. Gaelcean's asking for assistance felt more like a stern request. It all seemed too late now. He was responsible for them. Caleb Fields would never let harm come to those he cared about. Even if it meant standing up to the Diplomat.

CHAPTER TWENTY-FIVE

Setting Sun

T he sun had passed its peak some time ago. There was still plenty of daylight left to enjoy sitting out in the yard between Jaeger's house and the workshop. Cordelia sat with Jaeger and Andreas at a small fire in the yard. Cooler weather wasn't far off, and there wouldn't be many nights like this left. Even now Cordelia appreciated the warmth the fire was giving off. Not far from the yard several canvas tents had been set up. The sound of laughter and conversation carried across the yard from the Amber Waves camp. She had hoped Elina might come by after extending the offer; there was still time that she might.

"How much longer do you think you'll be staying?" Thin wisps streamed from Jaeger's mouth as he puffed on his vapor stick. She caught the scent of some kind of fruit. "Not that I *want* you to leave any time soon." He waved the wisps away and leaned forward. "I am glad I've been able to see you as much as I have lately." The light from the fire reflected off his green eyes and his beaming smile. He was a true friend and probably the only person she trusted without fault. Aside from her grandmother, anyway.

"I'm not sure. I still need to speak with Dimitri." Cordelia stretched her arms out in front of her and tried to stifle a yawn. She spoke once it had subsided. "Andreas, would you be alright finding your way back to Mountain Station on your own? I don't think Gaelcean is going to let Dimitri out of his sight any time soon."

Andreas was staring into the fire, lost in thought, and seemed startled when she had said his name. "I can manage. I'll take some time to rest up first. The Deep Scouts can get on without me for a few more days." He turned his attention back to the burning logs.

"Thanks again for going back to get our things. I had almost forgotten with everything that was going on." When she had returned from town, she had gone up to her room to find her satchel and helmet on her bed. Her Haze suit had been tucked away under the bed with the pack that she had originally brought with her when she came out to see Jaeger.

"Good thing too." Jaeger chuckled and more wisps shot from his mouth. "I spent a good amount of time on that suit." Cordelia's face felt warm, and it wasn't from the fire this time.

"I had been thinking about that." Andreas looked to Jaeger. "The Deep Scouts could really use suits like those. I couldn't help but looking the suit and helmet over a bit when I was bringing it back." He turned his body in his chair to face Jaeger. "Would you be willing to make equipment for us? I could make trips to come get them, and we could supply you with any old tech we find in the Fog. Anything we find out there we could give you."

Jaeger stared up at the night sky for a moment. Cordelia looked up too. Green and blue waves danced across the surface of the Shield. Sometimes she thought she saw purples too. Beyond that the night sky was deep blue and to the west the sun was setting. Pink clouds sat in a yellow-orange sky. "With what I have now." Jaeger paused again. "I could make three more suits similar to the one I made for Cordelia. Now

325

I say *similar*. They won't be exactly the same unless I can get in touch with…" He trailed off.

"Anything would be an improvement on what we've got now. Thank you, Jaeger." Andreas stuck out a hand and Jaeger shook it.

"Thank me when I have them ready for you. There are always problems that arise working on these projects." He rubbed his temples with one hand across his forehead while the other held the vapor stick between his fingers.

"I could also make the trips to get the supplies from wherever it is you get them from." Andreas sat back in his chair. "I think I could get used to spending time in here."

"I'm not sure it's a good idea." He was still rubbing his temples.

"I think it's best we save this conversation for another time," Cordelia said in a low voice and then raised it. "I'm glad you decided to come over. There's still some stew inside and Jaeger made a fresh loaf of bread this afternoon." Cordelia waved an arm to Elina and the others walking toward the fire. She hadn't learned all their names yet, but she remembered Caleb and Lucas. There was the bald dark-skinned man with shoulders so wide she was sure he would have to turn sideways a bit to get inside the house if they decided to grab some of the leftover dinner. He was good with that staff.

"There's a few extra chairs up against the workshop over there." Jaeger had stopped rubbing his temples and waved a hand in the direction of the shop. "Not sure I've got enough, but you can always roll a log from the wood pile over and use that."

"I don't mind sitting on the grass," the dark-skinned man said and sat cross legged. "Omar Cross. Thank you for letting us camp on your land, sir."

"Not a problem at all, Omar." Jaeger shook his hand and smiled. "It isn't often I get so many visitors who aren't looking for me to fill a job for them. The company is nice."

Omar introduced himself to Andreas and Cordelia as well.

"Just wanted to walk over and say thank you as well, Jaeger." Caleb nodded to the man, but the look on his face was serious. "There also something else I wanted to talk about."

Cordelia glanced up from the fire at Elina, who was looking back at her. *Oh no!* She must have been reading her thoughts, or Cordelia hadn't hidden her concern as well as she thought. Elina shook her head. The knot in her stomach unwound.

"Gaelcean has offered us more work with Weleya and her team." Caleb was staring directly into the fire as he spoke. "Weleya and the others have stressed secrecy, but after talking with the members of the Company that are here, we've decided it was best to involve a few others." He looked up to Cordelia. "One of the Upper District Families—most likely the Jorogumo—have been paying off governors in the Lower Districts. Perhaps rigging things to get them in their pockets." He looked around the group now. Even though Cordelia was sure the other Amber Waves had already heard this part. "If this is true. I imagine Gaelcean is going to want us to gather more information on them, which we have been having a curiously easy time doing." He continued on explaining how he thought the Jorogumo wanted them to find out about the members of Weleya's team they had in their control.

"I haven't spent time in the capital in years." Jaeger puffed on his stick again. "The Jorogumo. That's a name I remember. Now this is only rumor from when I was young, so it's probably even more so now. Apparently, the family that runs the Jorogumo goes way back to the founding of Amboy City. They called the people who were saved by the Amboians, the First Found, or The Founders. I can't remember."

"I've heard similar stories as well." Caleb nodded.

"Be careful. I hope you know what you've gotten into."

Jaeger shook his head.

"After we find the members that were placed into Weleya's team. I say we get out." Caleb was looking into the fire again. "Honestly, I don't even like getting this deep into it." He let out a long sigh.

Lucas stood up and put an arm on Caleb's shoulder. "You're not twisting our arms, Caleb. We all have an idea of what we're getting into." He shook Caleb's shoulder and smiled. "With what Jaeger just said, my bet is Gaelcean has been dealing with these guys since the beginning of it all and he's been trying to put a damper on them for some time."

Caleb seemed to try to smile, but he didn't quite fully get there. "We won't have to worry about it for a little while at least." He drew himself up. "We'll be here helping Elina get the chapter situated. When Gaelcean leaves, we'll be going with him. For now, I'm off to try and get some sleep." Lucas and Caleb said their good nights and walked off into the dark together. Cordelia could hear the sounds of them speaking as they left, but she was too far away to hear any words.

"I think those two have the right idea." Jaeger stood up out of the chair with a groan. "I'll clean up what's left inside and then try to get some shut eye as well. I tend to start work early in the shop, so I apologize now if I wake anyone."

Andreas stood up and agreed as well and walked toward the workshop where Jaeger had made a bed for him. He had also mentioned something about updating maps.

There was a long silence after Jaeger had left. The only sound was the crackling and popping of the fire. "Will you be joining the Amber Waves as well, Cordelia?" Omar was seated almost directly across from her. He had a comforting voice for such a massive man.

"Caleb had extended the offer, but I declined." Cordelia brushed some ash off her pant legs and jacket. She hadn't even realized how much had covered her. "There was a time when I would have, but I don't think right now is a good time for me." She glanced at Elina after she spoke. The woman seemed so unreadable at times. *Had* she told them?

"*A time for everything,*" Omar quoted and smiled.

"I'm not very familiar, but that's from the Salvation, right?" Cordelia asked. She didn't know much about the Salvation but knew enough to know the popular sayings.

"Yes, I spent some time with the Church." Omar smiled and looked into the flames. "*There is a time for everything.* I don't remember what the original text said, but that's what I've heard said more recently. I haven't looked at the original text in years. I had a hard time remembering it while I was studying with the Church." Omar's laugh was deep. Cordelia couldn't help but smile as well.

"It makes me think of what Jonas said earlier," Elina said. The two of them told Omar the conversation that had happened leading up to Jonas' death.

"It's been some time since I've actually read the Salvation. I can't remember the exact words, but it does tell of the wars in the Old World and the Amboians coming down to rescue the Humans who had survived. Maybe I should stop into the Church when we return."

Cordelia cleared her throat before she spoke. "I have heard similar stories to what Jonas spoke of. It would be surprising if any of that was in the Salvation." Neither Omar nor Elina had responded. The three of them were quiet for a time. Eventually Cordelia found herself humming *The Long Road.* Which made her think of Victor. It was odd, feeling sorrow from such a happy song.

"You know *The Traveler's Song?*" Omar asked.

"I heard it once, but it was called by another name." She smiled as she looked into the fire.

They continued to sit around the fire and talk for a short time longer. They shared stories, some of their own and others they had heard. Omar spoke highly of the other Amber Waves members. Being in the Amber Waves must bring people close together in a short time period. Caleb seemed almost ready to trust Cordelia after barely a day of knowing her. It was comforting to be around such warmth, but in the back of her head was the ever-present concern of letting her guard down too much.

Cordelia was alone with the dying fire. For a while she sat staring up at the now almost pitch-black sky beyond the perimeter. Flickering stars filled the sky. She took a deep breath in and could smell the smoky fire and the grassy fields around her. She had to enjoy moments like these, especially after the events of the past few days. She had a feeling there would be less and less of them in the future. She closed her eyes and listened to the chirps coming from the bugs in the tall grass around her and the occasional gust of wind that blew through it. What was left of the fire still gave the occasional pop or crackle. There was the sound of movement behind her.

Two people were approaching from the direction of the town. She shot up from her folding chair. It collapsed under her sudden movement and fell over. She picked up a decent-sized rock that had been placed around the fire as a barrier; luckily, she had grabbed the cooler side. It was still very warm in her hand. With the fire dying down, she was able to see well enough in the low light. It wasn't two people, but three. One of them too tall to be Human.

Gaelcean, Carter, and Dimitri stepped into the dying light of the fire. A second light appeared above Gaelcean. A glowing orb of dim white light that gave off a slight humming sound. Gaelcean was wearing a high-necked long coat and straight-legged pants, but a shade of blue so dark it seemed black. Dimitri wore a tan shirt with sleeves a bit too long for his arms and poor fitting pants. The neck of the shirt was unlaced revealing a fair amount of his chest and the brown hair on his head was tied back in a tail. Cordelia was finally able to breathe when she saw Carter wasn't wearing that matte-gray armor she had seen him in earlier. She couldn't see any weapons on them either. She dropped the rock, and it made a clacking sound as it hit the others around the fire.

"I apologize if we startled you." Gaelcean and the others continued walking toward her. "And for showing up at such a late hour. If you don't mind, there are some things I believe we must discuss."

She looked at Dimitri. He was trying hard to avoid eye contact. He seemed truly broken.

"I was about to let the fire die out. Let me grab a few more logs. There are chairs if you would like a seat." She was about to turn to walk to the wood pile by the workshop when Gaelcean held out his hand.

"That won't be necessary. Thank you." The orb floated in the air and placed itself over the embers of the fire. It seemed to have gotten slightly brighter as well. "Thank you for the chairs. It has been a long day and sitting down to speak sounds lovely."

She picked her chair up from the ground and sat back down. Gaelcean sat across from her with Carter on his left and Dimitri on his right. The floating white orb lowered a bit more once everyone was seated. Without the fire the night seemed much colder than before. She forced herself to keep from shivering. It was difficult though. Gaelcean's pitch-black eyes were staring intently at her. Carter's were as well. Dimitri seemed to be trying to withdraw into himself and stared into his hands that were placed in his lap.

"When you made yourself known today, I noticed Dimitri's reaction to your presence. As well as your name." Gaelcean began. "A person in a room who is able to fill that room, has power." Flashes of Jonas' crushed face shot across her mind. She thought she saw Dimitri flinch as well. "But when a name alone causes a reaction. That is something much more." He smiled. It felt like a cold smile. Like a wolf who had cornered a hen. "Dimitri has told me you are from Mountain Station." The knot in Cordelia's stomach returned. She had heard from her grandmother, as well as from Jaeger, what the Council did to those who had moved to and from the Haze. "I have known of you long before today, though. Dimitri has only given me a piece of a much larger picture." The knot tightened. "You are what they call a Haze Walker, in the city. I know this because your contact is part of a team. Part of my team." The knot seemed to loosen, but only a bit. "I have recently learned that some members of this team aren't who they say they are. These members have been pretending to be one thing, when in fact they are another."

She could see where this interrogation was headed. Why was Dimitri here though? Gaelcean didn't want him out of his sight. Of course. "I am not a member of the Jorogumo." She was surprised that her voice hadn't shaken. Gaelcean had even seemed to be taken off guard slightly. Only slightly. The knot was gone. "I take retrieval jobs for people looking for Old World tech and oddities." She had to keep from cringing when she let slip the part about bringing Old World tech in. That might cause an issue.

"I see. You are closer to the Amber Waves than my information has told me." Gaelcean sighed and then smiled. This smile wasn't as before. It was kinder in a way. "It appears my information has been lacking as of late. Well, Cordelia Faucher. I imagine you won't be staying long in East Edge. I would like to speak again soon. There are many things I would like to learn from you." Gaelcean stood and Carter along with him. Dimitri lagged behind slightly.

"Dimitri needs to answer for what he had done." Cordelia stood. "I need to take him back to Mountain Station."

"I'm afraid that won't be possible." Gaelcean shook his head. "He will answer for his crimes against us, but it will be in the capital."

"He isn't from the New Ring, or the capital. His own people will hold a trial for him." She thought she saw Gaelcean's face harden again. An image of Jonas returned to her thoughts. She pushed it down.

"Perhaps after he stands trial in the capital, we can work something out." Gaelcean turned to walk away without another word.

Cordelia couldn't let him get away just yet. "I need to know why, Dimitri." She glared at the man. "What were you *thinking*?"

"You don't understand what it's like." Dimitri finally looked up at her. His voice was hoarse, and it sounded as if he was holding back tears. "You and everyone who lives above the Haze have never understood what it's like. The Haze Line had only dropped below Tunnel Outpost recently, but they remember what it was like. I'm sure your grandmother can tell you how quickly the Haze receded from the Mountains. I bet even her grandparents didn't have to suffer like most of us have." The rasp in his voice was all too apparent now. The light from the glowing orb showed the dampness in his eyes and the wet lines running down his cheeks. She hadn't thought about it. He was right. The only time she spent in the Haze was traveling to and from. The longest she had spent in the yellow murk was when she was injured and stayed at the safe house only days ago.

"You're right," Cordelia said coldly. "I don't know what it's like." Dimitri looked stunned. He must not have been expecting her to agree. "The Elders will learn what has happened. I will stress the need for more aid within the Haze, and more shelter above."

"We *will* be allowing more of your people to enter East Edge, Dimitri." Gaelcean looked at the man. How could the Amboian switch from intimidation to kindness so quickly. "I cannot forgive what has happened here today. Many innocent lives were lost, but I will not punish those who were not involved." The orb lifted up and followed Gaelcean and Carter as they walked away. Dimitri still stood staring back at her. As the orb moved away his face was shrouded in shadow. "Come, Dimitri. You need rest. We have many long days ahead."

She thought she heard Carter mumble something about everything resting, but she wasn't sure. Whatever he had said, Gaelcean nodded and the three walked off into the night. Cordelia watched the floating orb hover over them, illuminating the tops of their heads and shoulders.

The fire had died out completely. Cordelia sat in the darkness with her thoughts. There was too much to process in the last few days and too much to get done in the coming days. She closed her eyes and tried to focus on the chirps in the grass and the wind moving through the fields around her. Perhaps, now she could finally relax.

EPILOGUE

A Meeting

There was a slight chill in the air in the Upper District. The Council had not seen the need to adjust the climate control system yet, but Rylae was sure that soon enough one of the Council members would propose they begin preparing for the winter season. His high-necked wool coat and pants kept him warm enough. The work done by the Human he had hired was exceptional.

Rylae's concern for the needs of the Humans in the capital and New Ring went as far as a blacksmith's concern for the condition of his hammer and anvil. It only mattered that they could do their jobs and meet the demands that were given to them. He never understood how so many Amboians could spend their time down here among so many Humans. Some had even taken up residence down here! Why any of them would ever want to leave Central Amboy was beyond him. If he wanted fresh air, he could lower the outer walls of his chambers in Central Amboy and relax in the open air.

Even though his task had brought him down into the Upper Districts, his mood was not entirely negative. The meeting had gone well, and he played his part. Humans were easy enough to manipulate and their short lifespans made them miss the much larger picture. Although those he had just met with had the blessing of Amboian technology to extend their lives, it did not compare to that of an Amboian. How long had it been since his first meeting with the Jorogumo? Twenty years? Patience came easy; it would all be worth it. He almost found himself laughing as he walked down the white stone path lined with tall oak trees. He would look like a fool laughing to himself. Still, he looked around to see if anyone saw him regain his composure. It seemed none were paying him any attention. *All for the best.*

Zaenin had not reacted. She was scanning the forested walking path around them. *As if someone would attack me in the Upper Districts.*

He could never be too careful. He would not put it past those Humans to try and take advantage of him during their meetings. Rylae thought Zaenin's presence had offended them at first; later he learned it was awe. The way they spoke of her it was almost worship. Asking too many questions about her augmentations. Especially that old man who had been in attendance more and more as of late. Who was he? Another one of their pawns? However, their interest in Zaenin was a useful distraction at times. Short lifespans and even shorter attention spans. This time Rylae allowed himself to laugh.

Davil Coram stood against the wall of the square room; he would have preferred to be a part of the wall. He made himself small and tried not to draw attention. He had only just recently been allowed to attend these meetings. The first time he had been called upon to attend he was tempted to sneak to his right, and out through the square entrance of the room.

He felt the cool black marble wall against his back and tried to ground himself with that, while he listened to the conversation that was happening at the lounge in the center of the room. The marble walls didn't quite meet the floor and in that space, white lights ran the length of each wall. In the center of the room a wide opaque bowl-shaped chandelier lit the middle of the room. The seating area was sunken into the floor, such that the servers had to kneel down to those sitting on the soft white couches that lined the square inset lounge. A server appeared from the left corner of the room. She glided across the black marble floor that matched the walls. She knelt down to hold out the silver worked tray that held several tall slender glasses filled with a yellowish bubbling drink.

A fair-skinned woman with waist-length straightened black hair took a drink from the tray without acknowledging the server. "His confidence will be his downfall." She took a small sip from the glass. "Wouldn't you agree, Mori?" She flashed her eyes at another woman sitting across from her.

"Yes." She waved a hand. Her almost shoulder-length brown hair bounced as she shook her head at the server. "Most Amboians are tough to read, but that one, he shows his thoughts very clearly."

The black-haired woman laughed. "It is a fun game."

"You can be overly confident as well, Taigen." A third woman seated beside Mori cut in. She also had waved off the server. She looked like she could be a sister—or even a twin—to Mori. Their brown, shoulder-length hair was styled almost identically. They both wore the same light-blue dress with lace along the low neckline and ends of the sleeves. Some unrecognizable flowers were patterned about the tight-fitting torso of the dress. It was difficult to tell from here and he dared not stare long enough to learn.

Taigen scoffed. "No, Haruka. *I* am confident. *He* is overly confident." The two maybe-sisters rolled their eyes almost in unison. Definitely some relation, Davil concluded. Taigen shifted her own dress as she got comfortable in the chair. The flowing white dress was almost as pale as her skin.

337

"Are you confident in your underlings in Port Amboy?" Haruka gave a wry smile.

"It is a shame I had to uncover my plans in the Port before I had intended, but if it puts eyes in another direction, it will be worth it."

"Your sacrifice hasn't gone unnoticed, Taigen. As for the Amboian, let him think he has the upper hand." When this woman spoke, the others straightened to attention.

Ten women sat on the white couches placed in the inset lounge, but only one sat alone. Three were seated to her left and right, and the other three were seated across from her. They were positioned so Davil could see all the women's faces except the one who sat alone. Her dark hair was long, but not as long as Taigen's. Long curls fanned across the back of her dark silk dress. The women were always here before he arrived; he had never seen her face since he had been allowed to attend.

"Coram." The woman had a brassy voice that filled the room. "Step forward." Davil almost stumbled for a moment as he took his steps away from the wall. She held up a hand from him to stop. He was never allowed more than a few steps into the room. "Although you failed to capture the Diplomat's personal guard, you have done well in your position. I am glad you reached out to us when you did. We will continue to fund your school. Your *interests* in these guards have proven more useful than we had thought."

He had to work some wetness into his mouth before he was able to speak. The repairs done to his neck weren't complete, he found speaking difficult at times. "They are truly masterworks. I found the Amboians' method of data processing to be quite interesting. The effects o—" Davil realized the women were all staring at him. His mouth went dry again and it felt as though he had swallowed a boulder. "Apologies, I get carried away sometimes." He gave a slight bow and stepped back. He had done it the first time upon seeing the servers on their knees and bowing before they left.

338

He had never been told to do it and there was no sign that he should or shouldn't.

"We will continue to act the fool," the woman continued. "He already thinks himself better than us. Better than any Human, no doubt. He will continue to let slip his plans, and we will use that to our advantage."

Davil was always made uncomfortable with all this talk of plans. Anything to do with Upper District dealings made him uncomfortable. He didn't know all of the Council members by appearance, but that Councilor's involvement in all this had made him feel even worse. His school would be funded, and he could continue the pursuit of elevating the Human species beyond their natural limits. He had failed them at capturing Weleya, but he wouldn't fail the next time they gave him a task. He would do whatever it took to realize his goals. Everyone was playing the game.

The only light in the massive room that held the gestation tanks were the dim lights that dotted the grated walkway. The most recent fertilized eggs were progressing well, only thirty percent had failed. That was something Paelle could be proud of. As she passed by the stacked rows of tanks, she looked each of them over and made notes of any irregularities. It was a difficult job do to alone, but she did not trust anyone but herself to do it. Without any complications, from fertilization to their Exit, there would be one hundred and twenty Amboians born each cycle. The accelerated gestation pods Paelle helped develop ensured rapid growth and allowed her species to be born into their young adult life. The new Amboians emerged as if they had been living among them the entire time. It would have insufferable to educate over one hundred adult-sized children. Something Paelle would never have the patience for. She always enjoyed meeting the newcomers.

If only the Council could somehow convince the Human

population to accept a birthing cycle. That would help the overpopulation in the Lower Districts. Perhaps they did not need to convince them? She could easily create a new *medicine*... No, thoughts like that could lead to a dark place. She could end up like Aelgan; banished to the Haze. Paelle would not be surprised if her old mentor were still alive out there after all these years. If anyone could find a way to survive it was Aelgan. Of course, it would also be just as easy to trick the Shield sensors to ignore your signature and reenter after the Banishing. She shook her head and continued down the rows of tanks.

She reached the last row and pulled a vial from her open coat and connected it to the nutrition delivery system. The other rows of tanks would not need anything else until tomorrow, but the future Knights of Amboy were always given extra. There was a hissing sound as any air was ejected from the tubes, and the blue-green contents of the vial were pulled up into the tubing that would lead to each gestation tank in the row. Once it was empty, the system released the tube and Paelle returned it to the inside pocket of her coat.

She entered the next room to check on the batch that was further along in their cycle. These would still need a few months until they were ready to emerge. Today she had to ensure the systems were giving them their in-tank education. She also checked that the motor control systems were stimulating their muscles so they would be able to function properly upon Exiting. The room after that held the Amboians that would Exit in a matter of weeks; this room truly excited her. She found herself humming a tune she was not sure had a name as she checked similar systems as in the previous room. After all the systems were checked and she updated the records on each row, she walked to the back wall of the room.

With Gaelcean gone, no one else would ever need to be down here, but as of late she always found herself checking her surroundings. She wondered when Gaelcean would return. The Council had been losing direction without him. It seemed more often than not arguments broke out and agreements could not be met. The only positive since his departure was that more Councilors had been showing up. Paelle was not sure if that was because they felt they needed to make up for his absence, or if they wanted to take advantage of it. At least Weleya was in attendance, not that she had any say in what was discussed. Her presence was a reminder to all that Gaelcean still sat on the Council. That would have to do until he returned.

Paelle sighed and put her hand against the wall in a spot that no other would know was there unless she or Gaelcean had shown them. There was no sound to indicate the mechanism release. No sound to indicate if she then walked five paces to the left and put her hand in another spot and pushed, a door would open on the wall.

Paelle stepped into the even dimmer room to inspect the gestation tank only she and Gaelcean knew about. She saw this as the culmination of her life's work. Gaelcean saw it as a sign for a bright future. She did not know what others may think of the Amboian growing in this tank. Looking over the systems, all seemed well. She *hoped* all would be well. When the newest arrivals of Amboians Exited, this one would as well. Gaelcean had to be there when he did. Paelle would not know how to continue without Gaelcean.

Thank you for reading Along the Perimeter! Please consider leaving a review.

The sequel to Along the Perimeter is coming!

Contact me at StevenJHealt@gmail.com with any comments or questions.

About the Author

Steven Healt was born in and raised in the Adirondack Region of New York State. He graduated from SUNY Oswego with a degree in Geology. He then went on to achieve a Masters in Geoscience from West Chester University. When he isn't reading or writing, he enjoys camping, hiking, playing the guitar and spending time with family and friends.